"This exciting story about the event that changed our world and the unforgettable man Noah, whom God used to make it come to pass, will captivate your interest."

—TIM LAHAYE
Co-author of the *New York Times*
bestselling Left Behind series

"The Antediluvian Legacy is an excellent introduction to and a fresh new take on fantasy-action. Taking the biblical pre-flood world and inter-weaving fallen angels and dinosaurs makes for a non-stop thrill read."

—IBPA BENJAMIN FRANKLIN AWARD JUDGE

"Full of fearsome beauty, conflict, and wonder, *Leviathan* is as engrossing as it is epic. A spectacular start to an adventure both ancient and new."

—TOSCA LEE
New York Times bestselling Author of *Iscariot*

"After reading the first volume of the Antediluvian Legacy series, I couldn't wait to get my hands on the second volume. It did not disappoint. Huffman has given us another rich and creative story about Noah and the mighty men of old who lived before the great flood."

—TIM CHAFFEY
Author of the Truth Chronicles Series

FALLEN

BOOK TWO
OF THE ANTEDILUVIAN LEGACY

FALLEN

‹ R. M. HUFFMAN ›

BROWN BOOKS
PUBLISHING GROUP

Fallen

Brown Books Publishing Group
Dallas / New York
www.BrownBooks.com
(972) 381-0009

A New Era in Publishing®

Publisher's Cataloging-In-Publication Data

Names: Huffman, R. M., author.
Title: Fallen / R.M. Huffman.
Description: Dallas ; New York : Brown Books Publishing Group, [2021]
    | Series: The Antediluvian legacy ; book 2
Identifiers: ISBN 9781612545325
Subjects: LCSH: Noah (Biblical figure)--Fiction. | Imaginary wars and
    battles--Fiction. | Ex-church members--Fiction. | LCGFT: Fantasy
    fiction. | Bible fiction.
Classification: LCC PS3608.U3547 F35 2021 | DDC 813/.6--dc23

ISBN 978-1-61254-532-5
LCCN 2021906399

Printed in in the United States
10 9 8 7 6 5 4 3 2 1

For more information or to contact the author, please go to
www.TheHuffmanLetters.com

For Meredith.

◂ ACKNOWLEDGMENTS ▸

I'd like to thank my dad, Rick Huffman, for once again reading chapters as I wrote them; Robert Mullin, who struck upon an inspired title; Richard Caponetti, Weldon Nanson, Janna Braudrick, and Brian Niro for their invaluable feedback on the novel's first draft; Lucas Graciano for once again providing the fantastic cover painting; all of the excellent publishing professionals at Brown Books; and my wife and four kids, who let me carve out time to write this (and provided plenty of adorable distractions when I needed a break).

‹ DRAMATIS PERSONAE ›

MISSIONERS

Noah: a preacher of righteousness from Eden.

Gilyon: Nephilim; last descendant of the *ben Elohim* Azazyel.

Eudeon: Nephilim; youngest son of the *ben Elohim* Samyaza.

Midash: member of the ruling house of Havilah.

Caiphes: Noah's young relative from Eden.

Emié: young woman from a menagerist family.

ATLANTEANS

NEPHILIM

Children of Samyaza

Dyeus: regal lord of Atlantis.

Pethun: commander of Atlantean naval forces.

Dedroth: reclusive naturalist of Atlantis's undercity.

Eila: sister and wife of Dyeus.

Temethe: sister of Dyeus.

Asathea: sister of Dyeus.

Children of Dyeus

Tehama: leader of the Wa-Mizhan huntresses; twin sister of Peleg.

Peleg: healer; twin brother of Tehama.

Mareth: war-minded commander of the Atlantean army.

Hamerch: fleet-footed friend to the Edenites.

Deneresh: decadent lover of wine.

Edenah: committed to Atlantean justice.

Eroch: enormously strong adventurer.

Hoduín: Nephilim mystic; son of the *ben Elohim* Barkayal.

Tiras: son of Hoduín; mighty warrior.

Tevesh: son of Hoduín; one-handed warrior.

HUMAN

Haphan: son of Dashael of Eden and Jet of Enoch; half brother of Gilyon.

Dashael: menagerist and animal tamer; originally from Eden.

Jet: mother of Gilyon; married Dashael of Eden after her first husband Gloryon's death.

Tubal-Cain: lame master smith; his sister Naamah birthed Samyaza's children.

Kiah: second-in-command of the Wa-Mizhan huntresses.

EDENITES

Methuselah: Greatfather of Eden; grandfather of Noah.

Lamech: firstborn son of Methuselah; father of Noah.

Hadishad: Noah's brother; longtime emissary of Eden to Atlantis.

Jonan: Noah's brother; an orchard keeper of Eden.

Rakeel: Methuselah's second son; an orchard keeper of Eden.

Elebru: face-scarred elder of Eden.

MIZRAIMITES

Ninniachul: inventor and ingeniator; war refugee.

Phiaphara: daughter of Ninniahchul; joins with the Wa-Mizhan after being driven from Mizraim.

‹ PROLOGUE ›

Gavai repositioned himself on the throne, trying his best to get comfortable. The golden seat had been built for a much smaller man, a lesser man—Gavai only wondered why someone had not wrested control of the tribes from the weakling earlier. Gavai himself was tall, with broad shoulders and a thick chest. So large was he, in fact, that more than one acquaintance had asked if he was part of an angelic bloodline. He never answered. He did not actually know, since his heritage was a mystery to him. Growing up among the airy tents of countless Zuthian oasis cities, stealing from merchants and following caravans like a carrion bird, Gavai had early on become resigned to the truth that he was either an unwanted bastard or an orphan. Still, this bastard orphan now sat on the throne of the Zuthian tribes, albeit rather uncomfortably.

Under the spacious cover of the white silk tents that stretched high overhead, the tribute procession had been moving along uneventfully for most of the morning. Each tribe's delegation waited for its turn to present gifts to its ruler, paid tribute, then exited the tent. Gavai's guards stood at the periphery of the tent's interior. Not much protection was to be had from drapes of cloth or skins; in Zuthi, the walls worth anything were made up of strong men worthy of trust. Such were the warlord's guards, handpicked by Gavai.

A line of men draped in bright cloth, dignitaries from an eastern tribe, knelt as one at the bottom step of the dais. They placed jeweled urns carefully down and retreated, pledging their fealty to the warlord. He waved them on.

Two of his concubines collected the urns as a slave called in the next tributaries. The scantily clad young women had proved to be the only interesting thing about this dull day. For a fleeting moment, he envied his generals, all former comrades in arms, still campaigning and conquering the leaderless rabble that resisted his rule. Those men had called him "the viper." Ironically, he hated using poisons. Before he had killed his predecessor in clean combat, Zuthian rule had often changed hands after poisonings, so in hopes of avoiding such a fate himself, Gavai had also murdered virtually every member of the former court—except the concubines, of course. Gavai grinned lustfully as they bent down to pick up the urns, bodies curving and stretching in fascinating ways. He abruptly decided that he had better things to do than collect tribute. "One more," he shouted to the slave serving as usher, "and then I shall retire to my chambers." He leered at the two concubines reclined on the steps by his feet. They smiled coyly back.

The usher nodded nervously and hurried the next group in. Gavai sat up. Eight slaves entered together, four male and four female, carrying a coffin-sized chest inlaid with shimmering blue lapis and blood-red rubies. They were naked but for loincloths, and their skin had a sheen as if they had each been doused in some sort of oil. All eight looked to be in peak physical condition, lean and muscular. Gavai did not recognize them to belong to any tributary he knew, but at the rate the outlier tribes were being conquered and added to his domain, that did not surprise him.

The chest was obviously heavy, and the slaves carried it carefully. Each of them tightly held two silver handgrips spaced around the chest's bottom edge, sixteen in all. Gavai found that he did not even care what riches the chest contained; what caught his eye was the four pairs of bare, oiled breasts bouncing slightly with every careful movement forward. He noticed his concubines' interest in the slaves, as well—mostly in the men, but not only. He beckoned a guard to him.

"Invite those slaves to my private chambers. See that no one disturbs us." The guard nodded. "And tell the waiting tributaries that I may be quite a while."

The oiled slaves now stood before the dais. Gavai smiled, benevolently, he hoped, at the nearest female. The cold stare he received jarred him. A warning horn sounded deep in his consciousness, not as clarion as it had been in the days when he was leading his warriors into battle but still clear enough that he stood, frowning.

"Drop that chest," he ordered. The closest two male slaves bowed their heads. Suddenly, all eight pulled their hands violently away, revealing the silver handgrips to be the hilts of wicked-looking long knives. They sprung away from the chest, burying knives into the surprised guards that tried futilely to defend themselves with raised shields and outthrust spears. One of the females ran to the back and tied the tall outer tent flaps shut, slicing the neck of the usher on the way.

While the slaves' knives were wreaking havoc, the chest fell to the ground. It cracked when it hit the sandy floor, but it shattered to pieces when one of the males threw a guard's spear through it. Gavai's battle axe was already in his hand, and three of the concubines had clustered behind him, when the swarm of beetles within the chest collectively realized it had been freed. Five guards had been downed already, but nine more had drawn their weapons and faced off against the armed slaves. One of the oiled women was already bleeding into the sand, dead or badly injured. Unnoticed by the guards, the swarm rose from the ruined chest as one black mass, then spread. The two concubines at the bottom of the dais were the first to cry out, slapping at the beetles that landed on their skin. Cries turned to shrieks of pure terror as the beetles covered them completely. They fell, screaming and writhing. The guards fared slightly better, if only because as soon as one's attention was drawn to the biting beetles, he was cut down by one of the oiled slaves.

Three remaining concubines rushed up the stairs. Only two reached Gavai and the others; the last was caught by the beetles that had finished stripping the fallen concubines down to bone. She screamed and fell, rolling down the stairs and leaving a trail of crushed beetles on the steps. More swarmed to her, though, and she soon was still and silent. Gavai was consumed by a jealous fury. He had been only a few minutes away from bedding those women, and now they were being devoured by flesh-eating insects!

Another assassin-slave, a male, had fallen, but six remained and now stood at the bottom of the dais. Gavai surveyed what remained of his court. Squirming black masses that were once guards lay spread around the ground. Shouts came from outside the heavy tent, and several blades stabbed through the fabric. Curious beetles flew toward the rents in the tent, exploring for an escape. "Stay out!" shouted Gavai.

"Why?" the warlord growled to the oiled man climbing the steps. He crushed the first beetle that had dared land on his person. "Why are you doing this?"

"For the jackal god," the slave replied. The answer made no sense to Gavai, gave no reason to this chaos. He roared and swung his axe. The slave dodged and threw a knife, blade sinking halfway into the meat of his shoulder. Five more knives spun through the air, piercing his chest and abdomen. He dropped to his knees, eyes on the buzzing black swarms rising behind the grim, knife-wielding slaves. As the swarms advanced, two of the females strode past him to the terrified concubines. They slashed at the curtains behind the throne, cutting out long strips of thick linen. Rudely shoving the concubines to the foot of the throne, they bundled each of them in curtain like a cocoon, then laid themselves sprawled on top of the bound women, all moaning in terror. "Quiet!" ordered the lead slave. "You will be gifts for the serpent god. Be thankful for your lives."

The black swarm advanced quickly now, ignoring the oiled slaves. Fighting sounded outside, and two more guards were thrown bleeding into the tent. Three enormous figures stepped inside, wrapped in dark strips of cloth and wearing evil-looking masks with wolflike visages. They held curved blades, bloodstained and decorated with rose gold. One held a jar out; the third female slave ran back to retrieve it, then ran up the steps and poured its contents on the wrapped-up concubines.

Gavai's lifeblood ran down the steps in crimson rivulets. He made no effort to stop the beetles that began to gnaw at his flesh. The lead slave dipped his fingers into the jar held by the female, then stood in front of the kneeling warlord a step below him, just above eye level. The slave tilted Gavai's head up, then wiped an oily hand across his face and eyes.

"You may watch your death like a man," he said, then stepped down the stairs. He paused, then called out over his shoulder. "The beetles are sated now, so it may be slow."

The giant black-swathed figures ascended to the throne, ignoring the warlord, and descended again carrying the bound concubines. As a group, the giants, concubines, and slaves left the tent. The beetles covered Gavai slowly, lazily, only nibbling at his flesh, but none came near his eyes. It was indeed slow. He watched as long as he was able.

‹ CHAPTER 1 ›

The city of Phempor sweltered and sweated in the morning sun. The morning mists crept through the alleys, prying into cracks in the crude wooden doors and empty windows with damp fingers. In other places in the world, the mists watered crops, orchards, gardens; here, they merely turned the filthy dirt streets into mud.

A man, neither very young nor very old, strode through the mud with a purpose, trying to avoid the patches of darker brown that marked where excreta had been tossed into the street. Working men and women were already about, trudging with dull, downcast eyes to toil in dry fields. The people of the city were impoverished, but they filled the warrens of their honeycombed dwellings with many children; after all, in a land such as this, what other entertainment was there to be had than procreation?

For eight years Noah had lived alongside the peasants. It was not the longest time he and his comrades had spent in one mission field, but it was longer than most, for the need was great. They had started in the small, dusty communities of the region and for the last few years had worked in the slums of Phempor itself. Much of his work had been of a practical nature. The application of sound farming principles, ingrained in him from his youth in the lands of Eden, to even this poor soil had led to markedly increased crop yields of the tubers and squashes that were staples of Phempor's diet, aided by regular animal sacrifices in the altar houses they had planted about the city. The strong arms of the missioners had helped build many homes and dig many wells, and parts of the clay slums now had rudimentary waste channels running to the sulfurous bogs outside of the city. Phempor's ubiquitous structures were the round-roofed clay hovels that clustered closely together and pressed almost to the high-walled palaces of the ruling class, like prostrate beggars clutching at the hems of noble robes. The palaces lay in the middle of the city, but for the peasantry that surrounded them, they might as well have been a thousand leagues away. After much work and prayer, though, Noah's invitation had come. He was finally to meet the reclusive prince of Phempor.

His destination loomed ahead, broad and dark against the cerulean sky. Messages of truth and hope, of the Creator God and His will for the world, bubbled easily to the surface of his thoughts. They were well rehearsed, given freely many thousand times and honed by study, prayer, and discussion to pierce a man's soul. Well it was, too, for times such as these, when the chance might not come again to witness the truth to these rulers of men. A good word well planted in fertile soil might bear fruit for an entire nation-state.

Noah smiled as he walked, reminiscing on the successes the Lord God Creator had blessed them with, on the many of His children who now called on His name and made sacrifice to Him out of fealty and love. This was his true work. Many others had joined the work over the last four centuries. Paths crossed and branched and began and ended, all weaving a holy tapestry for the Creator God's glory, and ancient truths had reawakened in many places they had been lost. Phempor was one such place. While its barren soil bore the curse of the land poorly, the souls of its people had been ready for harvest. Noah found that this was often the case; those without earthly needs seldom realized their spiritual needs, but poverty bred hearts hungry for hope and a willingness to listen.

At first, their message had fallen on deaf ears, but care and persistence had paid off. Now, Machmanis, one of the first of the peasants to take up the faith of old, had assumed full duties at one of the modest altar houses, and Felun's zeal was as great as Noah or any of the others. Young Gaen had expressed interest in continuing with them to their next mission field, whenever and wherever it might be, and some of the missions they had planted had even begun to plant missions of their own.

Still, this was the opportunity for which he had prayed. For all of its change for the better, Phempor was still dangerous and dirty. The populace was hard pressed enough, but crime was rampant. Women and children disappeared regularly. Gangs of brigands fought bloody, secret battles for control of alleys and muddy pools, answering only to rival gangs, since the Phempor guard remained within the confines of the palaces. There was much idolatry; clay was in abundance, and sculptors made a steady living crafting sun-dried figures, blind and deaf to their supplicants. These things did not have to be. Noah had seen it before: a righteous ruler, living as the Creator intended, could bless his own people, change how they lived their lives, in ways Noah could never do.

The palaces were enclosed by a tall guard wall built of red salt-glazed bricks that caught the sun like liquid. Iron lamps sat atop the angular buttresses that supported the wall every so often; whatever fuel filled the lamps burned bright blue. Dark doors set in the guard wall opened for Noah, seemingly of their own accord. He walked through them.

The courtyard was desolate and dry. No one greeted Noah as he crossed the dusty space to the wide steps leading to the palace's main entrance. Two bare-armed, leather-clad guards stood at the door, both holding barbed spears in one hand and long leather leashes in the other. At their ends, iron-grey wolfhounds strained against their masters and paced back and forth, roughly describing the arc that the leash length would allow. The courtyard stunk of dog feces; obviously little effort was made to clean up the droppings that littered the ground.

Noah took the stairs two at a time, smiling at the hounds despite their menacing growls. The guards' countenances were imperceptible in the shadows cast by their low-browed helms and faceguards that swept past their cheeks and nearly met a hand's length past their noses. The most striking things about the men were the symbols scarred into their necks, raised and waxy, clearly a result of branding. They did not acknowledge Noah, but neither did they move to stop him. He strode on, through the door that again opened for him with no sign of human action.

The palace interior was swathed in shadows, and a moment passed before Noah's eyes recovered from the daylight. As the darkness gained shape and hue, he raised an eyebrow in mild surprise. While the courtyard he had seen was in accord with the dirty quality of the city, the inside of the palace was opulent. Indeed, Noah would have thought he had stepped into a hall in Enoch—rather, Atlantis, as it was now named—or Havilah, had the stench of the courtyard not faintly followed him through the door. Sculptures and frescoes decorated the walls and columns, dim and dreamlike in the low light cast by more blue-flamed lanterns. Details of the art were difficult to make out, but each example was obviously done by a master in the form. Still, the more Noah looked around the room, the greater an uneasy sense of malevolence nagged at the edge of his consciousness. Whether the simple dichotomy of beauty in shadow, or some intentional twisting and warping of the figures by the artists, done too subtly to pinpoint, he was relieved when someone finally greeted him from a doorway across the entrance hall.

"Welcome, Noah of Eden. You are expected. Come, enter freely, of your own will." The man was thin and severe, dressed in a simple, straight black robe, and strikingly pale. He spoke with a heavy accent unfamiliar to Noah's well-travelled ears, but the invitation was an answer to many years of prayer, and Noah gladly followed him.

They walked quickly through a maze of hallways, and the missioner soon found himself completely disoriented. Rather suddenly, a turn took them through a high-arched stone hall, and Noah stepped blinking into a flame-lit room, complete with a coterie of courtiers, male and female, who stopped and stared as one at the newcomer, and the prince of Phempor himself gazing down from his ebony throne at the end of the room.

Like the rest of the palace so far, there was no source of outside light, but the lantern flames here were a comfortable, homey orange. Many of the courtiers' faces lit up at the sight of Noah, jovial and friendly. All of them were dressed in dark clothing of fine fabric and cut, fitting for an audience with royalty. Like the man who ushered him in, the people who smiled at Noah now were blanched of skin, as if none of them saw the sun. Many of them were fleshy and well fed, a stark contrast to the gaunt, bony physiques common to Phempor's peasants. Noah suppressed a frown. What secret store of food were these fat folk hiding in these palaces, and why had they not shared it with the starving populace?

A loud, light voice pulled his attention to the prince. "And you must be Noah!" he said. "Come closer! I am told that we have much to discuss, you and I. Come!" The prince stood. He appeared young, trim and starkly beautiful, and as pale as everyone else Noah had yet seen in the palace. His slender, almost effeminate, hands had clearly not known labor of any sort, and with one of them he patted Noah on the shoulder.

"What luck! You have arrived in time for our banquet. I know that you wish to speak to me—an honor!—so shall we walk and talk?"

"My message is for the ears and hearts of your courtiers too."

"Of course! All of you," the prince said, clapping his hands, "follow us, and listen closely to what this man says! Now, Noah, if you please. What message is this? A good one, I hope?"

"The best." Noah took a deep breath. This court was certainly the most informal he had ever experienced. A camaraderie seemed to exist among these denizens of the palace, and the prince was surprisingly friendly and open. Like the farmers from whose stock he came, Noah had planted the seeds with toil and sweat, and now he prepared for a harvest. "Prince, I will tell you an ancient truth. We are immortals under a curse."

"Intriguing! Do tell more."

"You and I, and all here, were made by the eternal Creator God in His very image. The first of us, the man Adam and the woman Eve, were placed in paradise and fellowshipped with the Creator Himself, wanting nothing. They were perfect of form, undying, happy and fulfilled, but they were not merely playthings for the Creator God, not puppets. They were free to choose to do what they would, to go where they wished."

"This sounds very nice indeed! What happened next?" The prince leaned closer as they walked.

Noah's tone took a grim timbre. "They were deceived into disobedience, Prince. Satan, the Serpent, once the highest of the Creator God's servants but now set in rebellion against Him, tempted the woman Eve with the forbidden fruit of the knowledge of good and evil. The man Adam followed. They disobeyed the one command that their Lord had given them. Fellowship was broken. The man and woman were cast from paradise, never to return, and a curse was set over the world. Death and pain, struggle and toil, was now the lot of man."

Quiet murmurs of disappointment and concern floated from the following courtiers. The prince frowned. "This story has become rather depressing, Noah."

"And depressing it was, Prince. No tragedy could have been greater. But with the curse came hope! To our great benefit, mankind was not to live eternal in this cursed flesh, sinking ever deeper into its sin, apart from the Creator. His justice demanded punishment for disobedience, but His love remained. He promised a Redeemer, who would free mankind, and indeed the whole of creation, from the curse. Even death itself, the last, final enemy, would be destroyed, and all would be renewed to be what it once was, to what it was intended to be."

Scattered clapping came from behind, as if the courtiers had witnessed a bard's bravura performance. The prince's interest could not be denied. "A very fine story. So, tell me—what are we to do now?"

"We obey the conscience given us by the Creator God," answered Noah. "We hope for the coming of the promised Redeemer, and we walk in righteousness while we wait. We treat our fellow men as we ourselves wish to be treated."

The prince slowed his walk and pursed his lips. "And this is why you have toiled alongside the people of this city?"

Noah smiled. "Earthly work can open minds to spiritual truth. If even one soul attains to the hope of redemption, I consider it well worth the effort."

"Ah." The prince grew quiet. His mouth twitched at the corners, as if he were suppressing some joke of supreme hilarity. "You believe all of this to be true, do you?"

"I know it to be true, Prince."

"Know it! Well, Noah, allow me to share with you what *I* believe." The prince glanced back at his fleshy followers with a conspiratorial grin. "I believe in what I see with my own eyes, and what I see is this. Each of us has a time, a thousand years at most, to suck as much pleasure from this life as we have power. I will waste no time thinking on a God I cannot see, nor the origins of the world around. It is what it is. That is enough. Might there be things that lie outside my perception? Perhaps, but why should I concern myself with them?"

Noah had a dozen ready responses that leapt to his lips. He was not surprised at the opposition that he now encountered, that he had encountered countless times before. Before he could speak, the prince abruptly exclaimed, "At last, we come to the banquet hall! I must say, I am *famished*."

The smell of meat and spices was heavy in the air, mingled with a faintly sweet, metallic scent. At first Noah couldn't identify the curiously familiar smell, although he knew that somehow he was no stranger to it. As he struggled to place it, the group rounded another corner and arrived at a wide hall. Long tables were spaced around the brick-paved floor, with short staircases leading to alcoves in the hall's corners. Fireplaces lined either side of the hall, and servants with the same sort of scars on their necks as had the palace guards stood at attention around the room.

The prince gestured to Noah with a broad smile. "Please, sit at my table." Noah could not well refuse. Each place was set with ornate silver settings, but the tables were bare of food. Two women were there already; they ceased their laughing and chatting with one another to look up at the prince and his guest.

"Who is this, brother?" asked one, a black-haired woman, fine featured and fair like the prince. The other, just as lovely, midnight-blue coif dotted with silver like stars, favored Noah with a lingering stare that discomfited him, all the more because he felt it tempt in himself a certain interest as well.

"This is Noah, a sojourner in our lands and, to hear him tell it, the mouthpiece of a god."

"He is older than your usual guests."

"He cannot help his age, sister." The prince glanced apologetically at Noah.

"On the contrary, we like older men," said the starry-haired woman. "Do we not?"

"Indeed," replied her sister. "So many interesting experiences."

"How experienced are you, Noah?" The women shared a glance and the hint of a smile.

"Please, sisters." The prince gestured at Noah to sit beside him. "Why speak of age? I have heard that Noah is possessed of twice the energy of a man half his years."

"Even better," said one of the women, though Noah did not see which. He had determined to pay them little attention, turning to talk with the prince as his sisters whispered with heads together.

Once the courtiers had been seated, the prince stood and clapped. "Bring food and drink! And be quick about it!" The servants disappeared into dark arched doorways.

They reemerged two at a time, carrying long platters that were placed on the tables before courtiers who licked their lips in anticipation. Noah abstained from eating meat, though roasted and seasoned it did please his nostrils, but the other strange scent wholly suppressed his appetite. Butcher shops would always be foreign ground for the missioner—those who kept the old and true ways held to a vegetarian diet—but what confused Noah at first was his surety that herds, of any kind of animal, sizable enough to provide for a feast as this simply did not exist in the fetid wastelands around Phempor.

Upon each platter lay a fat white fish as long as Noah's arm, still steaming, knife stuck deep between its ribs. A greasy-haired man at the closest table pulled out the blade with vigor as soon as the platter touched the table, carving slices and serving his tablemates. Noah thought he might ask the prince about the source of such bounty, and why it had not been used to help feed Phempor's hungry population. He preferred to do so before he himself was obliged to refuse the meat and risk hurting the prince's sense of hospitality, but his host cut off his question and motioned for his silence. Noah acquiesced.

Scarred servants began filing out of side doors carrying trays of silver goblets to each table. Suddenly, Noah recognized the smell. He feared nothing and no one but the Lord God, but a visceral terror clutched his heart in an icy, shocking grip, and a chill swept over him. The color drained from his face, and he stared at the prince with unbelieving wide eyes.

The prince returned his stare with a cold smile. "Welcome to our feast."

‹ CHAPTER 2 ›

One might have thought the goblets filled with wine, but a wine that was somehow too thick and viscous, too opaquely red. Clinking toasts to good health echoed around the hall. The feasters joined in cheerful conversation with one another, drank deeply, wiped crimson droplets from stained lips. Noah's gorge rose. He looked incredulously at the prince, who grinned large, and the nightmare continued.

The thin black-clad man appeared in front of their table holding a silver basin. This he placed before the prince, then clapped and beckoned toward a shadowed, high-arched doorway. A pair of servants emerged, pulling a tall apparatus slowly into the dim light. It was a bizarre, gangly thing, made of cord and iron bars set on small wooden wheels, somewhat resembling a gallows. A young woman, barely more than a girl, was suspended head-down, back curved and stretched over its metal framework. She was alive, moaning dreamily as if drugged, her face beautiful despite being swollen and red from hanging upside down. Her hair fell loosely down in satin curls that waved as the apparatus stopped, and through his increasing sickness, Noah caught the faint scent of roses.

The girl's head hung over the silver bowl; her curls almost brushed its edges. Almost delirious with incredulity, Noah whispered. "No." He shoved up from the table, scattering his silverware. A leather-clad fist hit him squarely behind the ear, stunning him. Hands grabbed him by the hair and neck and forced him back down. His cheek pressed against a silver plate; spittle from his quick, heavy breaths marred the girl's reflection upon it, but he could still make out the black sleeve and thin white hand, the curved knife that drew closer to engorged veins in a slender neck. Noah squeezed shut his eyes and cried out.

He blinked them open, hoping to awake. Instead, he saw blood. Pulsating rivulets of bright red mixed with steady flows of maroon, all meeting and mixing and masking the girl's face with macabre, meandering stripes that soaked into her blonde hair and turned it dark. The clear, sharp drips onto silver became the wet sounds of liquid pouring into liquid as the bowl rapidly filled. The prince put his lips to the rippling surface and took a sip.

"The rose is a very nice touch, Etien." He smiled benignly at the man in black, a crimson grin against white skin.

"Thank you, my lord."

"I think that will be all for now, Etien, this looks to be quite enough. Take it away—and please, do not waste any."

Servants returned, bowed, and dragged the apparatus with the dead girl away from whence it came; one held a wooden basin under dripping locks to catch the blood that still flowed from the long neck wound. Noah coughed, sick to his very soul and spirit.

"Let our guest up, if you please." The prince waved to the unseen figures behind Noah, still holding him against the table. Noah swayed in his seat as if he were drunk; some small part of his mind, some courageous subconscious spark, steeled him for whatever horrors were next, then his senses rebelled utterly. He vomited across the silverware and onto the floor.

With an animal's reflexes, the prince pushed himself from his seat. He frowned, a faint look of disgust edging his features. His sisters turned to each other, tittering behind bejeweled hands politely raised.

"Well, my appetite is gone." The prince stood, and a servant was at the table before he called. "Clean this up, will you? Noah, walk with me again."

A woman with drooping jowls and golden rings through her ears and nose noticed the prince stand. She turned and sent him an inquisitive look. The prince's handsome face beamed. "Excuse me, everyone," he called. "I leave you now, but please continue without me. Enjoy!" The woman happily resumed her meal.

Strong hands pushed Noah behind the prince. Two burly men in piecemeal leather armor, scarred like the servants and bearing scars of battle besides, walked to either side and behind the missioner. Their hands lay lightly on the hilts of sheathed, curving swords. Noah stumbled along, numb with horror. The prince seemed oblivious to his state, though, and began speaking once more.

"Noah, let me share *my* view of the world. It is this. We are animals—intelligent, cultured, but animals nonetheless. As the stronger predator thrives while the weaker starves and the prey is eaten, so it is with us. Those people outside these walls? They are as cattle to us, as sheep to be slaughtered. Your myths and fantasies cannot protect them, any more than they protect you now. What say you to that?"

An ember of defiance gave fire to Noah's defense of his faith. "Do what you will to me. I am a tool. The seed of truth has been planted in your lands, Prince, and it will grow, all the more if it is watered with the blood of martyrs."

The prince laughed, echoed by his sisters walking behind them. "Poetic! Vomit on your chin, but a gilded tongue! I will try to match you. You speak of your precious converts, yes? Come, let me show you why I will not worry on them."

‹ CHAPTER 3 ›

They came to a well-appointed room lit with candles that gave just enough light to illuminate the pallid corpse on the bed, bloodstained sheets maintaining its barest modesty. The prince's sisters, still lovely but for the red smears around their mouths, mounted the bed and gyrated beside the dead body. The raven-haired woman smiled lasciviously and beckoned to Noah with a finger.

The prince shoved Noah forward. "This man's name was Felun. He is known to you, I believe."

Noah made himself look at what had indeed once been Felun, his features contorted and frozen into a grimacing mask. "Monster," he spat weakly. "What did you do to him?"

"Nothing he did not enjoy, I assure you," the other sister said in a deep, smoky voice. The women exchanged smiles, stretching on all fours like cats.

The prince ran a fingertip over the bloody bed-clothes and licked it. "Your righteous, moral, obedient convert? It took only a glimpse of bare flesh and an invitation, and his pretentious self-righteousness was stripped away. Along, incidentally, with the clothes he was wearing." He jabbed his finger into Felun's covered corpse, sinking the sheet into some deep wound. "Then, after he partook of *my* favorite sacrament, his beautiful parishioners, still kneeling, sucked his very lifeblood from him." He put his face close to Noah's; suddenly, he smeared his still-bloody finger on the missioner's lips. Noah retched again.

Gleeful, the prince jumped back. Head spinning, Noah held himself up on the bedframe, and the women on the bed crawled over the body to kneel behind him. One jerked him by the hair, pulling the back of his head to rest between her breasts.

"Shall I ask you to join us, Noah?" The prince assumed a pensive air. "There are five more rooms like this, with the same scene played out. Your friend Machmanis? Your altar house stewards? Dead. But I need not end *your* life."

Noah shut his eyes, and the prince stepped closer. "I can reward you in ways much more real than your God has done. Will you bow instead to me?" Noah turned away from the voice, the foul metallic breath.

The prince gripped his face and whispered in his ear. "They say you have never had a woman—that you have remained chaste for nearly five hundred years! Astounding! Why is that, I wonder?" Cold hands caressed Noah's chest from behind. He shuddered.

"Are you uninterested in women, then?" whispered the prince. He darted his blood-wetted tongue into the missioner's ear. "Very well. Say that *I* am your god, Noah, and your god will love you, in spirit *and* in flesh." With nothing left to vomit, Noah dry heaved. He could not think clearly anymore, could not form the words of the desperate prayer his spirit was crying.

Unexpectedly, most of all to Noah, he began laughing. The sound was soft at first, almost as if he were drawing a hitched breath, but he then raised his face to the prince, looked him straight in the eye, and burst out in full-throated laughter.

"Oh, dear," said the prince, frowning. "I think we have broken his mind."

"You have not, Prince," Noah told him, with an edge of iron to his voice. "My message for you has changed. Turn from your evil ways. Fall on your face and repent. There is forgiveness for you, even now, even as your damnation pursues you."

The frown deepened. "Your confidence was rather darling before, Noah, but now it bores me."

"And yours is pathetic! Redemption slips away, Prince. It is not gone, but it is at the door."

The prince turned. "Yes, I am most certainly bored. Sisters, do what you will with him." The woman holding Noah's hair pulled his head back once more. The other ran her hand down to his thigh, then opened her mouth to reveal teeth that had been subtly filed to points.

A wolfhound's whine—a hollow sound, as if it echoed along a stone passage—caused the sisters to pause. They glanced toward an open portal, black with shadow, toward which the scarred guards started.

A thick grey body hurtled through the darkness, knocking one armored man down despite his size. The other began to draw his sword; he stopped, then stepped back, as a massive form filled the portal. Noah had regained control of himself, and he pulled away from the grasp of the women, whose eyes had widened at the sight of the new arrival.

Like a massive moth emerging from a stone cocoon, the giant came into the room, rising to full height once inside. The remaining guard made a spastic attempt to remove his blade once more, but before he could do so, the giant swung his own weapon. The crunch of bone on bone and the guard's cry of pain from his crushed hand spurred the two sisters off the bed and out of the ghastly room, fleeing half-naked. The prince spared a cruel sneer in Noah's direction and exited behind them.

A huge sandaled foot pushed down the guard struggling to rise from the dead wolfhound's weight. The heavy head of a two-handed hammer, swung again by the giant, came down with a crack on the man's shin, turning his efforts to agonized cries.

"My great thanks, Eudeon," said Noah. He glanced at the incapacitated guards and the still form of the wolfhound. "You killed the hound."

"I had no choice," replied the Naphil. "It has tasted human flesh, I am certain."

"I have no doubt of that. Help me." Noah grabbed a corner of a hanging tapestry, woven gold glinting in the candlelight. As one, he and Eudeon pulled it from the wall and covered Felun's corpse.

"Here." Eudeon reached up for the wooden rod upon which the tapestry had hung, pulling it down and handing Noah the makeshift staff.

"Lives have been lost here," said Noah darkly. "But perhaps there are lives to be saved. Come."

Eudeon led Noah out of the hideous chamber. Undeterred by wolfhounds' howls ahead, they followed the winding corridor, wary of each shadowed doorway that pitted the passage walls. With mortal threat came clarity of mind and renewed vigor, and both served Noah well when a meaty guard barreled out of a side door behind the two missioners. Bellowing and brandishing a pole arm with a rusted, hook-like head, the man attacked. Noah spun to meet him, blocking the weapon with his improvised staff, which proved solid. In a practiced motion, Noah pulled his parry away to sweep the guard's feet. The guard's back hit the ground; Eudeon dropped the top of his hammer down on the man's knees as if they were buttercream and the hammer the churn stick. The giant kicked the pole arm away, and they moved on quickly.

"A crossway lies ahead, Noah," said Eudeon. "If we hurry, we might gain it before the wolves. Our escape lies to the right."

"Then we shall go left," said Noah. "I will leave no other victim to die today at the hands of these monsters."

Even as he spoke, the crossway came into view around a bend, and with it a pack of slavering wolfhounds. No guards ran after the animals; if the wolves had handlers, such men had been left far behind. Retreat would only bare their backs to the beasts, so Noah and Eudeon braced for the onslaught.

The wolves reached the intersection; to the missioners' surprise, all but two of the pack peeled off howling toward something unseen down one of the cross corridors. Before either man could wonder, the remaining pair of running wolves was upon them.

Eudeon met the snarling snout of the first with the head of his hammer, spinning aside to let the canine corpse fly past him to the ground. Noah stepped back and swung hard at the wolfhound that lunged at his throat. The end of his staff hit the beast behind the ear; it shook its rough mane, stunned, but attacked again. Noah managed to bring his staff up in defense and thrust it lengthwise into the wolf's jaws, bracing with two hands against the angry animal. Eudeon struck again; the wolf collapsed, its spine broken.

"I like this not, Noah," said the Naphil, hefting his hammer. "This tool is meant to build, not destroy."

Noah did not give an answer, his silence implying agreement. They approached the intersection of corridors cautiously. From the silence, Noah guessed the rest of the wolfhounds had moved on.

Around the corner, wolf carcasses littered the blood-slicked floor. Another animal paced around the bodies, nudging them with its hawklike beak, sensing for signs of life. The beast was the size of a lion. Bristly hairs covered its body; long claws clicked on the tile, leaving bloody prints as it meandered. It was a fearsome creature, but not so much as the being beside it.

The giant was wiping the blades of his weapon on the wolves' hides. Not quite as tall as Eudeon, he still stood well over eight feet. Segmented iron pauldrons covered his broad shoulders and connected to iron-and-leather gauntlets, and an iron breastplate guarded his chest; otherwise, he was unarmored. The blades of his weapon connected to an ornate haft taller than a human; at the top of it, two swept to either side, and a third continued straight upward.

Noah almost laughed in relief. "Gilyon!"

"Praise the Creator—you are alive." Gilyon strode over the wolves to Noah and gripped his shoulders. "When we heard the stewards were missing, we feared the worst."

"A long story, and one which we must save for a later time." Another figure, human, came out from a shadowy recess in the wall. Metal glinted in the hall's torchlight under his faded duster. He carried a crossbow, its stock and magazine dressed in gold leaf and chalcedony, its ornateness in striking contrast to his worn clothing.

"Midash." Noah nodded at the man. "I knew you must be close. My thanks to you—and your griffin too."

Midash tilted his chin in acknowledgment, patted his familiar on its corded shoulder, and began plucking quarrels from the wolfhounds. He frowned, staring at Noah's clothing. "Are you hurt?"

The missioner glanced down at his crimson-spattered tunic, felt the cold, wet fabric sticking to his skin where he had been pulled against the bedsheets soaked in Felun's blood, and realized what a ghastly sight he must be.

"No, I am uninjured," he said. "Felun . . ."

Footsteps and the creak of hard leather warned of the soon appearance of more guards, so Noah and his comrades ran the other way. Their retreat had naught to do with fear; on the contrary, Noah had no doubt that any martial encounter with armed adversaries would be fatal for the other party, no matter their number. Eudeon was the most peaceable of his rescuers, and he had slain beasts thrice his size with only his hands. He followed now, still in a bit of a daze, only gradually realizing that none of his companions quite knew where they needed to go.

"The slave who guided me must have escaped the moment she was able," Eudeon was saying.

"As would any sane person," Midash said.

Out of a pillared opening ahead came a manslave balancing a pitcher on his head. He spotted the group fast approaching, squealed, and darted away, letting the vessel crash to the ground. It shattered, painting the floor dark with its contents. Gilyon put on a burst of speed, Midash's griffin close behind. The Naphil did not chase the slave; rather, he charged the portal out of which the man came. Noah rushed after them, steeling himself for more horrors, and the scene he found did not disappoint.

Gilyon and the griffin had discovered the kitchen, if such a place had been designed by the Serpent, his demons, and death itself. Blood covered everything: tables, floor, wooden blocks and red-stained basins.

Cages lined the walls, huddled men and women inside several. Others were empty; despairing, Noah breathed a prayer for the poor souls once contained there. A handful of kitchen staff, necks branded, paused in their work. A series of clay ovens heated the room to uncomfortable degrees, but the nightmarish centerpiece of the place was the ugly slab of wood in the center of the room, where two men held the feet and hands of a young woman while another brandished a knife over her smooth throat, his business mercifully interrupted by the appearance of the savage-looking newcomers. All inside the human slaughterhouse were frozen; the natural inhabitants of the place, greasy and meaty men stained with sweat and wearing belts heavy with all manner of knives, were still from momentary surprise, while Gilyon had been struck with abject disgust. The moment passed, as does the quiet prayer before the sacrifice, and chaos ensued.

Midash's griffin leapt over the butcher's table while kitchen workers scattered in every direction. The middle butcher raised a cleaver, to no avail; the beast knocked him to the filthy floor and ripped off a good portion of flesh on either hand with two strikes of its toothed beak.

The other two men dropped the woman's limbs and attacked Gilyon together. A harsh sound, a combination of cry of rage and scoffing laugh, barked out, and he swept his crossblade across their advance. Knives clattered to the ground. One of the men scrambled back, exiting the room through an arch masked by hanging strips of dried fish. The last had been literally disarmed; the stump of his right wrist bled freely, and he shrieked in pain. From the kitchen's entrance, the other missioners watched the oily man trip on his own severed hand and fall hard on his backside. While Midash and Eudeon ran to the occupied cages, Noah caught the maimed butcher under his sweaty arms and pulled him to the ovens. He heaved the man up, ignoring his agonized gibbering, and with a strain and a firm grip on the man's shoulder and elbow he forced the hemorrhaging wrist into the oven. The butcher squealed like a hog, but Noah set his strength against him. Flesh seared and fat popped as the stump pressed to the hot clay of the oven.

The wound cauterized, Noah let the moaning man drop to the ground. With his hammer, Eudeon had broken the locks on the cages, and Midash was now gathering the frightened captives together, soothing them in the gentle way that was his reputation among the missioners.

"Look at their eyes," said Midash to the others. Set in the sooty faces were pale violet irises still full of fear.

"You are from Seba?" Noah asked the woman closest to him. She nodded. Her striking eyes that marked her as a member of the Seban tribes pulled to the ovens, and she began to cry.

Gilyon pulled up the man he had maimed and threw him against a wall. "You know why she cries?" he growled. The Naphil took his groan as fearful assent. "What manner of . . ."

At that moment, Noah thought his giant friend would lose control and end the man right then. Gilyon checked himself, though.

"Your reckoning comes soon," he told the butcher. "But first, you will lead us to your master."

Midash stayed with the rescued Sebans, but his griffin followed Noah, Eudeon, and Gilyon. Their path cut through other food storage and preparation areas. From one room's ceiling hung scaled pangolin carcasses and ten-foot-long vipers. In another, vapid-looking women slowly cut a variety of cacti, barely registering the party making its way among the copper vats that filled the room. The wounded butcher halted at a pile of whitish powder in a silver bowl, addiction's lustful intensity in his eyes, but Gilyon roughly prodded him on.

The busy sounds of eating and drinking, mingled with a score of scandalized conversations, came from ahead. The butcher broke away in a burst of speed, screaming a warning and stumbling down the steps leading to the hall. Noah and the two Nephilim chased him, but Midash's griffin caught him at the bottom of the stair in a long pounce and knocked him flailing into the room, where he lay still. Their appearance in the hall interrupted the gossip and revelry, but not entirely; to his disgust, Noah noticed one pudgy man glance up while he continued to drink from his goblet, dark blood trickling down his chin.

Groups of leather-clad guards filtered into the hall, taking positions at the exits. They kept their distance, though, testimony to the dead wolves the missioners had taken no pains to hide. With Eudeon and Gilyon flanking him and the griffin at his side, Noah ignored the threat of the armed guards.

"This evil ends now," said Noah, letting his righteous fury melt into words, but the harsh laugh that echoed from hearth to canopy drowned them out.

"Welcome to my kingdom, children of the *bene Elohim!*" A voice like burnt honey, sweet and smoky and far from human, came from above them. When he had first come to this place as the prince's "guest," Noah had taken the bestial stone forms that jutted from the walls overhead as statuary. In actuality, as he now saw, they bounded a balcony, where the prince stood now. His dark eyes met Noah's. He began muttering, lifting up hands, the light from below casting his shadow on the ceiling like a wide-winged bat. Noah suddenly felt fatigued beyond what his exertion thus far would justify.

"That is no human prince only," gasped Gilyon. Eudeon struggled for breath also. Noah dropped to his knees and looked around him.

What little rosiness remained in the feasters' pale, fleshy faces had drained to stark white, and those lips not already stained crimson had turned blue. The blood from spilled goblets lightened to pink, then clear. Noah glimpsed a woman flopping about, still clutching a morsel of meat. Whatever sorcery this was, it knew no friends but the prince.

Tired, more tired than he had ever been, Noah felt a thin wetness replacing the stickiness of his blood-soaked clothing. Where red droplets had splattered his front, he now saw spots of water, like he had been caught in a light mist shower. He could do naught but pray as he succumbed to unconsciousness, lifting his eyes and pleading for deliverance from the demoniac above with the power to turn blood to water.

A polished blade appeared from the prince's chest. A weight lifted from Noah; he breathed anew, as if he were Adam newly formed from the dust. The prince's body tumbled to land hard among a jumble of fat bodies that showed no signs of life returning. Most of the guards were stirring, but these had been disarmed by the common men of Phempor, many familiar to Noah from the altar houses, who were rushing into the hall.

The man on the balcony wiped his sword on the cape he had ripped from the prince as he fell, cleaning the blood that befouled the blue of the lapis at the weapon's hilt. His features were hard, all that was not iron melted away from flesh and spirit by a missioner's life, but the family resemblance to Noah was unmistakeable. He saluted Noah.

Gilyon was already on his feet, supporting himself with his weapon planted on the bricks. Eudeon was sitting, his hand absently petting the panting griffin. "Perhaps," he said to Noah, "it is time for a furlough."

For once, Noah agreed.

‹ CHAPTER 4 ›

Where the frontier of the empire of Atlantis met the nation of Mizraim lay a swamp, at the foot of the mountains that rose above the mists and formed the border between the two lands. The Iron Springs flowed to the Atlantean side, feeding the vast expanse of bog and cypress forests. There was life there: pitcher plants and sundews supplemented what their starved roots could obtain with bog spiders and yellow flies; foxes darted about the forest thickets, never a human seen in their lifetimes; fat frogs fed on firefae beetles and were in turn fed upon by the tentacled creatures that hid themselves in the tannin-brown water. The swamp was useless for crops and herds, and so it had been left untouched by the waves of Atlantean pioneers, despite their ever-growing, never-slaked thirst to push outward into the wildernesses still unseen by any children of Cain. For the Atlantean border rangers—the virgin huntresses called the Wa-Mizhan—it was enough that the lords of Atlantis laid claim to it. For this reason, Tehama, daughter of Dyeus, now led a group of rangers to confront those who had violated Atlantean sovereignty.

Unlike the giant men of her kind, females with the blood of the angels grew to normal human height. The Nephilim huntress did have a preternatural beauty far beyond that of a purebred daughter of Eve, but that was all that set her apart from the women with her—that, and her age. Most of the Wa-Mizhan failed to protect their virginity for more than a few decades, although several with Tehama had served for over a century. She remained the standard, the first Huntress and the eldest, nearing five hundred years and never knowing a man, despite the countless who had made an attempt. She maintained that she wished to serve a greater good, and this was true, but her shame at her family's constant fornications and a desire to prove herself different from them drove her more than she would admit. Those in her company strengthened Tehama. From atop her elk she turned, surveying the huntresses behind her, strong women she loved more profoundly than anything romance could offer them.

The Wa-Mizhan wore no uniforms. Their tasks and surroundings informed their clothing, gear, and tools, both practical and martial, and what each of the women wore gave a unique history of her service. Most of the huntresses had bows, although some preferred slings, and long knives were ubiquitous on belts and thighs. In lieu of the gold and orichalcum of their pampered urban sisters and mothers, totems of wood, tooth, and bone hung at their necks and from their ears. Armor of boiled leather or drakehide or horn scale covered woolen hooded tunics. Hair was kept short or tightly braided; ornate and flowing was the fashion in Atlantis, but the jungles and forests demanded practicality.

Their line of light horses trotted on the higher, dryer paths, above the waterline but in the midst of the mists that never quite cleared. A predatory menagerie flanked the horses on either side. Every Wa-Mizhan chose her own animal familiars, invaluable partners in their patrols, supplementing the huntresses' craft with sight or smell, talons or teeth. Tehama noted that panthers had become popular with the latest generation, as had armored tarasq

dragons and wolf-sized badcats. Owls and falcons flew
low patterns above, and one veteran had trained a pack of
peccaries that skimmed the soft ground with razor-sharp
tusks.

Tehama rode bareback on her grand elk, the latest
in a centuries-old line that she bred herself. Despite
the colossal span of the beast's antlers, it could navigate
all but the densest woodland at speed, and no other
fleet mount established such dominance so quickly
without creating the fear engendered by a dragon, even
a saddled one.

"There," said Kiah, her *beth*, the second-in-command
of the group, riding at her side on a mist-grey mare. She
pointed at a cluster of lamps in the distance, the man-
ade lights discernible from the flickering firefae only by
their constancy. As they approached the lamps, peat-built
structures took form through the haze.

"No telling how long they have been here," mused
Kiah. "The mist never leaves the swamp, and peat houses
upon peatland is fine camouflage."

"There is telling," corrected Tehama. "We ask. They
tell. Come."

Tehama led her rangers down to the collection of
hovels, making no effort to mask their coming. They rode
slowly, stopping at a long, round-topped structure where
a group of men wearing high waders and damp-looking
cloaks huddled near the canvas-covered doorway. Scarves
swaddled their faces and heads, making it impossible to
ascertain from what peoples they came.

Kiah addressed them. "Who are you, and why have
you invaded the lands of Atlantis?"

The lead man, his eyes hidden by curious dark discs,
held up his lamp. "Do you intend us harm?"

"We are a skein, not a pack," Tehama said, "otherwise we would not now be speaking, and you would be dead. We are scouting, not hunting. Answer the questions."

"My name is Ninniachul, ah, ah, and we are from the tribes of Mizraim, across the mountains," he said. Tehama could not ascertain if the man was scared or merely awkward. "We need the iron from these bogs—bogs that belonged to no man forty years ago, when last I was here."

"You people have no turbary rights here," started Kiah, but Tehama stopped her. "Why do you need this iron?" the Naphil asked.

"Why?" sputtered Ninniachul. "Why? Because the, the hordes of Zuthi are raping their way through our lands! My people are murdered, our homes burnt, our herds slaughtered, our daughters defiled, our sons tortured. Are these reasons enough for you?" His anger gave him fluency.

"That is no matter for Atlantis," said Kiah. "This incursion into our territory is."

"Curse your 'territory!'" The protestation that came from a slight person behind the disc-eyed man was higher pitched than Tehama expected; the Naphil took him for a eunuch and stopped his complaint short.

"Let me finish. We are a fair nation. My Wa-Mizhan will take inventory of what you have thus far obtained. Your work will not go unrewarded; you shall be paid a fair portion, but the remainder will go to its rightful owners."

"Meaning you?" said Ninniachul angrily.

Tehama did not answer him, but continued. "Then this skein will escort you and your workers to the borders of your lands, and we shall consider the matter settled."

"We cannot leave!" said the slight man. He pulled his scarf from his face and stepped forward. To Tehama's surprise, he was, in fact, a she, and young. "Our loggers are missing." Ninniachul sucked in air through clenched teeth and placed a hand on her arm, but the girl brushed him off.

Tehama tilted forward on her elk. "Keep talking."

"What forests of our own we did not cut for walls to defend our villages, the Zuthians put to torch when they fell upon us. We need wood. We need iron. My father knew that this wilderness had both, so we came here. The men logging the swamp forests have been gone three days too long, and I am the only one willing to search for them."

"And neither do you have timber rights, even in a swamp," snapped Kiah.

"Our men might be *dead*," implored the girl. "Please. Help us."

A glance from Tehama silenced Kiah. "What is your name, girl?" asked the Wa-Mizhan leader.

"I am Phiaphara," she answered. "Please."

Tehama saw the truth of the matter in the girl's sky-blue eyes and the covered faces of the men behind her, downcast in shame but willing to suffer it in safety. She unslung her longbow.

"Wa-Mizhan, ready your weapons," she said loudly. "This skein is now a pack. We go hunting."

⋅ CHAPTER 5 ⋅

I will come with you," said Ninniachul. "I, ah, I mapped out the logging routes, after all."

Before her father could forbid her from coming, too, Phiaphara seized her chance. "We must take the boats," she called over her shoulder as she sprinted to the swamp docks. Already Tehama and Kiah were running beside her. "Mounts are useless in the swamps—more likely to drown in a quagmire than help us," she said.

"We are quite aware of that, thank you," replied Kiah. Tehama looked amused.

The peat bog was low and level, dominated by bushy moss with few trees, and the race was short. At the edge of the bog, the Mizraimites had constructed piers that were already being mastered by the green film that seemed to coat everything the swamp touched. The boats tied there were long and flat, designed by Ninniachul to float in just a hand's span of water. Phiaphara placed herself at the prow of the closest, with Tehama, Kiah, and the hare-eared panther that belonged to the *beth*. She had actually never been in one of the boats before; it proved surprisingly stable, hardly sinking down beneath its load. Then again, perhaps she ought not be surprised at all, considering it was conceived by her father. Tehama untied the docking rope, Kiah took up the pushing pole, and they cast off.

The transition to swamp forest was abrupt. While peat was still ever present, cypress and larch rose above the partially decayed plant matter. Lances of light beamed through the mist from the porous ceiling created by the canopy; but for these patches of illumination, the swamp was bathed in perpetual gloom. Four other identical crafts carrying three or four woman warriors apiece followed them into the flooded forest, with Ninniachul joining the crew of the last boat at a markedly slower pace.

Phiaphara felt a twinge of remorse. She had not waited for her father's approval to accompany them because she knew he would not give it; or, if he did, he would not have wanted to. Besides, how could she tell him that her primary interest in being there was to protect *him*? Ninniachul, for all his virtues, was virtually crippled by his poor vision. He also tended to miss details, and he did not know that for the last two days his headstrong daughter had carried a peat knife under her clothes. She peered to the end of the line of boats, the last one a monochromatic grey through the mists, and took comfort from his hunched-over, cloaked hump of a silhouette among his three savage and statuesque companions.

Mossy curtains and screens of fern hid the birds that called to one another incessantly but only seldom showed themselves. Griffinflies buzzed overhead and clung to half-submerged logs, watching the procession warily. Calm black pools punctuated the floating peat and collected the mist, reflecting the forest like fogged mirrors, as if an eerie world lay just beneath the surface. In a sense, considered Phiaphara, it did. While the men had mined the bogs, she had scoured the sparse land for food to supplement the meager dry goods they had brought with them from Mizraim, and she had found it: bilberries, cattails, paradise ferns, bog tea. Her searches had taken her near enough the water to witness the drama among the fish and frogs and suckermouthed eels that at times rippled the waters.

That was near the banks, though, in the shallows. When the water moved here in the deeps, she imagined, things died. In the swamps, the monsters were not overt, as in Mizraim—not like the green dragons of the Powder Plains, or the creodont gangs and miser-drakes that stalked the meadows—but their very clandestinity was what chilled Phiaphara the most. As such, she could not adopt the naive optimism about the logging crew's plight that the other men used to excuse themselves from looking for them.

For a while, the only sound in the swamp beyond the natural chatter of its normal denizens was the push of the poles that propelled the boats. Kiah broke the silence.

"It strikes me, girl," the ranger said, "that you have an uncommonly strong interest in these disappeared fellows, and I wonder why. Perhaps your lover is among them?"

"Lover?" Phiaphara sniffed. "These men are cowards and children, hiding from the war. If it were not for my father instructing them, they likely would have all drowned in the bog by now."

"I say, this girl is a bold one, Kiah," said Tehama, smiling. "A warrior's mistress. No doubt her man is on the front lines of battle right now."

"I have no *man*," said the girl. "My mother died birthing me, and my father is invalid. He needs me."

"You still have not said why," Kiah said.

The beginning pangs of a headache pressed the back of Phiaphara's skull. She squeezed the nape of her neck and rolled her head before she answered. "I am simply tired of *death*. I have lived only a score of years, but those have been so full of it."

"Beginning with your mother," Tehama said.

Phiaphara nodded.

"Tell us about the war—if you care to," prompted Kiah.

A new pulse of pain shot behind her eyes, but Phiaphara ignored it. "The Zuthians are winning it. They are exhibitionists of their violence, and they are very skilled at it. That . . . that is all I wish to say. I hope you will not witness such things." She looked around, letting the swampscape crowd out the more disturbing visions that threatened to surface. "And for some of my people, life has become cheapened. For me, though, it is more valuable than ever."

Kiah appeared satisfied with her answer and about to speak when a shout came from another boat. Tehama nocked an arrow as her *beth* poled their craft to a stop, and the panther laid its long ears back with a growl.

"That hillock?" asked Phiaphara, pointing at a small, bare black island ahead. Tehama ignored her until the other boats pulled even with theirs.

"That is no hillock," the ranger finally answered. "Sling!" she called.

A Wa-Mizhan warrior flung a shot stone at the shallow island. Phiaphara fancied herself brave, but she instinctively shifted to the very middle of the boat when the island proved to be a mass of armored arthropods, as long as she was tall, that scattered into the water in all directions.

"Scutum millipedes," said Tehama. "Not a danger to us."

Phiaphara craned her neck to peek over the boat's edge, unconvinced. "How can you be sure?"

"Because we are not dead."

"Scutums are scavengers," explained Kiah. "A bog swamp is a perfect habitat for them." She pushed them closer to the mass of material the creatures had vacated and prodded it with her pole. "Tehama, look at this."

The Wa-Mizhan leader balanced at the prow, examining the tea-brown water and whatever was in it. "Too big for a human," she mused. "They might almost be Nephilim men."

"But look at the jaws," said Kiah. "And the forearms." She used the push pole to lift up an object fully out of the water. Morbid curiosity overcame Phiaphara, and she came closer to inspect.

Nothing but stringy bits of waterlogged meat still clung to the bones, but that was enough to tell that the thing was an arm—but an arm that was three times as long as it ought to be. Skulls peered empty eyed just below the surface, and the jaws were indeed oversized and underbitten, with long, sharp foreteeth no human possessed.

"How many?" called a woman from another boat.

"Three," said Kiah. "None human."

"Ah, ah, and there are cut stumps," called Ninniachul. "We are on the right path."

"Let us move on," commanded Tehama. Phiaphara strongly agreed.

They pushed ahead slowly and quietly, scanning for another sign of the loggers and wary of any living specimen of the half-eaten carcasses. On the Mizhan plains, Phiaphara's keen vision let her see for miles; here, the mists and close vegetation, the monotone swampy green, made her efforts a struggle. She rested her eyes on the familiar figure of her father. He perched at his boat's stern, turning his head back and forth in a regular rhythm, like a gear-work toy owl set to an orrery's cogs. Phiaphara noticed that Tehama was staring at him too.

"How does your father see?" asked the Naphil. "You say his sight is crippled, but I cannot tell it."

"Are those black plates sorcerous in some way, or is he some sort of diviner?" asked Kiah.

Ninniachul noticed the three women's attentions and waved awkwardly, the large dark discs covering his eyes making him appear insectoid. Despite the grim setting, Phiaphara smiled.

"Those are occluders," she said. "My father designed them. Tiny pinholes in carved stone discs. He says the holes focus the light."

"How was he blinded?" asked Tehama.

"He was not. His sight has simply . . . diminished, I suppose, as he has grown older."

Kiah turned away, her brief interest gone. "Hm. I have never heard of such a thing."

"A curse?" Tehama suggested. "There are fine magicians in Atlantis who might lift it."

Phiaphara shrugged. "Just age." She stared at the water, clutching her cloak to herself and feeling uncharacteristically self-conscious. At home, people tended to mock her father's eccentric affect even while applauding his work. This huntress's questions of him had been sincere and kind, and in Phiaphara's mind they had shifted her from a heroic, distant, rather frightening stranger to . . . someone more familiar, somehow. As she considered it, she realized that Tehama was the woman she wished to emulate, to be. The thought was unexpectedly alarming; in that moment, Phiaphara felt everything about herself—her words, her bearing, her shabby clothing, her father and country—falling suddenly subject to the approval of the huntress. Cold butterflies erupted inside her, but she drew a deep breath and tried to let them escape. There was plenty to fear in this swamp already.

As if to prove it, a moldy face passed by her. She forced herself to whisper instead of shriek. "Push back, push back!"

The huntresses checked the boat's advance and poled it backward. All three women peered over the side.

"There!" said Kiah, wedging her pole in submerged roots for an anchor. Phiaphara used a short paddle to clear away peat and slime from the swampwater's surface. The corpse was statuesque in the shallow, motionless water.

"One of your loggers?" asked Kiah, who had drawn her horn-handled hunting knife. Phiaphara shook her head no.

By now, the closest boat had pulled beside them, letting its Wa-Mizhan occupants get a view of the body. "But he must be recently dead," said one. "His features are clear."

"Difficult to say. The tannin in these sorts of swamps keeps away decay," said Kiah.

"What about the scutum millipedes?"

Tehama looked about her, then above her. "Perhaps there is a reason they avoid this place."

A heron's creaky call startled Phiaphara. The Wa-Mizhan rangers looked to the sound expectantly; its maker was no bird, but rather a huntress with close-cropped olive-green hair in the boat furthest ahead. When she saw that she had their attention, she stabbed the water with a boar spear. The tip struck stone just beneath the surface, the sharp crack easily audible and unmistakably foreign to the swamp.

"A canal?" wondered Kiah.

"Road, more likely," said Tehama. "Drowned by a rising swamp. Let us follow where it leads."

The boats scraped along the slimy stone. Half-submerged totems poked from either side of their procession, weathered and ancient and filmed in a swamp green that failed to hide hideous, leering stone faces.

The first signs of the loggers' fates came soon. Whatever had turned the flatboat to flotsam had made no effort to hide it. In fact, its splintered planks seemed to have been positioned purposefully, stuck into the thick peat pointed straight up. Tehama caught Phiaphara's eye and held one finger to her lips, and the world around the girl suddenly went mute.

The swamp's birds and bullfrogs had long ceased their calls, ever since they had started down the drowned road. Now the pull of the poles through the water stopped too. Wa-Mizhan from each boat slipped into the boot-high water without the slightest splash, disappearing into the mists with animal familiars that moved with the same eerie silence. The rest of the rangers—seven of them, Tehama and Kiah included—formed a group with Phiaphara and her father that kept in the center of the sunken path.

Ninniachul pressed close to Phiaphara. "Stay with me, dear one. I like this none at all." A severe look from Kiah quieted him.

"Be as quiet as you can," whispered Tehama. The breathy admonition was somehow serpentine, and Phiaphara had the impression that they had reached the ears of their intended hearers and not a handspan further. Ninniachul nervously jerked his head yes, like a fowl pecking for grain.

The road ended in a ruin rising to the treetops, partly hidden in the shadows of the trees and further masked by the same thick coating of the slime that covered everything else. Despite the roots and vines grasping and weaving among the pitted stone blocks, the structure was intact, though for how many uncounted ages it had remained so was beyond Phiaphara's guess.

Phiaphara craned her neck to find the ruin's top. Shelters and halls in the Mizraim flatlands seldom rose above a single story, and she was rather awestruck that someone so long ago was able to build so high, and in a swamp of all places. The main structure was stacked in three tiers and capped by a enormous statue, details peeled away by time, but its presence and prominent placement suggested the ruin was once a temple dedicated to it. The arms of the temple curved away from the bottom tier and formed the walls of a courtyard, now a cove of dark brown water. Wrecked boats and logs were strewn about, new additions to the ancient tableau. The stench of the place assaulted Phiaphara like something physical. She folded her scarf across her face, breathing through her mouth, still tasting the foulness in the air.

A small splash broke the silence when a chalk-skinned Wa-Mizhan stumbled in the courtyard. She regained her footing, then looked down and jumped back. She waved her hand forward with urgency. At a nod from Tehama, three other huntresses advanced to join her. The four women and their animals—a speckled hound, a dire wolf, and two hunter tarasqs of different breeds—swept the proximal courtyard, pushing the peat into piles with legs and bodies, clearing the surface of the water that never rose past the knee. The huntresses trod gingerly and carefully; the hound and wolf kept up a quiet growl. Tehama led the rest of the group forward, but when Phiaphara saw what paved the flooded courtyard, she dared not step further.

Like the corpse in the swamp, the faces she saw under
the water had features that would have been recognizable, had she known them. Their bodies lay head to foot,
spanning the stone walls that bounded the court and
extending as far as she could see toward the ruins. None
was marred by much decay, but every one bore an identical grin-shaped wound at the neck, from one angle of the
mandible to the other and dipping almost to the top of
the sternum. They were naked.

"Take the wall," ordered Tehama, putting an arrow to
string and pulling it just taut. "All together—do not split
up." She leapt up green-clad stone shelves to the top of
the wall, followed by her *beth*. Phiaphara scrambled up
next, finding the way far slipperier than the two huntresses had made it appear, but she managed to attain the
wall without much difficulty and helped her father up.
The girl crept close behind sure-footed Kiah, stepping in
her footprints. She looked back past her father at the rest
of the Wa-Mizhan, then up at Tehama and Kiah; every
hand held a weapon. Phiaphara pulled her knife.

"Did you hear that?" Phiaphara overheard Tehama's
question to her *beth*.

"No," Kiah answered, in a way that connoted she
ought to have.

"I thought I heard grunting."

Phiaphara listened. She heard nothing, but as her
eyes drifted over the pockmarked ruins, a shaggy shape
passed across a gap in the rocks. Her knees began shaking involuntarily, threatening to tumble her off the wall's
slippery stone. She tapped the quiver at Kiah's back, not
daring to speak.

Any warning would have been too late regardless.
Enormous apes, stocky bodies half again as tall as a

human and covered with matted hair, spilled from the
ruins like termites from a broken mound, bellowing and
flinging some dark, clumpy substance. Some splashed
headlong into the swampy courtyard, others took to the
moss-draped branches that surrounded and overhung it,
but most charged onto the wall, shambling frighteningly
quickly toward them.

"Swamp apes. I count twenty-seven," said one of the
women behind Phiaphara, whose glimpse thus far of the
apes in the few seconds since their appearance had been
sufficient to confirm only that they existed, never mind to
number them.

"Off the wall!" shouted Tehama, loosing an arrow at
one brachiating beast above her and shooting another
as she dropped to the corpse-filled cove. The other
Wa-Mizhan and their familiars followed suit. Phiaphara
spared a glance to the other side of the wall, beyond
the ruins to the wild bog, hoping for a sign of the other
huntresses. She saw none; a sheet of mist and blanket of
slime and peat hid the dark waters of the swamp and its
horrors, and she could not imagine finding escape that
way. "Hurry, Father!" she cried, and she dropped.

Hoping she would not turn an ankle, she buckled
as she landed, falling on her side in the fetid water but
holding fast to her knife. She thrust it out blindly as she
got up and wiped her eyes, trying not to think on the bodies underfoot. She had fallen ten feet or so. The women
around her had formed a semicircle and were firing
arrows and darts and shot at the onslaught of giant apes.
Above her, Ninniachul hesitated.

"Now, Father!" Instead of heeding his daughter,
Ninniachul crouched on the wall. The apes came single
file. Their cheeks and foreheads swelled in fatty folds over

their noses and beady eyes, and yellow fangs filled their howling mouths. The leader sped up, ready to strike.

Ninniachul's hands flew from under his cloak. A flash and a loud blast erupted from the ape's chest; its speed carried its body forward, but it listed and fell to the outside of the wall. The next beast met the same fate, the meat of its shoulder exploding and showering the Wa-Mizhan below, two of whom were obliged to scramble out of the way of the tumbling carcass.

"Not a sorcerer, eh?" said Kiah, sending her blade through the eye of the fallen ape for good measure. The other apes paused. Ninniachul hurriedly sat on the wall, trying to make the distance down as short as possible.

A screaming swamp ape dropped from the trees above Ninniachul, who fell backward with a cry into the unseen swamp. The ape jumped after him in pursuit. A roar of bestial pain followed another explosion beyond the ruined wall, and then the stinking creatures were upon the Wa-Mizhan.

Phiaphara's shock gave her vigor and a certain reckless abandon. She screamed defiantly as she faced a monster ape twice her mass and thrice her reach. The beast swiped a feces-smeared paw at her; she swung her knife as she stepped back, cutting flesh but tripping over some underwater limb. She fell back, shallow swamp and human flesh cushioning her impact. Her elbow struck something hard. As she drew her hand over it, she felt a smooth wood grain and ran her fingers up to a metal head. The swamp ape reached to grab her, to tear her apart; with all her might, Phiaphara swung the logging hand-axe from the water, between the ape's outstretched arms and into its belly. She wrenched out the axe and swung again. The ape's simultaneous backhand blow hit her, knocking her to the side, but its blow had no real injuring strength, and hers had rent the animal's skull at its ear.

Sucking in air hard despite its oppressive rottenness, Phiaphara found another target for her new weapon in the exposed back of an ape that was attempting to fend off a badcat shredding its legs. The badcat's owner finished the animal with a spearthrust between the ribs. Phiaphara sidled close to her, steeling herself for another fight, but the apes had either died or vanished into the darkness of the swamp.

The Wa-Mizhan who had scouted ahead began appearing from hidden perches and gathering arrows and darts from the dead swamp apes. A few of their animal familiars sniffed at the carcasses, but even the scavenger dog turned its nose away. Phiaphara splashed back to the courtyard entrance and climbed the wall again, searching for a sign of her father.

"Hello, my dear," called Ninniachul. Phiaphara sighed in relief, but he was still in danger, limbs splayed out on his cloak and floating on a quagmire that had almost finished claiming the ape whose fingers still twitched weakly as they sank. "Perhaps you might find a rope." Before the girl could call down to the huntresses in the courtyard, Tehama had mounted the wall. Together they pulled the older man to safety and carefully lowered themselves into the corpse cove.

Ninniachul noticed the axe in Phiaphara's hand. "This tool is of our make."

"Time to look for bodies," said Kiah. With a few words from the *beth*, the Wa-Mizhan formed a perimeter on the walls and began the search. Ninniachul found a stone block, wiped it of slime with his cloak, and sat down to wait. Exhausted but still motivated, Phiaphara moved to help, but Tehama pulled her aside.

"You accounted well for yourself," the Naphil said. "Where did you get the axe?"

"Blind chance," answered Phiaphara. "When I needed it, it was at hand—literally."

"Fortuitous," said Tehama. "Perhaps some god has marked you for his."

"That would be fine," she said, then wrinkled her nose and spat as she looked over the dead islands of hair and flesh dotting the cove of preserved corpses. "As long as he had nothing to do with *this*."

Ninniachul identified the bodies of the loggers to a man, their throats crudely ripped and torn in bestial imitation of the wounds suffered by the unknown dead. The huntresses agreed that the ruins must have been a temple, the sunken courtyard a grave for victims of some ritualistic sacrifice; Kiah wanted to explore further, but Tehama forbade it. One of the Wa-Mizhan scouts handed out crushed leaves that exuded a strong, sweet-smelling sap that helped obviate the stench that now covered everyone. The return through the swamp was somber and quiet, but uneventful, and for that Phiaphara was thankful.

Between the swamp stench and the aromatic sap, Phiaphara's olfaction was stimulated enough that she doubted the new smell at first. When Tehama and Kiah both began sniffing the air, her doubts vanished.

"Smoke," said Phiaphara

Tehama grimaced. "Peat smoke. How much fuel do you use to smelt your iron?"

"It is no small amount, but I would not imagine that the smoke from it would carry this far onto the water."

"It would not," said Kiah. "The bog is burning."

Past the tree line the smoke was denser than any mist, and they had to find the docks by memory and feel. Phiaphara once again wrapped her scarf tight around her mouth, debarking quickly. The heat passed over her in waves, but she could not see flames; indeed, she could not see much of anything, which is why she collided hard with the man stumbling down the pier.

Phiaphara got back up, but the man did not. She knelt to him, not knowing how to aid him, unable to recognize him in his tattered cloak and scarf.

"Zuthians," he wheezed. "They torched . . . the camp. They . . . killed us . . . all."

"Help!" Phiaphara cried, and at once two huntresses were beside the man. Kiah barked orders to find their mounts, search for survivors, track the saboteurs, but Phiaphara barely heard the *beth*, or felt her father wrap his arms around her. She had withdrawn into a senseless cocoon of rage, hate, and self-pity; she dared not think what she would be when she emerged.

"We must inform my father and uncle that war is coming," said Tehama. "The Atlantean empire cannot ignore this."

"What about the Mizraimites?" asked Kiah.

"They come with us."

"So we give succor to one group of invaders, but will make war against the other?"

"Look at them, Kiah. They are not invaders anymore," said Tehama. "They are refugees."

‹ CHAPTER 6 ›

In the clay warrens that had hosted the missioners since they had arrived in Phempor, a young woman named Emié worked in the stables. The camels she groomed were of a lean, stringy breed, with pronounced humps ideal for traveling in the sulfur deserts, where water was scarce and cooling mists were few. She steeled her nerves with constant prayer while she brushed the hides, plucking the long hairs from the bristles and laying them aside for sale to the weavers. Various pets lazed close at hand: a jewelbox turtle had retreated inside its pearlescent shell, hiding from the afternoon heat; a tufted-tailed degu-rat engaged in coprophagy, happily nibbling at its droppings; and a lemur, nocturnal by nature, napped between the humps on the camel's back. She knew mankind had been lifted above the animals by the Creator; even so, she often found herself looking at life through the lens of that world, and in many ways the sight was true. Lately she had been thinking much on breeding pairs . . .

Her pets rested, but she could not, finding what little anxiolytic she could in the mindless routine of a simple task. She had been waiting—patiently, she fancied, but her heart had been racing since morning—for her companions to return, but thus far she waited for naught. Emié loved them: men of good blood and breeding, but set apart by character. Gilyon, her own blood, son of her grandmother's grandmother, a caster of demons and a mighty warrior; Eudeon, wise worker and brother of the three great Atlantean lords; Midash, minor noble of Havilah and, to her perpetual delight, accomplished griffin master. Noah, eldest of them all, served as the tip of their spear, their animating force, a man with relentless resolve to take the Creator's words to even the furthest frontiers of the Seeding. He was a preacher of righteousness, as wise and well learned as Eudeon, as keen a discerner of spirits and as powerful a caster as Gilyon, a more skilled ingeniator than Midash, and better with animals than herself, but most endearing to Emié was the fact that Noah was brother to Jonan, great-grandfather of her beloved Caiphes.

It was she who learned about the altar stewards' disappearances, news that had sent Noah's fellow missioners after him armed for battle. She implored the Creator God for their deliverance, the same prayer she had said a hundred times that day, and she wondered briefly if the repetition tired Him.

"Emié!" The voice from the outer gates was Eudeon's. He came alone. Dried blood stiffened his clothing, but he moved as one unhurt and with a firm purpose. "Prepare the wagon. There is need of it."

"Medicine bag, quickly!" Emié instructed the lemur. It scurried off, and she fell to the task. "What has happened?" she asked Eudeon while he helped her harness the wagon to the camels. The turtle peeked from its shell, as if curious to know as well.

"That field to which our friend Noah journeyed proved dry and fouled, and there was no harvest, I think," said the Naphil. "Even so, he completed his mission to preach righteousness to the nobles of Phempor, and for that we may give thanks." Emié sensed a dark undertone beneath Eudeon's adopted optimism, but she did not push him for details.

"And your own mission?"

"Noah is well. The others also." Eudeon pulled the last strap taut and buckled it down. "Shall we take a trip?"

The girl and the giant drove the camel-wagon through the muddy streets. Other sturdy carts, mostly pulled by mules, converged on their route, clustering and slowing each other's passage, all driven by agitated-looking men, all headed in the direction of the palace.

Emié's perch on the camels afforded her a clear view of the proceedings as Eudeon drove their wagon into the press. Outside the walls of the palace compound, the doors had been torn down. A shouting mob of peasants packed the space, making room for a rough parade of plain, drably clothed men of Phempor forcing pale-faced people to a line of carts and wagons. Of the latter, some were dressed in rich robes shredded to rags, others wore ripped bits of leather that might have once been armor, and a cheer erupted with every one of them thrown into the back of a wagon. The one before Emié's was marked as a sewage cart, still bearing a pungent pool of its daily consignment. A particularly boisterous yell burst forth as a tall, thin man in black, wrists and ankles bound, was passed above the crowd and tossed into the foulness. The sewage cart drove off, leaving Emié and Eudeon the last to accept their human cargo.

Through the broken gates walked men she knew well, but they were somber and bloodstained. Midash pulled a half-naked woman, stark white and beautiful, by the cord that tied her hands while his griffin stalked behind them. Behind him strode Gilyon carrying his crossblade in one giant fist and a screaming woman much alike to the first in the other. Then came two men, their eyes and the square of their jaws marking them as of the same bloodline, their stern faces masking the great compassion that she knew dwelt in both. The younger was the blood-priest of the missioners, Caiphes of Eden, whose hands were weekly stained with the blood of the altar house sacrifices, but the crimson on them now she thought came from no mere animal. The elder, the man she and the rest followed, looked to have been soaked in blood, not stained. She knew other men older than him, but she suspected that the four-hundred-and-eighty years of Noah of Eden would compare favorably for breadth and depth of experience to another man's full life of twice those years.

"You had better dismount now," said Eudeon. "This may become unpleasant."

Gilyon hauled up the woman he held and deposited her into the wagon, soon joined by the other. For a moment the two women lay there, crumpled and listless. Slowly, as one, they rose up and looked out at the crowd. In voices that seemed to turn the air to winter, they spat a language not human in a quickening chant. Noah immediately raised a hand to them and his eyes to the sky. He spoke the same tongue in a tone of rebuke.

"You will curse no one today!" said Gilyon angrily. At a word from Midash, his griffin crouched and leapt, knocking one of the women down and holding her prone. Gilyon's long arms reached easily over the wagon's side and gripped the other's face. The pop of a jaw dislocating was loud; the scream from a throat with no more tongue to give its words form was louder still. Gilyon did the same to the other woman, slacking her jaw with one violent motion and tearing the tongue out with only the strength of his fingers. He pushed both women facedown, letting the blood from their mouths run over the wagon floor instead of into their lungs. All the while Noah kept up his countercurse, spoken in the language of the angels and carrying the power of a faith that was assured the words would be heard and heeded by One who cared. He finished; only the garbled screams of the two women remained. Midash joined Eudeon on the driver's perch, and they set the camels to follow the long train before them.

Emié calmed herself, shuddering from the sudden violence. With a last prayer that her camels would be safe—she feared none for Eudeon or Midash—she ran to the men at the gate, elated that they had been successful in their own mission: Noah lived.

She stopped short of throwing herself in Caiphes's arms. His hand rested on the pommel of his ancestor Kenan's old sword; Emié noticed that it trembled.

"Are you hurt?" asks Emié, looking for a source of the blood that covered him.

"No, thank the Creator."

"What is all this?"

"Those who resided in the palace have been bound and exiled."

"They . . . killed men?"

Caiphes shut his eyes and nodded.

"Not men only," added Gilyon, wiping his fingers on his already-stained tunic. Briefly he recounted what they had found in the palace.

"I hope all of them are food for the leucrota before night falls," ended the giant.

"No one is beyond redemption," said Noah. "Not even such as they." He sighed. "Only once before have I seen so much death by human hands." He did not have to tell Emié to what he referred. She had heard it from

Greatfather Dashael, who had been there: the Battle of Banishing, when the men of Enoch—old Atlantis—took their city from the Grigori.

"The fiend prince's hands were possessed," said Gilyon. "No wonder he wanted no part of our message."

"Why ask you to the palace, then?" asked Emié to Noah.

"To know all goings-on in the realm of spirit is beyond me," answered Noah. "But I am thankful he heard the truth before he died."

"Before I killed him, you mean," said Caiphes. "I have never killed a man before."

"And does your conscience convict you?" asked Noah.

"No."

"Then trust it."

A shout drew their attention. A man in dress that marked him as a soothsayer of one of Phempor's many pagan faiths stood above the milling crowd that had not dispersed.

"How now shall we dispense with the governance of this people?" he cried, a thick length of animal intestine draped over his upheld hands. "The organs have shown the way! Let the Temple of the Ox lead us into a new age!"

Shouts against the suggestion drowned out those for it, the clash giving birth to a dozen loud arguments. An older man, long thick braids caked with mud and dragging at his feet, climbed up a crashed gate door. Emié recognized him: a local seer, not a worshipper of the Lord, but old and with some influence and true power.

"Look to the lion and the leucrota. The one who kills the leader of the pride takes its place." This pronouncement was met with more agreement than that of the soothsayer. The seer pointed at Caiphes. "This man will lead us! I have seen it! Blood and death and salvation come with him!"

A strange mix of fear, pride, and jealousy washed over Emié, her emotions already raw from the bloody spectacle she had witnessed earlier. She knew Caiphes well, but she dared not guess what response he might give to such a pronouncement as that.

Caiphes stepped forward, the people before him melting back, making a space. He raised his eyes to the seer; he stared for a moment at the dirty man, but then his gaze lost focus and drifted up to the azure sky. A hush fell over the worked-up crowd; to Emié, the silence felt somehow supernatural.

"Rule over thyselves and thy families," he said, in a voice that was his own, but richer, fuller. "Let thy conscience, knowing right and wrong, given to you by the Lord God Creator, dictate what thou ought do, lest mortal man subject thou to his will and bring thou to ruin."

He dropped to his knees, face in the muddy ground, chest heaving with sobs or laughter or both. Emié ran to him. The silence remained, except for Gilyon.

"Congratulations, Noah," the giant said. "You have another prophet in the family."

⸱ CHAPTER 7 ⸱

Every step was another away from danger, Phiaphara knew, but with each the weight of their loss grew heavier on her. Of the seventy men who made up her father's crews, six more besides herself and Ninniachul had survived the Zuthians. She could do nothing but count her horse's clipping steps through wet grass, wishing she were with Kiah and the Wa-Mizhan now tracking the saboteurs but knowing she would be useless in such an endeavor.

As a habit, the Wa-Mizhan traveled light, without extra mounts. A huntress, one of a pair of Wa-Mizhan twins with cheekbones as sharp as their curved bronze shortswords, had loaned Phiaphara and Ninniachul her horse and doubled up on her sister's steed.

The other Mizraimite men, none of whom had escaped uninjured, rode behind them in a long sled. The vehicle had been constructed quickly but sturdily by the women rangers, pulled by two thick-limbed horses that showed no signs of being bothered by the extra weight.

A keen whistle made Phiaphara's heart leap in panic, but it also momentarily snapped her out of her depression. "Ahead we make camp," Tehama called out from the front of the procession. "We have made the Harmouth Springs."

Phiaphara rose from the springs, exulting in the sensation of long-awaited cleanliness, the earthy scent of the indigo mushrooms sprouting in clusters from every bank erasing what stench remained in her nostrils from the peat swamp. She had finally loosed her tears—of mourning, of frustration, of loss, of relief that she and her father lived still—while she bathed, hiding them in the springwaters.

She dipped herself once more in the springs, then gained the bank, where the Atlantean women were redressing, some regearing. Tehama had called them a skein and a pack, and like geese and wolves they undoubtedly functioned as a unit—one to which Phiaphara did not belong. She sighed and picked up her still-damp clothes. Finding a dry, fungus-free spot a ways from the cluster of Wa-Mizhan, she dropped to sitting, pulled her knees in tightly, and tried not to sob.

"The sages in Atlantis say that blue is the color of sadness." Tehama approached Phiaphara with light footsteps, dressed in a clean tunic and leggings, unbound hair falling past her shoulders. "We rest in a fitting place, then. Here, eat." Tehama handed Phiaphara a mushroom cap.

The Nephilim woman spoke truth of the palette of this place, Phiaphara thought, taking a bite of the blue fungus and wiping a drop of mushroom milk from the corner of her mouth. In the twilight sky a fading pink sun cast dark-blue shadows about the springs, and already a curtain of blue light from the south wove its way slowly among the new night stars. Even the stone beds of the springs were shot through with lapis lazuli. Phiaphara followed the azure lines down the spring and gazed over the gentle falls at their end, beyond which her father helped the other Mizraimite tribesmen clean themselves and tend their wounds. She thought not of their safety; they were guarded by a dozen well-trained and deadly beasts. At least they could rest in peace tonight.

"You have been bold this day," said Tehama after a few silent minutes. "How are you now?"

"Tired," answered Phiaphara. "In my body and in my soul. I imagine you warrior-women are numb to such things as we saw today, but I feel the pain of it sharply, and I fear it shall never leave me."

"I do wish, child. It is not true, though. No, we are not complete strangers to death, but to acts of war . . ." Tehama's voice hardened. "This day was different. In ways, maybe, that even I do not yet completely understand."

This talk did not calm Phiaphara, and she sank her face back to her knees. When fingers touched her scalp, she started.

"Shh, child," said the huntress. "You must rest now. And since you rest with the Wa-Mizhan, I shall teach you some of their ways—starting with your hair." Tehama began dividing Phiaphara's wet tresses. She sang as she did so, some Atlantean lullaby that blended with the movement of her fingers, deftly weaving to create a hypnotic sensation that pulled Phiaphara inexorably toward slumber. She met it with thankfulness.

Phiaphara awoke as dawn broke, not remembering exactly when she fell asleep or how she had gotten to her borrowed bedroll. She did not particularly care; good sleep had escaped her in the peat hovels, dank and moth-infested, and she had missed it.

Her new companions were dressed and busy, and the industry with which the women broke camp and gathered supplies together spurred her to scramble to join them. As she rose from the ground covered evenly with flat, thick mushrooms, she took a minute to appreciate the bedroll's down inner lining that so ably kept her in the slumber's oblivion and what a surprisingly comfortable surface the spongy fungi had made. The moment passed;

she rolled up the bedroll, secured her belt, shrugged on her cloak, and went to find her father.

Wrapped in his owllike cloak and with a worn pack at his back, Ninniachul looked ready to depart. The lower springs, where the men had made their camp, no longer showed any sign of their presence, and five men sat or lay in the convalescence sled. A few noticed her, the one familiar female face among many, and hailed greetings. Ninniachul turned and smiled, but as he came to her, her heart fell. His slow step, the slump of his shoulders, marked a man getting too old for this much exertion. "Raw emotions are sensitive," Phiaphara thought, "and I shall ignore them," but she knew this sadness grew from truth. She hid it away for later, though, and greeted her father.

"Dear one, Betlishar feels much better and wishes to ride," he said. "Might you be able to find another willing to share her horse?"

"Not a horse." Tehama walked her elk toward them with the morning sun behind her, the beams framing her face, fierce and noble like some nature goddess. "Come, child. You may ride with me today."

Hours and miles passed, but to Phiaphara, the time flew like a swift. While they traveled cross-country, Tehama spoke to her of the woods and jungles and valleys; of all the beasts that lived and bred and hunted and died there, how to track, tame, or hunt them; of the herbs, flowers, mushrooms and trees that could kill a man or keep him alive; of the many kinds of earths, the flora that best grew there and the crawling things that made their homes there. When at last they struck a road—a proper Atlantean trade way, with a wide, paved portion for horse- and oxen-drawn wagons and a packed-earth path for the indriks, mammoths, and dragons that could carry whole trading posts on their backs—the Nephilim huntress told her of the history of Atlantis, of peoples from every tribe and nation melding and learning and building, shining the light of their civilization ever outward and brighter.

Tehama's stories absorbed Phiaphara and pushed away all thoughts of trouble. Such calm did she feel that when it was shattered by the fast clip of running horses on the road behind her, it caused her almost physical pain. She held her breath in fear; scenes of burning peat and dead bodies with faces she knew flashed in her mind.

"Be calm, child." Tehama must have felt her rapidly beating heart as she pressed forward on the Nephilim huntress's back. "It is only Kiah."

The hoofbeats slowed as Kiah's pack fell into place on the road, while the *beth* rode up to the front.

"We found no sign of the Zuthians," said Kiah. "We did find a Mizraimite transport team on its way to the destroyed camp. Even now they take that message back to their tribes." She directed this last piece of information at Phiaphara, but the Wa-Mizhan's expression turned cold when she looked at her. "Is something wrong, girl?"

Phiaphara realized that her own face was pinched in a look of disgust at the stench that could only have come from Kiah; she relaxed it, embarrassed, remembering that the *beth* and her pack had not enjoyed the luxury of a bath since the battle with the swamp apes. She opened her mouth, but she could not think of anything to say.

Tehama laughed. "The girl only wonders how you function surrounded by such stink. Can you blame her?"

"I grew up a tanner's daughter," Kiah said, losing her iciness. "Urine, dung, and rotting flesh, day in, day out. What of you, girl?"

"My childhood?"

"Your life. So yes, your childhood, since you are barely more than one."

"My father is an ingeniator. I help him." Phiaphara shrugged. "I suppose there is not much more than that."

"What sort of ingeniator?" nudged Tehama. "Tools, transport, weaponry?"

"Mostly transport," she answered. "Waterways. He builds boats, designs locks. Mizraim has many lakes and much trade among the tribal cities." Now she thought of home, of waterwheels and sails, and once more of the faces of the dead. "I have known his crewmen my whole life, and now most of them are killed."

"And are you content to flee from those who killed them?" Tehama asked. Phiaphara wished she could see the Naphil's face.

"I would rather see them avenged, see the murderers cut down with my own eyes," she answered, feeling new fervor. "I envy you—you who might be able to do such a thing."

"Anyone can become a Wa-Mizhan, Phiaphara," said Tehama.

"A Mizraimite?"

"Atlantis takes all who embrace her and her ideals. She has her flaws, to be sure, but they are borne from peace."

"Flaws?"

"A few."

"Young women, for example," said Kiah. "You say you have no lover in Mizraim. In Atlantis, a young, fit female like yourself could find a wealthy old man and live in pampered luxury. Perhaps she is obliged to bear him a few children, but she might keep younger men for playthings as she chooses."

"This is true," echoed Tehama. "Pretty girls want for nothing if they are willing to spend a few minutes a day in a rich man's bed."

Phiaphara again wrinkled her face in disgust, and this time she meant to. Kiah laughed. "You dislike the idea?"

"In Mizraim we are not such hedonists, nor so cynical about marriage," Phiaphara said. "Besides, I am the daughter of my father's old age." She glanced back at Ninniachul, swaying tiredly with every step of his horse. "I love him, but I would not wish that on my own children."

"Fathers mold their daughters in many ways," said Tehama. "My own family is full of bastards of my philandering father."

"At whose leisure we serve," said Kiah sternly.

"Nevertheless, it is truth," laughed Tehama. "I wished to be different. And so we Wa-Mizhan huntresses remain virgins always, sacrificing personal desires for the common good, choosing the purity of nature for the decay of urbanity. It is a hard life at times, but for her who has the strength and will, it has reward beyond measure."

Suddenly Phiaphara realized she was being offered something. "I want that," she said.

Tehama half turned on the elk, enough to meet Phiaphara's eyes. "What do you want, child?"

"I want to be a Wa-Mizhan."

"Are you sure?" asked Kiah. "It means nights spent in the cold mists, the dangers of the wild wilderness, never enjoying a man's touch."

"I am sure."

"Then welcome," said Tehama, her smiling face beyond beautiful.

"Welcome indeed," added Kiah, whose wry smirk was much less so. "Never say I did not warn you."

᛫ CHAPTER 8 ᛫

Once, the nation-state of Atlantis was constrained within its magnificent walls, its peoples content to live, work, and trade in the nine rings of the city, then named Enoch. That time was hundreds of years past. Like the rising sun, Atlantis cast itself and its influence inexorably further. Under the guidance of Dyeus, Pethun, and Dedroth—the sons of the fallen angel Samyaza, long disappeared from the world—Atlantis's coffers, libraries, wineskins, and tables filled to overflowing. When the Naphil Dyeus co-opted the secret stronghold of his Grigori father at Mount Armon for himself and his own family, Atlanteans drew after him. In the valleys, jungles, sinkholes, and foothills stretching out for the many miles between the city and the mountain, man enforced his dominion and molded the land for his own use. Shining bridges spanned cenotes and rivers rimmed and lined with Atlantean architecture; white stone towers, domed or spired, rose above the treetops; carven manors climbed cliffsides; and like arteries running from a beating heart, roads from the city connected all, bringing the vitality of commerce from a hundred lands along with them.

Noah and his companions traveled from Phempor down dusty caravan routes, game trails, and winding waterways, stopping at settlements to replenish supplies and visit many friends made over several centuries. When at last they reached the river Gihon and gained passage on a spice galleon for themselves and their mounts, their journey became easier. After an uneventful fortnight, the slow-flowing river deposited the missioners at Daras, the first port of call in the land of Nod and only two days' journey from Cain's city of Enoch—or, as it was now called, Atlantis.

"I used to like the smell of cloves," complained Caiphes on the second afternoon since Daras, "but now that it *still* seems to seep from my every pore . . ."

"Better than when we were chased by that Urkaddin wind cult and had to be smuggled out of the city in the goat trader's ship," said Midash, swaying on a silk-draped camel, his griffin traipsing on the road alongside. "For my gold, there is nothing worse than being stuck on a boat packed full of animals." Gilyon and Eudeon, each riding a hirsute camelid almost twice as large as Midash's, nodded in recollection.

"I should leave any ill feelings toward animals behind now," said Noah. Ahead, two tall wooden pillars, in form and size of behemoths' necks, swept up and toward each other, pushing into the blue sky where they joined together to create the frame of an enormous gate. Swaths of netting draped back from the grand gate to numerous towers beyond, covering treetops like a veil. Avian calls, everything from caws to whistles, reached them and seemed to beckon them forward. Emié grinned widely, and Caiphes suddenly looked nervous. Noah suspected why the latter, but kept his smile to himself.

"Is this the place, then?" asked Midash.

"It is indeed," answered Noah. "The menagerie of Dashael."

Past the gate, the wide entrance road to the menagerie's central grounds ran on a ridge, down either side of which inclined gentle slopes leading to lightly forested valleys where men in woodland greens and thick leather gloves, boots, and belts practiced falcons. Some appeared to be training the birds, and others performed demonstrations to groups of Atlanteans who Noah surmised were potential buyers. The expansive nets above that ably prevented the falcons from escaping cast spiderwebs of shadow over everything.

The center of the menagerie was a sprawling complex of thick-beamed corrals, stables, and enclosures built around the wide raked-dirt showgrounds just visible through another grand gate. As the missioners approached, a man on a white-maned stallion rode out to meet them. His form-fitting tunic left his shoulders bare; his burgundy leather riding skirt matched his horse's saddle trappings and leg sleeves.

"Welcome!" he called, in the friendly, impersonal manner of a man whose business it was to sell his wares to strangers. His show smile shaded genuine as he recognized two of the group.

"Uncle Haphan!" Emié waved excitedly at her father's grandfather's brother.

"Dearest Emié! Gilyon!" Haphan kicked his stallion into a trot, meeting them with an elegant about-face that made his horse seem to glide to a walk alongside Emié's camel. Noah, Caiphes, and Midash, horsemen all, were impressed, although their phlegmatic camels appeared bored at the display.

"It's good to see you, Emié," Haphan beamed. He turned and craned his neck to look up at Gilyon. "And you as well, half brother," he said formally.

Gilyon laughed. "Half brother, half angel. Shall I ever be a whole of something?" Eudeon and Midash chuckled while Haphan blushed beneath his blonde beard.

"Emié, I am eager to hear about your travels," he said, retreating to what he obviously considered safer ground, "and yours, Gilyon, and your fellows—but I shall not ask you to tell until more are here to listen. Until then, please follow me, all! And welcome home!"

Noah breathed deeply through both nostrils as they approached the bustling menagerie. The smells, to him, were of earth and life: straws and grasses, oats, sawdust and cedar chips, musk and dung. Each one brought back good memories, both specific moments and general feelings, of his first four-score years of life on his grandfather's farm. As he had not since Phempor before his encounter with the prince, he felt at peace.

Haphan led the missioners through the entrance, and almost immediately greetings abounded from all directions in the busy showground. Generations of Dashael's descendants employed in the family trade called to Emié, briefly interrupting their business with peasants and wealthier folk alike. Some called to Noah, Eudeon, and Gilyon too; every furlough the missioners had taken over their four centuries of labors and travel had always included a visit to Dashael and Jet, and every time they had taken a scion of theirs, or three or four, with them to the next destination. Now it was somewhat of a family tradition, on arrival of adulthood, to join Gilyon and Noah on a several-year mission. "Though not all choose to," thought Noah, glancing at Haphan.

"This place seems to be doing well," said Midash, his eyes following a rich-robed man directing three braces of fancy, brightly colored cock-drakes to an ornate carriage.

"Aye," said Haphan. "This has proven an ideal place for my father to settle and breed. Plow animals for the foothill farmers; pets, mounts, and carriage beasts for gentry; trained mounts and familiars for the Atlantean guards. He does keep to Edenic customs and mores, so he still refuses to breed animals for consumption." He laughed. "My apologies if you knew all this already, as I'm sure your companions do! The speech is routine."

Prominently placed stood an oversized painted map of the central grounds and the areas beyond, showing where different animal kinds were kept. Embedded in the proper spots on the map were facsimiles of the medallions denoting the masteries of the menagerie, and Dashael's were extensive: oxen, horses, indriks, camels, several dragon kinds—hornfaces, cresteds, tarasqs—bunyips, wolfhounds, cats, bears, riding birds and cock-drakes. While Noah and his comrades examined the impressive installation, new since last any of the party had been there, several youths in house livery—a blood-red bull on an undyed field—swarmed to them, one to an animal, taking their reins while their riders dismounted. The young man who had chosen Midash's camel suddenly made a strangled sound of alarm, followed by the Havilahn commanding, "Heel."

"A griffin!" exclaimed Haphan. "How did I fail to notice a griffin?"

"He likes to practice stalking," said Midash, as the predatory familiar quickly became the center of attention for the grooms and wranglers. "Ho there, not too close!"

The griffin drew the showground laborers to Noah's group, many of whom had spent years with the missioners in the past. Between salutations, Noah noticed Emié's father, a man in his sixties named Cohm who had joined them on a mission to Apitar three decades prior, embrace her with a smile. She pulled Caiphes over for an introduction. Noah could not hear what was said, but he could guess well enough as the three of them walked away that Caiphes had asked for a more private audience, and Noah had no doubt about what the subject would be.

Eventually, work called, and the remaining missioners were left with Haphan. He led Noah, Gilyon, Eudeon, and Midash and his animal partway around the perimeter of the open central ground, then up a broad, rustic spiral stair to an expansive low-roofed bungalow built on wooden pillars above pens holding moas and ostriches. Many tall fences impaired the view at ground level, but now, Noah could look across the entire menagerie, meeting the eyes of the dragons and indriks peeking above their pens. No stranger to the logistics of husbandry, he absently nodded to himself in approval as he realized just how many animals Dashael kept safe and secure in such proximity to one another. Haphan opened a polished ebony door set on the bungalow's curve and gestured to enter. The missioners went inside.

The interior of the bungalow smelled of sweet smoke, leather, and earth. A wide, carved slab of reddish wood surrounded by smaller stools of the same material dominated the center of the space, with stacks of scrolls, maps, and piles of contractual papers neatly arranged on its polished, ringed surface. The remainder of the room was decorated as a hunting den, much like the one in the sprawling farmhouse in which Noah grew up. Trophies from felldragons, dire bears, butcher swine, and other vicious predators packed the walls. One trophy in particular caught Noah's eye: an ancient, pitted leviathan tooth set on a plaque over a plate-sized scale. Memories from nigh on four centuries past, some good and many

terrifying, flooded to the forefront of his mind. A faint
clatter of goblets from behind curtains at the back of
the room snapped him from the scenes replaying in his
thoughts, and Dashael of Eden approached.

His skin was tanned, markedly so even compared
to fellows whose lives were spent under the heat of the
sun. What some men and beasts mistook for apathy
was evident in his nonchalant gait and half-closed eyes,
but Noah knew that in the beast master's breast beat a
lion's heart and in his wiry muscles was the strength of
an aurochs. Furthermore, despite donning the rough garb
of a hardworking husbandman, he had excellent taste in
finer things; this was evident in the quality of wine he
set upon the polished table. Noah, Gilyon, and Eudeon
greeted fondly their host, friend, and substantial benefac-
tor in their mission work.

Gilyon made the introduction of Midash to his
stepfather, who was as typically taciturn as the prince
of Havilah was effusive. Dashael became more talkative,
however, when Eudeon mentioned the griffin.

"You have the animal here?" asked Dashael.

"Just outside," answered Midash. "Would you come
out and see him?"

"Nay, bring him inside, please! I trust a fellow beast
master to manage his familiar."

Thus it was that the afternoon was spent in Dashael's
den, drinking Edenic wine and discussing the past few
years' work. As he did with all his major patrons, and
especially those to whom he was close, Noah provided
Dashael with a sheaf of papers: journal entries, maps of
their travels, lists of stewards from each altar house plant,
and, for Dashael, drawings of novel breeds of various
animal kinds encountered by the missioners.

Several hours and a few goblets of wine later, Noah and his two Nephilim friends were relating to Dashael the macabre tale of their encounter with the prince of Phempor, while Haphan and Midash discussed the possibility of importing pairs of griffins from Havilah and starting an Atlantean breeding program.

"The Lord Creator be praised," said Dashael, "that you came through all right. Whatever demon possessed the man sounds like one not lightly to be trifled with."

"Someone had to," rumbled Eudeon into his wine cup. "We have seen the Creator's truth drive out demons before. I know of no better tool He possesses for such matters than Noah the preacher."

"I do willingly engage in spiritual conflict," said Noah, "but I admit I do not relish the physical."

"That is why you have us," said Gilyon, tapping cups with Eudeon.

"Have some pride in your warrior's skill, do you?" asked Dashael. His expression did not change, but Noah heard the edge of disapproval in his quiet tone.

"Not pride, no," said Gilyon. "But as you yourself know, sometimes violence—"

Raised voices from outside and below interrupted the Naphil, escalating quickly to angered shouts. Chairs emptied as the men rushed to the door.

"—is necessary."

The people amassing near the yard's entrance surrounded a group of Dashael's husbandmen, four foreign fellows, and a flock of sheep, and Noah could tell that their words would soon turn to blows. With the two giants leading the way, he, Midash, and Dashael pushed through to the men in conflict. While Dashael's men protested loudly in a barrage of voices that proved impossible to separate into individual complaints, three foreigners were attempting to forge through the crowd to the exit as the fourth shouted back.

Eudeon and Gilyon had only to stand near the arguing men for their size to cause sudden silence. Between the giants stepped Dashael. "What seems to be the problem?" he asked, as casually as if he were inquiring on the day's birth count for cattle.

"These men bought sacrificial sheep on pretense of offering them on the altar, as is right and good," said the largest husbandman. "But several of the stableyouth overheard them talking about slaughtering them for some feast!"

"Sir," Dashael said, addressing the man who seemed to be the leader of the foreigners, "Dashael of Eden is my name, and these are my animals. Is this true?"

The man, like his fellows, had skin the color of pale stone and a long, thin, downturned nose that, to Noah's faint interest, was typical of the coastal tribesmen far south down the sea's curve. The men were dressed in that people's fashion, as well: leather trappings over sun-darkened chests held up loose skirts that fell to the knee. Rough fishermen's fingers resting on handles of fish-bill knives with shark-tooth handle guards did not escape Noah's notice, nor, he knew, the notice of his fellow mis-sioners. The tribes tended to violence, as fickle as the seas they fished; Noah and the two Nephilim had spent time in their coastal and island cities, but he could not fathom that any of the Atlanteans had. He prayed a brief word for peace, but readied himself to act.

Formality won for a moment. The lead man nodded his head to Dashael. "My name is Sibbe, once of the

island of Mame," he said tersely. "If we wish to feast on
our animals, what is that to you? We paid good gold." He
waved his hand at the pouch held by the big husbandman,
who handed it to Dashael with a jingle of coin. He hefted
it before him with another jingle, his face a cool mask.

"I do not sell my animals as food," said Dashael. "You
want that, go to one of Jabal's ranges." He held the man's
gold out, his argument complete in its brevity.

"The transaction is done," said Sibbe, chin thrust out.
"Unless you plan on keeping us by force, let us depart."
The men behind him eyed Gilyon and Eudeon nervously,
but the giants' lack of arms apparently gave them enough
confidence to draw their bill knives. A collective gasp
shuddered through the crowd, and most backed far away,
leaving only Dashael and the missioners with the coastal
tribesmen. A loaded crossbow appeared in Midash's
hands, and his griffin rasped menacingly. Dashael's hand
inched closer to the whip coiled at his side.

Noah stepped between the groups, showing empty
hands. "Is a meal worth bloodshed? Resist the sin that
beckons you, sir. Take the gold and leave."

"Who are you, to dictate to me?" sneered Sibbe. His
men advanced forward while he drifted behind them
toward the gate, driving the sheep with him. "We men of
the sea will be abused no more."

"Stand down, on the authority of Atlantis!"

Such command and strength Noah had seldom heard
in a female voice, but the woman it came from matched
it. He had spent enough time around the children of
the *bene Elohim* to recognize the otherworldly beauty of
a Nephilim woman; beyond that, this one was dressed
for either hunting or battle. Another woman—a girl,
really—similarly attired, stood behind her. She was

human, a moon to the other's sun, with a satellite of her own: a spotted feline familiar of a type bred for speed. The Nephilim woman interposed herself between the men from Mame and the missioners; weapons were not sheathed, but they were lowered.

"What means this?" she asked. "I will not countenance armed men from foreign lands making war in the very heart of Atlantis, where each man is free to conduct his business and practice his religion as he sees fit. If you desire to see your homelands again, put your weapons away."

"On whose authority?" demanded Sibbe, even as his fellows sheathed their knives.

"That of Tehama, mistress of the Wa-Mizhan, of the house of Dyeus of Atlantis," said the woman. "If you know not those names, you ought not be here, considering your people enjoy their current succor in the very shadow of our home. Now take your gold and get yourself gone."

"Leave the livestock, if you please," added Dashael.

Sibbe scowled as he accepted his gold, then brushed under his nose with two fingers. He stamped away quickly, and Noah wondered if the man suspected that at least a few there—himself, Eudeon, Gilyon, and he guessed Tehama—understood the coarseness of the gesture. None followed him or demanded apology, though; Dashael went to help his men herd the rescued sheep, and Haphan began dispersing the crowd with light jokes and laughter.

He turned to where a miniature family reunion was proceeding. "Eudeon!" exclaimed Tehama. "I did not expect to see you here!"

"When *would* you expect me, my niece?" He smiled, and she returned it. As he had been born decades later than many of his aunts and uncles, as a child Eudeon had taken to referring to these elders always as his niece or nephew, in truth but also in jest; centuries later, to Noah's amusement, the habit persisted.

"Point taken. Noah, Gilyon, well met. Shall we trade introductions?"

"Midash, of Havilah," the griffin master said with a courtly bow, mirrored in bestial fashion by his trained familiar, which clearly impressed the two women.

"This is Phiaphara, late of Mizraim, now joined to the Atlantean border guard," Tehama said. "This happened to be the day she chose a hunting companion."

"Well met to you," said Noah. "It is a fine animal. A better breeder than Dashael you could not find." The girl nodded; the lithe cat pressed its head up to her stroking hand as if in agreement.

"When will you come to Mount Armon?" asked Tehama to Eudeon.

"My comrades and I had not discussed it," he answered. "Within the week, certainly."

"Make it today if you can," said Tehama. "A council of chiefs begins today, the likes of which I have never seen. All the colonies from Old Enoch, the tribes of Nod, a dozen others—including that man's islander tribes. Even some from Eden, Noah. No doubt my father will appreciate the presence of each of you."

"Council? For what purpose?" asked Gilyon, looking questioningly at the other missioners, who had no more knowledge of such things than he.

"War," answered Tehama. "Atlantis prepares for war."

CHAPTER 9

Caiphes had succeeded in securing Emié's betrothal; the happy couple opted to stay with her family to begin the wedding preparations. Gilyon felt obliged, even eager, to visit his mother Jet—his only living blood relation—and chose to forgo the short trip to Mount Armon. So it was that Noah, Eudeon, and Midash joined the company of the two huntresses, Tehama and Phiaphara, to the Atlantean seat of power, home of the children of Samyaza.

Noah, Midash, and Eudeon accepted Haphan's offer of a riding carriage, pulled by crested dragons of a hatchet-headed breed. "I can drive it back," Haphan explained. "I doubt you should find an open stable anywhere near Armon." Midash cocked his head in quiet query. "You shall see when we get there," said Haphan.

With the two huntresses behind them on elk and horse, the party made the hour-long trip to Mount Armon. The foothills of the mountain had been heavily built upon, but the Atlanteans had obviously taken pains to preserve their natural beauty. The land settled by ancient Cain and his children had been cursed for crops, but the greenery that did grow was no less beautiful for its thorns and nettles. Carnivorous pitcher plants, whose natural home lay beneath the sinkhole falls that punctuated the land, had been transplanted to decorate fountains and tiered pools. Climbing blooms of roses with talon-like thorns embraced alabaster columns and sculpted stone walls. Atlantis and her people had ably tamed her wilderness, then incorporated it into her opulence.

As the group followed the winding road toward Armon, ornate pools became plentiful. Occasionally, half-naked figures lounging in the bright sun lazily lifted heads at their passing, then fell back to drinking or napping.

"Modesty has suffered since last I passed this way," noted Eudeon.

Tehama nodded. "Pethun claimed this land for public bathing." The statement was factual, but the manner in which she said it seemed to Noah to suggest that she shared the missioners' disdain for exhibitionist nudity. "Strange from a daughter of Enoch and Dyeus," thought Noah. He suspected these Wa-Mizhan had their own ways of things, but how closely they hewed to the uprightness of the Creator he could not yet guess, so he made no comment.

At last Mount Armon came into view: shimmering veins of white stone, wreathes and patches of olive groves and vineyards, and at the very peak the shining sprawl where lived the children of Samyaza. Noah could not recall exactly how many scores of years had passed since last he visited the mount, but he did remember the forest valley surrounding it. The estates of families of mistresses and bastards of the Atlantean Nephilim, as well as villages that housed the host of servants who worked at their palaces, clustered and clutched up the flat slope of Armon's base, but the woods and fields beyond had been kept pristine as long as Noah had known of them, for hunting and other outdoor pastimes. Now, though, a solid coverage of tents and dwellings hid the green of the valleys, at least the portion they could view, and the haze of campfire smokes rose thickly above the forests.

They descended into the valley. Walls of wood and stacked stone, hastily constructed off either side of the road, did little to obscure the camps from the missioners' curious eyes, although the constant presence of grim-looking Atlantean guardsmen at the interval gates deterred any desire to make a detour for a closer inspection. They kept to the road.

The faces from beyond the walls that raised up as the party passed were far from those of the leisurely Atlantean bathers. They were dour, sad, streaked with the dust of travel and primitive living. That none were of Cain's people was obvious, but neither did the people at each new cluster of fur tents or branchy huts bear much resemblance to the next group. However, Noah found that he could name the likely lineage of all but a few. He and Eudeon began speculating aloud from where each new group might be; between noteworthy physical distinctions and differences in building styles and materials, the missioners placed them all with a fair degree of certainty before the road began its ascent up Mount Armon.

"By the moon," swore Tehama as they passed the last rough wall into the first servants' village, "how do you recognize all of them?"

"Spend four centuries traveling among all the sons of Adam," said Eudeon, "and you could as well."

"What is this, Tehama?" asked Noah. "Did all the peoples north of Zuthi decide to uproot their homes and move to Atlantean lands?"

He meant the comment mostly in jest, so he was taken rather aback when Tehama met his eyes in stern and earnest seriousness.

"Yes."

⋅ CHAPTER 10 ⋅

Haphan drove the dragon-pulled carriage up the winding road, past gardens draping down the mountainside like curtains, through ice-green forests where sprawling chateaus housed bastard bloodlines of the Atlantean giants. The man-made buildings at the base of the mountain were ever growing, built in the style of the original Grigori's dwellings at Armon's peak, where resided only the children of Samyaza and a select few of their offspring. The greatest Atlantean artists, sculptors, and architects had spent centuries attempting to duplicate the styles of the angels. Noah was reminded of watching his great-great-great-grandfather Jared with his pottery apprentices; the pupils' best attempts at duplicating Jared's work fell short, victim to the subtle, almost imperceptible touch of a true master of a craft. Like that were the lower buildings to the true Grigori palaces, pale blue at Armon's peak, even seen from a distance. Noah had never been up to the Grigori palaces, nor did he care to; if the *bene Elohim* who had built them had followed their Creator's ordained roles, the place would not exist.

As the group climbed, Armon's defenses became apparent. Sentry posts spanned the road, arching high overhead, thrusting out from towered and fortified barracks built into the mountainside. Atlantean mountain guards secured the road at their posts there, some manning ballistae perched above, others checking each traveler as he passed. These men were much changed from their common counterparts in the valley, whose forerunners were the guards of Enoch; in place of the fur-lined capes, the thick bronze, the sturdy leather, the guards of the mountain wore thin, silvery shirts of fine chain, shimmering like fish scales. Their armor was metal, blue-tinted, formfitting and artistically asymmetric, decorated with waves and circular patterns. Many wore longswords, slightly curved, at their sides. Some carried short bows and crossbows of the same bluish metal and white wood, and others held elegant pole arms. They exuded an aura that foolish would be the person, human or Nephilim, who might wish to cross them. Even Tehama afforded them a certain deference as they passed.

The road circled around a broad, cascading waterfall. Its spray scintillated in the sunlight, sweeping its coolness over the travelers. Tehama guided her elk close to Haphan's carriage. "For those of you who have been away," she said, "and those who come to our land for the first time: behold you now the glory of Atlantis."

The sparkling mists cast up by the waterfall failed to hide the splendorous buildings of the colleges of Armon, clinging close to the mountain as they rose toward its peak. Busy streets and plazas—built to accommodate dragons, indriks, and other steeds fit for giants—separated the magnificent structures. While the missioners drank in the sheer awe inspired by enormous edifices, Tehama spoke almost to boasting of them. Built into a cleft of the mountain large enough to engulf a village, the highest center of Atlantean knowledge was kept close to her leaders. Here were the libraries of the philosophers and clerics; here were the repositories of medical and herbal lore, the smoke-wreathed dens of Atlantean high sorcery, the cacophonous, cavernous ingeniators' workshops. Here were the forges where the pupils of the master smith Tubal-Cain of Enoch turned metals into tools of every trade, both civil and martial. Here was a testimony to mankind's ability to derive knowledge from the Lord God's creations, yet attribute no part to Him. The more Tehama talked, the stronger the jealousy that arose in Noah for his Lord. He saw the same feelings in his fellow missioners, especially Eudeon. "My home fields have grown great weeds while I have been away," he murmured to Noah. "Perhaps after this I ought to tend to them."

They came near a monolithic structure pressed against the mountain's side, like Armon's white rock had melted, then been molded by a master sculptor. It stretched from the mountain in two great wings and dripped upward into elegant towers; whether the structure had been carved from the mountain or built from stone quarried from it, the seamless and decorated form gave no clue. To its entrance led Tehama down the plaza that preceded, past a long mirrored pool and through mingling crowds of myriad races, all kept in close order by the presence of the silvery guards. Near the cavernous entrance, three of these approached. Tehama and Phiaphara slid from their mounts; two guards led the animals away. As the third stood expectantly, Haphan's passengers exited, and after thanks and farewells, he drove his dragons back down the mountain.

Nothing inside the entrance hall had not been touched by an artisan of the highest skill. Murals and gilding adorned a sky-high ceiling supported by sculpted pillars; bright lamps, built into the walls, illuminated where the sunlight failed to reach. No stranger himself to ink and papyrus, Noah drew closer to a mural with an artist's appreciation. It depicted bright figures over an eight-ringed city.

"Eudeon, look here. The descent to earth of the Grigori?"

The Naphil grunted his agreement. Together, they tracked the murals to the first of them while Midash examined the gold-flecked stone pillars. The wall-long paintings proved to show the entire history of Enoch-turned-Atlantis, from its founding by exiled Cain, to the birth of his son—the city's first namesake—to the arrival of the *bene Elohim* and the wondrous works they wrought while on earth. Noah lazed behind his giant friend, basking in the artistry, wondering how many hours and how many masters had contributed to the murals.

"Midash, look. Here is Noah!"

The mural before Eudeon showed a rough-dressed man standing defiantly before five shining figures; in the next, the same man, now wearing a bright white cassock and the ornate robes of an Atlantean mage, raised his arms to heaven while the previous shining figures burned rather graphically to ashes beneath him.

Noah felt no pride in the images. "This honor does not belong to me. What glory does a vessel have when it fulfills the purpose its maker intended?"

Tehama walked over from where she had been conversing with guards, the young woman Phiaphara behind her. "If you three are finished perusing the history depicted in this hall, you can come see it being made."

They passed through a winding hall, up spiraling stairs, to a gallery where they were ushered to seats by a man in deep blue livery of Atlantis. The gallery was one of scores within a cavernous forum (and Noah did not doubt that once it was an actual cavern). Men from disparate lands filled the upper galleries above Noah; at his own level the audience wore mostly Atlantean garb in a wide variety of regional styles. On the floor of the chamber, Atlantean ingeniators in caps of leather and iron wrote in their loose-leafed draught books, and diviners from the colleges of sorcery tended small, ornate lamps whose tongues of flame created ever-shifting light patterns in the crystals held above them. Behind these sat row after row of humans and Nephilim listening intently to an account by some sort of tribal chief. Clearly cowed by the setting and the company, the chief stumbled through an account of barbarity after barbarity. Whatever people had visited such atrocities on his tribe had already been named. Noah was about to ask Tehama about whom the chieftain spoke when another man took his place.

"Greeting to my Atlantean hosts, and to all free sons of man who gather here today." The man's booming voice matched his physique, the disconnect between his rather primitive dress—scaled loincloth, ropes of teeth and shell over bare chest—and his oration already evident. "My name is Doude, appointed leader of the cities of man at the edge of the southern sea. I come to you today as a prideful man from a prideful people, whose ancestors feared neither gods nor demons, dragons nor sea monsters, so accept that I come before you at all as proof enough of the magnitude of the threat about which I speak. Our people inhabited the coasts and islands from the Rim Sea to the Daet-Mame archipelagos. Now our cities are empty, our nets broken, our piers and ships splintered, by the cursed armies of the Zuthians. I will tell you now our tale, that perhaps you might gain some knowledge of their tactics, methods, and weapons. What course you then take I must leave to your own wisdom, O Atlantis.

"Our coastal villages were attacked first by the ento-
mancers. These fiends are cowards, sorcerers who send
before them swarms of pestilence: biting locusts, scour-
ing beetles, scorpions, giant centipedes, flies. After these,
hordes of slaves were driven by terrible giants—slaves
who were men we knew, men we traded with, whose
lands had been swept asunder and who feared more what
their captors would do than the shame and danger of
making undeserved war. Also there were Zuthian assassins, dressed in rags so as to blend in amongst the slaves,
who slaughtered many in the chaos. Their weapons are
of glass; they know not defense, only aggression and
bloodshed, and they visited much upon us. Whoever of
our people could do so escaped to the islands; we thought
we would be safe there beyond the deep channels.

"The onslaught on the coasts took only a day, and
we fell back throughout the night, fighting where we
could but rescuing few. My own island fortress provided
refuge for several villages. In the morning, through the
mists, giant warriors came as if drifting on the water. The
spines behind them proved to be the backs of great river
dragons, submerged beneath their riders and pulling rafts
of Zuthian warriors behind them. We fought. We lost,
and we fled. This is the account of Doude."

The big chieftain stepped away to a group of his countrymen that included the man Sibbe and his companions.
"That explains some things," murmured Eudeon.

"But it does not excuse anything," said Tehama. "You
ought not be so soft, Eudeon—not in these times."

A curious fixation by Phiaphara on the floor of the
chamber drew Noah's eyes there. An older man walked
from where the ingeniators sat. "That is Phiaphara's
father," said Tehama to the missioners. The young

woman's calm stillness belied her emotions, given away
by a slightly trembling hand and held breath. For some
reason—perhaps her youth—Noah felt sudden trepida-
tion at the prospects of hearing what horrors she might
have experienced in her short life.

The man, Ninniachul, gave his account. It was not so
terrible or graphic as much of what the missioners heard
throughout the remainder of the day from a further
score of foreign men, but being so near a victim of the
Zuthians' violence made a sharper impact than the more
anonymous reports.

After the river of grim recollections finally finished,
Noah felt exhausted. His spirit swelled, though, when he
saw what Nephilim leader addressed those gathered.

"My friends, thank you for reliving these horrors for
the benefit of us all." Dyeus, son of Samyaza, looked almost
unchanged by the centuries. His bearing was straight and
proud, his manner and dress befitting his status as a regent
of Atlantis. "Until such time as your lands are returned
from the bloody hands of the Zuthians, this valley may
be your refuge, and I assure you we will keep it safe. Now
please, go back to your peoples and assure them that the
Atlantis turns her eyes and strong hand to your cause."

Most of the men there—those from foreign lands
who had testified against the Zuthian armies, who had
no other ties to the Atlantean children of Cain other than
needing succor from them—rose and exited, guided by
the guards. As he scanned the faces of those left, Noah
began to feel a strong sense of familiarity, despite the
years that had passed. He recognized many: Dyeus and
his brother Pethun, in urgent conversation with Dyeus's
giant son Mareth and Tubal-Cain the smith; his old
Nephilim comrades Hoduìn, Tevesh, and Tiras, dressed

in heavy furs and solid iron, from their stronghold in the north, at the Assyrian border; and to Noah's great pleasure, his own brother Hadishad, talking animatedly with other men in Atlantean garb, but with features that marked them of Eden's heritage. Two other groups of men, variable mixes of human and Nephilim bloodlines and none of whom Noah knew, remained as well.

The last of the refugees left. "Stay," said Tehama to Midash, half out of his seat, the only one of them obviously unsure whether he ought to be privy to whatever followed. "Havilah is a friend to Atlantis. Take note of whatever happens now, to carry back to your land when you may."

As if Dyeus took his daughter's words as a cue, he spoke again.

"My great friends," Dyeus said, spreading his muscled arms to their full enormous span. "The sand drakes of Zuthi have driven the hares before them, but they come now to us, the lions. For many of us here, our fathers were the Grigori, the Watchers of mankind, but long, long ago they abdicated and fell. Shall we take up now their roles? Shall we succeed where they failed? I wish to listen to your wise council; here is mine. Let us make war on this murderous horde—not for our own gain, but to protect the weaker among us, as a Shepherd does his lambs, to help them reclaim what is rightfully theirs. My brothers and sons are agreed. Who now shall stand with Atlantis and the sons of Samyaza?"

Tiras, who Noah had held in high esteem for twenty-score years now, rose. "All at this mote have been duly chosen by their people to speak for them. I do now for mine, in solidarity with my own father Hoduin and brother Tevesh. My people will bring an arm of iron to bear against these murderers."

The tallest of one of the groups unknown to Noah, a wild-looking giant in skins and furs, stood next, and Noah's mind flashed back to a Naphil in the streets of old Enoch, bringing down a dark assassin with a sling of leather and chain. "The kingroups of Tuath stand with you," the giant said. "Lugh declares it."

"Are those the sons of Asaradel?" asked Eudeon quietly.

"Aye," answered Tehama. "Now bred among the woodland tribes of Tuath Danr."

Another giant, identifying himself as a representative of Gilgamesh, lord of Uruch, gave a quick pledge of support for the city-states on the Euphrates for which he spoke.

The turn came for Hadishad; Noah suppressed his sudden strong urge to call out a greeting. His brother kept silent for a moment, then said, "I cannot promise that Eden will join you in war, even if I myself would gladly. We are, and have always been, a peaceful people, by the grace of our Lord God Creator. I beg leave to consider further and to consult Eden's Greatfather and elders."

"Eh, the Edenites are all human anyway," interjected Lugh. "What help could their small arms give?"

"Eden is strong," countered Dyeus. "It was Eden who joined with us to remove our Grigori fathers, remember." Lugh shrugged.

Tehama rose. "There is another from Eden present. What says Noah, whose name and deeds are known to many here?"

Noah wished he could hide from the faces that turned up to meet the unexpected interjection. He glanced at Eudeon, but the helpless look he received back showed no clue how he might escape. As was Noah's habit, he dealt with his own surprise with a quick prayer.

"Loath am I to council you strong warriors in matters of war," he said, "or to supplant the words of Eden's emissary with my own. I have seen evil things and evil men. We are all of us fallen from righteousness; some, though, are depraved beyond allowance. If these Zuthians be such men, they must be stopped."

Heads nodded, and several voiced assent. "I do not promise that my homeland will join you in battle," Noah continued, "but I think they ought not stop you in doing so. For my part, I would go to what places need warning, who are unprepared. I would rather save lives than avenge them." He sat back down, meeting Hadishad's eyes and afraid he had spoken too much, but his brother's smile assured him he had remained within his bounds. The attention of those gathered turned back to Dyeus, for which Noah was thankful.

"I thank you all," Dyeus said, "and I invite you to put the heavy thoughts of this day away for the moment. It is time to enjoy the peace and pleasures of Atlantis. Pethun?"

"Follow me, my friends." Flanked by guards, Dyeus's brother swept out of the hall, his blue hemicape trailing behind him.

"Do . . . we follow?" asked Midash.

"I go because I am expected," said Tehama. "You *men* may enjoy it." Not knowing what she meant or what else to do, and eager to see his brother Hadishad, who had already followed Pethun out, Noah nodded to the two huntresses and gestured toward the staircase leading down from their gallery. "Lead the way," he said.

‹ CHAPTER 11 ›

They entered an expansive hall, where those who preceded them were already availing themselves from central tablescapes abounding with food and drink. With Tehama leading, they meandered about, eventually finding a quieter corner somewhat secluded by potted plants and pillars. Noah scanned above the heads of human height for any of his Nephilim friends of old: Hoduìn and his sons, or Dyeus, Pethun, or Dedroth (had Dedroth even been present?), the three sons of Samyaza. To his disappointment, the only giants he saw had the unfamiliar elongated, leonine faces of the delegation from the Euphrates cities or the long, matted tresses of the wild scions of Asaradel.

The rich smell of roasted meat drifted to them, working the opposite of its intended effect on Noah. His appetite thus suppressed, and finding no one he knew who he might wish to greet, he took in the details of the hall. The architecture was flawless, the artisanal flourishes bold and admirably executed. Statues, as lifelike as stone could be shaped, marched one after another around the hall's diameter, presiding from their plaqued pedestals over the lavish display of Atlantean state hospitality. Noah examined the nearest statue.

"Irad, son of Enoch," read Noah aloud from the stone-set bronze plaque.

"This is the Hall of Heroes," said Tehama, who had made no move to leave the missioners. "The greatest soldiers and statesmen of our people's history are commemorated here."

"Do not feel obliged to play hostess if you do not care to, Tehama," said Eudeon. "Your time in Atlantis must feel all too short."

"On the contrary," answered the huntress, "I am far more at ease in the forests and plains than these gilded halls. What have I to do with politics and pampering?"

"I might be able to become accustomed to it," said Midash, eyeing a fountain of amber-colored liquid. "I shall be right back." He excused himself, weaving his way to the tables.

"I would beg leave as well," said Phiaphara. "My father is not a man for the public eye. He might care to see me."

"Of course," said Tehama. "Your duties as a Wa-Mizhan do not always supersede those of a daughter. I shall see you back at the lodge."

The girl left the way they had come. "She seems older than she is," said Eudeon.

Tehama nodded. "A green branch from a burned tree. She and her father are the only survivors from Mizraim to make their ways to Atlantis thus far. They seem to be an able people, though—we hope they fight still."

"She must be fearless, too, to join the Wa-Mizhan," said the giant. "Hardly a safe occupation."

"I am glad she did. Believe me, she could have found herself in far more dangerous positions . . ." Tehama looked into the shadows created by rows of pillars; Noah followed her gaze, but whatever she expected apparently did not materialize. What fears she had thus ostensibly allayed, Tehama fell into a familial conversation with Eudeon, leaving Noah to his own devices. Happy to have a new friend in an unfamiliar place, Noah continued to round on the statues.

"Ho, Eudeon! Look here," he exclaimed. Eudeon and Tehama came over. A stone giant, nude but for a fur-cowled cape and holding a massive axe above his head, stood atop his pedestal in some moment of triumph.

"Gloryon of Enoch," read Eudeon. "Gilyon's father?"

"He died when you were a babe," said Noah, impressed at how accurate the carven features were. "He was my first ally in Enoch—my first true Nephilim friend." Noah smiled up at Eudeon. "But not my greatest."

"Try not to become emotional in front of my kin, lest she think we missioners soft," said Eudeon, eyes twinkling.

"We ought to show Gilyon this."

Midash returned with a dribbling goblet. "What, this Naphil's sculpted genitals?"

Eudeon cocked an eyebrow. "Some propriety, Midash."

Tehama laughed. "Here? In the shadow of Armon? Worry yourselves not—such a thing does not exist. Besides, those are nothing compared to the ones on Pethun's statue."

"My brother has a statue?" asked Eudeon. "Hnh. I had assumed these were posthumous tributes."

Tehama gave him an enigmatic glance. "Then you must also assume that we Nephilim die beyond injury and illness. Why, though? No descendant of the *bene Elohim* has yet."

The apologist in him lit aflame, Noah gathered up a preacher's words. Before he could begin an exposition on his understanding of sin's universality and bodily death that must follow as its consequence, he heard his own name shouted.

"I say, Noah!"

Noah turned to see his brother Hadishad, a second later embraced in embroidered silks. He returned the rather crushing hug as best he could.

"So good to see you!" Hadishad pushed away to arm's length. "Come, eat! You seem all tendons." He laughed.

Noah glanced at Hadishad's paunch, stifling an uncharitable reply. "No, thank you, brother. Ah, have you met Midash of Havilah?"

The answer negative, Hadishad greeted Midash warmly, then Tehama and Eudeon in turn.

"Your coming is providential, Noah," his brother said. "When news of the Zuthians began reaching Atlantis, I considered sending racers to find you—and you, Eudeon. Atlantis and Eden will need every able ally soon. And the two youngest generations of my family have yet to meet their uncle!"

"Have I really been away that long?"

"Aye," said Hadishad. "But our Creator has as impeccable timing as ever."

A lyre began to play. Soft red lamps on the walls alighted. Hadishad's smile did not fall, but Noah sensed a sudden tension in his brother. The redness of his cheeks could have been from the new lights, or perhaps a flush. Other men around them, human and giant alike, looked pleased. Various curtains about the hall rustled and parted, and the cause of Hadishad's discomfort was immediately clear.

"We must find an exit before they are upon us," said Noah, stepping closer to his fellow missioners. They drifted back a bit to one of the many other hangings about the hall, now proven to be doorways as well as decoration. Eudeon pulled it away; it hid an alcove with a small table set with wine and wide cushioned benches, but no egress.

"Too late," said Noah.

"Really, Noah," whispered Hadishad harshly. "I have seen you fearlessly face lions, drakes, and dragons. Surely you are not afraid of a few pretty girls."

A swarm of beautiful women spread throughout the room. Bits of silk, gems, and gold barely served to maintain their modesties. They flowed across the hall, attaching themselves to different dignitaries by ones and twos, lilting and laughing, like buzzing bees to flowers' stamens. Perfume, sweet and strong, enticed men from the food, their interests too clearly turning from their stomachs to other organs.

"Are these Atlantis's pleasures Dyeus spoke of, brother?" said Noah.

"Not just of Atlantis," says Tehama, disgusted. "Look there, and there. Your brothers, Eudeon, have wasted no time in leveraging the refugees' gratitude." Indeed, many of the women, especially the younger ones, possessed features and skin tones that marked them from the displaced nations. "Thank the moon Phiaphara is with the Wa-Mizhan, else she very well may have ended up here . . . with *her*."

"Who?"

Tehama's contempt was palpable as she glared across the hall. "Voluta, Armon's mistress of courtesans."

The woman was beautiful beyond humanity, her walk smooth and sinuous, every motion seductive. She wove her way with a touch on the arm, a silvery laugh. Thus far, none of the courtesans had approached the missioners, roughly dressed compared to the other men there and already in the company of a beautiful woman whose despising look was hardly inviting.

Such things did not deter Voluta from coming right to them. She was clearly a Nephilim woman, too physically perfect to be otherwise. Her clinging gown caught the soft light in the hall and seemed to direct it to what parts of her body Noah wanted his eyes to avoid most.

He felt a sudden kinship to Eve's temptation; he, unlike her, knew good and evil, and he crushed the seed within him that threatened to blossom into lust.

"Tehama, so good to see you!" The mistress of courtesans exuded sincerity and charm. "And Hadishad!" She leaned to him, kissing him on both cheeks and causing his now-definite flush to redden further. "Who are these friends of Atlantis?" Her smile virtually shone, in heated combat for attention from her voluptuous form. To Noah's great satisfaction, both Eudeon and Midash were giving the Nephilim woman a wide berth, Midash having actually backed into a stone column. Phempor was fresh in all of their minds, and they had each seen the bodies of the dead altar house stewards. They knew what price it could cost to succumb to temptation.

Hadishad answered her with an emissary's smoothness. Voluta's eyes sparkled wide open, especially at Eudeon's introduction. "Such persons as you three must enjoy the very best hospitality Mount Armon has to offer. I should be happy to arrange chambers for you all tonight, as well as a hostess to guide you as needed. I would even be willing to give you a private tour of Armon myself." Noah doubted her expectant, and exceedingly lovely, smile was often met with denial. He allowed himself a small bit of pleasure at the thought of doing so.

"We will be making ourselves known to the xenist at the altar house when we leave here, thank you. He shall provide us lodging there."

Voluta made no reply as if she expected more. When nothing else was forthcoming, she said, "Eudeon, I must consider you almost family, as I do your brothers and sisters. Shall you come with me to the peak of Armon? A warm reunion awaits there, I can promise."

"I will stay with my fellow missioners."

"Look around you, woman," Tehama snarled. "There are plenty of soft men ready to be plied by your pretty claws. Leave these alone. Leech your lips to someone else."

The two beautiful creatures faced each other, one a lithe lioness and the other a jeweled palace cat. The cat backed down with an angelic smile. "So pleasant to have made the acquaintance of each of you," she said, again with off-putting sincerity that almost caused Noah regret at his coldness.

"You must come visit me soon, Hadishad," Voluta said in parting. "I do miss you so. Give Boehta all my love." She drifted back into the crowd.

Noah exhaled. He turned on Hadishad, who now looked rather pale.

"Have you slept with that woman?"

Hadishad raised his defenses at the directness of the question. "Things are different here, Noah," he said. "She is a great favorite of Dyeus. By the sword of fire, her parentage is unknown, but still she lives atop Armon! Many currencies are traded here, and we pay what we must to do our jobs."

Noah's eyes narrowed. "Does your wife know?"

Hadishad set his jaw. "Boehta plays this role as well as anyone when she needs to." A profound pity welled up in Noah's breast, bringing with it a tinge of guilt for even introducing his younger brother to the Nephilim all those many years ago. "But it is a role only!" added Hadishad.

"Man and wife," said Noah softly. "One flesh." He put a hand on the nape of his brother's neck, pulling his head in closer and locking eyes. "There is pain when that is torn." With one quick motion he pinched Hadishad's skin and ripped. Hadishad spun away, stifling a cry and clasping the back of his neck. He pulled his hand away, examining his open palm. Noah saw the smear of blood there, but was not sorry for it.

"Nettle-headed prude!" said Hadishad harshly, then tried his best to regain his decorum. "You are a hard man, Noah. Do not force your sexual exile upon the rest of us." He nodded curtly at Eudeon, Midash, and Tehama, and walked away holding a honey-colored kerchief to his neck.

"May we leave now?" asked Midash.

"This way," said Tehama. "If my father meant to address us again tonight, he would not have sent his whores."

They pushed through the press of people whose high stations were threatened with embarrassment by drink and flesh. Tehama led their way to a tall archway covered by tapestries hanging from the vault high above. "Let us out," said Tehama to one of a couplet of guards, who was standing by a thick silver rope. Midash pushed his half-empty goblet into the hands of the other.

"Let us in!"

The heavy tapestry muffled the refined voice hidden beyond it, but still it jarred old memories that Noah could not quite place. The guard—whose command he obeyed, who could say?—pulled the rope, and the hangings parted.

"Leaving so soon, dear Tehama? But the festivities are only beginning! Wait, wait, wait . . . Eudeon? *Noah*, of *Eden*? Oh-ha! This *does* call for celebration!"

Noah recognized the voice now, but he could not quite reconcile it with the Naphil before him. Ringlets of perfectly arranged golden curls framed a face with bleary eyes and smiling mouth that seemed too small for it. A bulbous red nose protruded from rosy round cheeks. The giant had no chin; rather, he had a great many folds of fat, all crowding for space and forming a bulging collar of flesh where his neck should have been. He wore an enormous ruby on a golden chain, and the robe draped around his puffy shoulders served his modesty poorly.

With the obese giant was a tittering group of thin men and women—a few of whom defied easy distinction as one or the other—that smelled of herbsmoke and alcohol. As scantily dressed as their fleshy patron, they swayed and moved like wavering satellites around a gargantuan sun, laughing and dancing drunkenly with no rhythm or care.

"Move aside, Deneresh," said Tehama impatiently. She shooed away the revelers to the left of the enormous giant, allowing them to push through.

"That was Noah of Eden!" said Deneresh loudly and jovially, his high voice carrying to Noah as the missioners hurried out. "Although I do remember him being more fun than that!"

‹ CHAPTER 12 ›

Outside of the hall—the spacious, cloying, noxious hall—and after promises to Midash and Eudeon to meet soon at the altar house's domiciles, Noah wandered. He followed the rush of the waterfall they had passed when they came to this place, an aural beacon that drew him past the monolithic buildings to the mountain's edge. At a lattice-lined outlook, overgrown with orchids and bordered by a short, stout stone wall, he listened to the cascade, watched it career down the rocks. The clean, constant cacophony of the water cleansed the memory of the evening's noises, lustful laughs and clinking goblets, until his mind was still. The outlook provided him a view of the valley at the foot of Armon, the foothills beyond, a dark line far away that might have been the sea, and above that, dusk's starry night sky, a bright new moon taking a fading sun's place.

The world was changing before him, and he had not realized its extent. The stories told today, the Zuthians sweeping across the earth like a line of locusts, seemed to him as the onset of night in an untamed wilderness fraught with dragons: foreboding, but not immediately so, with plans yet to be made and precautions that might be taken. His encounter with Hadishad, though, had wounded his spirit. His brother possessed all good things the world could offer; why reach further to what was forbidden? Noah looked to heaven's starry expanse. "I suppose You might have asked the same thing of Eve and Adam."

He closed his eyes and turned his thoughts to the one thing he knew to be immutable and true. The words passed over him, through him, bringing him the peace of the One to whom they belong. "In the beginning, *Elohim* created the heavens and the earth."

Noah completed his recitation of the toledoth. Saying the words aloud calmed him, but with the calm came a keen fatigue. He released the night sky from his gaze and leaned on the wall.

He was not alone there. The realization hit him like cold water. He looked to his right, slowly. A shadowed silhouette leaned lazily on the lattices, raising itself to full height as it noted Noah's notice. The giant stood a third again as tall as Noah and was twice as broad; even in the darkness, Noah traced a star-shine outline of arms as big around as his torso. From sheer size alone, Noah knew that he had no chance in a fight. He stepped back. Atlantean lands had historically been safe for any traveler, but with what the missioner had seen today, he trusted no longer to history. Noah tensed to bolt.

"So are you an astrologer, or are you mad?"

The missioner paused. "Excuse me?"

"You mumble into the night sky. That's astromancy or madness." The giant shrugged. "Not that it matters to me. Just curious."

A preacher of the Creator's righteousness was always eager for conversation that might be steered to spiritual matters, and here was an opportunity as good as Noah had ever seen.

"I speak to myself the words of the Lord God Creator, Who made the stars themselves," Noah said. "Do you know of Him?"

"I know that people believe such things." The Naphil stepped from mottled moonlit shade of the orchids and into the starlight. He was massively muscled, his face calm and confident, dressed in a cloak and clothing of a traveler's cut. "Are you from the altar house, then?"

"I shall bed there tonight, but originally I come from the lands of Eden."

"And how came you here?"

Noah thought across the last day, and he realized he had no good answer. "There is a need here. Perhaps I can help in some way."

"And partake of the palace girls. I can smell them on you. I thought altar worshippers avoided such."

Noah was jealous for few things; his good reputation was one of them. "Your pardon, sir, but—"

"Nay, I do not judge. Atlantis has needs, you have needs."

"You misunderstand. I did not demean myself with those sad women. I fled from them."

The giant apparently found this amusing, letting out a deep, rumbling laugh. "'Fled'! Whatever for?"

"Would you drink wine from a bottle passed around by slobbering consumptives?"

"Ha! Just so." The massive figure kept chuckling. "This is what I keep saying! Where is the honor? Where is the conquest? Voluta's girls are employed as objects of pleasure. Bedding one would be as pathetic as mounting the head of a pet house-hare over the hearth and calling it a hunting trophy."

Noah was uncertain if his own meaning had been fully understood, but the giant continued.

"So what *do* you want?"

The giant's candidness asked for his own. Noah studied the deep purple hill-broken horizon as he considered his answer. "I want to save them," he said.

The Naphil stared out too. "Many folk need saving, from many things. Who do you mean?"

"Those girls. Atlantis. Mankind. From themselves, from sin, from death. I fear for the souls in this place. I fear for the lives of those outside it."

"You refer to the Zuthian offensive?"

Noah nodded. "If all that is told is true, they are a flood that will cover the earth if it is able. Someone needs to warn those in its way, to lead them to higher ground."

"And Atlantis?"

Noah sighed. "Drowning in a different way. The body is vital and strong, but the soul is gasping."

"So what comes before—saving Atlantis's soul, or saving those who remain in the path of destruction? What is the next task for you? Do that."

Both of them, human and Naphil, fell silent. Points of red light flared one by one into existence about the valley, becoming a crude terrestrial mirror to the heavens above. "How many fires have been stamped out already?" wondered Noah to himself.

With only a "your pardon" for warning, the Naphil flung himself over the wall. The movement, violent and sudden, shocked Noah, and he feared that he had been the last conversant with a suicide. He thrust himself against the stone guardwall, leaning over and peering down. At first he saw nothing and felt sick; then, already near the canopy of the valley's forests, he saw a billowing traveler's cape, black against the moonlit mountain, almost flying from ledge to ledge downward. The Naphil, whoever he was, made a final lionlike leap from the stone slope into the treetops and disappeared. The single sign left of his presence was the memory of his conversation. Noah gathered that, then walked away toward Armon's altar house.

‹ CHAPTER 13 ›

D ashael's estate sprawled about the hills, a testament
to affluence gained by skill and labor. The lands held
homesteads and hamlets of descendants who had
stayed in the family business, as well as many private stables and herds of wild mounts kept on the property. The
open-walled main house, where Dashael and Jet resided,
combined Atlantean luxury with Edenic style, equal parts
rose marble and white wood. The house rested on a high
hill, overlooking a rambling path that marched down a
slope filled with orchards, pools, and gardens. It felt like
home to Noah.

For three nights at Armon he had divided his time
between clerics from the altar house, who descended daily
to the valleys to offer prayer, sacrifices, and healing to the
displaced peoples there, and the councilors and commanders of Atlantis and her allies, sallying words of war.

Gilyon had joined them on their second day, plung-
ing headfirst into the martial planning. His near-lifelong
absence from Atlantis had made his lineage largely
unfamiliar to younger generations, those who had never
known their city as Enoch. However, his father Gloryon,
son of the *irin* Azazyel, had never been forgotten by the
guardsmen, many of whom now led as captains and battle
marshals.

Seldom during the three days did Noah see any of his
Nephilim companions of old. Deneresh, certainly no warrior, had taken a large party to the wild woodlands to the
north for what Hadishad had called "revelry" and Tehama
"debauchery." Noah had taken a pleasant meal with Tiras

and Tevesh, sons of the Nephilim mystic Hoduín, at the emissary hall they kept at Armon, but the brothers were as thickly involved as anyone in the war planning and had little time to spare. Hamerch, son of Dyeus, friend of both Gilyon and Noah, called twice at the altar house between what he called "endless errands," both times staying for just a few minutes and sprinting off.

Dyeus and Pethun remained at Armon's peak. Noah saw them once, summoned by a brace of palace guards, right before he gained retreat to the lands of Gilyon's stepfather. Having been badly battered by his ordeal in Phempor, a lengthy journey, and three days' immersion in nonstop talk of man's violence against man, Noah now rested at Dashael and Jet's table with Gilyon and Eudeon, Midash of Havilah, and Caiphes and Emié. The meal—a half-dozen different cultivars of custard fruit, some thick and sweet, some firm and tart—had been cleared of all but wine, and the newly engaged couple had been briefed of their fellows' last few days at Armon.

"So what did Dyeus and Pethun say?" asked Caiphes.

"They asked me to fight with them—'as once I did against their fallen fathers.' I agreed to take warning," he said. "Toward Havilah and beyond. Nothing more."

"How far? Until you meet the Zuthian armies?"

"I hope not. I must entrust that to our God." Noah shrugged. "Eudeon comes with me, and Midash—at least to Havilah."

"Did they provide you with provisions or travel means? Weapons?"

"Weapons we will not need, beyond what we have," said Eudeon. "Ours is a dangerous undertaking, a race with an unseen competitor. By every account the Zuthians move fast, their numbers swollen with slaves, exiles, and bandits. Success is dependent on speed, not strength."

"My own stables will provide the mounts," said Dashael. "Better than any state-bred animals, no matter the kind."

"Gilyon, shall you not go with them?" asked Jet. Noah suspected she already knew the answer, but wished not to seem selfish of her son in front of his closest friends. Noah could picture his own mother doing the same. Looking at Caiphes and Emié, Noah was suddenly tempted to envy. He had no wife, nor a son she might love and cling to. He stifled the feeling; thoughts of what might have been would lead him down a path that stopped at a beautiful girl from Eden hanging at the end of a rope.

Gilyon put an arm around his mother and pulled her to his side, her head coming barely past his hip. "I have no respect for the magicians of Atlantis," he said. "What if the Zuthians fight with more than swords? Whether demons or dragons, I know I can defeat them with the Lord God beside me. That is something few in Atlantis will say, so I will stay here and make ready for war." He looked down and said, more quietly, "And you are the only blood I have left. I will not leave you."

Noah waited until the moment passed, then said, "I did ask for one thing from Dyeus and Pethun." He excused himself from the table and quickly returned with a felt-wrapped bundle. "Careful with the wine." He untied a knot of twine and set down the parcel's contents.

Sheaves of crisp, folded paper, labeled at the edges, made up the bulk of the bundle, and underneath rested a leather-bound folio, cream colored, with a silver sigil imprinted on the cover.

"I borrowed these maps from the cartographers' school," said Noah, unfolding the first one on the table and giving the rest to the other men to look through. "And this from Dyeus's treasure room."

He unbound the folio's leather strap that secured it shut, supple and strong as if it were made yesterday, and lifted the cover.

"An atlas," said Gilyon, tracing a snaking line of pale blue on the first map. The opened atlas spanned a good portion of the table, enough to give all there a decent view. The Naphil leaned closer, inspecting the page through squinted eyes. "Human hands did not make this. Who did?"

"Samyaza," answered Noah.

"And Dyeus let you have it?" Gilyon straightened, letting Dashael have a closer look.

"Samyaza was my father as well," said Eudeon. "I have as much right to it as Dyeus."

"What do these symbols mean?" asked Dashael. The first map showed a mass of green shaped as a thick crescent and a field of blue that surrounded it and filled its middle. Like star points, silver symbols similar to that on the cover dotted the green, most of them clustered about the middle of the crescent. "Quite a number of them."

"Two hundred exactly," answered Noah. "The sigils of the *bene Elohim*. When Samyaza made this, he must have marked where he and his fellows settled."

"What place is this?" asked Jet.

Gilyon smiled at the petite woman half his height. "The earth, mother. The lands, and the seas God pulled them from."

Jet raised her eyebrows. "And how much of it have you traveled?"

Gilyon laughed and looked at Noah, who, with a moment of thought, traced a hesitant outline with his finger that encompassed most of the inner coast and a good deal of the northern horn.

"It is a big place, mother," said Gilyon.

The next page showed the earth again, but this time the land was done in dull reds and browns. Symbols covered this map, too, more evenly distributed and dark like burns rather than silver.

"This is accurate?" asked Gilyon, bending over Midash and Caiphes, both pressed against the table.

Noah nodded. "As of five hundred years or so ago."

"Every caster in the world needs a copy of this," said Caiphes.

"What does the map show?" asked Dashael.

"These," said Gilyon, pointing out a few dark symbols, "are the marks of Satan's princes. Diabolic politics are somewhat of a mystery, but if this is still remotely correct . . ."

"We spent last night at Armon's altar house making copies with the Scribes," said Noah.

"A fine job we did too," said Midash. "I plan on doing some hunting when we get to Havilah."

"Where to after Havilah?" asked Emié.

Noah flipped through the atlas. The rest of the pages were split between regional maps and star maps broken into quadrants. "Zuthians have made it here, at least," he said, showing a page crisscrossed with rivers. "With these topographical details, our missioner's maps, and Atlantean trade maps, we think our small party can stay ahead of them—"

"—or hide from them—," interjected Midash.

"—to spread the warning."

Emié pursed her lips. "Will you go to Phempor?"

Eudeon smiled at the girl. "There was no word that they are in danger."

Emié shared a look with Caiphes, brief, but noticed by Noah. A griffin's piercing cry preceded the animal itself padding into the room. "Company," said Midash, and it was true: Hadishad's voice called from outside, bringing Noah and Dashael to the front room. Up the path came Hadishad, leading his wife Boehta by the hand. Behind them were Tehama, the girl Phiaphara, and a Nephilim man, face hidden by the hairy hood of a lion-skin cloak that seemed little altered from when it had been part of a living animal.

The arrival of visitors compelled Jet to come play hostess in the front courtyard, and while her existing guests swarmed out to greet the new ones, Hadishad immediately pulled Noah aside, to where the babble of a fountain and basin afforded their conversation a modicum of privacy.

"You are right," Hadishad said. "About my marriage, its sanctity. My wife agrees. We need to have a respite from Atlantis and her lusts. We leave for Eden within the week."

"I think you do rightly," said Noah. "Who will take your place as emissary?"

"Nobody. Dyeus and Pethun have agreed to commission me to go to Eden in my official capacity. I am to do what I can to convince Methuselah to aid the war effort. Hoduìn, Tiras, and Hamerch will accompany us, and Atlantean dignitaries and soldiers too."

Noah raised a brow. "Do you escape from Atlantis, or do you take it with you to Eden? No, I am not judging your action. Just . . . be careful."

"And you as well. I heard what task you and Eudeon have taken." Hadishad glanced over to the mass of people conversing in the courtyard. He caught Tehama's eye; she strode over. "Speaking of which."

"They say you are a master of persuading for an unseen cause," said the huntress to Noah. "I hope it is true—my own tongue is wild, with no bridle. I suppose I shall see soon enough."

"You are to accompany me?"

"Indeed." Her radiant smile held a hint of wild danger, like a sunbeam warm enough to burn if left on bare skin for too long. "Myself, Phiaphara, my brother Peleg."

"Is that him?" Noah pointed to the giant, hide-clad back to them.

Tehama grimaced. "No, Peleg gathers supplies in the city as we speak. He is a healer and chirurgeon, and there may be much need of his skills where we go. *That* is—"

"Eroch!" said the Naphil. "Son of Dyeus! Well met again." It was the unnamed giant from the night before; upon this realization, Noah took better stock of him in the daylight. Not tall, as Nephilim went—perhaps eight feet or so—but muscular breadth made up for what height he lacked. He wore a belt and breeches under his leonine cloak and well-worn sandals; a strap around his bare chest denoted a weapon at his back.

"My apologies for my exit," Eroch said. "That vantage is good for dragon spotting as they come into the valley. I saw one. Hardly healthy for our refugees, would you say?" He laughed.

"You alerted the guards?" Hadishad asked, concerned but unsurprised, as if the problem had occurred before.

"Ha! No. I killed it, of course." He unslung a cudgel as thick and long as Noah's leg and held it out. "And its killer is at your service! We will be seven, and none will stand before us."

"Fighting is what we are trying to avoid, not search out," said Tehama. "Remember that, or you will *not* accompany us."

"Ha! And who shall stop me?" said Eroch jovially. "I jest, dear sister. War is predictable—no doubt it shall overtake us eventually, and we shall wage it. This task strikes my fancy. Onward to it!"

Tehama stepped close to Eroch. "In Dyeus we may share a father, young bastard, but *never* call me sister. He and Pethun may favor you, but I do not have to." Eroch continued to look amused.

At the mention of the two sons of Samyaza, another face passed Noah's eyes, one conspicuous by its absence at Armon. "Where is Dedroth? It occurs to me that I have neither seen him nor heard word of him since we arrived."

"Oh, he confines himself to the city," said Hadishad. "A man of the mind, not of arms. But he will contribute to our cause in his own way—of that I have no doubt."

His experiment was a success. The anastomoses had worked, and the beasts now shared viscera. The joining wounds were healed and scarred, and he no longer feared any suppurative breakdown. He had avoided any attempt to join nervous systems, previous tries suggesting the futility of such efforts. This had led to some initial difficulty with coordinated movement, but he felt confident that the pack mind would soon overcome each individual's confused struggles to act independently. The key, it seemed, was using littermates. He would explore that link further at a later time, but for now, today's breakthrough brought with it a sense of completion for him, at least for a while.

Indeed, he could even be said to be in a good mood, an uncommon state for such a racing mind.

Dedroth chose a newly picked pomegranate from the bowl outside his chambers. He pulled off an edge of rind to get to the jewels of seed beneath and pondered. The day's success put him in an amorous mood, he decided, and he considered a suitable courtesan he might send for. He did not indulge as often as the rest of his family (his brothers Pethun and Dyeus more than picked up his slack!); he had much serious work to accomplish, with little time for dalliances. A face and form came to his mind, though, and, following quickly after, a name. Ah, Iltha. Just blossoming into the flower of her womanhood. Likely overlooked, too, by his brothers and nephews, due to her youth; the others tended to enjoy the company of more mature women, although they typically kept a young boy or two around. Yes, she would do nicely. He sent for her and prepared the wine.

Iltha arrived quickly after the summons. Dedroth had recalled correctly. She was young and vital, a red rose in full bloom. No, not a rose, he considered; more like a pomegranate, his favorite of fruits. The girl was beautiful to behold in the sunlit courtyards, as she was now, full of unspoken promises to satiate his hunger. The smell of her, too, was delicious, all the more so in these more intimate quarters. His appetite, so often denied, began to increase, and he poured her wine.

She danced for him at his request. "Drink, my dear," he offered. She smiled at him and took a sip of the wine, never taking her eyes off his. Yes, just like a pomegranate. He could think of no better comparison.

Her smile faltered, and her wide eyes began to drift closed. Quickly Dedroth rose and caught her as she fell.

He tenderly laid her on his couch. She breathed slowly, then slower and shallower still, then no more.

Dedroth took the still girl's hand in his and gently felt for a pulse, finding nothing. He bent his head, touching his ear to her lips, listening for any faint exhalation of air and hearing none. Carefully he reached out his hand and held open one of her pretty eyes, forcing the lids wide apart; with the other hand, he drew the edge of the nail of his first finger across the surface of the globe. No response. He sighed in anticipation.

A pomegranate, as with any fruit, he contemplated, is indeed beautiful on the branch, and its fragrance may suggest more tangible pleasures to come. However, only at that moment when the fruit is separated from the life-giving mother tree does it leave distant theory, merely *potentially* satisfying, to become a thing to be actually tasted, eaten, enjoyed as it was meant to be. The girl was now, as it were, ripe and freshly picked, ready to be savored. Dedroth wondered what his brothers might say about this particular use of a court girl, but only briefly. Would they find it distasteful in some way? Surely not. After all, it wasn't as if he were digging up corpses; he had no more interest in that than he would in eating rotten fruit. This was different, as any reasonable mind could see. This was special. This—she—was for him and him alone, and he would savor every moment with her.

Hungrily, he loved her.

‹ CHAPTER 14 ›

Atlantis was much changed since last he lived there, Gilyon thought. He laughed to himself at the understatement. In his childhood, the city had been named Enoch, taking its current name at the same time he departed with Noah. Perhaps it was only fitting that he recognized almost nothing of it now.

Of the old rings of Enoch, only the ninth outer wall—the one built under direction of the *bene Elohim*—remained. Gone were the centuries-old architectural ripples that had spread outward from the center built by Cain. The wall of the Grigori had reflected them back, and the entirety of the city of Atlantis had taken the same form and style of it. Gilyon admitted that the transformation had been admirably done.

The arched spans that he and Haphan passed under as they rode together proved to be just one of many evidences that Atlantis had been built for a citizenry where giants were common. Dressed stone walls stretched in rows like cave-marked canyons; columns as thick boled as redwoods supported promenades and walkways overhead. These seemed to hold as much activity as the wide streets below. Gilyon saw no pack animals or mounts on the suspended walkways, but familiars and pets followed their owners there. The ground-level streets sloped from their centers to the walkways at either side. As Haphan navigated their hatchet-crested dragon through the busy thoroughfare, Gilyon saw now and again wagons pulled slowly down the middle of the street at its slight apex. Men in the back of it tossed constant pailfuls of water—seawater, from the tang in the air—onto the tightly paved stones, washing the refuse from the perpetual parade of animals to the street's sides and away through metal gratings placed every so often. "A world above," thought Gilyon, looking up at a delicate bridge perhaps fifty feet above, flowering greenery flowing across and hanging down from its siding, that connected one alabaster tower to another. He passed a grate accepting a small river of filth. "But the one below must not be so pleasant."

"This place has changed since my childhood," he said aloud, inwardly cringing at his feeble attempt at casual conversation. Haphan should be a man he knew better than any other. As it were, he was a virtual stranger, and Gilyon felt limited to banal observations.

If Haphan noticed the giant's discomfort, he took it in stride. "Mostly stables and carriage houses at street level. The commerce is conducted on the upper levels."

"Levels."

"There is *much* commerce."

They passed where old Enoch's eighth wall used to be, then its seventh. Stacked and tiered edifices climbed skyward, many built from monolithic blocks whose transportation Gilyon found difficult to fathom, even with the aid of indriks or behemoths. Gardens, replete with songbirds and squirrels and tamarins, hung from raised rose-marbled plazas and sprung from multileveled pools. Cain's cursed city of Enoch had been dead, relying on the trade of other tribes and lands for its lifeblood; somehow, as Atlantis, it had come alive.

Now the buildings became less grand, the bustle and hum of activity more pressing. Strips of bright patterned cloth draped from walk bridges overhead, still or billowing as the sea breeze blowing from the harbor dictated. Haphan pulled their dragon to a halt under a banner of intricate designs done in the colors of sunset. A stable master took the dragon's reins, and Gilyon and Haphan dismounted.

The stairway from the street took them to an open platform, where workers deposited rolls of fabric on dragons and mammoths whose laden backs rose to the heights of the upper level. A veritable village of tents and flags lay before them on the plaza, riotous with colors and symbols denoting different sellers and bordered on three sides by shopfront buildings. With Haphan in the lead, Gilyon took a breath and waded in. The place was loud and crowded. Merchants called to them as they passed; at one point Gilyon was obliged to listen to the pleading of one of them for half a minute while his way was blocked by a line of servants, each with a colorful carpet rolled at his shoulder, winding like some enormous segmented worm. Men and women, all well built and attractive, patrolled about their employers' stations and drew attention to the wares they modeled. Some of these had animals with them, fancily dressed as well: cats on leashes, monkeys perched on shoulders.

They came to a merchant's shop whose extended awning thrust into the busy market and presented its colorful wares like the rest. Haphan bypassed this and led Gilyon into the proper structure which housed the main part of the shop. A well-tailored attendant met them immediately, addressing Haphan as befit a regular patron.

"We would see Ryim, if he is able," said Haphan. The attendant glided off.

Gilyon ran his eyes down rows of robes and tunics, their quality evident even to his rough taste.

"These are—"

"Exquisite, are they not?" Haphan fingered the material.

"I was going to say 'not very fit for labor.'"

A thin man wove through the manikins toward them. "Labor! Not here, my lord. Here we sell luxury," he said, coming up to Haphan and clutching his shoulder in friendly greeting. "And who is your tall friend?"

"This is Gilyon, for whom we need a livery."

"Good, good." The tailor circled Gilyon, leaning in to examine the sleeveless tunic worn by the Naphil. "This is a fine cut. Old," Ryim noted. "Very old."

"I have little opportunity to refresh my wardrobe," said Gilyon.

"Clearly. Where runs your lineage?" Ryim asked. While he talked, he ran his hands up and down a knotted string as he held it to Gilyon's back, chest, arm, his motions fast and fluid.

"To Adam," Gilyon replied.

Ryim chuckled. "I meant a little less distant. Who was your father?"

"My father was Gloryon of Enoch. *His* father I will not mention."

"Gloryon!" Ryim looked at Gilyon with new eyes, then returned to measuring. "A legend in Atlantis and in Eden!"

"I have spent little of my life in either of those places. I would not know."

"And how do you come to be with Dashael's house?"

"He married my mother."

"Lady Jet! I had no idea she had a first husband. How could I . . . so you two are . . ." He looked to Haphan, then up to Gloryon.

"Brothers. Yes."

"Half brothers, technically." Haphan grinned at Gilyon, who decided in that moment that he liked his mother's second son.

"My, my," said Ryim. The information apparently pleased him. With deft hands he continued to measure dimensions, which eventually necessitated two stepladders and an assistant. Talk turned to business, alternating between husbandry and haberdashery.

"I refuse to do it," said Ryim. "I make clothing, not . . . *not*-clothing. The courtesan who works at the palace? The harlot at a pagan temple? Why must I drop my mores and standards to accommodate her?" He grunted. "The Creator God's explicit commands are few, and these I shall keep without fail."

The words of Adam's toledoth came to Gilyon's mind: *A man shall leave his father and mother, and be joined to his wife; and they shall become one flesh.* "And for this your guild gives you trouble? Do they think this the Garden, that nakedness ought bring shame no more?"

"Your market seems busy enough without such tawdry trade," noted Haphan.

"The issue is politics, not money. The guild attempts to please the council, and the council enjoys its flesh." Another grunt. "It wants its war too. This Zuthian threat stretches us taut almost to snapping, but again, I refuse."

"Refuse?" asked Haphan.

"To make armor from my leathers—arms down, please—for private commissions. I expect that such a refusal will finally result in my expulsion from the guild."

"But it cannot prevent people from purchasing your wares. The market seems busier than ever."

"The markets are busy, yes, but their natures change. In the smithy district, for example, men are bringing tools to be forged into weapons. The households that can afford to do so are equipping themselves as militias. Arms and armor ought not to be for public consumption, do you not think? Is the guard corps not sufficient?"

"Arms, armor—my own household has these things and uses them," said Haphan.

"Yes, but you fight drakes and lions on a daily basis. You hardly count."

He proclaimed himself finished with Gilyon by deftly wrapping his measuring line around his hand and stepping back, though he continued opining. "Besides, the Lord God would not wish His creation to war with one another. We are men, not beasts. We ought to behave as such."

His limbs and torso once again his own, Gilyon folded his corded arms over his chest. "My soul too possesses the knowledge of what is good and what is evil. I have warred, and it weighs none on my conscience. Ask your own: What wrong can be in protecting the weak?"

Ryim cocked his head. "Can you protect them as well as our God? Leave it to Him."

The Naphil passed several seconds in silence, but before Ryim could claim a victorious argument, he spoke. "You have a dagger in your left sleeve. Not a tool of your trade, since those you wear at your belt. You are a successful merchant, no doubt engendering some envy among your peers, not to mention the displaced peoples in your city who have lost all they possessed." He bowed, his enormous size almost making the gesture seem

patronizing. "Conviction is admirable. Hypocrisy, less so."
A curt nod was the full extent of his goodbye to the tailor.
He left in the long strides of a Naphil.

"Sorry to run," said Haphan, hurrying to keep up.
"We shall return this evening for the livery, yes?"

They left the tailor shaking his head.

Regarding his treatment of Ryim, Gilyon knew not if
Haphan felt insulted until his half brother said, "So, we
have time to spend. The smithing district is not far . . ."

Gilyon grinned. "Lead the way."

‹ CHAPTER 15 ›

In a small, sparse land called Raphut, a swelling of the
earth overlooked the sea. Beside a mirror-calm lake,
pressed into the peak of the swell, the human colonists
of the place had built a sanctum. Naturally, the rising of
earth was bare of life but imbued with a particular attrac-
tion that connected, quite literally, with the earth itself.
Smoke and steam rose from the water, and the chimney-
like rock stalks around it, in constant plumes. No matter
how cold the wind above or the sea below, the warmth of
the water was ever unchanged. It was a good place to pass
from the world.

This had been when the fourth generation of man had
become close to death, and some of them had wished for
a place for their withering bodies to rest and prepare for
when their souls would depart them. Gilyon, Noah, and
four sons of Nicah the Seer had spent a decade or more
at or near the sanctum: cultivating the colony's oceanic
orchard; driving off cliff wyverns in the winter and sea
serpents in the spring, beasts that saw the dying as easy
prey; and talking about the Creator with men and women
who would soon meet Him.

More than anything, the smiths' district of Atlantis
reminded Gilyon of the sanctum at Raphut. The cluster
of forges was seated over the Atlantean ports, over which
a charcoal trail of wind-drawn smoke never ceased as
of late. A spiral street ran down and ever tighter to a
depressed plaza, as cacophonous as Raphut's pool was
calm. Atlantean smiths sold wares from shops along the
man-made crater, their thick stone walls and iron-barred

windows proof against thieves, hollow pillars providing egress for plumes pulled away by sea winds. Men of many colors streamed like water down a drain into the plaza, some inspecting tools, but most in the market for more deadly instruments.

Gilyon and Haphan joined the flow.

"I was not unfavorably impressed by Ryim," said the Naphil. "He is a man sure in his work."

"He is a true friend as well," said Haphan. "Those are too few here. I wish to keep all we have, especially in these uncertain days."

"Perhaps I shall buy him a new dagger," said Gilyon. "I jest!" he added, seeing Haphan's uncertain expression. "If anything, it will be a stout sword." Haphan did not appear amused.

The mood about them was jovial. Many of the refugees they passed, although conspicuous by particular skin and hair coloring, had otherwise adopted Atlantean garb. Gilyon overheard merchants discussing new trade routes, both to the refugees' lands soon to be reclaimed as well as to the unexplored Zuthian lands, free for the taking when the hordes met the "Atlantean wall" and certain decimation. In every conversation, Atlantis was a savior and a symbol of prosperity and power.

Where the textile district's buyers were mostly Atlantean, the smithing district was primarily packed with the displaced men of other nations. Guards stood about, maintaining the calm that no one wanted to risk losing to any chaos catalyzed by the proximity of warriors to weapons.

A guard wearing a captain's cape made his presence known to the new wash of men circling down into the arms market. "Welcome, all, to the bones of Atlantis," he called from astride his charger, short maned and Atlantean white. "Above she is beautiful, yes, pleasing to the senses, but her sinews and strength lie here underground. Enter in peace." He bent down to a group of scarred, scowling men. "Or do not enter at all."

Gilyon had not spoken with a guard of Atlantis in four hundred years—not since the city was called Enoch and his father Gloryon was a legend in it. He diverted his path toward the horse-mounted captain and beckoned Haphan to come with him. His half brother made a poor protest but followed.

The guards' conversation was necessarily loud to be heard above the crowd's din, and Gilyon, his keen Nephilim ears a chest and head above that din, picked out the words easily.

". . . a joke. These wretches have never used iron arms, or even bronze; stone, bone, wood, no wonder the Zuthians keep marching," said the captain. Three of his men on foot below him said nothing, but their agreement lay on their faces, plain by the disdain with which they watched the flow of foreigners.

"Ah, well. They can have what iron they will," said the captain. "As long as their *gold* is good." One guard laughed. "Besides, chances are, if there's any fighting done, we'll be gathering these weapons back from their cold corpses."

Gilyon stopped; people walked around him, a stream against a pillar of rock in its midst. He stared at the captain until he caught the man's eye.

"You embarrass your station and those who came before you with your uncharity," he said.

The Naphil could tell that, had they been only two, the captain would have been shamed into silence. As it was, his men present and listening propped up his arrogance beyond the proper response of a corrected conscience. He glared at the giant. "Just who d—"

Gilyon cut him off. "I did not intend to begin a conversation with you. Think better of strangers and aliens. This city would never have survived without them." He rejoined the press of men headed to the forges, Haphan behind him.

The street emptied into what Gilyon saw now was only the atrium for the true smithing district, the shops beside the spiral street only a taste. Yawning gates lay open beneath rough-hewn stone porticoes and beckoned men to enter, and they did. Inside was like a cavernous cathedral to some god of war, whose incense was forge smoke and whose paean was the clash of hammer and metal. Instead of priests, smiths and dealers attached to each foundry shouted to attract buyers, proselytizing in a manner to make any clerical order proud.

"Sir! Sir! Here, sir!" A leather-clad smith held a long sword out to a trim, middle-aged man with a sizable entourage. "Try this blade and you will never try another." The man accepted the sword, weighting it, then handing it to a comrade. He made a show of considering, stroking each upcurling tendril of an ornate beard in turn. At his command, another of his men drew a wooden cudgel, arm long and studded with stone, and took up a defensive position against the fellow with the sword. With a stroke that Gilyon deemed painfully awkward but powerfully delivered, the sword cleaved through a good portion of the wooden weapon.

"There, see?" said the smith. "That's Atlantean iron, and I have enough of it for your entire cortege."

"Wait, sir, wait!" Another smith, apprentice in tow and sword in hand, hurried up to the bearded man. "I see you want the best. You shall not find it with *him*, this I promise. May I see that cudgel?" The weapon was produced and taken up by the apprentice, who held it aloft. With one swift stroke, the second smith cut full through the cudgel's thickness.

"Hold a moment!" The smith in leather took his sword back from the man who held it. "A clumsy striker's blow against a seasoned swordsman's? That is no way to measure a blade against another."

"The outcome would be the same," said the second smith.

"The deuce it would!"

"It would, and these men would be better off wielding their sticks than your poor work!"

"Gentlemen!" The bearded foreigner raised his hands and spoke as one accustomed to obedience. "Truth, my men be not trained in blades, but surely there are here some whose prowess is equal to your excellent weapons." A crowd was gathering around the commotion, and a few of its members shouted aye. "My name is Cirrat of Marah. Give me two fighters now who might show me and my men what can be done with a blade!" Men in groups began to look at one another; the crowd's chatter rose. Gilyon felt uneasy. This was a mass of strangers, fighters burdened by an aggression born of defeat, with no immediate object upon which to release it. Cirrat continued. "And I shall bestow upon the victor any weapon of his choosing!" The clamor that erupted then caused Gilyon to glance back at the Atlantean guards. He expected to see them pushing forward to abrogate the violence about to occur, but the captain kept his mount in place, and the other guards were climbing to better vantage points.

While humans comprised the great majority of those present, a few giants rose above the crowd. None of them were known to Gilyon, although he thought he could guess with reasonable certainty from where they came. Two of these pushed through to the open space that had formed between the smiths: a lithe hunter from one of the long-heeled grassland peoples, and a thick, hair-covered brute. Cirrat and his men had vacated to form the area's far edge. Few traits were universal among the descendants of the *bene Elohim*, but in Gilyon's experience, one had proven invariable: whatever their maternal heritage, a Naphil could fight with a sword. "Heaven's weapon," his father's father Azazyel had called it—one of the few memories Gilyon had of that evil creature. Now the smiths handed blades to their adopted champions, who took up battle stances to roars of approval.

"Gilyon, I cannot see over this crowd," Haphan said. "What is happening?" Truth be told, Gilyon did not pay much attention to human height; compared to the Nephilim, such differences among Adam's purebred sons and daughters were insignificant. Still, he noted, his half brother did seem to have inherited their mother's slight stature.

"Nothing yet," he answered. "Call those guards over, will you?"

"I will try. What will you do?"

"Keep peace. Somebody must." With a nod at Haphan, the Naphil waded further into the crowd.

At first there was no animosity in the spar. The hairy giant took the role of aggressor, testing his taller opponent with a series of common-form attacks. When these were parried adequately and returned in kind, the audience grew louder. The participants broke from each other smiling, having taken one another's measure. The grasslands giant crouched like a cat, sword back; the brutish one ran his weapon through a vicious pattern movement that even Gilyon found intimidating.

"Impress us!" cried Cirrat. "There are healers here. Fight!"

The Nephilim obliged. Each escalated the severity of his attack and was matched in turn. The graceful, fluid style of the first giant proved effective against the efficient, brutal strokes of his more muscular foe. Gilyon watched, appreciating their skills but analyzing weaknesses as well. His hope that this would remain only a martial performance seemed to be winning over his fear that bloodshed was inevitable; the lithe Naphil's sweeping strikes slowed, and the other pressed in with a series of short, powerful blows. Cirrat and his men cheered. Surrender was inevitable.

A shouted curse quieted the crowd. The brute broke away, clutching his hand. His eyes, wide with rage, shot up to the other Naphil, whose sword's edge showed the smallest smear of blood.

"The blade must have slipped over his crossguard," thought Gilyon. The possibility that such a slight mishap, as might happen during any sort of bladework—whether cook's kitchen, harvest field, or training ground—would be forgiven never entered his mind. This was for pride and honor, not to mention a material prize. A glance behind showed the guardsmen paying no mind to Haphan's entreaties, which were becoming more insistent, to no avail. No aid would be had from that quarter.

He turned back. The combatants held to the outside of the closing circle of the crowd. A group of men dressed in the same grasslander garb as their Nephilim champion were railing and pleading with the first blacksmith to give them weapons to join as well; when he refused, several drew bone knives and pressed to the circle's inner rim. "Blood for blood!" shouted a voice in the crowd from where the hairy giant had come.

"Mine soul, this is about to become a gang brawl," said an Atlantean in front of Gilyon. "Let us depart."

"Not I," said the man beside him. "Our taxes support these refugee leeches. At least they might provide some entertainment in return."

"Not today," said Gilyon. "Move aside."

Without his crossblade, Gilyon was loath to step between the Nephilim fighters. Now was his chance, though, for he feared the next lull in the giants' battle would be when one of them lay dead. He waded through the packed onlookers, his great arms pushing people to either side like a dragon-pulled plow through deep soil. He broke into the ring.

"Enough!" He shouted it twice more until a quiet fell. "This is Atlantis, Cain's city of old! Blood is not shed here. Put down your weapons."

"Blood *has* been shed here!" bellowed the brutish giant. He held up a fist, gripped tight and dripping blood from a gash between knuckles. "If you wish yours to remain within you, you'll back away."

Gilyon stood his ground, locking eyes with the bleeding giant, who broke the stare and slumped his shoulders slightly as tension ran from taut muscles. Without warning, the butt of his hilt struck out like a flared cobra, but Gilyon was ready and reacted. Rather than backing or dodging, he sprung forward before the other giant could bring his full strength to bear behind the blow. He stepped into his attacker's body and ducked as they collided, using the hirsute giant's own momentum to power a throw that landed the brute on his back near Cirrat.

The lithe giant had not abandoned the fight. With the speed of a plains creature, he fell upon his downed foe. Whether the grasslander meant to kill or only to maim mattered not to Gilyon. He leapt and grabbed the second Naphil from behind, pinning the long arms before they could bring down the blade held at the end of them. Gilyon planted his own feet and pulled the giant up, then, turning, slammed him to the ground.

Both giants had kept ahold of their blades; both were rising from the sooty stone ground, blackened where their bodies and clothing had hit it. The fury on their faces showed Gilyon exactly who the new target of their ire was. He stepped back to the edge of the circle.

He needed a weapon. He scanned over the heads of Cirrat and his men, and the smithy workers that had gathered behind them, deeper into the forges. Weapon racks were gated, guarded, or otherwise closed to him, but he saw a wooden wagon filled with iron bars that were the length of the missioner giant's forearm and half its thickness. The men in his way parted, laughing and jeering at Gilyon's perceived retreat, then shouting angrily when he pushed back through with a black bar in each hand.

With the attentions of the two other Nephilim divided between himself and one another, the work was shortly done. Gilyon avoided delivering strikes that would break bone, limiting his attacks to butt-ends to the gut and half-strength blows to thigh and upper body. He tried his best not to mar either sword, although he was obliged several times to block a blade with edge-dulling force. He disarmed one giant by locking an arm and dislocating a shoulder, replacing the joint at the end of another body toss. He kicked the dropped sword across the stones toward Cirrat's feet, the blacksmith who had made it darting in to retain it.

The other giant, limping, made a last futile swing at Gilyon, who turned inside the strike and wrenched the blade away. He kicked the Naphil hard in the backside, sending him careening into the crowd, then strode calmly over to the second blacksmith and handed him the sword.

Gilyon towered over Cirrat, whose men backed from him. "Remember that all here have a real, common enemy," said the giant. "This pettiness you instigated might have resulted in death."

"Hie there!" The call was backed by the clip of hoof on stone as the guard captain at last presented himself. "Break the peace of Atlantis and suffer the consequences. Behold the trouble you have caused!"

A few seconds passed before Gilyon realized the guard was addressing him.

"He's injured two refugees!" shouted someone in the crowd.

"And he threatened me personally," said Cirrat to the guard.

"He has stolen my iron!" The man from whose wagon Gilyon had taken the bars appeared the only one who was not feigning offense.

"And here they are back to you, sir." Gilyon handed the black bars, none the worse for wear, to the ironmonger, whose wiry muscles strained as he replaced them with the rest.

"I know you saw all that happened," said Gilyon, at eye level with the mounted captain, who tried not to appear intimidated. "So I know that you know I am not at fault here."

"I saw nothing, save you brutalizing two of this city's guests and abusing the goods of honest merchants."

"You saw nothing, Captain? We saw everything." Two figures cloaked and hooded, one a giant and one who walked with a limp and a cane, emerged from the foundries. The Naphil motioned the guards to follow him; he spoke as they walked, and Gilyon saw the captain turning white at the words, even in the firelight of the foundries.

"Who knows who this fellow is?" said the lame man to the congregated smiths. After a moment of uncertain glances among one another, an older blacksmith said, "He has somewhat the bearing of Gloryon, son of Azazyel Grigori, but I think that line is vanished, honored Tubal-Cain."

"Not at all. This is his son, Gilyon."

Red light reflected in more than a few wide eyes. The two smiths who had lent their weapons to the beaten giants offered those swords to Gilyon, who refused both. By now the halted crowd had renewed its press into the forges, and Tubal-Cain waved the smiths off to resume their usual business.

"How many years has it been?" asked Gilyon to the cripple. "Twenty-score?"

"A man does not forget one who helped save his life."

"Excuse me." The ironmonger planted himself in front of them. "I mean no disrespect, but I alone suffered true hurt here. My iron I sell to the smiths for six gold apiece, but no one will pay that for a stressed bar. I insist you buy them yourself, or at least pay me the difference on a short sale."

Not every smith had drifted away, and a few approached. "Did you say six gold for a bar?" said one to the ironmonger. "I will give you eight for one of the bars used by Gloryon's son."

"I will give you ten for the other," said a second smith.

"Ten apiece for both!" said a third. Now half a dozen smiths came near, their hands placed on the iron seller's shoulder or reaching into pouches of coin.

"I will give you twelve for every bar in your wagon."

"Thirteen."

"Fifteen!"

Tubal-Cain looked pointedly at the ironmonger, who bowed to them and turned away to the eager smiths.

"We heard you had returned to Atlantis," said the lamed smith. "You can offer more to us than you realize. Come with us to Mount Armon and see."

Gilyon could not fathom what he meant. "My half brother and I must finish business here."

"Your half brother may accompany us, and I will arrange for completion whatever business you might have."

Without a reason to decline, Gilyon assented.

"Gilyon!" Haphan skip-stepped to keep abreast of the cloaked giant's strides. "Know you who this is?"

Gilyon peered at the unhooded Naphil, square jaw shaved clean, dark and frozen eyes at odds with a handsome face. "Mareth, son of Dyeus."

"And the High Commander of the Atlantean army," said Mareth. The giant turned a cold stare down to Tubal-Cain. "Will he come?"

"Yes."

Mareth nodded. "Then let us away, that you might see where the real preparation for war against Zuthi goes on."

ᛏ CHAPTER 16 ᛏ

Seven riders set out from Atlantis at the forefront of a stream of messengers and soldiers. The cities of Nod were many, and its borders long. Outposts needed strengthening, southern regions wanted warning, and the strength centered in Atlantis was demanded beyond the city walls.

The band of seven—Tehama and Peleg, twin children of Dyeus, and Phiaphara, Wa-Mizhan ward of Tehama; the missioners Noah of Eden, Midash of Havilah, and the Naphil Eudeon; and Eroch, the adventuring bastard—were soon left alone as the other Atlantean runners and riders peeled off to their own paths. The humans rode horses, beasts of fine and careful breeding. Eroch and Eudeon were mounted on duck-billed dragons with most of the party's supplies, but as such things would be easily replenishable in Atlantean lands, this was a relatively light burden. Tehama rode her grand elk as always, and Peleg, a physician, drove a gold-trimmed horse chariot with wooden wheels that shared the hue of his honey-colored cloak.

"A Wa-Mizhan woman belongs only to herself," Tehama had told Phiaphara. "Listen to everything and learn from everyone, but decide as you will." Phiaphara was trying. The soldiers and messengers who had peeled away as they went—hooded and helmed, anonymous in their uniforms and liveries—she did not miss, but every man who now remained fascinated her in some fashion.

The Nephilim healer Peleg presented himself as the most learned of the group, but Eudeon was the best teacher, recognizing when a conversation flew beyond Phiaphara's experience and helping her with an explanation or history lesson. Eroch's long stories invariably featured himself, but they made the travel pass by quickly, and if they were remotely true, she need not fear any beast on the road. She made fast friends with Midash, the quick-witted missioner by far closest to her in age, and her hunting cat seemed to find a companion in his griffin. His fellow, Noah, was least interesting to her by virtue of his silence, but there was something powerful about him; he struck her as a plain skin filled with strong wine, and Tehama regarded him with great respect.

As replete with violence as her last few seasons had been, Phiaphara had expected that talk of war would consume the group's conversation. Rather, much of their time on the road was filled with song. Peleg's trained voice rivaled any Atlantean bard, and Tehama's wild anthems were as much bird whistles as human language. Eroch made one attempt in his rough bass, but his bawdy ballad was shouted down by several voices at once. Of all of them, the missioners captivated her most. Never did they sing alone, and their harmonies rose and fell to braid cords of music that seemed to bind her. The words, when she listened to them, spoke of a Creator, His glory, and the history of the world that was believed in their religion. Tehama and Peleg often rode ahead or dropped behind when the missioners sang, but Phiaphara thought their devotion noble in a way, and it certainly had led to the composing of some nice melodies.

Their planned path to Havilah took them through the river country south of Nod, by way of the port city of Pey-en-Pishon. Long days at a brisk pace pushed Phiaphara to the edge of her stamina, but she was young and fit—every day becoming fitter—and her desire to impress Tehama added to her strength. They spent nights in Wa-Mizhan wayhouses. These structures, the girl learned, dotted Atlantean lands as safe lodges for both huntresses on the move and travelers on the road. Some they found full and others nearly empty, but every one had well-stocked pantries and warm fireplaces.

The first open discussion of the Zuthians took place at the last wayhouse within Nod's borders. Phiaphara had gotten up from the worn wooden table, where they supped on dense nutcakes, honey, and cheese, to refill the watered wine. When she returned, Peleg was speaking.

". . . river country will slow down the Zuthians," said the Naphil.

"Not all of them," said Midash. "Not if they have river dragons."

Tehama leaned in on her elbows, hands clasped. "We should hope that they are stopped before they reach it."

"What sort of terrain lies beyond Havilah?" asked Peleg. "Who has been that far?" He looked at his sister, who shook her head.

"My tasks seldom take me beyond the borders of Nod," said the huntress.

"That is further than I can claim," admitted Peleg. "Midash?"

The younger missioner shrugged his hooded duster. "Noah and Eudeon have traveled further south than me."

Eudeon gestured his deference to Noah, who said, "Lands south of Havilah are mostly wild. I think not even the Seeding would have settled them much. The beasts are larger there, grown to fill the vastness of the forests and deep valleys. What roads there are lead through as quickly as able to more hospitable lands."

Tehama nodded. "So it might prove a barrier to the Zuthians."

"If they were careful with the lives of those forced to go with them," said Eudeon. "Perhaps what overlords and slave drivers there are will simply push through and use the captives as expendable protection from the environment. What reason have they to believe they will not be able to replenish their ranks once beyond?"

"They have Havilah," said Midash coolly. "And if they underestimate *her* strength, they will regret it sorely."

"And Havilah has Atlantis," said Peleg, raising his wine cup.

"Right!" said Eroch, who forewent his own cup and took up the pitcher just refilled by Phiaphara, sloshing it over his beard as he took long, gulping swallows. He set it down hard with a hollow, empty thud. Phiaphara decided that she was done with drink for the evening.

Ignoring looks of annoyance from his twin half siblings, Eroch asked, "Now, is there any meat around here? Girl, go find us some meat!" Phiaphara realized she was being spoken to.

Tehama glared. "There is no meat. Wa-Mizhan only eat meat that we have hunted ourselves, and we are not in the habit of storing it."

Eroch frowned. He turned to Eudeon, lowering his voice. "I know you missioners care for the poor and hungry. Do *you* have any meat? Dried, salted perhaps?"

"Have you seen them eat meat? Ever?" asked Tehama.

Noah smiled, his patience a study in contrast with Tehama's exasperation. "We who follow the ways of the Creator abstain from consuming flesh. When Elohim created living things, to them He gave all green things for food. Only after man's Fall did animals begin to eat meat."

"Right, right," said Eroch. "Animals eat meat." He looked at the missioners in turn, as if he expected further explanation.

"But we are not animals," said Eudeon.

"Ha! Of course we are!" laughed Eroch. "We bleed, we piss, we rut, we—" Tehama stopped him cold with a vicious stare. "Hnh. Right. Virgin huntresses. But we *men*—"

Noah stopped him before he went further. "Followers of Elohim remain chaste until married."

The muscled giant's eyes went wide. "But you . . . Eudeon . . . well past four centuries . . ." He sat back on his haunches. "Well, some of us rut, anyway. I rut." He looked at Peleg. "You rut. Anyway, what do you think?"

"I try not to judge others, or expect much from them," said Peleg. "I have my own standards, but I ask no one to hold to them but myself."

"Like what, brother?" asked Tehama.

"For example, I follow a vitalist diet. I eat nothing that causes the death of a living thing: only honey, milk, and fruit; no flesh, stalk, or root. I do not condemn Noah here for killing the carrot or taro, or Eroch for killing the deer."

Phiaphara glanced at the deep orange of a dying fire and felt fatigue wash over her. She wished not to excuse herself and it be taken for rudeness, but Tehama rescued her.

"Enough. Come, Phiaphara, let us retire. We have a long day tomorrow if we wish to make Pey-en-Pishon by week's end."

"And after that," said Noah, smiling at Midash, "Havilah at last."

CHAPTER 17

Look at all that game," Eroch moaned. "For the last time: we ought to have gone by the river."

"If only it *could* be the last time," said Tehama, so only Phiaphara could hear. The girl marveled once more that the Wa-Mizhan's lips did not move; Phiaphara had been practicing, but to her it seemed impossible. Still, as she looked back at her time with Tehama thus far, she counted many things she might have once thought beyond her that seemed of no consequence now. Though she felt her transformation inwardly, she recognized its reflection without too. Her body was leaner, harder, and she had traded her Mizraim linens and watercloaks for leathers and tough wool. The training was constant, even on the road with these strangers, and the hardness Tehama adopted during such times was severe—of necessity, Phiaphara knew—but occasional moments of levity like this broke through like sunrays through mist.

Today they had traveled through wet country. The road between Nod and Pey-en-Pishon wound around the raised edge of a vast, flat plain veined with streams and springs. The tops of plants, deep purple and green, peeked above thick, low mists on the ground. Tall, straight trees sprouted cones out of reach of the minor behemoths that dominated the flat land, far from the only beasts to be seen. Animals were everywhere. Herds of cattle, antelopes, and bulbous-headed moschops grazed, while indriks and giraffes searched for higher vegetation or stooped to drink among wading birds. Eroch had wanted to cut through, but navigating the waterways and the animals sounded daunting and not at all expedient, and Peleg's chariot was not suited for it.

"No one is stopping you, Eroch," said Peleg. "If you want to hunt, go hunt."

"We will not wait for you," said Tehama.

"Ah, my sister, your graciousness astounds!" Eroch dropped from his dragon, unslung his cudgel, and started down the slope to the riverland.

"Hold, Eroch, I shall join you," said Midash. The older missioner, Noah, looked his way with a furrowed brow. "My griffin might do with some hunting as well," said Midash. "Does your cat care to join us, Phiaphara?"

Phiaphara started to ask Tehama's permission, but she held herself. One of the Wa-Mizhan precepts was self-reliance, on both physical abilities and matters of judgment. She pulled her horse off the road behind Midash's, their familiars running ahead to catch up with Eroch.

Phiaphara had enjoyed the company of Midash more than the others, for many reasons. He was closest in age to her, and was well spoken on broader subjects than war and politics, which dominated the discussions among the Atlantean Nephilim, or on his religion, the perpetual subject of talk between Eudeon and Noah. She knew why he had offered Eroch his company. One of her daily exercises—perpetual, really—mandated by Tehama was to *listen*, and she had heard, more than once, discussions among the missioners of Elohim about how to address the eating of meat in their party. Noah preferred a firm approach, demanding its abstinence entirely from everyone with them, while Midash argued that the missioners' good example and grace on the issue might help win minds to the Creator. When Eudeon finally pointed out that Eroch would almost certainly not acquiesce to any demands of the sort, Noah deferred to Midash. Phiaphara suspected that he was now taking an opportunity to "find a common ground," as he had said; she considered that his invitation to her was much in the same vein. Still, perhaps it was more . . . But that sort of thought would not do, she told herself, and she thrust it away from her once more, hoping it would not return as it had every time before.

"I saw the look that Noah gave you," she said to Midash. "He is quite judgmental, is he not?"

Midash gave her a smile, but she knew that she had spoken poorly. "Noah," said the missioner, "is a man who sees right and wrong as easily as day and night. Abstinence from the eating of flesh is one of the few explicit directions from Elohim, not dependent on conscience. So yes, I suppose he is judgmental, but I have never known him to judge incorrectly, or out of any evil motivation. If you perceive this to be a flaw in his character, consider this: If to judge a person is a wrong, have you not done the very same in so naming him?"

Phiaphara's instinct was to argue, but she admitted to herself he made a fair point and kept silent.

She saw Eroch ahead, crouched in the low foliage near the edge of a wide, still pool. Animals drank in droves a stone's throw across the water. They slowed their horses to a walk.

"Hie, Midash," the giant breathed. "What are those?" He pointed to a group of antlered deerlike creatures, several with a conspicuous, curious forked horn at the end of its snout.

"Those are yale," whispered Midash. "But I have never known them to come this far north."

"Driven by the Zuthians?" asked Phiaphara.

"Perhaps."

"The important question is," said Eroch, "do they give good meat?"

"I would not know."

"Right, right." Eroch turned his attention back to the herd.

Phiaphara gently prodded her horse forward. "I wish to see these closer," she said.

"Do not frighten them away!" whispered Eroch. Phiaphara did not care to lend particular aid to Eroch's hunting, but it behooved her to practice moving quietly anyway.

One of the straw-striped beasts—a female, judging by the lack of a front horn—pushed a small stick-legged yale, surely a newborn, into the shallow water. The calf— "Is a baby yale called a calf?" wondered Phiaphara— entered with reticence, proceeding only when nudged by its mother. It stopped, looking back and making a mewling sound. Phiaphara smiled, suddenly missing her father. She tugged her reins to the side, pulling her horse between the animals and where she knew Eroch was watching; these two, at least, would not be prey for hunters today.

More yale stepped into the pool to drink, muddying it quickly. A few wandered closer to Phiaphara, where underwater plants grew to float their leaves just at the surface. They saw her and her horse, but their wide-eyed glances were unafraid, finding her far less interesting than the water weeds upon which they began to graze.

Here the yale stood with the water almost to their bellies. Phiaphara thought back to her time with her father in the Iron Springs, to the many denizens below the water's surface and to the predators that fed upon them.

She was no seer, but no sooner had the thought passed her mind than the yale sprung in all directions from the pool, except for one animal that made attempt after attempt in vain. Phiaphara noted this in a second or two, which was all the time she had before two frenzied yale bounded past her horse. It bucked, and she was not ready for it. She pitched into the water, in her mind perilously close to whatever had captured the single unfortunate creature. "I hope Tehama is not watching," was her last thought before she splashed in.

She hit face first and submerged. Her booted feet felt the pool's soft bottom but found little purchase, and with a shock in her chest she felt movement in the water near her. A strong arm—human, not Nephilim— gripped her around the waist and pulled her out and to the bank.

Phiaphara assumed her rescuer was Midash, and with a very different feeling in her chest she turned to thank him, breathless from her brief submersion and other reasons besides.

It was Noah. Midash, dismounted, hurried up behind him. Her wounded pride wished to reprimand the older man for unneeded service, but she knew he deserved thanks. Noah did not wait for either, but interposed himself between her and the water. "He is strong for one his age," thought Phiaphara, and at the same time, "He seems quite cowardly of water."

The trapped yale had pulled itself free, hobbling away on three legs, its wounded leg maimed and stripped in some places to bone. The beast did not travel far; a lithe cat and a griffin flashed in tandem and took it down.

Eroch's attention had turned from the yale herd, now scattered, to the water. He crept to where the weeds floated, arms outstretched to either side, then leaped in headways. He emerged seconds later, holding an enormous snapping turtle over his head upside down, its beaked mouth champing in futility and its stumpy, clawed feet writhing at the air. The thing was monstrous, ancient and gnarled, almost as wide as Phiaphara was tall. The burly giant grinned.

"Who wants turtle soup?"

‹ CHAPTER 18 ›

"Again, I must say no."

Methuselah stood at the side of a fallow field, where the young men of Eden had mastered the sling, bow, spear, and dart ever since long-passed Seth was a boy. Learning the tools of death was a task taken seriously, which is why the youngest Greatfather in Eden's history insisted on training the local youth himself.

Greatfather. Hadishad, his third son, now more of Atlantis than Eden, had never known him as such. Indeed, this ought not to have been Methuselah's time at all, but his father Enoch was gone, and so the mantle had been passed on Jared's death to him. The yoke of leadership was a heavy one, especially in these later days. In Eden, as in the rest of the world, death had settled as an ever-growing part of daily life, no longer a rare occurrence as it was in the first millennium of human existence. Methuselah's thoughts flew back over the centuries, to Adam's deathbed; the first man's passing had been novel and terrible. Now, though . . . He had seen every one of his sires, save his father, pass from the earth, along with every one of their siblings, cousins, peers. Entire generations were gone, their bodies turning to dust and feeding the roots of Eden's grave groves, vast orchards sprung up from the saplings planted over the corpses of the deceased. These places were treated with great respect, and as Greatfather, Methuselah was master over them. While his sires who had served before him busied themselves with care for daily life in Eden, he felt at times that his responsibilities had more to do with death.

All of this he wished to tell Hadishad, but it seemed that the "no" was the only word his son could comprehend, and all else fell upon deaf ears.

"But we do not ask for aid for Atlantis alone!" said Hadishad.

"I know this, my grandson."

"Then why—" Hadishad bit his lip—in frustration, Methuselah knew—but he was unmoved.

"Son, come here," said Lamech. Eden's Greatfather was glad at his son's presence, especially as these matters would pass to Lamech one day. Usually Lamech could be found overseeing the vast vineyards and endless herds that his father had abdicated into his care, but he had many other sons and grandsons to aid in those endeavors. Lamech and Hadishad walked together to a group of Atlantean soldiers watching the ongoing practice, leaving Methuselah with the Nephilim giants Hoduìn, his son Tiras, and Hamerch son of Dyeus.

Hoduìn, ever hooded, said, "He wants your approval very badly, you know—more than your granting this particular request. He fasted and prayed the whole fortnight we were on the road."

"And he looks more like the farmer we first met, rather than the portly politician he had become," said Hamerch to Tiras under his breath, but Methuselah's hearing had not aged so greatly that he could not hear it.

"Will you not consider the matter further, Methuselah?" asked Hoduìn.

Methuselah looked up at the giant. "I know death, Hoduìn—as I did not when first we met. I will not send my grandsons and their grandsons to face it." The Greatfather felt the eyes of a boy bowyer, not yet five, upon their conversation.

"Focus on the target, Ammob, not us."

"But they are so *big*," whispered the child, as if his words would travel only to Methuselah and no higher.

"A mammoth is bigger," said Methuselah, "and an indrik, and a behemoth, and a dragon. And if you are to become able to fight the last, you must keep practicing."

Hamerch knelt down to the boy and smiled. "Yes, a dragon is bigger than me, but watch this," he said, then stood and stepped away. He withdrew a metal disc from where it was secured at his back and heaved it toward the wooden pole that served as the child's target. In a shower of splinters, the projectile cleaved the pole in two. More than one boy cheered, and when Hamerch told Ammob that he could keep the disc for himself, the child's face beamed bright enough to break through a thick mist.

"And a leviathan is bigger as well," said Hamerch, returning to Methuselah and the other giants. "Methuselah, once you asked us for aid."

"Which eventually led to death on a scale I had never seen, nor wish to again."

"Death is already come," said Hoduìn. "If you could have heard the stories . . ."

"It is a good thing to repay a debt," said Tiras.

Methuselah stood firm. "A debt four centuries old, if it exists. Nations have risen and fallen in that time."

"But none from war," said Hamerch. "None like this."

Methuselah stroked his short beard. "Eden goes to war. War will follow back here. Hoduìn, if you wish for a story from *me*, I will show you why this is *the* Fallow Field." At a word from the Greatfather to hold fire, the other adult trainers handed out staves and wooden swords to the youth, and Methuselah led the Nephilim upfield.

He took them to a barren spot, well past the last target. Dry dirt spread out in a wide circle. The ground plants that had reclaimed the field sent forth a few feeble green feelers here and there, but the dead ground defied their progress more than a few inches.

Hoduìn gasped when his steps hit the bare dust. He breathed in deeply, eyes closed, almost trembling. "This is . . . This is . . ."

The mystical giant's agitation did not surprise Methuselah, and he finished the Naphil's sentence. "Where Cain killed Abel. An event tied to Enoch as closely as it is to Eden."

"You do realize the city has been called Atlantis for nigh on four centuries, yes?" said Hamerch.

"It will always be Enoch to me."

Tiras paced the circle's circumference. "And you keep it this way as . . . some sort of reminder? A shrine?"

"I do nothing. The mists do not come here. Where blood is spilled, the Creator God ceases to send mists to water the polluted ground. Here the land is cursed, and the curse followed Cain to Enoch, so you would not know of its consequences."

Hamerch smirked. "I value the legends of my grandmother's people as much as you do, but this is simply a dead patch of ground. Such a thing need not be attributed to supernatural causes and ancient curses."

"Unless the true cause is as such," said Hoduìn severely. He looked at Methuselah. "I know that there is great power in the religion of Eden. I saw it long ago, when Noah's cries led to the Grigori's demise after I and my fellows could do nothing. If you will not fight with us, perhaps you might help in a different way."

"How?" asked Methuselah.

Hoduìn looked at his son, who was lost in thought, then back to the Greatfather.

"Pray for us."

The three Nephilim met Hadishad and the Atlantean soldiers at the edge of the field, by their convoy of chariots and pack-dragons.

"I am sorry, Hadishad," said Tiras. "He did not consent."

"It is no matter," replied Hadishad. "My father feels differently. We are to speak with him at his home tonight."

"On what?" asked Hamerch, stepping into a gilded chariot with sides fashioned as the wings of birds.

Hadishad climbed into his dragon's saddle, coming eye to eye with the giant. He smiled.

"Eden might go to war alongside Atlantis after all."

‹ CHAPTER 19 ›

Atlantis's centuries-old societal structure, built on peace, scholarship, and robust trade, allowed its people to engage themselves in whatever pursuits their natural inclinations and talents led them to. In war, thought Gilyon, this fact remained the case.

Mareth's hatchet-headed dragon led in front of Gilyon's and Haphan's own crested beast. Tubal-Cain sat on a passenger saddle behind Mareth facing them, calling out notable structures and describing what work went on there. They saw several ingeniators wheeling contraptions of mirrors and lenses from cavernous halls into the daylight, taking measurements and tracking the sun's rays. Another group performed what appeared to be a disastrous attempt at sending a manikin off the side of the mountain strapped to an enormous sail-like apparatus. Its precipitous fall and the rocky impact that obliterated it did not appear to perturb the men, who simply scribbled on their slates and went back inside. "Ingeniators are divided into three schools," said Tubal-Cain. "Sun, air, and earth, and they're all busy adapting their technologies for military application."

Gilyon shook his head. "If the Zuthians fear their own reflections or come so near the mountain that we might drop man-sized objects upon them, then I am sure these men will contribute much."

"I am partial to forged iron and a strong arm as much as you," said Tubal-Cain, "but be slow to mock. There is great power in the earth that remains to be harnessed by man."

"And what powers do you attempt to harness in *those* places?" asked Gilyon, pointing ahead. Magicians' towers wreathed in colored smoke darkened against the bright sky; down the mountain slope, under expansive glass-domed atria, diviners by the score sent birds flying about.

"We are almost to the barracks," said Mareth, and it seemed to Gilyon the question was purposely ignored.

Ahead of them, the mountain slope had been sheared away in places to create vast vertical faces and wide outcrops. These had been lengthened to project out far from the rock face, the stone arches and massive columns supporting them beneath also serving as conduits for supplies which moved slowly up from the valley on chains and ropes. Masses of shining silver moved on these gargantuan platforms, like vast pools of molten metal. As they came closer, Gilyon saw that these were in fact large groups of armed Atlantean soldiers, exercising with sword and spear and shield.

"I wonder if the same skills used in fighting beasts will translate to fighting men?" asks Haphan. "I still pray it will not come to such."

Tubal-Cain laughed. "Think you that a nation famous for its peace cannot learn to shed the blood of man? You shall soon be surprised."

"As will the armies of Zuthi," shouted Mareth.

Gilyon frowned. Much of the culture of old Enoch—a culture that Atlantis still respected, as far as Gilyon had seen—had been founded on Cain's curse. The city of his offspring accepted the premise of great vengeance on the man who would visit violence upon his neighbor, and surely nothing—not the constant migration from other nations, not the long years—could shift that bedrock.

"I trust you have not abandoned belief in the promise made by the Creator God to your forefather, to your namesake," said Gilyon to the crippled smith.

"But we are not Cain, and he is long dead, my friend. No one can suffer for killing him," said Tubal-Cain. "Times change."

"Anyway, I suppose the Zuthian murderers share none of his blood," said Haphan by way of concession, but Gilyon heard no conviction in his brother's voice.

The dragons passed into a cavernous cleft in the mountain, past beast masters showcasing mounts and saddlers selling armored trappings for them. At the dragon stables, Haphan excused himself. "My place is with animals, not warriors. I will wait for you here." Thus taking his half brother's leave, Gilyon followed Mareth and Tubal-Cain as they winded into the mountain.

"How will your armies learn to fight men?" asked Gilyon as they went. "Who here has done so? It is no small thing to purposely wound a man, much less take his life from him."

The metal head of Tubal-Cain's cane clicked on the stones with every other step. The crippled man's ability to keep up with the giants impressed Gilyon; he found the sense of purpose that possessed the smith infectious.

"The answer is closer to you than you think, son of Gloryon." said Tubal-Cain. "We shall see it shortly, but you must promise to keep your peace when we do."

A stone passage widened, and they were outside once more, on one of the great stone platforms built off the mountain. Activity was everywhere—the ring of mail as soldiers walked, the click of iron-toed boots striking stone, the clash of metal upon metal—but Mareth had a determined destination in mind.

Ahead, a gathering of foreigners by dress watched an older man, his fit form clothed in a loose tunic. Six others, in similar attire and much younger, stood behind him. He spoke to the foreigners softly enough for his words to be carried away by the mountain wind before they reached Gilyon. One of the younger men faced his elder, at whose word the foreigners—a score, perhaps—separated into groups. With every eye still on him, the speaker lashed out violently with a stiff hand toward the neck of his partner, stopping just at the skin. He did it again, then barked a sound. The foreign men began to copy the motion, one at a time facing the older man's fellows, who corrected the motions as they practiced. Mareth ignored these and approached the speaker.

"Gilyon, I wish you to meet Ibon-Azazyel. It is he who is teaching our armies how to kill."

The man bowed. "I know who you are. The honor is mine, Master Gilyon."

A series of straight scars cut from the man's lips down his chin and from the corners of his mouth to his ears. As understanding took him, white-hot rage coursed through Gilyon, and only a lance of prayer for self-control prevented him from grabbing the man, carrying him to the edge of the platform, and tossing him to the valley below.

"You are *bene Sheol*." Gilyon turned to Mareth and Tubal-Cain. "What is this?"

"Listen, Gilyon, listen!" Mareth held a hand out.

The towering giant glared down at Ibon-Azazyel. "I am listening."

The older *ben Sheol* showed no sign that he was intimidated, though the top of his head reached only to Gilyon's navel. "Then I will tell you how we were all orphans," he said, "unwanted, starving, and that Azazyel showed us how to live in a way that he valued; thus, we saw our lives as valuable."

"Live? You took *away* lives!"

"You had killed two men before you reached a score of years," reminded the scarred man. "One was your grandmother's brother, was it not?"

"Yes, and they were attempting to kill my father! One succeeded, damn him, and his fellow almost killed me!"

"And I am sorry," said Ibon-Azazyel. "The *bene Sheol* were monsters, but we paid dearly—with our own lives, the lives of my friends, my brothers. I have lost more people who I cared about than you, I promise you this. But now we—you and I—can reshape Azazyel's legacy into something good. There is good and evil in the earth, and we *bene Sheol* have seen both. We choose good now."

Gilyon looked at Mareth. "Did you not spend all those years hunting these murderers down?"

The Atlantean giant cocked his head up. "How think you they came to be reformed? Who do you imagine they now follow?"

"They have written down what Azazyel taught them about war," said Tubal-Cain. "Through them, we can fight Zuthi as no one else has been able to. Through them we have the tools to protect the defenseless."

"Please consider this, I ask you." At last Ibon-Azazyel craned his neck up to meet Gilyon's eyes. "We would follow you as well. Teach us what you have learned. Teach us what is in your blood."

The Nephilim missioner considered all of this, though it was much. By natural gifts and long practice, Gilyon had proven himself a skilled fighter, but his conscience struggled with the proper role of one such as he if nation were to war against nation. What lasting peace could

come through death? Seldom had it been necessary for
him to visit death upon a man, but when he had, innocent
lives had been spared—lives he knew, lives in which he
played a role. Should Haphan—or anyone in peaceful
Atlantis—be obliged to bring arms against a stranger, in
defense of strangers?

These were questions that would be long in answering, but Gilyon trusted in the Creator God to provide
them in His good time. If acceding to this state of events
would allow him to influence the behavior of his ancestral
people toward Elohim's righteousness, he must do so.

"I will teach you," Gilyon said. "About the tools I
know to use for war, and about the Creator Elohim, that
you might use them rightly."

A smile flitted across Ibon-Azazyel's serene face. "The
bene Sheol await your instruction, son of Azazyel," he said.
"And we thank you."

The way back to the stables was tortuous, and Tubal-Cain
escorted Gilyon back.

"You wonder if there can be a right war," said the
smith after a spell in silence.

Gilyon nodded.

"Consider this," Tubal-Cain said. "I am not a humble
man, but I think I do know my place in this world. I have
always found great amusement that my family is included
in Adam's holy writings—in *your* holy writings. I do not
believe everything in them, but I know them, and I ask
you: When my father Lamech asserts that he was justified in killing another man for striking him, do you see
any condemnation of him for doing so?"

Gilyon ran the words through his mind. "No. I do
not."

"Perhaps that is because killing in defense—even of oneself—is weighted differently than killing in aggression, as Cain did."

"Perhaps." Part of Gilyon resisted accepting exegesis from one who did not believe the words, but he also knew he would think upon what Tubal-Cain said.

"You spoke of tools for war," the smith continued. "I remember when your father Gloryon brought you to my first smithy. And you may not know the answer to this, but I must ask. Do you know what became of Azazyel's weapon? It was a long staff, with two wide blades to the side and one coming straight from the haft."

"Why would you want to know?"

"I want to unlock the secret of its making—duplicate it, if I can. I have Azazyel's forge in Armon's heart, and I have his armor. The *bene Sheol* have shown me examples of his lesser work, but that was his personal weapon." Tubal-Cain sighed. "Ah, well. Even an angel's blade would rust after four hundred years."

"On the contrary: it is as bright and sharp today as when I first took it up."

The smith quickened his crippled step to walk in front of the giant and face him directly. From his belt he pulled a token of crystal and silver. "Take this, then," he said to Gilyon, a sudden eagerness speeding his words. "It will allow you to bring arms past the mountain guards. Bring it to me, and I will grant you whatever boon you wish."

"Peace, Tubal-Cain." Gilyon pushed the outstretched hand down. "Shall I at least sleep upon it? I have seen none other weapon like it, and it is what I have used for near my entire life."

"I will make you anoth—"

"Let me think upon it."

The smith was not pleased, but he was at least appeased. They continued on, passing under the spires of the magician's college.

"Diviners," said Gilyon, letting the disdain he felt drip into his words. "I hope you are not placing much trust in what comes out of those halls."

"I do not see how they differ from Elohim's prophets," says Tubal-Cain. "Does the source matter, when the results are so often the same?"

"Yes, absolutely," says Gilyon, narrowing his eyes at a trio of mages walking the other way. Dressed in robes of the palest grey and adorned with so much silver they shone, their skin coloration was an odd, unnatural purple of differing hues. When one of them noticed the giant, they quickened their steps away from him, the tallest giving a furtive glance that Gilyon perceived just the same; at the same time, the Nephilim missioner sensed a filthy presence, a rot-tinged miasma, trailing behind the mages.

"Who are those?" asked the Naphil.

"I believe they come from the Silver School," Tubal-Cain answered. "The highest magicians in Atlantis, though I have no knowledge or part in anything they do."

Gilyon thanked Elohim for giving him a solution before he was aware of the problem.

"I have decided. I will bring you the weapon you ask for." Gilyon took the token from Tubal-Cain, whose face was lit like a forge's fire. "Until tomorrow," was all the smith could say.

Gilyon nodded. "Until tomorrow."

◂ CHAPTER 20 ▸

Between the angel-blooded members of the house of Dyeus and the missioner Noah, who may as well have been of some otherworldly origin for all she had in common with him, Phiaphara had only a single fellow traveler she might consider her peer. As the small band drew closer to Havilah, she grew closer to Midash. When Tehama was not attempting to impart the wisdom and ways of the Wa-Mizhan to her, Phiaphara rode beside the younger man. She made known that she wished to learn more of the lands to which they traveled—at least, this is what she told Tehama, and herself.

Midash was a patient teacher, and she found herself eager to please him. She learned much of geography with him, studying maps unfolded over her horse's neck while he spoke of the places depicted, and where he loved to speak of most was Havilah. He told her about his homeland in a manner that painted a picture for her that she found glorious: of the gardens, the quiet villages and winding white streets, storehouses of glittering gems, mines that bored down to caverns resplendent with crystal pillars and diamond pools, made and hidden by the Creator for the discovery by his children. The country lay south of Eden and Nod, bordered by the river Pishon, by which Havilah exported its richness to Eden's southern cities and beyond. A fact more interesting to him than her, Havilah itself was named after Eve, whose ancient tomb was in that land. Phiaphara did not care to talk about the lady in eulogy, though, and although she did not voice the thought, the idea of a single woman being the bearer of the children from whom the entire population of the earth was descended felt so odd.

Phiaphara admitted to herself that she was attracted to the young missioner, and why not? He was well spoken and kind, a righteous man by the standard of her conscience, and though Tehama had sheltered her under the wing of the virgin Wa-Mizhan, Phiaphara had taken no oath yet. She imagined, too, that the fit, intelligent girl she fancied she was—or at least, was becoming—played a part in Midash remaining so accommodating, even to the extent of eschewing his missioner companions.

Perhaps it was when she noticed Tehama and Noah riding together the way she and Midash had been doing, speaking together in hushed voices; perhaps it was when she realized the others in their party had stopped participating in conversations obviously more pleasant for only them two. Either way, when Tehama requested a private word, in a way that brooked no argument, Phiaphara knew what the subject would be.

"There is a thought," said the Nephilim huntress, "that has taken root in your mind, like a weed with bright blossoms, and it threatens to kill everything you have cultivated over these last moons."

Phiaphara nodded, blushing. What point was there in denying, especially when the voicing of it made clear to her how obvious her feelings had been showing? "Midash."

"He is a fine man, Phiaphara. He has many gifts, and he has devoted them to his God. Should you turn from our ways and be his woman, his devotion would become yours, and you will be responsible for tearing him from the purpose of his life thus far."

Tehama paused, and Phiaphara suspected that the huntress wanted her to consider this, or refute it. Her mind could come up with nothing better than an unreasoning, "No, I would not."

"Or," continued Tehama, "you might bind to him, and his God would win out over you. Shall you travel with him as baggage while he works for a cause he deems higher than you? Or stay at a home, alone, raising children he might give you when he returns every . . . how long? A year, ten years?"

Now Phiaphara felt the advent of tears, but she dared not cry in front of Tehama.

"Shall I remind you that we ride toward a seething nation of violence that every day grows nearer? Shall I tell you how my freedom under an open sky differs from the slavery of the wifely hearth? You are on a path now. You have walked it well, and you are beginning to run. I am loath to see you turn from it. I miss that fearless, headstrong girl you were when first we met. I would have you find her once again."

She left Phiaphara to her thoughts. She had the aching feeling that something, intangible but beyond price, had been denied her, but she lacked an object upon which to place blame. Midash she considered a victim as well as she, and Tehama had given her too much for her goodwill and honest concern to be questioned.

Tehama had ridden up ahead to where her brother Peleg and Eudeon were. She knew Eroch was far, far behind them all; since he had eaten of the turtle he had found, his personal trips off the path had been frequent, returning each time smelling anew like rotting onions, and Tehama had insisted he "bring up the rear," which he had found uproarious.

That left Midash and Noah, who were set a ways behind her and no doubt having the same sort of talk Phiaphara had just finished. She listened, as she had been practicing, focusing only on those sounds she wished to hear, shutting off her consciousness from the birds, the clips of shoed hooves on stone road, the rustle of fronds. The words she picked out were few, all from the older missioner: distraction, unfit, wild. Still, they were enough for her to attach upon Noah the responsibility for the diffuse hurt she felt.

The river country was passed, and only the Pishon remained. At the riverport city of Pey-en-Pishon, the band of seven boarded a vessel bound for the interior of Havilah and its capital of the same name. Tehama's grand elk and Phiaphara's cat came aboard with them, confined to the boat's stalls; all other beasts, and Peleg's chariot besides, were sent to a stabler, to be returned to Atlantis with the earliest caravan.

Eudeon, Tehama, and Peleg suggested that they ought to stop at every port to give warning, but Noah, Eroch, and Midash thought that direct travel to the capital, from where messages could be sent at once in all directions, might prove the quickest way to spread word of the Zuthians throughout the land. Phiaphara did not consider herself a vote worth counting, but the rest insisted. Tehama seemed surprised, but not upset, when she sided with Midash. Thus, they made all speed to the city of Havilah.

"Who are all those people?" asked Phiaphara on the second night, watching a mass of plodding bodies that stretched along the west riverbank road, then curved to the west to the farthest hillcrest that she could see. She directed the question to Tehama, although the three missioners stood on the deck with them.

Midash answered. "That is the road to Eve's grave-shrine, but I have never known it to draw such a pilgrimage as that."

"It may not mean anything," said Eudeon. Phiaphara had her doubts, and the dampened mood that settled on the group proved to her that the others did as well.

After another three days of haste, Midash's spirits visibly picked up. "The Havilah canals approach," he said. No stranger to the river trade of Mizraim, Phiaphara wondered to herself why every ship they passed went the other way. The answer appeared as the Pishon widened into a lake and the entry canals came into view: frigates, turned sideways with flags unfurled, blocked every waterway.

"Those are ships of Havilah," said Midash. "What are they doing?" The captain of the vessel, a man named Nul—a stout man, but clearly without bravery to match his physique—wished to leave the question as it was. Tehama changed his mind through "diplomacy," as she presented to the others, but Phiaphara heard her whisper, "I will offer you our silver, or you will get our iron instead. Approach that frigate."

The ship did so; Midash took his place on the prow, still well underneath the large Havilahn vessel's deck wall, but nobody returned his hails or peeked over the rail.

"Did they simply dam up this canal with the ship?" asked Peleg, and it seemed to Phiaphara that they had. It was indeed a very large ship. High stone walls rose on either side, flush with the frigate, and a thick chain from the boat to the water denoted a heavy anchor.

"Come, we can climb to the bank," said Eroch.

Noah shook his head. "We could not carry enough supplies with us," he said.

"And my elk cannot climb that," added Tehama.

Peleg nodded. "Somehow we need to move that ship."

Eroch stared blankly at his half brother and breathed the deepest sigh Phiaphara had ever heard. "I do not see Peleg's words justified *that*," she thought, but then the giant repeated a dozen more. Then, to her surprise, he leapt into the water. Half a minute of confusion passed before the anchor chain moved, the grinding of wood on stone was heard, and the frigate began to turn. A dark shape emerged from the water between the ship's side and the bank; Eroch, grunting but progressing inexorably, was climbing the stone wall with a massive iron anchor over his shoulder. He reached the top, pulled the anchor's chain taut, and heaved. The frigate, slowly but surely, started to move back up the canal.

"He is as strong as the stories say," said Peleg.

Tehama sniffed. "I still do not like him."

Midash smiled at Noah. "The Creator uses every tool to prepare our path before us."

"I still do not like him," said Tehama.

‹ CHAPTER 21 ›

We are going the right way, yes?" Hamerch asked.

"I think so." Hadishad stood on his stirrups to peer over stone walls. "Never would I have thought I might say this, but I do not know this place anymore."

"One does not appreciate the empty field until it is built upon," said Tiras.

Gone were the dirt roads and open meadows of the Eden of Hadishad's youth, the Eden first visited by the Nephilim so many years ago. Instead, smooth highways of seamless stone wove through fenced orchards and plots of farmland, partitioned pastures and hillside homesteads. Every inch of Eden, it seemed, had been pored over by man and set to specific use. The land remained unmistakably pastoral, but had become tamed entirely.

As the Atlantean party made its way to Lamech's home, common botanical themes emerged, and chief of these were vineyards. When the road rose, it rose above valleys of vines heavy with clusters; when it dipped down, entrances to cave cellars and winepresses overlooked it, each marked with its vintner; and though the evening hour approached, the highway was still busy with bulls pulling barrel carts and cock-drakes porting laborers with feet stained red from a long day of crushing grapes.

The Atlantean delegation to Eden traveled en masse, since for all intents and purposes this was to be a state visit. Lamech also treated it as such. He and fifty mounted men of his household met the other company on the road, and together they rode the short distance to Hadishad's childhood home.

"It is mine in full now," said Lamech to his son as the rambling estate, its lanterns lit against a lavender star-speckled sky, came into view. "Since your grandfather took up residence in Adam's old home, his time is taken by the tasks demanded of Eden's Greatfather—solving disputes and arbitrating trade deals and the like."

"And did he turn his home into a village, or did you?" asked Hadishad. Everywhere around them were buildings, most long and single story and others enormous, fit for housing dragons or storing food enough for a city.

Lamech's grin reflected his pride. "I have been blessed by the Creator in abundance, and that is the form it has taken."

"Where do you find such stone?" asked Tiras as they reached the stables. "Have some of your farmers turned quarrymen?"

"In Eden we all learn to do what work is needed," replied Lamech, dismounting his horse and rubbing its shoulder. "With wine comes the need to store it, which means caves must be dug and carved. I considered that good stewardship would demand use of the byproducts, so I began building. Likewise, when we clear hillwoods for terracing and crops, shall we waste what God seeded? True, there is nothing here like the palaces of Enoch," he said, using the city's archaic name, "but then again, only true human hands did the work."

"Father," reprimanded Hadishad quietly.

"I refer only to the Grigori, of course. Their sons are eternally welcome in our lands. Ah, here is a bit of hospitality now!"

A throng of Eden's elders awaited them in the grand hall, a round and multileveled space. A gargantuan tree grew within, ascending through the open ceiling through which flew two monstrous ravens to perch above Hoduín. Lamech's wife Betenos met her husband with a kiss and her son with a cry and embrace.

"Decorum, Mother," said Hadishad, glancing back at the regiment of scale-mailed soldiers, but she was already clutching his own wife to her and inquiring on their children and grandchildren.

"An unreasonable request of a woman in matters of family," said Tiras, smiling and bowing. "Go with them, Hadishad. War is my domain."

A nod from his father sent Hadishad with his wife and mother to the tables around the hall, where men of Atlantis and Eden were striking up conversations and filling plates with food and cups with wine. The spectacle of the presence of the three Nephilim drew a crowd, mainly younger men; Hamerch took the brunt of their questions upon himself, leaving Hoduín and Tiras with Lamech.

"Come," said Lamech, once the Edenites' interest had coalesced around the gregarious giant. "Let us find privacy." Into the house they went, Lamech tapping two Edenite men to join them. Lamech led them through the maze of rooms until they came to a small one, plain but for the unlit lamps and a dark tapestry on the far wall.

"Is this not . . . a bit cramped?" asked Tiras, ducking into the space with a ceiling too small to allow him to stand upright. Lamech pulled back a hanging tapestry, revealing the entrance to the top of winding stairs. "Watch your heads."

The staircase accommodated single-file only, the two giants obliged to descend walking sideways. "Your soldiers are free to visit whatever stables, blacksmiths, bowyers, or wine cellars they wish tomorrow. I know the travel takes its toll. If you haven't engaged an inn, I have an empty bunkhouse for seasonal workers. Perhaps a barracks or a royal keep might suit you better, but Eden has neither."

"We do not come for shelter," said hooded Hoduín.

"I know why you come. Here, sit."

This new space was all unadorned stone, and not all of that touched by man. Torches were set alight, and they showed a wide table with maps neatly set upon it. Around this they sat, the three men of Eden on one side and the two Nephilim on the other.

"Now we may speak plain," said Lamech. "Hoduín and Tiras, this is Elebru, and Halhannah." Elebru, an older man whose head and neck were swathed in cloth wrappings that hid everything but his face from brow to chin, sat as stone; Halhannah gave greetings. "We are all for helping your war effort, but if we are to do so without the Greatfather's blessing, we must be delicate."

"Speak you as Methuselah's son and future Greatfather?" asked Tiras.

"He does not," said Hoduín, eyes shut. "Nor does he speak as a warrior."

Lamech nodded. "I speak to you now as a Shepherd of Eden."

Tiras raised his brow. "I would say you were more of a winemaker than a shepherd."

"Noble giant, we are the protectors of our land," said Halhannah. "We are called the Shepherds."

"Rangers, spotters, hunters, runners," explained Lamech. "We serve within the roles to which the Creator has called us and with the skills He has given us."

"Eden grows, ever expanding," said Halhannah, "and the beasts displaced have no fear of man. The Shepherds protect our people from the predators too great for one household to manage: dragons, rampaging mammoths, wolf packs and the like."

Tiras frowned. "But Eden is a peaceful land."

"Peaceful?" Elebru broke his silence. "The Garden. Abel's altar. Eden is the very birthplace of evil."

"Elebru is right," said Lamech, sighing. "And we do more than hunt beasts. There are pockets, sharply defined, where killers are banished. Not all stay there willingly. We ensure they do."

"Surely Atlantis does the same with your own murderers," said Halhannah.

"At times, yes," answered Tiras. "As well as the lands of Assyria, but often not. Shall a man forever be denied his family, his friends, for a moment's offense?"

"Thus you let the rot remain," Elebru said.

"Yet rotten grapes can make the sweetest wine," answered Hoduín.

"No philosophy, please," said Tiras. "Let us remember who the proven killers are. Lamech, how many men can the Shepherds bring to help our cause against Zuthi?"

"Thousands," said Lamech, "but a few hundred will suffice. We will not fight, but we can let you know their numbers, what manner of soldier they be, which beasts come with them and where you might best strike them."

"We have scouts in abundance."

"Not such as us," said Halhannah.

"Would you fight if Zuthi marched upon Eden?"

Lamech shared a look with his companions that suggested this question had been asked among themselves already. Elebru answered. "Yes."

Tiras stroked his red beard. "I hesitate to even speak the thought . . . No people on earth can rival the strength or will of Atlantis, except perhaps Eden. If we divide the Zuthian horde, split their advance to crash and disperse upon the strong rocks of both Atlantis *and* Eden . . ."

Hoduín shook his head. "The war must be fought in Atlantis, my son," he said. "Lamech, if your father is right, then bloodshed will not affect our land, since Cain's curse is already upon it."

"The curse is upon the lands of old Enoch," said Tiras, "but crops and orchards grow beyond it. Or would you suggest risking the city of Atlantis itself? Would you fight a war outside it?"

"Under its very walls, if I could," said Hoduín. "Is there another place on earth where such strength dwells?"

Tiras did not answer his father. Instead, he turned to the men of Eden. "Atlantis accepts your offer with thanks."

"Then come, friend Tiras," said Halhannah, standing. "Let us council together, that peace may soon return." Followed by Elebru, they ascended away up the small staircase.

"A word, Lamech," said Hoduín, leaning his robed figure over the man like a tent canopy. "Your scouts are not the only thing you might offer."

"What else?"

"Your God. I have seen His power. We all have. Where is the center of His strength? Who wields it? This place I wish to see above all others."

"I . . ." Lamech paused in thought. "Meet me here tomorrow. I will show you what few outsiders have seen."

Hoduín drew his hood over his head. "I greatly anticipate it." The giant sorcerer turned to the spiraling stairs, and Lamech quenched the lights. The stone room turned to black, and he heard the wings of unseen birds fluttering away in the darkness.

· CHAPTER 22 ·

Gilyon faced the line of bare-chested men. Most were slight, and the crossblade carried by the giant stood taller than any of them. Of these, the acolyte mages of the Silver School, only one met Gilyon's eyes with anything other than fear. His defiance did not give him the boldness to step in front of his fellows, but it did help him find a voice.

"You cannot be here! This is a place of the spirit and the mind. Your weapon desecrates this sanctum!"

"Give me no reason to use it," Gilyon answered, closing the distance to the acolytes as he spoke. "Stand aside."

Gilyon had found no guards, no gates, no security whatsoever to impede his entrance to the Silver School towers. He had found the acolytes in the middle of some arcane liturgy, the circular hall's white torchlight glinting on their thin silver belts, the only adornments on the grey garments wrapped around their waists. Apparently, the pagan magics they wielded gave them ample confidence; in Gilyon's experience, such confidence bled out quickly at the sight of a second-generation Nephilim caster carrying an angel-forged weapon.

"You cannot enter the inner tower!" The acolyte's voiced cracked.

"Will you stop me?" Gilyon spun his crossblade in a full circle, a useless maneuver in a fight, but like a drake's frill display to a rival, it was an intimidating show.

Another one of them, at last, drew strength from his conviction. He raised a white pendant that hung around his neck down to his belly and spoke words clear as the crystal within, but with no meaning in human speech. Gilyon watched, amused. The little mage pinched his mouth and uttered the words again, holding the crystal yet higher.

Gilyon rolled his eyes and strode forward, every other step tapping the butt of the crossblade on the marble floor for emphasis. The Naphil passed the sputtering acolyte and his fellows, who backed up to give him a wide berth. From behind him, the raging man shouted in one last attempt at potency. "Familiar spirit, come forth! *Come forth!*"

The missioner kicked the ornate doors that led to the inner spire of the Silver School mages' tower, satisfied to hear the crack of splintering wood and the shriek of now-ruined metal mechanisms.

"Surely all of your diviner friends told you I was coming, did they not?" He turned to the exposed and unarmed men. "Your 'familiar spirits' are demons, and they are cast far, far away now. Your power is gone, but be thankful your souls may yet be saved."

A spiraled incline wrapped around the circular wall of the tower's inner cone. As far as Gilyon could discern, it rose to the very top. He ascended it. Doorways showed him glimpses of what this branch of Atlantean magic valued, though he cared for none of it: studies with alcoves, lamps, and shelved walls of books and scrolls; rooms of mirror and clear crystals; great glass pools in which swam schools of silvery fish flashing to and fro. The pull that Gilyon felt came from none of these. Whatever awaited him did so from above.

No missioner's role gave him as much satisfaction as casting, and he was gifted at it. Perhaps the blood of angels aided him, or perhaps the Creator had simply seen him as a fit tool for the purpose, but either way, no demon yet had stood before him and his fellows. He wished Noah were with him, but only for the company; the only Ally needed in this endeavor was eternally with Gilyon *and* Noah, wherever his old friend might be.

His ascension ended at the top of the tower in a wide antechamber. Polished platinum bases held lenses pointed at the sky through the open ceiling. Two mages— no acolytes, these—stood before a silver portal. Gilyon recognized them from earlier, with Tubal-Cain. They were armed, after a fashion: one with a thin, decorative short spear, and the other with a chain of woven metallic strands. Gilyon sensed no possession of either of them, and neither posed a threat to him, so he ignored them and went on, mildly curious as to the whereabouts of their third companion. To the Naphil's surprise, the spear carrier actually opened the portal for him. He ducked his head as he entered this final chamber, thankful for the ease with which he had proceeded, though more than mildly suspicious.

Fear never entered his most fleeting thoughts, and not for some misguided sense of hubris. His size and strength, abilities and arms, simply existed as fact; his confidence lay in the Creator.

The lamps shone brighter in this space, which was larger than the giant had expected. An apparatus of mirrors and crystal prisms dominated the chamber, but the reflections and refractions were odd and dark, incongruous with the light in the room. The third mage stood before the construct. His skin was the color of a deep bruise, silver patterns and figures painted upon it. He wore a loincloth latched with a crystalline girdle, but nothing else. A great owl with trailing tailfeathers glided to his outstretched hand; the other stroked the head of a lithe-looking panther, lightly spotted, with erect ears pierced by rings that connected by webs of thin chains to a silver collar. Gilyon heard the two other mages enter behind him and shut the portal.

This was a demon's abode—of that, Gilyon was sure. He felt the sick, earthy mold of its presence. This man, at least, had descended from the vulgarity of magic practice to the abject obscenity of sorcery, and it would surprise him none to find it true of the other pair.

"The scion of Azazyel has come," said the purplish sorcerer.

"By all means, let us forego introductions," said Gilyon. "I need not know your name. Let me speak to your master. I feel him. I know he's here."

The sorcerer's eyes rolled back until only bright white orbs showed. "Greetings, Gilyon, son of Gloryon. I knew your grandfather Azazyel well. My name is Asaradel."

"Asaradel." Gilyon knew the name. "You were banished and chained in Gehenna."

"Clearly I was not. The Lord God Creator forgives . . ."

"Oh, just cease your prattle. Always with you demons it is the same lies. 'He has shown us grace and restored us. We who were present at the world's creation know Him fuller than you do.' I know not how you escaped banishment, but damned you were and damned you remain."

The possessed body of the sorcerer paced in front of the mirrors, the owl and panther doing the same. "Very well. I have indeed thrown in my lot with the Prince of the Earth, but we are a house divided. The Zuthians have a magic that is deep and evil. They control creeping

things. They are in league with powerful princes of air. To
fight them, we must use their own devices, else they fall
upon Atlantis and snuff out the greatest beacon of hope
for free men. Make no mistake, we want men free—free
to reject the Creator's enslavement and do as they will,
not as He does."

Gilyon frowned. "Is this meant to compel me? Do I
strike you as a stupid creature? Have I no discernment? If
the Zuthians march with demon princes, I will do what
I can to free them. My task now is to free *these* men. Go
of your own will now, or be satisfied when I cast you into
a moth."

"Fool! We are on the same side."

"Is that correct? On which side do you perceive us
both to be?"

"Atlantis! Humanity!"

"Hardly. Be gone."

The Asaradel-possessed sorcerer raised his voice in
frustration. "I will not go, not when I am so close. I do not
wish to harm you."

Gilyon saw no utility in prolonging this conversation.
"In the name of Elohim," he started.

A silver spear left the mage's hand in a flash. Gilyon
had already leaned to miss its path when it somehow
shifted, like a shaft of light passing through a waterfall.
A head snapped at Gilyon as a viper, rather than a mere
spear, flew by him. The bite missed, and the fanged snake
disappeared into a fold of hanging curtain.

No sooner had Gilyon registered this sorcery than a
silver chain wrapped around him, thrown by the other
mage. The cold metal changed to smooth scales and sinews that slid and contracted around his body, trapping his
arms to his sides. He kept hold of his weapon, although

he had no leverage to use it. A tickling tongue darted behind his ear.

"I do not wish to harm you," said Asaradel through the sorcerer. "I only wish to explain myself, to convince you. This construct behind me is the result of long work by myself and these mages, and in it may very well lie the salvation of Atlantis."

"By such words are many evils undertaken," said Gilyon. He heard a snake's hiss and felt it slither at his feet. The constrictor tightened. He grunted.

"Evil? You judge without knowledge."

"Then give me knowledge."

Asaradel was considering it, Gilyon could tell. His fellow mages looked hesitant, but unwilling to naysay the demon, they stayed silent. The Naphil kept any expression of disdain or arrogance from his own face, hoping to appear amenable to whatever reason this being might bring forth.

"Nineteen," the possessed sorcerer said at last. "Nineteen of my companions, nineteen angels under my command, are enchained. Nineteen beings of power, who will follow me to aid the cause of Atlantis, lie trapped just without my reach, but I am close—so very close."

"Nineteen new demons to lead men astray."

"No!" The sorcerer waved his hand angrily, as if to disperse blasphemous words. The panther and owl came nearer to Gilyon. "Not demons. Recall you that day, long ago? Recall Samyaza against his sons? Recall your own grandfather Azazyel, resplendent in his armor and carrying your very weapon, victorious and untouched against his own rebellious children? Nineteen Grigori, immortal, unkillable, could stand against the Zuthians alone! Think on the lives that will be spared. Their demons will flee! Their slaves will be freed! Their strong men will fall on their faces and repent!"

"And then they will follow you into service of Satan." The constrictor's head floated into Gilyon's vision, which swam as the snake's body tightened around his neck.

Asaradel's passion grew almost too great for the sorcerer's human body to contain. The man jerked as the demon shouted, spittle and blood flying with his shouted words. "No! No! Their sin was love—not hate, not wrath, not rebellion! Do you not see? I became a slave to the Serpent because it was the only way I could remain free!"

In the mirrors and through the crystals, Gilyon saw countless eyes blinking and flitting out of a deep darkness, as if from the depths of some watery pit. Inside, he thanked the Creator for showing him his path.

"Help us," said Asaradel, calmer now. "Elohim has bestowed you with a connection to spiritual things that is unlike my own. With your aid, we can save Atlantis, and all free men. We can save Zuthi from the night that has fallen upon it. Otherwise . . . it will be unfortunate to hasten your steps to Sheol, but I will do so."

"Have you considered," said Gilyon slowly, "that all of this—everything you have built here, the years of work you all have done—has simply been in preparation for my coming here this day, all in the Creator's perfect timing?"

"Of course," said Asaradel. "That you might help us free those imprisoned."

"No, no." Gilyon chuckled. "Quite the opposite. So I might send you to where you ought to have been for the last four hundred years." At once, Gilyon flexed and strained, hearing the snap and pop of serpentine spine and muscle. The snake turned back to metal, now rent and ruined, and Gilyon shrugged it to the floor. A sweep of his blades cut the viper in two before it could strike. Gilyon kicked its pieces, wood once more, across the room.

The mages retreated as far as the chamber's walls allowed, but the panther pounced. Before it could land, the Naphil's blade had separated its head from its body. Bloodstained chains slid on the slick floor, painting a dark pattern. Gilyon scanned for the owl, but it had wisely taken its talons as far away as possible.

The possessed sorcerer staggered back, pressing against the central, largest mirror. The other mirrors radiated outward like eyes on a peacock's plume. Shadowy, inhuman hands reached within them; glowing spheres pressed like faces on glass.

"You cannot," said the sorcerer. "You *must* not. Please!"

Gilyon focused on his spirit, his true eternal self, to whom the Creator gave his crude vessel of flesh. When he spoke, he invoked the greatest person, the greatest Spirit of all, by name. "Elohim! In the name of Elohim, depart from this man to the banishment that was meant to be your lot!"

The terror in the scream might have been from Asaradel or the Silver School sorcerer; the hoarse groans from the man after he dropped to the ground were certainly from the latter. Almost every mirror had cracked, but the reflections from them had lost their strangeness. The owl was doing its best to hide in the shadows near the ceiling. Gilyon smiled at the mages yet standing, both cowering under his attention.

"I shall leave you to clean up, yes?"

Both mages nodded eagerly.

"Then I bid you all good night, and remind you that the altar house is always open."

With that, Gilyon left the top tower chambers with a tune of praise to the Lord God Creator on his lips.

‹ CHAPTER 23 ›

The mists lay thick on the river Pishon. From their ship's deck, Noah peered out over the featureless grey that grew lighter as the new sun began to rise. His hood was up to keep the wet chill at bay. Despite the fervor of his morning prayers, he felt in his spirit an unease.

The heavy footsteps of a giant sounded on the stairs leading below the deck. The voice that belonged to them was Eudeon's, who joined him at the prow's railing.

"For one who dislikes the water, you come up here often," said the Naphil.

"I have seen a river forced empty of boats before," said Noah. "The water can hold unwelcome surprises."

"And have you seen such?"

"Nothing," said Noah. "The morning is quiet."

"But you doubt it is the quiet of peace," said Eudeon.

Noah nodded. "For Havilah traders, this is the last leg of the journey from . . . how many mines? Where are the gem barges? When we have come this way before, the mists cannot hide the glint of lapis and gold on the water. I will remain hopeful, though. What lies ahead might be unknown to us, but not to our Master."

"For the sake of Midash, I too hope all is well," replied Eudeon. "Will you come below? Peleg has prepared breakfast."

The rest of the company was up and present at the table below, with the exception of Midash, who had risen early to aid the captain of the vessel.

"Here you are, Noah," said Peleg, placing a bowl of syrupy broth before him. "Hot honeymilk. It will warm your innards."

"But it won't fill them," said Tehama, tilting her bowl to her mouth for the last sips.

"I hate when your brother cooks," complained Eroch. He raised a spoonful of the syrup and let it pour back down, frowning. Inside, Noah was amused; here at least was one thing upon which Eroch and Tehama shared a like mind. He found the substance pleasant enough, though. It was almost medicinal, and it did warm him.

The light meal was finished and the dishes washed and stored. As soon as they were, Midash's shouts stirred them. Noah rushed deckside after Eroch. Whatever the giant's faults, hesitance to action was not one of them.

Midash was working the sails while the captain, Nul, was at the wheel. The younger missioner pointed. "Other ships at last!"

"Seen you any like them before?" asked Eroch. "Are they friendly?"

The two ships, the furthest barely visible through the misty curtain, were deep hulled and had no warlike appearance. Their decks were hidden, draped over with silken sheets. A few moments of observation showed Noah no sign of human direction; they drifted as though abandoned.

Noah wondered at this, and it foreboded ill to him. He reminded himself of the mission they had undertaken and the danger inherent to it and that the point at which they turned back would necessarily involve some flavor of Zuthian slaughter; so close to his grisly trial at Phempor, he did not relish it. He asked Elohim for strength—for himself and for his fellows, and especially for Midash.

"Those are not traders," said Midash. "They look to be peacekeeper transports—unwieldy, but quiet and vast. Those covers are used when cold-blooded mounts are aboard, to keep out the chill of the river mist."

"Do they not take great care to keep obscured and silent?" asked Peleg. "Could they be fleeing? The Zuthians ride river dragons . . ."

"Bring the ship aside," said Tehama to Nul. "Let us see if they need aid. Quietly, now."

The huntress's command was met with the captain's curse. The drape on the far ship burst into flame in one, two, three places, each of them spreading to engulf it in a matter of moments.

"Captain! Get alongside that ship now!" Tehama jabbed a finger at the nearer barge.

"I'll not risk my vessel for all your gold," replied the captain, watching the black smoke from the burning boat billow toward his ship. Tehama's hand went to a knife at her belt, but Peleg stopped her.

"Sister, we have no time. Look!"

Points of light, faint through the mist and smoke, arced through the air and fell upon the near ship's covering. Perhaps they had come too late to Havilah—for how many, only the Creator knew—but every soul was worth his best effort to save. Noah shed his cloak and dove into the water. The rush of sudden submersion filled his ears, followed by several more splashes beside and behind him. He was the quickest to action, but he was not alone.

The dark hull of the nearest barge was close. The momentum of his dive covered half the distance, and a few strong strokes completed it. His head broke water, followed by those of Eudeon, Eroch, Tehama, and Midash.

"Eroch, you and I take the far side," said Eudeon, and both giants disappeared under the water. Noah scanned the side of the ship. Time was precious if they were to save it from the flames, and Noah thanked Elohim for the carvings and flourishes that provided ample handholds.

He pulled himself up with little difficulty, outpaced by Midash and Tehama. The thin rail was the only place their feet could purchase; the silken cover rose like a small hill over the barge, tied near flush with the rail by thick ropes sent through the spaces between the weatherworn wood.

The knots were wet, and untying them would be impossible. Noah glanced up. The fires were spreading, but perhaps whatever—or whoever—lay underneath could be salvaged. The smoke from the other burning ship was upon them now, and Noah pulled the neck of his soaked tunic over his mouth and nose. Since his youth, he had carried a pair of knives at his belt. His first two he had long since retired, but his current blades, forged by a starsmith of Mu from iron fallen from the sky, he unsheathed.

"Cut the cover, the rope is too thick!" he heard Midash yell, and he was happy that another had his same thought. Between Tehama's hunting knife and Midash's short saber, Noah hoped they might prevail. He slashed at the cloth wherever it held a rope. The river was in the calm of the morning, and balance on the rail proved no difficulty as he moved. The work seemed to take an eternity, but when his progression met Tehama's, the flames had still not spread beyond hope.

"Eroch! Eudeon! The cover is free on our side!" Tehama yelled. Her answer was the rapid departure of the cloth in the far direction; the giants must have simply jumped overboard holding the other edge. The fires left with it; when Noah saw what it had been hiding, he counted as providence the smoke that had caused him to cover his nose.

What had seemed like a hill was in fact a mound of corpses. Bodies in a state of rigor were stacked ten or more high above the railing, with no way to tell how far they continued below it. If he held out a hand, he could touch the face of a woman fixing him with a death stare. Her jaw had fallen and her lids drooped, giving her an expression of idiocy but for the yellowish crust that surrounded her eyes and mouth. He heard a splash; Midash was no longer on the rail. Either his comrade had jumped away or had lost his balance, but Noah thought he had the right idea. With a grimace, he leapt away from the ghastly cargo.

Noah joined Midash in the water, and Tehama followed right behind. Midash breathed heavily, and Noah thought it was not from exertion. "What . . . what . . ." spluttered the younger man, horror marring his even features. Noah had no answer.

Nul's long scream, higher pitched than his bulk would have suggested, prefaced his plunge into the river. The ship's captain emerged, gasping, eyes searching until he found his bearings and the vessel he commanded. Peleg towered at the bow.

"This rat would have left you all," the Nephilim physician shouted. "I do not relish violence, sir, but few things spur me to it as ably as cowardice and disloyalty."

"Rats!" Eroch's voice boomed unseen. Treading water and mind rather misty and numb from his morbid surprise, Noah oriented himself to where came the shout. Between the mists and the smoke, visibility on the water was poor, and he heard the splashes of strong strokes before he saw the great arms of Eroch and Eudeon churning the water in a mad swim. The captain spewed curses, then yelled up to Peleg, "Throw us a rope!"

Another sound chittered through the mists, and it came from everywhere. Eroch did not stop swimming until he reached the side of their ship, Tehama in his wake; Eudeon grabbed the tunics of Noah and Midash and, with a few kicks, propelled them all there as well.

"Whatever was aboard that vessel, rats kept it company," said Eudeon, panting. "They abandoned the ship in droves when it burned. We need to get aboard now."

Noah realized that the two Nephilim had not seen the cargo before pulling the cover off of it into the river. Now that Eudeon was close, Noah saw countless red marks upon the giant's shoulders and neck, many bleeding. The knots of a single rope knocked against the wooden hull as it dropped. The captain clambered aboard first, then Tehama. Eroch forewent the climb, simply using the span of his arm to reach a porthole high above them and pull himself up, then once more to the deck.

"You first, Eudeon," said Noah. The cacophony of the rat masses grew closer, but they still were unseen, and Noah knew they would remain so until they were right upon them. Eudeon wasted no time in arguing, but barely had he pulled his feet out of the water before a roiling wave of rodents materialized through the mists.

"Under, Midash! Make for the bank!" Noah took a deep breath and submerged, hoping the rats did not swim too deeply. The bank here was steep, and on it somewhere near were men with the means to shoot flaming darts or arrows, but the thought of being swarmed by rats just finished feasting on diseased corpses made the decision easy. Diving as deep as he could, Noah swam. The diffuse light of morning above turned dark, and Noah prayed that the countless creatures responsible would find the slick sides of Nul's ship unclimbable.

Midash matched his pace underwater. In a minute that seemed interminable, their hands touched the vertical stone of the walled bank, a man's height still beneath the river. Here, too, above them was black and churned by fear-maddened rats, but Noah could not ignore his air-starved lungs for long. Sharing a look of determination with Midash, together they kicked up hard to the surface.

The rats saw them as islands of salvation even as their fingers found purchase where the stones joined. Noah pulled up, shaking and jerking in an effort to dislodge the foul-smelling rodents. At first he felt only their claws as they clung to him in surprise, but the piercing pain of their bites soon followed. His inability to bat them away, needing both hands to ascend the bank, was almost as torturous as the injuries themselves, but not quite. Finally, Noah rolled onto flatter land, writhing and slapping at himself until he was rid of the rats. He tried to knock them off back into the river below, but more than a few escaped into the grasses and bushes lining the river's edge. He glanced beside him; Midash had made the bank, too, and he had suffered the same. Gasping, Noah got to his feet, then pulled Midash to his knees.

"Down! Down! On your belly!"

Noah complied, his exhaustion making the command easy. He heard faint shouting from the river. Boots in front of him were of supple leather and stitched with golden details on the sides, and cloaks of the same sort flowed about them.

Midash failed to join him on the ground. "Hold!" said the younger man. "Are you not peacekeepers of Havilah?"

"Yes, and we are keeping the peace. To the dirt with you!"

Noah took a chance to look up. Five figures held crossbows, two trained on himself and Midash and the others pointed toward the river Pishon. They all wore the same sort of garb: dark cloaks, wide-brimmed hats, gem-studded leather plates covering chests and legs. Cloth masks hid their faces but for their eyes, which showed fear as much as anger.

A different peacekeeper jabbed his loaded weapon near Noah's face. "Tell your companions to lower their arms!" Noah glanced behind him. Their boat was drawn close to the bank now. Tehama and Phiaphara had bows nocked and drawn, and Eroch and Eudeon both crouched at the near railing with cudgel and hammer, ready to leap ashore.

"Hold, everyone!" Midash held out an outstretched hand to the peacekeepers, but his palm faced to him. "Look!" Noah realized that Midash was displaying the ring upon his middle finger. Midash wore jewelry at times, but he did not often speak of the riches of Havilah, especially when among the poverty of the mission field; Noah had always assumed that the habit was tied to Havilah's famous culture of goldworking, but he had never asked if any of the pieces had any personal significance. The peacekeeper leaned in, eyes narrowed.

The ring showed a golden circle inside a crescent, inset with an orange corundum. Whatever it was, it resonated with the crossbowman.

"I am Midash son of Tobrash, a fifth scion of the House of Dono-Vothuna. Where are all the tradeboats? What has happened here?"

The five peacekeepers dropped their bows to their right sides, clasped a fist to their chests, and declined their heads, eyes downcast.

"I said I was a *fifth* scion," said Midash, standing tall now. "Not first."

"My apologies, but you *are* first," said the chief peacekeeper.

"What mean you?" asked Midash, but Noah knew the man's meaning was clear to both of them, and his hesitancy in answering the question confirmed it. Noah carefully put a hand on the peacekeeper's cloaked shoulder, willing the Creator's strength to all of them. The man raised his head, and their eyes met.

"Tell *me*," said Noah.

Shed of his authority, the peacekeeper loosed a shuddering breath and answered.

"Every ... everyone in House Dono-Vothuna is dead."

· CHAPTER 24 ·

The canopy filtered the sun like a sieve, and Lamech thanked the Creator for it. The culled bulls, rams, and lambs would slow their journey down. Between himself and Elebru, they could have supplied enough sacrifices for the entire Atlantean contingent; Halhannah, who often served as bloodletter at the altar houses, assured them that twelve of each animal would suffice.

The giants met them on the road, absent the soldiers that had come with them. "Magnificent beasts," said Tiras, placing platter-sized hands on the upswept horns of a pair of pure-white rams. "To where do we take them?"

"Men make plans," answered Elebru, "but it behooves them to search for Elohim's approval."

"For cryptic speech, you match Hoduín, friend," said Hamerch, taking a lamb from the shoulders of one of Lamech's Shepherds and placing it on his own.

Lamech smiled. "Our destination is the Tree of Knowledge."

Hoduín spun to him, cloak billowing, and crouched to the level of his eye and clutched his arms. "In the Garden? Can you really take us there?"

From behind him, Halhannah chuckled. "We would not complete that journey. No, we call this place the Tree of Knowledge, but there is only good there, not evil. The toledoths of the Creator and of Adam are kept there."

Hoduín rose. "The very words of God."

Lamech nodded. "There we may sacrifice and supplicate the Lord God for assurance that this path we have chosen is one He would approve. You wish to see the center of His power in Eden. If there is one, that is it."

To Tiras, Lamech gave two rams, and Elebru gifted a bull to Hamerch. Hoduín alone did not claim an animal for his own from among those the Eden men had brought; instead, he loosed his two monstrous ravens to disappear into the forests. Lamech asked what aim he had in doing so, but the Nephilim sorcerer, as was his wont, only smiled mysteriously.

The road upon which they traveled passed through no towns. Stalked fields of crops raised up on either side, then became berry bushes and orchards, and finally wild wood. Midday came and went, and the noon meal was taken from whatever overhanging fruit tree each traveler fancied. At one point, for a brief moment, the livestock caught the attention of a pack of drakes crossing the road on a patrol of their dark domain of the forest floor. The creaks of drawn bows from Lamech and his Shepherds moved them along.

Just as the golden sun turned rosy and set behind the highest boughs, the forest road opened. The evening light cast all in deep, long-shadowed hues, and still the sight remained breathtaking. A meadow, vast and flat, stretched around and ahead, bordered by tall, thick trees and a green wall of undergrowth. Bright birds and serpent gliders flitted and flew high above, and an avian choir was singing the evening's entrance. Gathered around pools were horses, billed dragons, camels, and a mammoth, all possessing the tamed demeanor of trained mounts. Other beasts, too, ran about, each at home: deer and antelope, ape and okapi, minor reptiles and mammals of every kind. Lamech's smile grew wide.

Through much labor, the people of Eden—his people—had tried to replicate what the lost Garden must have resembled, and every time Lamech traveled to the place, he felt an assurance that, in at least a small way, they had succeeded.

"This is our destination?" asked Tiras.

"Almost, my friend. There," pointed Lamech across the fauna-filled meadow.

Hamerch frowned. "I fail to see the difference in that particular edge of forest."

"A little further, then."

Lamech led the group across the treeless space. He and his men gave the apples, roots, and nuts that had not been eaten on the journey to whatever animals came near, and soon their food was gone. They passed groves and incense gardens, then the rose hedges protecting and hiding the altars; then, at last, nothing lay between them and what Lamech considered the grandest sight in Eden.

He watched recognition light upon the giant faces above him. He remembered the first time he had seen this place, the home of the two toledoths: the patterns in the trees showed first, then the facade of the citadel that kept expanding in the vision as limbs and trunks settled into columns and stairs. The mind's difficulty lay in making sense of the lack of straight edges. There were none, since the structure, in its entirety, had not been built. It had been *cultivated*.

Since this was far from Lamech's initial visit, he recognized the new additions: circles of saplings, new grafted branches, shaping supports and limb ties. All of these were afterthoughts in the face of the arboreal grandeur of the Tree of Knowledge before them.

"A living temple," breathed Hoduín.

"Here we will offer sacrifice to Elohim," said Halhannah, running a hand along the shoulder of the flawless bull aurochs beside him. "We might find wise council as well."

"Father, shall you not make sacrifice too?" asked Tiras. "Pick a beast from what has been provided."

Hoduín's eyes glinted, despite the deep shadow cast over them by his hood in the dusk. "My son, I have done so." He raised his arm high. Flapping followed loud caws from the canopy; the Naphil's two enormous ravens harried and drove a pair of doves, bright white even in the dark-blue evening, from the trees into Hoduín's waiting hands. He held them gently, fingers curled into cages, and looked at Lamech. "Lead us to the sacrifice."

Night fell. Altars' smoke filled the sky, and prayers offered in turn by each man from Eden pealed across the quiet meadow and echoed among the trunks and great roots of the toledoth's temple. The bloodletter of the temple, a man named Dadi, expertly wielded a leaflike blade upon the necks of the sacrificial animals. Each man carefully collected the lifeblood of his animal in clay vessels. Oil was poured, fires were lit, and Lamech considered each crack and pop of burning flesh a hymn to the Creator and a cry for His aid.

Lamech's turn came, and he asked Dadi if he could perform the bloodletting himself. He lifted the lamb he had chosen and placed it upon the virgin wood of the altar. It bleated and met his eyes. Lamech was moved—no man could not be—but this innocent creature no longer belonged to him, and his hand was not stayed. He took the blade and drew it across the short, soft hair of the lamb's neck. He supported its head with one arm; with the other, he held a bowl tight against its flesh, where the beginnings of downy fleece grew. Lines of blood flowed down the beast's neck into the bowl. The lamb's eyes closed at last, and the bleeding ceased. Dadi held a pitcher of olive oil above the animal and poured. The lamb thus doused, the wood below soaked, Lamech put a torch to the altar and stepped back.

"Lord God Creator," he said, in a clarion voice that all could hear, "I pray that You bless this path we consider. I ask that You refine us and remove any hubris and hypocrisy from our spirits. If this not be righteousness in truth, show us now a sign, that we not go astray, led by imperfect consciences." He stepped back in silence. His prayer did not end until the sacrifice had been turned to ash and blackened bone, but the rest he kept between himself and his God.

"Welcome, all," said Dadi, the sacrifices over. "You are free to find rest here—not that it is mine alone to offer such." He spoke mainly to the giants. "This place is open to all Eden, and any of her friends."

"And exactly where might such rest be found?" asked Hamerch. After the last prayer had been made and the final animal killed and burned, the now-unburdened group of visitors entered the Tree of Knowledge. Hamerch had not ceased taking in his new surroundings since then, Lamech noted with some pride. His world in the city of Cain was one built of dead stone, no matter how elegant its shaping. Here, the only man-made furnishings inside the living cathedral were at the very center, where Eden's parsers and scholars kept the toledoths themselves. The mesmerizing greens of moss-agate slabs formed a low-walled atrium in which hardwood tables with polished tops hosted copyists throughout the day and night. The native scholars, some of whom lived in this forest paradise for years at a time, allowed no lamps or flames anywhere inside the Tree of Knowledge but at night, and only within the boundaries of the stone. The granite tablets of the toledoths of the Creator and of Adam, the latter far cruder than the former, rested in an ornate wooden setting several heads above human height, but both remained easily read.

Dadi pointed to several dark impressions in the moonlit wood-walls. "Those lead to sleeping eyries in the canopy and branches. I recommend the lower limbs for you, if you please. I would be loath to discover our graftwork on the upper trees proved insufficient support for one of your size."

Hamerch bowed and went off, along with Elebru and several of Lamech's Shepherds.

"I want to see them," said Hoduín.

"The toledoths?" asked Halhannah. The Naphil nodded eagerly. "Come! These words are for everyone." He led the giant into the greenstone scholar space. Lamech, Dadi, and Tiras followed, if only for the better light from the lamps of the scribes still at work.

Tiras folded his arms, at far less ease than his father. "Who are these men?" he asked.

"Most are parsers from Eden," said Dadi. "They copy these scriptures constantly. They also read prophecies for visitors, opine on morality . . . wisdom of all kinds is their purview." He pointed out several groups of differently dressed men.

"'They?' Are you not among them? I thought you a high priest of some sort. A speaker for your god."

"Not I," said Dadi. "The words of the Creator are plain and easily understood. No man needs another to speak for Him."

"Are those not your robes of office?" Tiras gestured to the deep magenta tunic worn by the bloodletter.

Dadi grinned. "My 'office' is that of healer, human and animal alike. I am also the son of a berry farmer. This is our family's dye."

Lamech looked over the working scholars. Foreigners were present, but fewer than what Lamech suspected was usual. "Dadi, are many others here?"

Dadi pursed his lips and looked about, as if he had not considered the question before. "No, I think all the Tree's guests are here now, excepting your men who have retired."

"Does that strike you as odd?" Since Hadishad had brought the Atlanteans to Eden, and more so after his meeting with the Nephilim last night, Lamech had begun placing observations into the context of the threat from Zuthi.

"No . . ." Dadi tapped his lips. "Why are you so eager to make war, Lamech?"

"I am not eager," said Lamech. "These Zuthians are."

"Then why are you so eager to oblige them?"

"Please!" The owner of an elderly voice from several tables away set down his stylus with a sharp rap. "There are those here who would work in peace and quiet."

Dadi bowed. "Apologies, Jezar." The old man picked up his instrument, muttering and scratching on his parchment.

Tiras leaned in over Dadi, like a tilting wall made of flesh. "Have you heard of what these hordes do? Have you seen forest ants swarm upon a wounded animal? It is much the same."

"Thus these unruly killers must be killed themselves, yes?"

"You kill," said the giant, pointing at the scabbard at the man's belt that held his freshly used blade.

"For sacrifice only. I would rather be killed than kill a man. Would you become ten thousand Cains, that you might fight ten thousand Cains? I would instead be part of an army of Abels."

At a nearby table, a bull-necked man sitting closest to the conversation turned toward it. "But through Adam's words, the Creator records that the Lamech who was Cain's descendant killed a youth in self-defense, and he is not explicitly condemned."

Dadi frowned. "But neither is he praised, Maban. Can we not assume from the text that the line of Cain is condemned?"

The new man, Maban, shifted his seat to face them. "Condemned in all things at all times? I am descended from Cain. What matter is it? Each of us is created in the image of Elohim."

"What image is that?" asked Tiras. "A coward? A weakling? Give me instead a warrior god who will strive against evil."

Dadi did not speak for a moment. "Tiras, you think this earth is the battleground, and we the warriors. *We* are the battleground, and our souls are the spoils. Some of us, yes, have chosen sides, but they might choose again, for right or for wrong. The Creator does strive with you: he strives with your heart, your conscience. My own is ground he holds, but even still the battle rages, for I have lived barely three hundred years. What new temptations do the next centuries have in store? No heart is impregnable." He looked at Tiras, uncowed by the giant's sheer height and breadth. "Has He won yours?"

The light changed. Lamech almost failed to notice; the others certainly did not. Still, there it was: where only the moon's grey glow ought to glint off the surfaces facing out from the lamps, an orange light began to shine stronger. The altars' fires had long died down. Innocent explanations abounded—late travelers, a guided trip to the outhouses—but again, that constant presence of Zuthi in his mind colored everything.

"Bring out the toledoths, men of Eden!"

The command came from outside, and the grating rasp of whatever throat spoke them sucked the breath from Lamech's lungs. He and Tiras looked at one another, and he was grateful. Whatever fire of resolve he saw in the giant's eyes kindled its kin in himself, sending a warmth back into his body.

Dadi's jaw fell open. "Jezar, stop!" Lamech spun to see the fluttering robes of the old scholar exit the tree-temple and disappear into the night. He ran after, followed by Tiras, Maban, and Dadi. Short, thick stubs of branches along the wood-wall held cloaks and bags, and Lamech grabbed his quiver and bow as they passed. The elderly man had been outside only a few seconds, so he could not be lost.

"You do not have the toledoths," said the rasp. Tiras had passed the humans and was almost at the front portal.

"No, I—" Jezar's wavering voice was cut off. He stumbled back into the inner chamber of the Tree of Knowledge, clutching his belly, Tiras obliged to catch him as he fell. Dadi and Maban immediately dropped to him.

"Do not . . . do not let . . . my blood spill upon . . ." The old man struggled to draw air. Dadi untied his scarlet sash and pushed it hard against the wound. Lamech did not see its full extent, but what glimpse he had did not engender hope. Dadi looked lost for answers. Maban, however, had become hard as flint, and Lamech remembered faces much the same from four centuries prior, among the followers of his grandfather Enoch's teachings in a city of the same name.

"I say again," said the harsh voice, "to bring out the toledoths, else we burn all of you alive!"

"You wish to avoid war, Dadi, but it has come," said Maban, rising with a half staff in either hand. Tiras already clutched his axe, glaring stone faced to the shouted ultimatum. "Let us thank Elohim that He has sent men such as this to aid us in waging it."

‹ CHAPTER 25 ›

Gilyon walked with head held high into the spacious spheroid theater in the shadow of Mount Armon's peak. Mareth and Tubal-Cain, the human too short to catch his eye as they walked but whose dysrhythmic limp marked his presence, flanked him as he approached the center of the room. Mareth lay a hand on his shoulder, indicating he ought to sit. Gilyon did so, the level of his gaze dropping to Tubal-Cain's standing height.

"Say nothing," said the human smith. Gilyon nodded, and his two companions took their positions on the front row, facing him.

The theater's walls swept upward steeply. Two hundred finely sculpted seats—"Almost *perches*," thought Gilyon—were distributed about them in a pattern. Most were filled, and space on the floor was taken by a few Atlantean giants whose size obligated more solid seating, but more striking than the room's inhabitants, as varied as they were, was the room itself. Gilyon knew its origins, and his escorts gave him details on the way: formed by the *bene Elohim* with arts known only to them, by skill possessed only by them, beyond the wildest creative imaginings of humans or Nephilim. The chair in which he sat, while ornate and impeccably crafted, was imported from plainer regions, made by mundane hands. It was built for a giant's proportions, for which he was thankful, but it stood out in the otherworldly setting like a lump of iron in a jeweler's gem case.

He had been called here, to the Council of Atlantis, by the diviners' guild. Unsurprisingly, that body proved to be rather put out on the account of the silver sorcerers' tribulations at Gilyon's hand, for which he felt no remorse. Still, the amassed power that these petty mages and demon followers wielded corporately was enough to prompt a response from the Atlantean leadership, which seemed to Gilyon to have retained many of the same cues from the centuries-defunct Grigori council. So be it, though. As his father Gloryon had defied the *bene Elohim*, so too would he defy the Council of Atlantis, if need be. At least he had allies who sat upon it.

The row of seven faced him, with Mareth and Tubal-Cain taking two places at the end of it. At the opposite end was the other giant present, his old friend Deneresh, who waved happily and whose corpulence required an enormous couch akin to a dragon's nest.

Four women made up the rest of the present council, and all displayed the aching beauty characteristic of Nephilim women. Three he recognized, although he did not know them well: Temethe, Eila, and Asathea, daughters of Samyaza and the Cainite Naamah, who died birthing Gilyon's great friend Eudeon. For this relationship alone, Gilyon felt some regard for the women, whose faces were no less stunning for the severity with which they looked upon him now. The final woman, the seventh member of the council, occupied the center seat. Mareth had named her as Edenah, his much-younger half sister and a favorite of his father Dyeus. Gilyon did not believe in signs or omens, unlike the audience that faced him. Still, he considered her name to be favorable, and she seemed to match it: her features were lovely but not lustful, the lines of her face soft, her eyes bright and deep like pools, her dress modest yet flattering. Gilyon smiled at her. She did not return it, but she did speak.

"You before this council are Gilyon, son of Gloryon and Jet, both of Atlantis?" asked Edenah.

Gilyon nodded. There was to be no more preamble, he gathered, which was well, though he must not waste time. His gaze glided slowly over the assembled factions of the guild. The augurs sat between the entrail readers and astrologers; root workers mingled with crystal gazers; the tantric seers, shunned by the others, were left to themselves; the sorcerers of the Silver School glared at him from just behind the council; and the one group Gilyon knew he could ignore were quiet at the periphery of the chamber. He began his work.

"Let the accusers give their account," continued Edenah. The sorcerer who had been the vessel of Asaradel stood up. He recounted Gilyon's assault in severe language, then related the hopes and plans of Asaradel and the silver mages in soaring terms, all dashed in a night by the Nephilim missioner. He plaintively placed Gilyon's actions in the context of harming Atlantis's well-being and helping the threat from Zuthi. He pleaded for restitution for the violent death of his panther familiar and the violation of the sanctity of the Silver School's tower stronghold. His words carried passion and weight, and few there seemed unmoved by them.

Gilyon ignored the entire speech. He focused instead on his true self—not the flesh he simply possessed while on the earth—and let the light of his spirit faintly glow within the realm where dwelt his true adversaries. One by one he sensed them, silhouettes on the paper screens of their hosts' minds and souls: arrogant, fearful, cowering, deceitful and mistrusting. Yet they would come out, come to examine the glow, like a moth to a flame. He waited.

When the silver sorcerer had ended his diatribe, Edenah said, "Who else wishes to speak against the accused?"

"In these troubled times, Atlantis must use every help available to her!" This from a portly, thin-bearded cleromancer, pouches full of runed lots rattling as he stood.

"A spirit from the Grigori would be invaluable. This was their home! Why would they not wish to defend it, even now?" This from a thin, dour astrologer almost lost in his billowing blue robes.

"What about the pronouncement?" This from an augur, whose words were punctuated by chirps from the birds on his shoulders. Murmurs rippled among the seers and mages.

"What pronouncement?" growled Mareth.

The blue-robed astrologer stood, after no one else seemed to be willing. "The various disciplines represented here, my lord, have each, by their own particular means, received the same words: 'Freedom to slaves.'"

Mareth shared a look of disparaging doubt with Tubal-Cain. Deneresh appeared to be daydreaming. The female Nephilim, though, seemed struck.

"What meaning have you derived from the message?" asked Eila. The answers came fast, each struggling for supremacy.

"It has been fulfilled by the Zuthians enslaving the southern nations! *From* freedom, to slaves!"

"No, no. This people, our people, shall *bring* freedom to those nations. Let the Zuthians come!"

"They come to add *us* to their masses! Atlantis—the world!—is doomed! Our time has ended!"

"Peace!" shouted Edenah. "Order, please!" A semblance of such fell upon the diviners.

A trim, bare-chested man stood up. "Honored council, our visions—"

"What visions?" interrupted a high-collared mage. "You 'tantric seers' care only for how many maidens your farcical claims let you deflower." Argumentative clamor erupted again, louder than before.

"Enough!" demanded Asathea, scowling at the mage. "The tantric seers are a valued thread in the tapestry of Atlantis." She visited the shirtless man with a beatific smile, which he returned in a way that made Gilyon suspect that she had visited other things upon him before.

With eyes locked on Gilyon, Eila asked, "What does the Silver School have to say of this?"

The chief sorcerer rose gravely. "We had not been clear upon it. We believe now that it might refer to the matter we have brought before you, where the free spirit of a *bene Elohim* of Atlantis, his aid offered, was banished to Gehenna's chains by the one before us." He turned about as he spoke, addressing all. "You see how much import the stars themselves place upon the actions of this Gilyon, once of Atlantis but now a wanderer of the world! Shall his actions be without consequence?" He cast furious eyes upon the Naphil. "I tell you that his actions have already *had* consequence. Where will Atlantis get the power to best the mages of Zuthi now? All we here have scryed and searched the stars for ourselves. Zuthian sorcery is powerful!"

"Scryed?" scoffed Tubal-Cain. "More likely you have heard stories whispered among the survivors that gather in the valley below."

"Do not mock us, smith. You deny their power at your peril, and that of us all."

Edenah held up a porcelain hand. "Thank you, all. Be assured that this council appreciates the great contribution daily made by the diviners' guild to the well-being of Atlantis. Now, Gilyon, son of Gloryon." Her countenance was like a perfect pale rose, distracting Gilyon from his task for but a moment; he reminded himself such flowers have thorns and resumed his quiet, unobserved work.

"I understand you are a missioner of Elohim," Edenah continued. "You will appreciate that I was named for Eden, and, fittingly, my task—and that of this council—is to keep peace in Atlantis, as there once was in the fabled Garden. We cannot brook any *serpent* upsetting things. Seven of us are enough to pass judgment; if serpent you are found to be, your lot will be banishment beyond our borders. Permanently. Are we agreed?" The rest of the council nodded.

"He has broken a few mirrors and killed a beast that attacked him," said Mareth. "I find no guilt worthy of banishment."

"Neither do I," said Tubal-Cain.

"Gilyon is one of my oldest friends," said Deneresh. "His mother is from an old Enoch family. Why deserves he banishment? What a gloomy thing to do!"

"Why deserves he banishment?" echoed Eila. "We have heard why, nephew. I am convinced. I would banish him. Alathea?"

Serene beauty poured from Alathea's pitying face. "Atlantis is better off without you, Gilyon. Banishment."

"And I agree," said Edenah. "It is left to you, dear Temethe."

At last the moment had come. Whatever the council decided, he cared only slightly. This very trial had been an opportunity he could never have created for himself. Only Elohim, working all things for His good, could have orchestrated this work He was allowing Gilyon to perform. Gilyon let himself be a conduit for the light of his Creator to shine, turning his spirit's glow into a fiery flare of inexorable brightness. Every demon, every dark and rebellious spirit that aided these diviners, prodded them to sorcery and debauchery, twisted their thoughts and deeds against their Maker, loosed unheard shrieks and fled madly before the flood of light. So sudden, so absolute was the mass casting that for a few moments, as with a quick, deep cut from a sharp blade, no pain was registered by the many diviners who were now without their familiar demons, or whatever name such spirits were called by them.

"I could not be the voice that separates a son from the homeland of his mother," said Temethe, in the seconds when the realization of what had happened began to fall like ash upon the diviners. "No banishment."

Edenah nodded. "The decree of this council is final."

"Nooo!" screamed the astrologer.

Edenah turned and looked upward severely. "Sir, do not question—"

"NOOO!" The panicked cacophony began in earnest, feeding upon itself. Mages dashed madly out of the amphitheater. Trembling fingers pointed at Gilyon, and one wide-eyed seer rushed toward him, fists flailing. Mareth felled him with an outstretched arm as he ran by, and the man writhed, gibbering, on the polished floor. All seven council members stared at Gilyon.

"I thank you all for my freedom," he said solemnly, and rose from his chair.

Mareth began to laugh.

‹ CHAPTER 26 ›

The change that fell upon Midash broke Phiaphara's heart. Not for herself only, though that was true in part, but for his missioner companions and his countrymen. The latter she had known only for the few days since they had debarked onto Havilah's banks, but they had shown themselves to be a capable, resolute people.

Well it was, too, for those few days had shown her horrors.

Their ship's captain, Nul, had fled back down the river as soon as he had been paid and his passengers on land. The peacekeepers initially encountered by Midash and Noah had led them all to the head of their order, a broad-shouldered, well-built man named Kieb. It was he who relayed in full the plight of the Houses of Havilah.

"At first," he had told them, "the young men fell. After that the rest, in every house."

"Were there none left alive?" asked Noah.

Kieb's dour gravity lightened. "Children. Only children, and only a few."

Eudeon placed a huge hand on Midash's shoulder, who reached back and gripped it, seeming to siphon strength from the giant. His spirit thus bolstered, he raised his head out of the darkness of his grief.

"And the people of the cities?" he asked, a new edge to his voice.

"Fewer deaths in proportion, but still they died in the thousands."

Peleg stopped pacing. "*Died*, you say? They die no more?"

Kieb nodded. "Many families fled. The cities are largely empty now. Some stayed, and we peacekeepers make daily rounds to the gates to collect new corpses left there, gathered by the citizens who will not leave. The curse lies much less strongly upon the farmlands and villages."

"A curse," said Noah. "How know you this is the work of a curse?"

"What else could it be?" answered Kieb.

"This is not a curse," said Peleg. For nine days the seven of them had made do in peacekeepers' lodgings outside the city of Havilah, once the seat of the decimated house of Dono-Vothuna. Few hours were spent inside the lodgings, though: the three missioners of Elohim worked tirelessly among the diseased living, quarantined in fields of gold-threaded tents and silken pillows fouled with the seepings of open wounds. Eroch lent his strength where he could: to displaced city dwellers wishing to build shelters of more than sheets, to farmers who were left shorthanded and disheartened by death. He was an endless fount of useful energy, to be sure, but Phiaphara suspected that more than a few newly bereft widows and despairing maidens had experienced the physical "comforts" of his ever-searching loins. Peleg, to his sister's dismay, insisted on making forays inside the city walls, to speak with survivors still there and to work what healing he could. The Havilahns had then given up the Naphil for dead, but each night he returned hale and animated.

All in their party were loath to relay the further bad news of the threat of Zuthi. Midash took the burden of relaying it upon himself, and Kieb and his captains shouldered it well, immediately dispatching messengers whose absence left the peacekeepers stretched even thinner. The need therefore obvious, Phiaphara and Tehama worked with them, taking up patrol duties and hunting predatory beasts displaced from their territories by the efflux of people. The peacekeepers, in turn, labored to quarantine anyone stricken anew by this land's affliction and to dispose of the previous day's dead. Neither, judged Tehama and Kieb alike, was appropriate for a foreign volunteer.

Life adapted here, as it had for Phiaphara and her father in the peat swamps, and now with Tehama. Tapestries and lush carpets that once graced manor walls and marble floors now stood lonely vigil against the chill of the thick southern mists, accepting their ruination for the sake of families happy to be alive. Like them, Phiaphara wished desperately for a diversion to keep her mind from the disease and death around her—the thought of Midash only brought such things closer now—and she found one. She discovered a fascination with the Havilah peacekeepers' mechanical crossbows, cleverly engineered to keep their missiles pulled back without effort until they were loosed with impressive power and accuracy. Her enthusiasm somewhat faded when Tehama showed her that in the time it took to load and fire a single crossbow bolt, the huntress could loose five arrows with equal precision. Still, she acquired one for her ingeniator father.

She saw Midash when he visited the peacekeepers; each time, he had shed more of the quiet missioner she had so admired. Slowly, he was taking up his duties as the first scion of the leading house, asking questions.

"Why burn the ships?" Midash asked today, cornering four peacekeeper captains. "Why taint the river?" From beyond a doorway and well across the central great room, Phiaphara listened with a huntress's ear.

"We blocked it off, honored Midash. Nobody was supposed to be traveling the river. We had to do *something* with all the dead," said a captain.

"It was a shortsighted thing. Did you give no thought to Havilah's future, when trade would ply the river once more?" No answer. "Why was the ship not manned?"

The captain's frustration broke through. "Because my soldiers were too busy trying to save their families!"

Phiaphara did not care to listen to what the pregnant silence that followed the ill-spoken excuse would birth. She rose to go, but even outside she could hear Midash shouting.

"And who saved *my* family? *Who saved my family?*"

A weight fell from Phiaphara as she walked away, free from a temptation she had been ignoring but had not yet defeated until now. She derived no satisfaction from it, but the fact remained: the Midash she had known so briefly was well and truly gone.

◄ CHAPTER 27 ►

Dadi upheld outstretched hands. "No one must die here!"

"I shall let Jezar know," said Maban, but he halted his advance toward the tree-tower's main bole-arched and branch-wound egress.

Lamech, Elebru, and their companions who had not yet retired took places near the separations in the trunks that served as windows. "I see six humans and two giants," said Elebru, a count confirmed by two other Shepherds.

"Weapons?" asked Tiras.

"Both giants carry torches. The humans . . . I cannot be sure. They have empty hands, but their belts look heavy."

"Only eight," wondered Gregan.

"This is a scholar's refuge," said Dadi. "Seldom do we host men bearing arms."

"Providence, then, that these creatures come this night," said the Scribe.

Dadi grimaced. "Or perhaps a trap of the deceiver Serpent."

Lamech cursed inwardly, but he agreed. These murderous trespassers must have expected no resistance, and now he and his men might cut them all down with a flurry of arrows before they knew the danger, but the blood that would be spilled would wreak untold havoc on the earth it stained.

Tiras looked back toward his father and Halhannah, both attempting to order the chaos around the wounded Jezar, who was now lying supine on a cleared table.

Tablets that had been quickly removed were stacked upon the floor.

"Give me two copies," said the giant. "There are so many, and how are they to know?"

Dadi shook his head vehemently at the many voices of agreement among the Shepherds. "No! Shall we use deception to protect sacred truth, and thus make a mockery of it?"

The hellish voice from outside cut through to them. "Scholars of Eden! I await your action!"

"We fight or flee," said Tiras, looking around at each man, then back at his father and meeting the older giant's eyes. "Is there egress into the forest?"

"Not to any man-made paths," answered Maban. "This place is no more a fortress than the original Garden, nor was it created with escape in mind."

Tiras hefted his axe. "I shall make a path for us . . . through woods, beasts, men, or Nephilim."

"Tiras, no!" Dadi's firm hand on the giant's elbow provided no actual physical restriction, but Tiras stopped. "Not an axe. The cutting edge . . ."

"I may be leading a retreat, but I *will* have a weapon with which I might fight a man," said the Naphil.

"I shall find something," said Maban, who ran off.

Lamech had seen several small mallets, used to chisel characters into stone for those scriveners who preferred more permanent reproduction of the toledoths' words, scattered about. The thought of Tiras carrying one into battle with an unknown enemy was laughable. However, the tool that Maban the Scribe rushed back carrying proved to be more serviceable. Having secured his two fighting sticks to his broad belt, he gripped a long-handled wooden sledge with both hands and passed it to the giant warrior, who took it up in a single fist.

"For stoneworking the altars when needed," he explained. Tiras weighed it, bouncing its handle upon his rough, thick fingers, and nodded.

Halhannah and several other Shepherds of Eden clustered around the fallen Jezar. Hoduín, with a few other parsers, was attempting to calm the several dozen unarmed scholars congregated near the toledoths. Maban and a few men who seemed to be his fellows stood with Elebru, whose sword was drawn, and the remainder of Lamech's Shepherds had begun to appear from dark hollows, half-dressed and carrying staffs and crooks and bows. Such were their forces and numbers, and their assailants remained in place before the cathedral of trees.

"Let us go then," said Lamech. "Hoduín, take the toledoths. Tiras, Dadi, lead the way."

Despite the danger, Hoduín wore a wide smile of supreme pleasure at Lamech's command. His hand stretched up, reaching twice the height of the human scholars around him, to be silhouetted by the glow of the lamps that perpetually lit the stone-carved words of Elohim. With a curse, he pulled it back. A black spot crawled upon the stone, then another. More cries emanated from the scholars, who began slapping bare limbs or pulling hoods over uncovered heads, but the moonlight did not shine strong enough for Lamech to understand what was causing such reactions, until he felt the insect's mandibles chewing violently on his own neck. He struck it to chitinous pulp, wiped it away, and looked up.

"Everyone out! Now!"

The cloud of beetles did not announce itself with chirping or clicking, but the sheer number of their pulsing wings and champing pincers added in total enough to break the night's silence. It descended quickly, and pandemonium ensued. Hoduín abandoned the toledoths, and his ravens sailed away in a weaving flight into the outer darkness, by their avian instincts escaping while they could. Hoods went up, arms flew about down-turned faces, and cloaks swept closed; nothing, though, could keep the insects from finding flesh somewhere. On the table, Jezan screamed, and Lamech watched several beetles burrow into his open bowels.

"We cannot fight these!" cried Maban, his long sticks blurring in movement but having no noticeable effect on the swarm. Elebru, whose burn-masking head wrapping afforded him a modicum of protection more than the others, had dropped his blade and taken up two stone tablets, one in each hand. He was trying to crush beetles between each resounding clap of the sturdy slabs, but the success marked by a few oily smears paled when compared with the sheer mass of insects still descending. "Then let us," said the older man, "attack something we *can* fight!"

It seemed to Lamech, in that chaotic moment, that time slowed as does a rushing river when it suddenly widens. His heart hammered like a woodpecker's bill, but he felt each beat as distinct as a blacksmith's steady strike. In that moment, too, he took the measure of those around him. The scholars ran about terrified, fear and physical pain overwhelming their wits, their great learning offering no solution. The conflict between a need to protect the defenseless and a respect for sacred ground tore his Shepherds in twain, and they looked to him for guidance as they engaged in futile struggles against the hideous swarms. Outside, the strange Naphil's compan-ions remained silent ciphers, but the giant himself had begun spewing revolting, arrogant blasphemy that could only be borne of the Serpent's persuasion. Men would die, whatever Lamech's action or inaction, and his clarity showed him no options to circumvent that outcome. He could, however, affect whose deaths might be, and in what numbers.

In that moment Lamech knew he could kill a man.

He forced himself to refrain from shouting, so as not to give away his intent to the adversaries waiting beyond the portal. "Halhannah, help everyone without arms flee behind us. We fight." he said. His men were too busy fending off the ravenous bugs to signal their assents, but he knew they heard him. "Elohim will not be mocked."

Tiras barreled outside before Lamech had finished speaking. Time snapped back to a more familiar pace, and Lamech, exhaling through grinding teeth, followed with his Shepherds.

The distance to the semicircle of strangers was short, and the outpouring of Edenites covered it quickly. One human was down already, his chest caved in by a blow from the hammer swung by Tiras on his way to engage the giants. The other humans—both male and female, Lamech now saw—wore fitted tunics with thin belts, from which they drew knives carried behind them. As he had surmised, they must have expected unarmed lambs running to the slaughter; his Shepherds' crooks and staffs felled four immediately, and three quick strikes by the Scribe Maban disarmed and downed a female with limbs angled in ways that the Creator did not intend.

"Garden mice!" screamed the rasping Naphil, holding his torch outstretched above him. "You come before Zuthi to have your lives spilled out before you, like water on dry sand!" He threw a skin, round and full with liquid, arching to burst at the base of the living cathedral. His torch followed, the line traced by the fire burning into Lamech's vision, and flames roared up.

The Zuthian warriors had been surprised, but only two remained prostrate and still. They moved like water, or mist, flowing wherever the swinging blows of wooden staffs were not. The blunt blows that landed did so glancingly; the strikes of their knives upon the Shepherds and Scribes began to drop bodies, swarms of beetles descending upon them as they fell.

Lamech shrouded himself with his hood and cloak, made to hold off Eden's wet mists and not the chitinous jaws that now rent the cloth. He ran half-crouched to the line of altars. The swarms thinned here; Lamech suspected the mundane lingering of the pungent sacrificial smoke, rather than the sacred nature of the place, had more to do with this. He withdrew an arrow. He wished not to draw blood here, but a bow was his weapon of mastery, and his fury raged in him like the flames that had so recently risen from the altars near which he now stood. With an archer's eye he assessed his targets, and he noted that the insects harried and attacked his forces, but not his enemies. The bare limbs of the Zuthi fighters caught the moonlight in a subtle sheen. Whether planted by a divine impulse or from witnessing the Zuthian giant's arson, the thought struck Lamech regardless. He stabbed his arrow into the still-orange coals of the altar. With a prayer to his Creator, and a hope that its martial nature would not be an affront to Him, he loosed the missile at the nearest knife-wielding warrior. The coal blazed to life in the wind of its flight and hit the Zuthian in the shoulder. Whatever oils protected the fighter from the insects proved highly flammable; burning and screaming, he ran a dozen steps away toward the meadow and its pools before crumbling to the ground.

Tiras had been victorious in his assault on the other giant, who writhed upon the ground in senseless agony, his face crushed to pulp. However, the fight between Nephilim had kept Hoduín's son static enough that beetles had fallen upon him in a thick blanket. Lamech saw two of the Zuthian warriors sprinting toward him, leaving their fellow human adversaries, a handful of Shepherds and Scribes, behind to deal with the insects. Lamech loosed another coal-tipped arrow, dropping a fighter midstride to stumble wreathed in flames. The other ran on, knives flashing, a thousand champing mandibles distracting Tiras from the killing strike that neared him. A sheet of flitting insects obscured Lamech's view, and he turned away to wield them off with a sweep of his cloak.

Through slitted eyes and a rising panic, Lamech saw another dark, undulating mass against the black backdrop of the forest's edge, and it moved toward him. A cry—of fury, of command—rose up from below the mass, and Lamech recognized it just as it flew past him toward Tiras: Hoduín. The insects' biting ceased as they fled the avian army that the Naphil had somehow summoned to accompany him. Lamech exhaled in relief, feeling no pity for the doom about to befall the giant's human attacker.

What father would do less for his child?

Hoduín swept past the altars, gaining speed as he waved his arms at the flocks of birds that swirled above and dived in the dozens below. In the chaos, Lamech saw hook-billed parrots, knife-beaked hawks, even the occasional bat and gliding serpent, and, more than all the rest, ravens. The huge black birds wove patterns that the Zuthians' flesh-eating insects could not escape. The feathered onslaught obscured everything, so Lamech simply bowed his head and thanked his Creator.

The beating of wings and cracking of carapaces quieted. Lamech rose. Two Zuthian fighters stood up from the roll of the terrain where they had taken refuge during the storm of birds. Slowly, painfully, other figures, ragged and bloody, rose and faced them. With one last cry, Hoduín advanced upon them, robes billowing, and every man still able to wield a weapon contracted toward them.

Lamech ran to Tiras, who had given up his attempt to get to his feet and was sitting, head bowed, on the ground. The giant's sheer size did not lend itself to sleeves or cloaks, and he had fought with bare arms and exposed neck. Nowhere was his skin intact or smooth; blood oozed evenly, meeting into beads and dripping slowly down limp-hanging limbs. Lamech removed his tattered outer garment and began tearing it into rough strips.

"Thank you, Tiras," whispered Lamech. "Here, let me wrap these tight." The Naphil made a noise that Lamech took for assent.

Dark mounds littered the rolling ground. As he ministered to the wounded giant, Lamech prayed that Dadi was not among them; a typical farmer—and that is how Lamech regarded himself, despite his lineage—knew enough rudimentary medicine to be useful, but the bloodletter was a trained and practicing healer. His eyes leapt from body to unmoving body, looking for the bold purple-red robes, but in the moonlight every color drew near the same deep, dark blue.

Suddenly, one shape exploded from the grass and toward the Tree of Knowledge. "The last giant!" shouted Lamech to the mass of men still fighting, but he knew it was in vain. The final Naphil of Zuthi, the rasping speaker, was moving too fast for any human, never mind one battle weary and wounded, to hope to catch. Lamech watched in pained futility as the giant raced to the sylvan home of the toledoths, now unprotected. Whatever desire stirred in the murderous monster's foul heart for the sacred tablets must have been strong; only one other of the Nephilim had Lamech seen ever move with such speed. Only a lone young giant, long ago, in a race for his life with a leviathan in pursuit.

Only Hamerch, son of Dyeus, who burst out of the tree-temple at a sprint.

The two Nephilim collided at full speed just outside the broad, twined boles of the entrance, then fell to the ground clutching one another like pythons. They rose together quickly, Hamerch's long, powerful arms wrapped around the Zuthian giant's neck and head, the other clawing weakly at his captor's forearms.

"Help me, Lamech," grunted Tiras. Lamech aided the giant to his feet, as much as he was able, and together they limped hurriedly toward the tree cathedral. Halhannah and Dadi met them en route; the side of Dadi's face and neck streamed blood that stained his clothing a different hue of moonlit red. Lamech gave thanks that they lived still.

"Most of the scholars are safe away," said Halhannah. "Down a trail leading west. Four Shepherds go with them."

Halhannah had said "most," and Lamech knew the fate of the remainder. He gathered that knowledge as kindling for his anger, picking up the pace.

"What . . ." choked Dadi, turned round himself like a stumbling drunk, aghast at the still bodies. "What . . ."

"Would you still be an Abel?" asked Lamech. "Rather,

be Dadi of Eden."

They gathered around Hamerch with the battle's other survivors, Maban and Elebru among them, and none unscathed. The giant of Zuthi had ceased struggling, but he wailed wildly, sounding more animal than man.

"My lord, my lord!" he screamed. "Why, why! I have done all you asked of me!"

Lamech felt a calmness of conscience despite the cold rage that enveloped him. "I know not the foul gods to whom you cry, but be assured: they are not here in Eden. They cannot hear you, and you alone will answer for what you have done here."

The Naphil snarled and writhed, and Hamerch had to strain to hold him. "Hoduín, help me," grunted Hamerch, then a wet snap like a sapling's branch echoed among the boles. Silence fell, and so did the limp body of the Zuthian giant. Hamerch's eyes came up, wide and unbelieving. Hoduín, who alone seemed untouched by blade or bite, placed a hand under the giant's arm and lifted him up.

"He did it to himself," said Hoduín. "Like a beast in a trap."

"The toledoths," whispered Dadi, and rushed inside the Tree.

Lamech followed him, prayers of thanks seeming to him more appropriate than those of lamentation or for retribution. Men had died—most would say *good* men, but Lamech knew there were none—as the curse on men demanded, but the eternal words of the Lord God Creator remained safe.

The cry from inside the Tree of Knowledge made the dead Zuthian Naphil sound genteel in comparison.

Dadi ran madly out, nearly knocking Lamech down. The bloodletter was barely intelligible, but after twice repeating himself, Lamech understood. In a daze, he found himself shouting—to the Shepherds, to his Nephilim friends—and although he knew he must have confirmed Dadi's news himself, he could not remember details. Nevertheless, the certainty remained.

"The toledoths . . . the toledoths are gone!"

‹ CHAPTER 28 ›

Back at Armon's base, Gilyon mounted the dragon given him by Dashael. The valley road stretching before him bustled with refugees readying for war. It was not the preparation of soldiers, neither the gathering of arms nor the training in them. Rather, men of disparate nations reinforced walls and forged alliances with one another while women and children ran to and fro gathering foodstuffs. Gilyon absorbed every detail. He knew these nations, had traveled their roads now riven, had lived in their villages now decimated. Death approached, wielded by Zuthi's armies; of that, he was sure. For these people he would fight, else they would surely die. He could almost hear Noah's voice, imploring him to consider the eternal soul over the temporal body, and he knew how he himself would reply to his old friend: the souls of the dead are beyond saving.

"Gilyon! Wait!"

The voice was not familiar. It came from the leader of a trio of men in robes secured with thick leather belts, each atop a shaggy, single-horned mammal that snorted as it shuffled. Gilyon turned his dragon around, its clawed feet stomping the earth.

"Do I know you?" he asked.

"Once you did, long ago," said the man, hooded and bearded. "My name is Merim. I speak for the Scribes of Enoch. I have a proposition for you."

"Why so sober?" asked Haphan. Gilyon sat with his half brother in a roofless upper room in Dashael's greathouse, a tall and sprawling structure nearby the menagerie and still the primary meeting place for family. Their only other company was Haphan's familiars: two blue foxes sunning themselves atop the home's resident tortoise and the eagle perched upon the beast master's leather pauldron. Surrounded by fields and forest, being there was a breath of fresh air for Gilyon, literally. Forges had seemingly sprung up everywhere—inns, bathhouses, temples—and a smoky haze drifted constantly from within the walls of Atlantis. The giant took a long draught of a dry wine before answering.

"I spoke with the Scribes today," he said. This information failed to solicit any particular reaction from Haphan. "Do you know anything of the Scribes of Enoch?"

"A small bit," Haphan answered. "They breed various animals and sometimes come to us for supplies or advice. Odd kinds of stock, but they do it well." He signaled the eagle to flight, which it did with a great flap of wings.

"What sorts of men are they?" asked Gilyon, picking out a bit of down from his wine.

"Scholars, mostly. Insular, sectarian. They worship Elohim as we do. Zealous, though. Once I heard that everyone who embraces their order must have the words of the toledoths burned onto the skin of their chests." Haphan poured himself another cup, then tossed a bundle of skins in a long arc over the roof's edge. From high above dropped a blur of feathers. "About what did they speak with you?"

"They told me," said Gilyon, "that the coming onslaught from Zuthi is but a symptom of the disease. That ever since the Grigori, the Watchers, were cast into Gehenna—this was a few years prior to your birth—the remainder of the angels charged with watching over humanity pulled back, for fear of falling to the same temptation. Since then, demon princes have strengthened and spread their positions about the face of the earth."

Haphan frowned. "And then the Seeding began." His eagle returned, and he absently raised his wine to let the bird dip its beak to its contents.

Gilyon nodded. "The Scribes say that in many places where the pioneers of humanity settled and multiplied, demon princes had already gained influence." He searched his half brother's face. "You are inclined to believe these men."

"They are known to be wise," said Haphan. "Not like the seers and diviners of Atlantis, whose livelihoods depend upon a constant production of predictions. The Scribes are more careful, more discriminating, especially in mystic matters. Do *you* believe them?"

Gilyon studied the red reflection in his wine. "I have seen what demonic influence can do, but men are able to wallow in depravity all by themselves. Either way, whatever evil animates Zuthi is coming here, and the Scribes of Enoch are adamant that they will stand against it. They wish me to lead them to war."

At this, Haphan sat upright. "The Scribes have an army?"

Gilyon nodded. "A vast cavalry of horses and great woolly unicorns. Their war beasts have no claws or teeth, and they use no blades, as to not spill blood that will corrupt the land."

"Stone-skulled drakes. Hammertail tarasqs. Spiral-horned dire goats. Now their choices of breeding stock makes more sense." Haphan looked over at Gilyon's weapon leaning near the doorpost, its three blades sheathed in oiled leather. "Spilling blood may be a problem for you." Gilyon laughed.

"So, then," said Haphan. "Will you do it? Will you lead them?"

Gilyon could not give an answer he himself did not know.

⟨ CHAPTER 29 ⟩

Peacekeeper, have you seen Tehama?" Phiaphara asked the man standing guard before a tent city newly erected around the manor house of a Havilahn root farm. She had not seen the huntress since early morning, before Midash's eruption at his captains, but she had discovered that the men often knew where the breathtaking Nephilim woman was, despite her practiced coldness to even the most genteel of advances. The mention of her name flustered him, a man whose profession it was to fight dragons. Phiaphara suppressed her impatience and, though she would not claim it, a hint of envy.

"N-no, I'm sorry. Did . . . did she mention me?"

"Phiaphara!" Tehama strode to them through the blanket of mist between the tents, knee-high leather boots sending eddies through it with each step. "Greetings, fellow hunter." The huntress cuffed the peacekeeper's arm in the manner of comrades in arms; the man's smitten head likely translated its meaning into a lover's caress, judging from his slack jaw. "Understand you the meaning of 'virgin,' man? Show respect for yourself," thought Phiaphara, immediately shamed at her flirtations with Midash while under the auspices of the Wa-Mizhan.

"Come with me, Phiaphara," said Tehama. Together they left the peacekeeper tongue-tied at his post.

Tehama led her to the manor house, a spacious and solid residence now serving as everything from treasure hold to armory. One wing had been converted to a house of healing, as the city of Havilah's own healing houses had been either abandoned or fouled with fetid piles of the dead. To this place they went, passing into several rooms with tubs of boiling water that smelled of strong herbs. Two healers, dressed in their profession's tunics of deep black that showed no stains of ichors or humors, exited a low hall as the women entered. At the sight of the huntresses, the healers paused their conversation until out of the room, but Phiaphara cast her attention and heard one last wondering whisper between them.

"How are those men still alive?"

The morbid curiosity of the Havilahn healers caused Phiaphara more annoyance than worry, but when she saw the patients of whom they had spoken, she could not deny they had reason for it. Noah and Eudeon faced away from her on palettes, bare backed, dressed only in hardy missioners' breeches. The sunlight streaming in the open skywindows painted their wounds—countless scabbed claw scrapes and bite marks from the rats in the river, stretching from head to beltline and down both arms—in bold and grisly detail.

To the side, Peleg worked at a polished table with piles of crushed leaves and boiling water. At her arrival, the giant physician glanced over. "Midash has had his treatment already," he said. She blushed.

"I . . . I saw him at the peacekeepers' quarters earlier. I am here with your sister." Noah propped himself up on his elbows at her speaking, looking at her, then over at Eudeon in a telling manner that showed her they were more concerned about him than even she.

"Healing is an important art in the wild," said Tehama, either missing or ignoring the silent concerns in the room. "Peleg is a master at it. Learn from him today." She gestured to the long table, its gleaming surface surely more familiar with crystal decanters of fine wines than the apothecary ingredients there now.

Phiaphara hesitated; males and females, whether home in Mizraim, with her father's crews, or on the road with her current companions, bathed and dressed separately, as was proper, and she was unused to this state of even modest undress. The clinical setting and the presence of such ugly wounds cleared her head. She watched as Peleg worked.

Raw red marks covered the missioners' backs, relics of their brush with the rodents in the river. The giant Eudeon's body was so broad, so big as to seem otherworldly. "And half of him is," she thought, "if the tales my companions tell about the *bene Elohim* were true."

Noah's wounds were worse than the Naphil's. Half-healed sores blanketed his neck and upper back and covered his arms like sleeves. He bore them without complaint, as he had done since he had received them, earning him pity and admiration from Phiaphara that she would prefer not to feel toward him. She blamed him still for the distance she felt between Midash and herself, though only in part and in no specific role. She put all that away and focused on her task at hand.

While Peleg administered a salve to Noah's upper back, she listened to him discuss its components. She was expected to keep her eyes upon the older missioner, and as Noah remained prone for the treatments, he could not see her doing so. This voyeur's freedom was at fault, perhaps, but as she watched, the path down which her thoughts traveled surprised her. A missioner's life, full of labor, had kept Noah fit and lean, though his years approached five centuries. His waist was lean, his musculature defined. She wondered briefly what Midash looked like under his tunic, then she caught herself. She gave her head a slight shake.

"Attend to this, Phiaphara," whispered Tehama.

Her thoughts refocused.

"Cats," said Peleg. "Where cats dwelled, and other eaters of vermin, is where little of this crusting disease spread. I become surer each day."

"But if rats spread this plague through the cities, why do we yet live?" asked Eudeon. "Neither we nor Midash has shown sign nor symptom."

"Your god shows you favor, perhaps," said Tehama.

"Havilah has many worshippers of Elohim," said Noah. "Why would the Creator spare me? I am no one."

"It could be that we shall yet see," said Eudeon.

Peleg beckoned Phiaphara to begin applying the salve to Eudeon, then shook his head. "I doubt your good health is from divine protection. Different bloodlines? But Midash remains hale, so it cannot be. This is a puzzle, and I am still missing pieces."

"After speaking with how many survivors?" asked Tehama. "Scores? Hundreds?"

"Yes, and I will speak to more," said Peleg. "For the dead number thousands, and they are forever silent." He backed away from Noah, the missioner's wounds covered, his scabbed skin now with an oily sheen.

"I know you do not believe in Elohim's protection," said Noah to Peleg, rising and shrugging on his tunic. "But I will continue to pray for it, all the same. I am thankful for your gifts, Peleg, but the Lord God is the giver of them, and the provider of the tools you use."

"A green and living nature provides."

"Yes, and on creation's third day, the Lord God made it. If anyone must find me, I will be at the altar house."

He inclined his head to the Nephilim siblings, then Phiaphara, who kept her eyes on her work.

"Keep at it, Phiaphara," said Tehama. "Young uncle Eudeon has much flesh still to cover. Brother, may I steal you away? We have been longer here than I anticipated. We must discuss what must next be done in service of Atlantis."

"Eudeon?"

"It is fine, Peleg. Go." The giant smiled kindly at Phiaphara. "I am in good hands." Thus encouraged, Phiaphara continued while Tehama and Peleg took their leave.

She worked as the Nephilim physician had shown her. She rubbed the ointment in deeply, palms running over sores that must have hurt Eudeon, though he showed no pain. Living in peace in Mizraim, she would never have imagined touching fresh wounds with bare hands, but she knew word of her effort would reach back to Tehama, and her wish to impress her mentor buried any squeamishness.

After a while, Eudeon spoke. "You know, you remind me of someone, Phiaphara."

"Who?" She wanted to add "my lord" but knew that the Naphil would disabuse her of using the title on him.

"Myself."

Phiaphara stifled a laugh. The arm to which she was applying salve was as big around as her body; the being to which it belong had spent four centuries roaming the earth, and she had grown up in a single plains town.

"How is that so?" she asked.

"When I began my travels with Noah, I was no older than you. My companions were more experienced, more skilled, and wiser, so I did what you have learned to do. I listened."

"I cannot imagine you being other than wise."

"Yet so I was," said Eudeon. "And still I learn from those around me. The healing arts from Peleg, the wonders of wild creation from Tehama. The ways and mind of the Creator from Noah."

"From Noah." She did not intend to scoff, but when her lips formed the words, she immediately wished she had not loosed them in the company of one so perceptive.

"You have little like for Noah," said Eudeon.

Phiaphara saw no use denying the fact. "Noah . . . seems like a good man. He is not unkind, but he has no warmth to him. Certainly he has no regard for feelings of romantic attachment—not that we Wa-Mizhan need worry on such things. Is he a eunuch?"

Eudeon's slow answer made Phiaphara worry that she had overstepped her bounds. "No," said the Naphil. "To understand Noah, you must understand that he was heartbroken beyond what any man ought to bear. You have heard of Samyaza?"

"Tehama's grandfather."

"Yes, and my father."

"The angel."

"Angel. Indeed, he was once. Have you heard the name Emzara?"

"No," said Phiaphara.

"Then listen, and I shall tell you," said Eudeon. She moved on to his other arm as he spoke. "Emzara was a woman of Eden, betrothed to Noah. The third constant member of our mission, Gilyon, is a paragon of virtue and devotion, but he is descended from villains. His grandmother, the sorceress Lilith, was the wife of a foul *ben Sheol* called Azazyel, Samyaza's closest companion. When Samyaza stole Emzara from Noah, Azazyel saw the opportunity to wrest the earth from humankind for himself. Noah stopped him."

Rather oddly, Phiaphara had no problem believing that Noah would stand up to angels.

"With her husband banished," said Eudeon, "Lilith hung Emzara by the neck off a balcony, leaving her to strangle just out of Noah's reach." He sighed. "She held me once, Emzara did. When I was an infant, so my grandmother Zillah told me."

Phiaphara gasped. By now, the presence of death was neither new nor uncommon, but Eudeon's tale was more visceral, more personal, and all the more awful for it. She ignored her shame at her uncharitable words and focused on her newfound pity for the older missioner.

"I do understand," she said. "He closes himself to those around him so he cannot be hurt again. I cannot blame him. I ought not to have felt so poorly toward him."

Eudeon sat up, his treatment finished. "Closes himself? No, young Phiaphara. He is not closed to anyone. Losing Emzara resulted in a sort of universal empathy. That is what animates him. He serves the Creator, yes, and upon that foundation, he desires to make every effort so that no person can be hurt so badly as he was."

Phiaphara handed the giant his voluminous—to her, at least—tunic. "Still, it is terrible," she said. "His betrothed stolen, then strangled to death in front of him. I cannot imagine."

"To death?" asked Eudeon. "No, no, my girl. Strangled, yes; but who said Emzara was dead?"

‹ CHAPTER 30 ›

From the very moment that the Garden had been shut to Adam, life in Eden had never been easy. Hadishad knew this truth firsthand. Seasons of planting led to seasons of harvest, every day a toil. The herds were never safe, the labor never ended, the thorns always regrew. The mists and the sun, both vital for the growth of crops that fed each family, rotted house beams and burned backs. Hadishad's people were resilient, though. They knew their lot was due to the sins for which they sacrificed, sins that returned again and again like weeds. Adam's curse lay upon them all, but so did the Lord God's promised redemption, and thus despair met their hope as water met oil.

Until now.

News of the toledoths' theft spread like nightfall under a crescent moon. It had badly shaken Hadishad, especially upon learning of Zuthi's involvement, but throughout the rest of Eden's lands, grief and horror had swelled across fields and villages until it seemed as if every soul was broken. The toledoths were gone. Eden's most sacred place was desecrated. His father Lamech's Shepherds, so recently promised to the Atlantean cause, had spoken no more of fulfilling that promise, drowned in mourning for their fallen fellows; Lamech himself had not spoken at all.

Of the men who had fought at the Tree of Knowledge, old Elebru seemed to be holding up the best, but he had been a hard man since Hadishad's youth. Too, the manner in which Methuselah had worn his mantle of Greatfather since the attack won Hadishad's admiration, in both official and familial capacities. Despite his distressed soul and the troubled times, Methuselah proved that his aging bones held strength. Still, he held no power to stop the inevitable.

The time had come to bury the dead.

At final count, twenty-seven men of Eden had been murdered, along with six scholars from friendly lands. Eight Zuthian corpses, two Nephilim and six human, moldered in an abandoned silo while Methuselah and Elebru argued about what to do with them, until persons unknown put a torch to the building. No one fought the fire.

Hadishad travelled with the rest of his family, along with throngs of wailing kin to the dead, to the grave orchards of Eden. He had been there last at his grandfather's grandfather Jared's funeral, when the trees numbered few enough to be rightly named "orchard." With passing years and generations of mankind that had multiplied, then died, that orchard was now a forest. Before him now, a line of graves, dark dirt upturned upon verdant grass, stretched along the front tree line. Saplings potted in clay rose like silent sentinels over bodies wrapped in rice paper and bereft of the spirit of life. The burials were about to begin. Hadishad tried to pinpoint his sense of growing dread. He decided that it was due to the *finality* he would feel when the last tree was planted, and the recognition itself helped decrease the sensation. "At least," he thought, "the endless crying-out might abate."

The Atlanteans who had traveled with him had stayed behind, none showing a desire to intrude upon the mourning rites of ones who were strangers to them.

Without them, although he was surrounded by a crowd of countrymen, Hadishad felt strangely isolated, as if he belonged to Eden no more. He wished at least Tiras had come, but the giant had been badly injured, and Hoduín forbade any travel.

"I have never seen it this bad," said a man's voice. Hadishad turned in some surprise; all the faces he had thus seen were either twisted in grief or frozen in stoic stone. Elebru's scarred visage was neither. "Never," he repeated. "Not the grain blight, not the year without mists, not the leviathan—you were there, yes?—not the laming plague."

"We will stop Zuthi," said Hadishad. "With Eden joining Atlantis, they cannot win."

"Yes. With Eden . . ." Elebru said, and Hadishad disliked his tone. "I myself would pay back these vermin from Zuthi, but Hadishad . . . I would not count on help from the Shepherds, were I you."

The crowd quieted, but for a soft chorus of muffled sobs. An elderly man awaited its attention before the middle grave. Hadishad recognized him, though more from his deep-green hooded cassock than familiarity of kinship, as Elidiah, the second son of Enoch, and Methuselah's younger brother. The two other second sons of that bloodline were beside him, dressed in the same green vestment: Rakeel, Hadishad's eldest paternal uncle, and Jonan, his brother.

Elidiah's face was cut with the lines of ancient age, but he held his back as straight as the sapling by which he stood, and his clear voice carried over the quiet crying.

"Today we mourn," he said, "and rightly so, for the loss of our beloved sons, husbands, fathers, friends. We mourn that they have fallen, as we all must one day do.

But let us also be thankful that the Lord God Creator had mercy on us, not allowing man to live in these vessels of flesh, in separation from His presence for all eternity. And let us pray that these souls have peace in Sheol, faithfully awaiting the day when the Seed of Woman will at last crush the Serpent's head and restore creation to what once it was. Until then, we still living must toil, but their toil has ended. They have eaten their bread by the sweat of the faces, and now we must return them to the ground." At this, he named each of the decedents in turn and beckoned forth all who would aid in the burials. Groups of somber men dispersed from the front of the crowd and spread out to each prepared body. "From dust we came," finished Elidiah, "and to dust we will return."

The burying of the bodies began. Elebru had disappeared during Elidiah's address, leaving Hadishad alone in the thinned crowd. With so many heads bowed in sorrow, he easily spotted Lamech weaving his way to him. His father's friend Halhannah—Hadishad had only met him once, at Methuselah's reception for the Atlantean delegation, but a few centuries' worth of diplomatic gatherings had skilled him at skewering names to faces without fail—walked behind him like a brawler fighting off a concussion, dazed but trying to hide it.

"A word, my son."

Hadishad, unlike his brother Noah, was no prophet, but he regardless felt quite certain that this "word" would be one he did not wish to hear. Nevertheless, he nodded.

"I must ask you to convey a message to Atlantis. Eden cannot fight beside her."

"Cannot?" asked Hadishad. "Or *will* not?"

"Our people, our guests, were slaughtered, Hadishad!" Lamech kept his tone to a harsh whisper, but it would have been a shout in any other setting. "We were surprised in our sacred place, our most treasured possession stolen in front of us! It must not happen again. Eden is unprotected. The Shepherds' task lies here."

"Or it might be, father," said Hadishad, "that you are simply afraid." The petty taunt was beneath either of their stations and the respect he had for his father, better left to teasing children, but it slipped past his lips regardless. Perhaps fittingly, the look Lamech gave him took him back to times he had misbehaved as a youth.

"And justifiably so," hurried Hadishad. "The Zuthi fighters are ruthless and reckless. No people has yet stood before them."

Lamech rubbed his bearded chin slowly, as if he were guarding his mouth with his hand until he was sure of what he would say. "Do you know what I fear?" he finally asked.

"This," said Hadishad, waving at the masses of people. "The tears, the anguished screams of the kin of the dead, spreading across Eden until no one is unaffected."

"No," said Lamech. He clutched his son's head with both hands and pulled him close to himself, noses near touching. "I fear the time when death is so common that the mourning *stops*. When there are not enough hands to plant a tree for every soul gone down to Sheol, when life is lost so easily that we stop clinging to it, stop caring when it ends."

"Father . . ."

"No, my son." Lamech dropped his hands and stepped back. "The Shepherds stay in Eden."

"Father!" But Lamech had drifted into the throngs, looking for friends and neighbors to whom he could give a bit of comfort.

Hadishad's hopes were dashed, his mission failed. His instinct was to pray for Lamech to reconsider, but he was not at all sure that the Lord God would take his side in the matter.

Having always been rather outgoing and gregarious, Hadishad was accustomed to enjoy seeing kin, especially during his rare visits to his homeland. The bitter pit inside him was a new sensation, and it grew stronger as he watched his father disappear into the crowd. New too was the sickness he felt when he spotted Methuselah coming toward him, with Elidiah, Rakeel, and Jonan in tow.

"No need, Greatfather," said Hadishad, deferring to title over familial address. "Father has already told me."

"How could he," said Methuselah, "when we have only now decided?"

"Decided what?"

"I will not leave the toledoths—the very words of God Himself!—to be defiled and desecrated by villains." The resolve in Methuselah's voice was reflected in the faces around him. "I will hunt down Zuthi like they were a pack of feral dogs, and I will take all of Eden with me if I must. Elohim will not be mocked."

Hadishad's ill feelings dissolved in an instant, yet even in his happiness he found himself echoing his father. "And if that hunt leads Eden to war, to death?" he asked. "What then?"

"So be it," answered Methuselah.

The burial ended. The mourners dispersed back to their villages and farms, left to pick up broken pieces of lives cut short. Hadishad secured a promise from his grandfather to gather together elders and leaders from villages across all of Eden, then bring them to meet with the entire

Atlantean delegation. Thus, his task as Eden's emissary to Atlantis ended.

He found himself walking among the grave-trees with Jonan. The last time he had been in the role of younger brother had been with Noah, and that had gone more poorly than he had wished. Jonan had never been as rigid, though, and despite his daily proximity to reminders of death, he had retained his easy manner.

"So you prod us to go to war with you, little brother," he said. "Congratulations. As if I did not have enough work to do here." He plucked a thick brown pod from a low-hanging branch, cracked it, and began to eat the cottony pulp inside. "Courtesy of Hugoth, daughter of Nabu, of Seth's line. Care to try?"

Hadishad declined. "You really eat the fruit here? From trees fed by dead bodies?"

"Which make wonderful fertilizer, as it happens." Jonan talked between mouthfuls. "Once we had to replant a jaca tree a behemoth herd knocked over. The roots had wrapped up the bones like a nest of constrictors."

At this, Hadishad felt a bit queasy, and the brothers ambled in silence while Jonan finished his fruit. The macabre nature of the place notwithstanding, the orchard was well tended, productive, and quite beautiful. Still, remembering the addition of so many trees today saddened Hadishad. He was glad the corpses of the Zuthians responsible had not desecrated the orchard, and he hoped that their souls were now trapped in a particularly dark and cold corner of Sheol.

"You saw Noah, I hear," said Jonan, dispersing Hadishad's morbid musings. "How is he?"

"Honestly? Despite four hundred years of tromping about the earth, he is . . . the same, really."

Jonan grinned wryly. "I am glad to hear it. When next you see him, you might let him know we need him to have two sons. I need an apprentice here."

"Ah, but he would need to find a woman that would have him first." The joke fell flat as Hadishad's mind flashed back to a young girl called Emzara; from the look on his brother's face, Jonan had the same thought. "You might tell him yourself," Hadishad continued, "if you come to Atlantis."

"Atlantis," repeated Jonan. "Where the men of Eden shall face the onslaught of a murderous horde. It does sound delightful. Many thanks for involving us in that. Already I have begun plotting out the new additions to the orchard."

"Could you do it?" said Hadishad. "Could you kill another man?"

"To regain the toledoths?" asked Jonan. "Oh, I doubt I would need to. There are so many other ways of crippling a person, after all. Kneecaps, for example, are fragile, and you might be surprised at how much of man's face might be obliterated without threatening his life."

Hadishad stared at his brother, then shook his head and laughed without mirth.

"What?"

"You jest about such things," said Hadishad. "I would have thought your many days in this place would have destroyed your good humor, but I see that they have simply burned it black instead."

Jonan gave Hadishad a sad smile. "How else could I face this enemy death, day after day, knowing it comes for me too and I cannot stop it? Better I mock it. Each of us orchard keepers copes with our calling in his own way. Rakeel is as silent as the bodies we bury here." His eyes roamed through the trees, as if expecting to see something. "But he has more reason than that."

They fell silent again.

"Does Emzara have a tree yet?" asked Hadishad quietly.

"No," answered Jonan. "Not yet."

Hadishad nodded. "Good. That is good."

He could think of nothing else to say.

‹ CHAPTER 31 ›

"Curse this waiting," muttered Eroch. He peered to the top of Havilah's city wall. Confirming that no guards stood atop it as witnesses, he struck the thick gates thrice in succession with his iron-banded cudgel, sending dull echoes into the unseen city beyond. The sounds were hollow to Noah, unpleasantly so, like a carrion bird's beak pecking bits of flesh from an empty skull.

"Bide, Eroch. Midash will be here soon," said Eudeon.

Noah sat high upon the hornfaced dragon he rode. The beast's saddle was secured at the apex of its back's curve, so that anyone mounted might avoid the line of long horns that swept back from its bony frill. In Eden, most hornfaced breeds had hidebound edges, with facial horns safely pointed away from the rider, letting him sit closer behind the head. Noah sighed. In this, as in so many things, life had been simpler in his homeland.

The view afforded him by his perch was excellent. Peleg and Eudeon rode hornfaces of their own, Tehama sat upon her grand elk, and Phiaphara rode a horse that, like the elk, had been fitted with bracers upon each foreleg as protection from the vermin bites they expected once inside the walls. All of them, Noah included, had encouraged her to gain the thick-skinned safety of a dragon mount; Noah had even procured a tandem saddle from a stable, but she had declined. At least she had the good sense to remain close to Tehama.

Eroch alone was unmounted, shod in iron-toed boots that went to midthigh. He began beating a rhythm with his cudgel onto the ground. "I *wish* to *crush* some *rats*," he chanted along. "There are scars that need repaying!"

"Scars?" asked Peleg, peering down at the other giant's swells of shoulders, sun-bronzed in uniform, unbroken hue.

"Not *my* scars," said Eroch. He pointed his cudgel up at Noah. "His. Noah's, and—"

"Midash," said Eudeon. "Listen."

Faint, but rising, a clean, piercing pipe grew louder as it came closer. "That," said Eroch, "is the least solemn dirge I have ever heard."

"They play as if they come to celebrate," said Peleg.

Tehema prodded her mount to approach the gate, and Phiaphara followed. "Midash returns to his home, and his people have a leader again," said the Nephilim huntress. "Why not find a bit of happiness in dark times?"

"No happiness will be found beyond those walls," muttered Peleg.

The mists were thinner in Havilah than in Eden, and the men, beasts, and enclosed, spheroid carriages first appeared as if the color had been leeched from them. A stern Kieb led the way, followed by the pipe player and a block of spear carriers. Behind him came the carriages, three in number, each pulled by a team of horses and flanked by lines of peacekeepers.

Midash stood above and behind the driver of the first carriage, eyes locked forward. He was dressed in gold-trimmed robes, jewels at belt and neckpiece. "Open the gates," he said, in a voice of command Noah had only ever heard when he cast out demons.

"Eudeon. Noah." Midash raised a hand, his fingers bearing so many rings that his hands appeared gloved in gold. "I beg your forgiveness, brothers. In the darkness I lost hope." He looked away to Tehama and Phiaphara, setting jeweled chains ringing. "I . . ." Whatever he saw in the younger woman's face turned his head back to the shut gate. He paused there, took a breath, and smiled. "I have found hope again. Let us now bring it back to Havilah."

At Midash's command, Kieb and another peacekeeper went to dual keyholes, holding two sword-sized keys with heads of crystal. Other armed men took positions behind them, three to a side; still more, these in heavy cloaks and masks, pushed long steel grates along the ground with poles, aligning them with the edge of the gate. The metal shined as if oiled, and lit torches were secured to the poles.

"Turn keys," commanded Kieb. The gates cracked open; though enormous, the head peacekeeper and his counterpart could push them inward. As soon as they did so, the men pushing the grates set their torches to the metal and rushed in. A cacophony of squeaking retreated before the polemen as piles of rats scurried away, washing over each other in waves. With a yell, Eroch ran in right behind, smashing his own gory path among the fleeing rodents.

Their path thus cleared, the carriages passed into the city with a corona of guardians surrounding. Several peacekeepers held leashes attached to the harnesses of dark, lean griffins of a smaller breed than Midash's familiar, which was padding alongside Kieb.

"After you, my ladies," called Peleg. Tehama and Phiaphara obliged, followed by Peleg, Eudeon, and, last of all, Noah.

In Noah's mind, the villages in Eden were like the farming men who built them: low and close to the land, hewn stone and timber imparting a rough appeal. Atlantis, then, was a city like the Nephilim: enormous to the point of overwhelming, grand towers and walls retaining the grace and beauty of the angelic fathers of the giants, fallen though they were. Havilah, though, was a woman, appropriate for Eve's namesake. Structures here featured rounded curves with few sharp edges, created by builders obviously interested in beauty that was sometimes subdued, sometimes extravagant. As the procession made its way through paved and empty streets, low domes and half domes bubbled overhead, and tree-filled gardens abounded. Indeed, *above* the streets, Havilah remained lovely. The streets themselves, however, were unkept and littered with all manner of grisly detritus, testament that the city existed only as an empty, lifeless shell of what she had been.

If lands were people, this one had been murdered.

"Be on the lookout for vermin," warned Kieb loudly enough for the entire procession to hear. "Stay well away."

"We will not be the only ones doing so," said Peleg to his companions. "In my forays here, I have seen snakes and feral cats in abundance. This rodent explosion has brought predators to keep it in check. Even in chaos, nature finds harmony."

Eudeon inclined his head down a shadowed alley. "I find nothing harmonious about that," the Naphil said. Human limbs, desiccated and partially devoured, spilled out of a doorway; a few looked too small to be those of adults. Without thinking, Noah covered his mouth and nose with the back of his hand, as did Eudeon, and the two huntresses pulled their riding scarves higher.

"No one need protect their faces," said Peleg. "Breathe freely. I am confident the plague is not borne through the air."

"Perhaps not," said Tehama, "but the smell certainly is."

Indeed, the stench of stale rot permeated their path, made all the more noticeable to Noah by its contrast with the splendor the city still displayed. Upon the buildings in Havilah, gold was everywhere. It decorated the domed roofs in sculpted sheets and lined the lamps hanging over gilded doorways. Even the solid stone that formed the structures' foundations was shot through with it. All of this was put to shame by the interior of the grand ancestral house of Dono-Vothuna.

The domes of the house—in truth, a palace—proved to be supported by a dazzling array of arches and columns bathed in gold, no inch of which lacked some ornate flourish. Despite the embarrassment of space and the soaring ceilings, Noah's party contracted to themselves once inside; even Phiaphara's cat pressed close to her.

As if that body of people created a stronger pull by becoming denser, Midash approached them.

"Each of you honors this house by being here," said Midash, giving no feeling to the words. "Noah, Eudeon, would you come with me?" He regarded the others, blinking eyes that flashed lids dusted with gold or something like to it. "My friends, the greathall would much benefit from your presence." He gestured to the backs of native Havilahns ambling en masse through large carved and gilded doors, then turned to a side room. Midash's boots clicked a brisk pace, matched easily by Eudeon's giant strides; Noah hurried to keep up.

They went into a smaller room, its dome closed to the sky, but with circular windows set in patterns like jewels in a brooch. Privacy loosening his tongue, Noah opened his mouth; Midash held up a golden hand. "Please," he said. "For a moment, I would be just a man returned home after a long absence, and I would have you simply be . . . my friends. Please." Noah's words died upon his lips, and he nodded.

"Then let me show you my home," said Midash.

The next minutes rivaled in wonder what the previous days in Havilah had shown them in horror. Midash had taken them to the house's leisure room, filled with devices wrought in gold and orichalcum and stone of myriad bright colors, with hidden mechanisms that imparted motion, or sound, or some other clever artifice. While Noah and Eudeon examined the objects, a silver bird fastened to the edge of a small basin flapped its jeweled wings and sang a thready note. "The sun's light," explained Midash, "is focused through the sapphires, and it steams the water." He smiled, but sadness wearied his eyes, despite their new golden luster. "I spent hours as a child staring at it, trying to fathom its mechanism. My father banned me from this place for a month when he caught me about to pry it from its perch. Would that I could have told him goodbye . . ."

All peace fell from his face. He turned to Noah and Eudeon, chin uplifted. "My house is decimated, mine and the houses of the three young women with me."

"*Young* women?" asked Eudeon. "One is certainly past that description, and another fits it far too well." The women must have been in the carriages. Noah had not noticed, but neither would he have, as his long practice of purposeful and studied ignorance of the opposite sex had created a habit now several centuries old.

"Pabania is older, true, but still of childbearing age, and Careth has but a few years until womanhood."

"Childbearing?"

"You are not fools, neither of you. Today I will marry those three daughters of Havilah and begin to rebuild our house. I ask not for your approval; you know to Whom I answer, and my conscience is my own."

Eudeon seemed disappointed, but not surprised, and that in itself surprised Noah, since he truly had not fathomed that this was Midash's purpose.

"I must tell you, I feel deceived," said Eudeon.

"A lack of complete disclosure is not a falsehood," said Midash, "and every matter is not communal business, especially here."

Still taken aback, Noah feared his speech would be mostly babble, but he spoke anyway. "Midash, the work we have been doing . . . I understand seasons come to an end, but you know the words of Elohim as well as we do." His thoughts found a familiar rut, and he traveled that path. "When a man marries a woman, he becomes one flesh with her. What of himself, then, is left to be joined to another, and still another? Does your conscience absolve you, or is it clouded by pain, or grief, or anything else rightly felt but better treated by less . . . drastic measures?"

"Have I forgotten the toledoths? No. But as you mention Elohim's words, I ask you, Noah: How many explicit commands have been given us by the Lord God? Few indeed. I will quote one: 'Be fruitful and multiply; fill the earth and subdue it.' Have we been obedient? No. Have *you* been obedient? No!"

"My blood ought not to be here at all," said Eudeon. "My celibacy does not denounce me."

"And I have been fruitful in spiritual things," said Noah, "and multiplied worshippers of Elohim in every land touched by man."

"Semantics!" Midash accused. "You mask your disobedience with wordplay. Whose conscience is clouded?"

Noah felt off, as if he had had one too many cups of wine. He was no stranger to conflict, but from these quarters it came unexpectedly. "It is not disobedience! Midash, you know what happened to me . . . to my beloved, my betrothed."

"And thus, you have made yourself blind to all things female. You think *you* know the pain of loss? Look around you! Look at me! I have *no one!*" Midash raised a fist of gold and cast about, as if to strike down one of the beautiful things around them, but at last he dropped his hand. He took a breath. "I will do this thing."

Noah quelled his own anger brought by the sudden thought of Emzara's fate. "Yes, but . . . with three?"

"Yes."

The younger man's eyes stared pikes at Noah's, transfixing them. Finally, Noah shook his head. He embraced Midash, and Eudeon knelt beside them.

"Midash, you look . . ." The giant paused, searching for the right word but apparently unable to find it; Noah supplied, "Noble," at the very same time Midash said, "Ridiculous."

They laughed, but it was a mirthless thing. Though no one was fully assuaged, there was nowhere to go but forward.

‹ CHAPTER 32 ›

Noah and Eudeon found their companions standing near the painted wall of the greathall. The top of Midash's head bobbed above those of his countrymen as he walked to the wedding altar, his head and chest finally rising into view when he reached its dais at the center of the hall. The three women followed him up, and the ceremony started.

Noah's dissatisfaction with Midash's decision prevented him from engaging mentally with the words of the marriage rites. Midash spoke, each woman followed in turn, and Noah could not affect it. He knew his countenance displayed his perturbation; with a twinge of satisfaction about which his conscience convicted him, he saw that the others with him showed a varied spectrum of discomfort as well. Tehama, looking rather like a raptor momentarily trapped and planning its escape, felt most at home in the wilds, and this gilded palace of Havilah was as far from that as humanity had yet escaped. Phiaphara echoed her mistress's morose, surely deepened all the more with whatever she felt toward Midash at the moment. Peleg was bothered, but it was the muttering consternation of a man in great effort to solve a problem. Half-heard phrases like "cats, no rats" and "which pathway came first?" surely meant nothing to anyone but the giant healer, but Noah wished him success in his ponderings. Eudeon was subdued, unsurprisingly, but not far from his normal self. Only Eroch, blood speckled about his booted shins and calves, seemed in high spirits, but while Eudeon's eyes remained fixed on his fellow missioner on the dais, Eroch's roamed about the room, no doubt identifying the more attractive guests.

The ceremony could not end soon enough for Noah.

Loyalty to their friend Midash pulled Noah and Eudeon into the banquet hall, following the Havilahn crowd familiar with the procession of events. Peleg and Tehama protested briefly, but when Eroch saw the array of food-stuffs displayed on each low table scattered about the hall, the group's course was set.

"I am ravenous," said a grinning Eroch, moving two lounging couches together to accommodate his massive frame. The action brought a man over to them. His dress was simpler than that of Midash, but in a similar style, and others around the hall wore the same, so Noah deduced that he was a steward of some kind.

"Excuse me," said the man, seemingly unimpressed by the Naphil's bulk. "Your boots. If you please."

Eroch looked down at his bloodspattered boots and chuckled. "My apologies, man." He unlaced them to his calf and turned them down, the clean inner leather now to the outside. "I would take them off, but my feet could match all those rotting bodies out there stench for stench!" His booming laugh was cut off by a sharp rebuke from Tehama. Noah felt for the steward—and every person of Havilah within earshot, which likely was most of the hall—and searched for a word to mitigate any pain caused by the reminder of death carelessly voiced by Eroch, but before he could, Peleg was arisen.

"Sir," he addressed the man, "you are of this house-hold, are you not?"

"I am."

"I wonder if I might inquire about the habits of this place." He led the man away, talking gently.

When they had gone, Tehama shook her head. "Eroch, your lack of thoughtfulness amazes me."

"Perhaps it is the context," answered Eroch. "In the bedroom, women say the very opposite of my thoughtfulness, and remain likewise amazed."

"Enough, Eroch," said Noah. "Have a modicum of propriety. This is a wedding banquet."

"A triple wedding at that," said Eroch. "Our friend Midash will be busy tonight, eh? Hands full, and wishing he had more than two of them? Sorry! I am sorry, Noah." Eroch raised the hand that wasn't prodding through a broad basket of fruit. "I spend most of my time by myself, you see, and when I do, I'm not surrounded by such . . . such . . ."

"Prudes?" asked Eudeon drily.

"Yes, exactly! Thank you, Eudeon." Smiling, the Naphil's focus returned to eating, then again he looked up. "I say, is there no wine? Man! Man!" He beckoned another one of the stewards to their table. "Where is the drink?"

"The wedding wine will be served at the apportioned time, sir," said the man stiffly. "As is custom in Havilah."

"And is that time soon?"

A hush fell and pipes began to play. "Excuse me," said the steward, and walked briskly away.

"It is Midash," said Eudeon, easily able to see above the tables of reclined guests. "And his brides."

Sitting up, Noah watched his friend proceed slowly to the center of the hall, the three women behind him. They greeted no one on their way, and nobody shouted their congratulations or well-wishes or stood for a toast. In all

Noah's centuries, it was a singularly somber experience, but Noah never enjoyed weddings anyway—not since Emzara.

With courteous aid from Midash, the brides reclined at their appointed table and descended out of Noah's view. Before the groom could join them, a towering figure strode through the hall. A clutch of perturbed men and women of the household skipped at his heels, trying to keep up. A frowning Midash met them, and though the words were intelligible, it was clear that everyone began to speak at once.

"What is Peleg doing?" asked Tehama, rising up to go answer her question herself. Eudeon looked at Noah.

"Go on," said Noah. "I have used up my portion of contention with Midash today."

Eroch sat up, his overstressed reclining chairs protesting with an ominous creak. "Wait for me," he said to Tehama, and Noah and Phiaphara were left together.

Peleg had gained the sole attention of Midash over his protestors, and while he spoke, the hum and buzz of whispering, questioning guests filled the hall like mists in a valley. Momentarily left alone with the girl Phiaphara, Noah recognized that here was a chance to make a move toward peace with the somber young ward of Tehama.

"Phiaphara, you appear in thought. What of?" he asked.

Her eyes remained fixed on nothing in particular. "I was noticing," she said, "that all of us are woefully underdressed for company such as this." She pointed at one woman's ostentatious coif, piled high with strings of jewel-set gold woven about. "Where does the hair end and the gold begin?"

"That is the truth," replied Noah. "But I feel less badly when I consider: there is not a single garment I possess that would change the fact."

"Nor I." Phiaphara showed a hint of a smile. The common ground was plain and pedestrian, but it had been taken.

"Still, our company is good too," said Noah. "Surely Midash, Tehama, and Peleg could adorn themselves likewise if they so wanted. I have found, and I think they as well, that the paths worth traveling seldom lead through palaces and fountains."

Tehama returned, and she motioned Phiaphara up. "Noah is correct, and these palaces and fountains will be soon behind us." Noah rose too. He craned his neck and glimpsed Midash hurrying out of the hall behind Peleg and the other two giants, Kieb and a stream of peacekeepers behind them.

"So where does our path take us now, Tehama?" asked Noah.

"To a vineyard. Peleg says he has found the source of the plague. The wedding wine . . . it is taken at funerals too, and only at those two occasions. Peleg says that the sicknesses started right after the sudden passing of an uncle of Midash, a friend to many high men of the Havilahn houses."

"So that single death . . ."

Tehama nodded. "And disease spreads to all the mourners, then those who mourn them."

"And before long, entire families are destroyed."

"That is my brother's assertion, and we have known Zuthi to use nefarious and clandestine means before." The huntress looked pointedly at Phiaphara, whose expressionless face masked an anger that her quickened breathing and clenched fists could not hide.

"Come, girl," Tehama said. "You need your cat, and I need my elk. Noah, we will see you on the road." They left, but at least Phiaphara had thawed enough to acknowledge the parting with a small incline of the head, which was good; with such real enemies prowling about them, any perceived faults in friends ought to perish.

Outside the house of Dono-Vothuna, all was a flurry of saddles and arms. Midash, seated upon a horse and holding the reins of another, wore a heavy cloak as ornate as his old missioner's duster had been plain. He called to Noah.

"No hornfaces now," said Midash. "We need speed, and I need you with me." He tossed the horse's reins to the older man.

Noah mounted the animal. "Tehama told me what Peleg told you. Do you think it is true?"

"Yes."

"Then you know what else is true." Reality was painful to voice, Noah knew, and he took no pleasure in it, but a happy deceit served no one, least of all his friend, now leader of a leaderless land.

"That we came too late," said Midash. He secured his crossbow to his saddle's side and called for his griffin. "That Zuthi is already here."

A steward rushed over with a felt-covered parcel. "As you requested," he said as he handed it up to Midash, then hurried away.

"Here, Noah." Midash unwrapped a bow, compact and intricately carved, gilded on its raised edges and with a full quiver to match it. "Eudeon told me you used to prefer this weapon." He held it out.

Noah shrugged the quiver over his shoulder and took the bow, feeling its weight and balance. He turned it back and forth, letting sunlight play within the jewels set above and below the grip and in the faces of the limbs. "This is beautifully made."

"More importantly, it beautifully fires. This bow was my father's. It is yours now."

Noah nodded his thanks, feeling that the gift was grand beyond the adequacy of mere words. "One of many benefits of traveling with Nephilim as companions," he said, "is that the protection of their presence is far greater than any I could give myself. It has been many, many years since I went about armed."

"That time, I think, has come again." Midash gestured to his crossbow, then pulled back his cloak to show a silver sword's hilt and two gem-bladed daggers.

"Midash," said Noah, "remember who is the One who goes before us in this, and in everything. I will not cease praying to Him as we ride."

"Nor will I, Noah, and in answer He will smite the abusers and murderers of my people with His just vengeance." Midash's voice lowered, as if he were talking now to himself. "Or else I will."

‹ CHAPTER 33 ›

I just cannot understand," said Dono-Vothuna's pantry steward, who had insisted on coming along. "It seems impossible." Noah suspected that the reason the man talked to him now was that the steward had already loosed his insistences upon Midash, Kieb, and the rest of his peacekeepers that rode to the vineyards of Asoth.

"The vintners are so particular—perfectionists, even," continued the steward. "In fact, only months ago did one come to replace all the barrels at no expense. A rot had contaminated the interior of a few barrels, and they must replace all of them."

"And have you considered since," asked Noah, "that the good was exchanged for the bad instead?"

"Impossible!" protested the steward again.

"It is nearly assured," Noah locked eyes with the steward. "What was done is not the fault of you, but you disserve the truth and those who died because of it when you deny what is plain to everyone else. The evidence must dictate your conclusion."

"No. I cannot believe it."

"You will not believe it, but you can. You must—lest the truth wrench your stiff neck when it turns your face to it, as it will eventually do."

The steward decided to end the conversation there, so Noah once again traveled in silence and prayer.

When at last they came upon the vineyards, the only green that met their eyes was that of the short grasses and moss that overgrew the hills. The wooden supports that once held clusters of grapes were barren, rotted by the mist that should have fed those clusters' growth, jutting out like bones of a great serpent whose corpse had been haphazardly laid among and atop the hills.

"This place has not produced new wine in a very long time," said Peleg, riding upon a hatchet-crested dragon. He spoke not as if this were an insightful observation that needed to be shared, for it was surely obvious to everyone, but rather as if *someone* were obliged to deliver a eulogy for a once-precious thing now dead. Birds hopped about, picking in piles of decaying vegetation and perching on posts, but nothing else stirred. Even in civilized lands, travelers remained wary of beasts outside the walls of cities, but if there had been any creatures nearby worth any concern, they would not have been able to hide in the skeletonized vineyards.

A paved path took the procession in and carried it past several buildings uncared for, as empty as everything Noah had seen in the vineyards. The path ended at a wide court occupied by broken barrels and a few canvas-covered wagons molded from the mists.

"Spread out," said Kieb to his guards. "Search for life." Midash shifted in his saddle as if he would spur his horse to join them, but Kieb stopped him. "Havilah needs you safe."

As the men obeyed their commander, Tehama dismounted and circled the open court on foot. Noah was examining a derelict wagon, its rotted wheels stained with wine like blood, when the huntress called out.

"Tracks," said Tehama. "There." She pointed to the edge of the court and one of many wagon paths leading from it. Noah went to look, but though he tried, he saw nothing. A glance at the rest showed he was not alone in his failure, save perhaps Phiaphara, who moved slowly in Tehama's direction, eyes cast down.

"There is nothing," said Kieb, after a few moments of his futile squinting at the ground. "It is stone. It bears no tracks."

"You can doubt me," answered Tehama, "or we can follow them."

A nod from Midash commanded the latter. Thus instructed, Kieb appointed three captains to complete the search of the grounds, then follow quickly. He, a handful of his peacekeepers, and Midash and his companions followed Tehama, confidently leading the way.

The stone road became soil, and the tracks became obvious to all. Deep lines made by wide wheels partially obscured the muddled footprints of many beasts of burden. Tehama said that she could not identify them, so Noah did not bother to try. Wisps of mist blew across the loamy soil, but nothing obscured the trail for miles, and the mounts made good speed. After an hour or so of riding, the back of a impressively large transport wagon came into view. It was covered, moving slowly. The group of riders split and overtook it from either side. The animals pulling the wagon were the size of large cattle and heavily muscled, with hideous tusk-replete snouts, and at three wide and four deep presented a rather terrifying engine for the transport. "Stay back from the dire pigs," shouted Tehama, and several Havilahns pulled at their horses' reins to do so.

"Hold, you!" shouted Midash to the hidden driver. At a guttural command, the harnessed animals slowed to a ponderous stop.

The driver's seat was a high-walled perch at the front of the cart that rose well above even the giants' heads and afforded a poor view of the man there. A hooded cloak and traveling scarf obscured him further. Kieb trotted his horse to the front of the monstrous team of beasts, keeping distance between him and the slobbering tusks. "State your business," he commanded.

"Why?" replied the hooded driver.

"Because your lord commands it."

"No one here is *my* lord," said the driver, "even if I were of these lands." His tone was educated, with a lack of affect that might mark him from any civilized place— Eden, Atlantis, Havilah, or a score of others.

"We will know your business at the vineyards from which your travel began," said Kieb, undeterred. "Your tracks were easy enough to follow."

"And why should I have hidden them? My business is, like yours, my own, but you seem pressed to know it, so I will tell you. I drive a wagon. I picked up a shipment of wines and vinegars. Now I travel to where I was paid to take it."

"You are a liar!"

"I am many things," said the man, standing, his head rising above the walls of the driver's seat to stare spears at Kieb. A wisp of straw-blonde hair escaped the penumbra of his hood. "But I am not a liar, and I have no interest in ceasing my business to be interrogated by strangers."

"You are the stranger here," said Kieb, who then pointed at two of his peacekeepers. "Search the wagon."

"I often find," said the driver, sitting back down out of view, "that the man most comfortable with giving commands is the man most ill suited to be giving them." The peacekeepers began undoing the ropes that held the wagon's back in place. "Yet those underneath him are the ones who seem to suffer."

The ropes fell slack, the wagon gate swung down, and two barrels dropped out behind it. The men beneath them cowered in reflex, throwing up arms that had no power to stop the enormous wooden containers from crushing them into the earthen path.

Eroch's arms, though, had that power and more. Before either barrel could strike a man, he caught each one in a massive cradle of an arm, then heaved them onto his hands and pressed them above his head, a feat as much of balance as of strength. He placed them back in the wagon heavily, rocking it.

"My apologies for such haphazard arranging of goods," called the driver from the front of the wagon, despite having had no possible way to view what had happened. "I hope nobody was hurt."

"No, no harm was done," called Eroch, his tone jovial but his countenance dark.

"My great thanks! Please, take a barrel in gratitude."

Peleg dismounted. "I would strongly advise against that," he said, walking to the wagon's open back. "Come assist me, Noah. You know the making of wine." With some effort, he pulled himself up into the loaded wagon, raised high even for a giant.

Noah rode over to one of the loose ropes, entering by means of it from horseback and prompting an overloud comment from Eroch about his being "nimble, for an older man." Inside the wagon, a narrow aisle separated large barrels stacked two deep on either side and two high, enough to be taller than Peleg, who was able to stand upright without hitting the canvas ceiling.

"I see nothing amiss," said Peleg. "I cannot test the wine for poison here. I would need to bring a barrel back with us. Do you see anything wrong, Noah?"

"No," Noah replied. "Not *see*."

The making of wine, at every stage, was accompanied by smells: grapes, yeast, oak, bone char, honey, a hundred others, as varied as the many kinds his grandfather's vineyards had produced over the years. He closed his eyes and inhaled, slowly making his way to the front of the wagon one barrel at a time, crouching and standing tall with his face almost touching the oak staves. An abrupt sourness marked which barrels contained vinegar instead. Something else was present, though, lost within the vinegar's acrid odor ...

"This one, Peleg," said Noah, touching the barrel before him. He put his face almost to the curve of oak and sniffed once, then again. "No, the one behind it." He was certain, but the barrel he wanted was at the bottom of its stack and trapped behind another stacked pair. He leaned back, wondering how to access it.

"Afford me the aisle, Noah," said Peleg, "and you shall have it." He gestured gallantly to the open back of the wagon, and Noah obliged him. He dropped to the ground, Peleg's labored grunts above him.

"Eroch!" shouted Peleg. "Catch!" The massive giant stepped up with a grin. Peleg tossed out a barrel with some effort, and Eroch caught it with none, placing it on the ground. Another followed a moment after. Peleg appeared with a third. "Not this one, Eroch," he called, and as soon as the other Naphil had stepped back, Peleg thrust the barrel into the air. It crashed hard down onto the dirt path, splintering and breaking but not bursting entirely. Thin, dark liquid poured out of the rent seams, but less so than Noah expected. "Something else is within," he said. Eroch nodded, then found a split that would accommodate his massive hands and ripped the ruined barrel open.

"Were you expecting a man's body, Noah?" asked Eroch, stepping back for all to see. "Because this is a body."

Midash's face contorted, and not at the sour stench of the pickled corpse. He wheeled his horse around and galloped to the front of the wagon. He looked to want to board it, but before he could cross from his saddle to the steps that would let him reach the driver's perch, a sudden loosening of the reins let a dire pig snap at his horse's neck. The horse reared; Midash kept his seat, but drew his animal back.

"Stay, if you please," said the driver. "I need no company up here."

"You will pay!" cried Midash, near the breaking point of his rage. "And I will be damned to Sheol if I let you leave to spread your disease in other lands!"

"Disease? You have naught but conjecture and assumption. I will be on my way now. Keep those barrels as a gift—drink up!" He whipped his fistfuls of reins and the huge vehicle jerked into motion.

While Peleg leapt down and remounted his dragon, Noah kicked his horse to join Midash, Tehama and Phiaphara behind him.

"Stop!" shouted Midash, trotting as the dire pigs picked up speed.

"No," the driver shouted back. "Consider this, man of Havilah. Say that you are correct in all you must suspect. Say that I killed the vintners of Asoth and fed their corpses to my pigs, save a few preserved for study. Say I used my arts to bring Havilah to its knees, prostrate and unprotected, through a plague that struck down entire bloodlines. Blame countless deaths upon me. But then what? Your people are followers of Elohim and will not put a man to death! What would you do for justice?

Banish me? But I am leaving already, and you attempt to prevent me! At day's end I shall pass beyond the borders, and you should be rid of me as surely as if you had taken my life from me."

Midash halted his horse abruptly, and Kieb rode to his side.

"My lord, you cannot—" said Kieb, as Tehama said, "Surely you will not—" With a raised hand, Midash cut them off.

"He is right." The leader of Havilah called four peace-keepers to him. "Follow," he said, through gritted teeth. "Follow until that man is far away past our borders. Tell me everything he does. If he is met, prevent it and detain that person."

"Take him!" said Tehama. "Take him and make him confess."

"And then what? He was right. I serve the Creator God still, and I cannot take his life."

"Midash has conquered, Noah," said Eudeon softly. Noah concurred. He knew Midash's course was righteous and obedient; with some difficulty, he pressed that knowledge down upon his flesh's desire to see the driver cast to his own pigs. He moved his mount closer to Midash, wanting to give words of encouragement to the friend who had just faced the most difficult trial of his young life and triumphed. The young leader and the rest of the party had stopped entirely, except for the four peacekeepers tasked with following the wagon. With a glance around the morose group, Noah amended that observation: four peacekeepers still followed . . . and also the girl Phiaphara.

The quartet of Havilahns rode their horses at a trot, and Phiaphara galloped past them. As she did, she drew a handful of arrows and, in the space of seconds, had fired them with good grouping behind the lead right pig's ear. It dropped soundlessly, but the snapping of leather and the squealing of the beasts that trampled upon their fellow were anything but quiet. The animals panicked in their harnesses, trying to break free; the wagon's mass and momentum crushed at least one dire pig's back legs under its front lip. More arrows flew from Phiaphara, dropping another beast.

Noah's surprise at the girl's action evaporated in the face of the danger they would all face if the mad pigs broke free of the harness, as their thrashing threatened soon to do. He kicked his horse and gripped his gifted bow, calling, "Midash!" as he did. The other man nodded, taking out his own weapon. "Men of Havilah, bring those animals down!"

The cacophony of the beasts' bellows and squeals reached its crescendo when the firing started, but streams of arrows soon quieted it. Only one dire pig managed to escape its chains and leather strappings, immediately felled by Eroch's club to its skull. In moments, a pile of dead pigs lay before a motionless wagon and its dumb-founded driver.

Phiaphara was dismounted, gazing upon the work she had begun, but she eventually noticed the many silent stares surrounding her, Noah's included.

"You say he may escape with his life," she said, plucking an arrow from a pig's carcass and pointing it at the man on the wagon. "Very well. That need not mean his beasts and cargo escape with him while he rides in ease." She went back to salvaging arrows.

The driver had obviously lost his arrogance, but had picked up a long whip and backed up, wide eyed, to the far edge of his perch.

"Drop the lash and come down," Midash commanded. "The points of our arrows will be behind you while you *walk* to whatever foul place you go." He raised his loaded crossbow. "Do it now, or I am inclined to put a bolt through your hand." The man climbed down, a pack at his back, and began walking at a brisk pace, four mounted peacekeepers behind him.

"What do you wish us to do with this rubbish?" asked Kieb, inclining his head toward the pigs and wagon.

Midash fired his pulled bolt into the wagon's side and pointed his horse toward Havilah.

"Burn it all."

· CHAPTER 34 ·

Now they rode as five.

Midash had pushed the pace back to the city of Havilah, sending off peacekeepers at the road's every branch. Their task was simple: compel anyone outside village walls to get back inside them. His farewell to Eudeon and Noah, and Tehama, Phiaphara, and Eroch, too, was sincere but brief, then he was pulled away by Kieb.

Peleg had decided to stay as well. He had saved a few barrels of tainted wine from being burned. These he took to the city's best-regarded physicians and alchemists, whom he convinced, frightened, or threatened until they reclaimed their studies and laboratories to help the Naphil in his work to divine a cure for the plague.

The five remaining in their party agreed that war was come sooner than anyone in Atlantis would expect. Although none of them regularly resided there, they each had enough ties—even Phiaphara, with her father Ninniachul—to worry what insidious tactics Zuthian agents might have loosed among its populace. Their decision was unanimous: their mission had met its end, and they must make their return to the lands of Nod with all haste.

The maps of Havilah matched well with those from Atlantis, but neither showed a marked route between the two lands any shorter than those following the meandering Pishon. A straight line cut through a swath of unexplored wilds, but as the two missioners and Tehama were used to rough travel through unmapped lands and Eroch showed no fear of anything, their route was chosen, and a straight line it was.

In the high-roofed stables of the peacekeepers of Havilah, they prepared for the trip ahead. Four river dragons had been supplied to them. The beasts were lean and long, with narrow jaws designed for fishing and scales the color of algae. "Swamps, lakes, jungle—who knows what terrain one might find out there in the wilds? These can get you past all of it," reasoned Kieb. "Take them, and if you happen across any Zuthians . . . let them feed freely."

"What can we expect from these wilds, Eudeon?" asked Tehama. The huntress secured the last of her provisions to her elk's saddle and swung atop it. "Noah? No people, certainly. What beasts?"

"I thought you were the expert at all things barren and alone, dear sister," said Eroch. "Is that not the Wa-Mizhan code?"

"To start, the wilds are hardly barren," said Eudeon, heading off a fierce reply from Tehama. "Green is everywhere. We might come across people, too, unlikely as it may be, but they will be strange, if we do. The Seeding traced its trails upon maps; if any settlement lies in the path we go now, it was founded by men who did not want to conform to an established society, or were thrust out of it. Either way, they will be best avoided."

"True of most things we might meet in the wilds," said Noah. "Beasts to challenge even you, Eroch. Drakes, bears, dragons. We must travel fast, for Atlantis's sake and ours."

Shaking her head but biting her tongue, Tehama rode away to where Phiaphara worked on her animal's cargo.

"Speaking of dragons, this breed is robust," said Eroch in low tones, patting his mount's hide. "We ought to carry the small people with us, Eudeon. Noah with you, and Phiaphara with me. What say you?"

"Surely you would prefer Tehama as company," said Eudeon.

"Not at all," replied Eroch, the wryness of the other giant floating past him unimpeded. "She has her elk, and I know not whether dragonhide is thick enough to protect my animal from her prickles."

"I am fine with the mount I have," said Phiaphara. Eroch turned her way in surprise. "I am *not* fine with men making plans for me without my say." Tehama made no sign that she too had overhead the men, but she nodded at her ward with approval.

"We will have no time to hunt, and we cannot count on easy foraging," said Noah. "The dragons will be able to carry food enough to feed us all for a good while—your appetite included, Eroch."

"Oh, my appetite hungers for one thing only," growled Eroch, his eyes following the girl as she mounted her animal. Eudeon noticed it too. "One last push to Atlantis, friends," the muscular giant said. "Let us be off!" He leapt upon his dragon and kicked it into motion.

"I suppose our journey begins, then. Be ready," Eudeon told Noah. "For anything."

"Even if we are," thought Noah, recalling Eroch's predatory gaze upon Phiaphara, "what could we do?"

They made good speed for the first few days, through valleys and over ridges empty of people or predators. To Noah's satisfaction, Phiaphara stayed at Tehama's side when camp was made, teaching her the wilderness ways of the Wa-Mizhan.

"Will you *stop*," said Eroch, reclining on a slope of turf, "with that interminable chirping, sister?"

"Bird calls are our method of communication," replied Tehama. "And the beasts of the woods know when the sound is false, which means perfection is vital, so we practice. Again, Phiaphara."

The girl put her hands to her mouth and blew, making a sound that was less warble and more wheeze.

"Your time would be better spent with me," said Eroch, turning on his side.

"Keep going, girl," said Tehama. "Pay no mind to creatures who speak in bellows and grunts."

Amused, Noah watched her for several more attempts, then got up and went to her. "Here, Phiaphara, watch my hands." He spread them palms up, then clasped them just so and put them to his mouth.

"That is good, Noah!" Tehama exclaimed. "Whatever he did, Phia—do that."

"May I?" asked Noah. He took her hands and guided them into a semblance of his own, with marked improvement in the sound she produced.

"Do the gibbon," said Eudeon. Noah grinned and made a short, high-pitched whooping sound.

"Mammoth!" shouted Eroch.

"It is not my best one," said Noah, but he obliged, to Eroch's immense enjoyment.

"I thought you were just a stuffy old mystic," the giant said, "but you, Noah, are a regular menagerie!"

"How know you to do these?" asked Tehama.

Noah shrugged and looked at Eudeon. "We have spent the last four centuries traveling like this, for days at a time, from one mission to the next. One must find amusement on the way." He let loose with a stuttering cry.

"Dolphin," declared Tehama. "Uncanny."

"Most people cannot guess dolphin," said Eudeon.

"The Atlantean navy has trained pods."

"It is fun," said Eroch, "is it not? Discovering your companions' hidden talents?" He pushed himself up, the muscles of his arms defining themselves with the effort. "Alas, most of mine are suited to show only a very . . . *particular* sort of person. If you care to experience them, Phiaphara, you know where to find me." He patted the turf beside him. Phiaphara's cheeks flushed faintly. "Come on, Phia," said Tehama. "Let us leave this pig to wallow alone." They retired to a pair of cots set under a canvas canopy strung up among a small grove's trees, per Wa-Mizhan practice.

"I will take first watch," said Eudeon, rising up and bending his longbow—another gift from Midash—to string it taut.

"Would that I and Phiaphara could give you something *to* watch." Eroch chuckled.

"Master yourself, man," Noah said, without anger. "You stoke the fires of Tehama's ill will, and Phiaphara is just a girl."

"That girl is a woman," said the Naphil. "One I would never force to do anything she did not want, and all here know I *could*."

"Why antagonize her so?"

"On the contrary, I mean to entice her." Eroch looked over his shoulder to where the females rested, then met Noah's eyes. "Not everyone has the will to deny his natural passions until they wither and die inside him. In that, *you* are mightier than *me*. And if a battle cannot be won, why should I fight it?"

"Why fight it?" asked Noah. "Because your Creator and Master requests it of you."

Eroch shook his head. "I know you and Eudeon believe that, but I am my own master."

"Again, then master yourself." Noah turned toward his own bed—a mat of leaves covered with a cloak, its hood rolled up as a pillow—but paused. "So you know, my passions are not dead. I have simply tethered them. Sleep well."

"How can I sleep well when I sleep alone?" called Eroch after him, then promptly lay down and began snoring.

The next morning's riding set them upon a path that traced a wavering line upon a forested ridge. Below it were mist-filled valleys, tree canopies pushing through the drifting fog like islands. On the ridge, prey animals congregated around hilltop pools that sent leaping springs down slopes of swirling green stone and flakey blue crystal and shelves of colorful lichen clinging to it all. Retreat for these animals was close by; when the band of travelers passed, they scurried and scampered into the thick, tall-treed forest that pushed almost to the ridge's edge.

"I like these trees," said Eroch, steering his dragon mount alongside Phiaphara's and dangerously close to the steep slope leading down to the hidden valley. "Tall and erect, with enormous girth. They remind me of how *I* am most of the time."

Eudeon groaned. "Eroch . . ."

The other giant turned in his seat. "I refer to my spine, Eudeon. Another Naphil with such good posture you will be hard pressed to find. I very seldomly slouch."

"I am literally begging you for your silence," said Tehama. "Next time you open your misogynous mouth, a sincere part of me hopes Phia will put an arrow in it."

The younger woman kicked her dragon to speed up past Eroch's. "My arrow would be aimed at somewhere other than his mouth."

This elicited laughter from the heavily muscled giant, though Noah did not think she meant it in jest. He started to speak to change the subject—any subject—but Tehama beat him to it.

"Stop," Tehama said, reining in her elk. "See there." She pointed at a shape like a rough-hewn pillar just inside the shadows cast by the forest canopy.

"Someone has been here?" asked Phiaphara.

"Someone very disturbed, or who means to leave warning," the Naphil huntress answered. "It looks to be made of bones."

"There, another." Noah dropped to the ground and in a strong, practiced motion strung his bow.

"Outcasts." Eudeon's voice was quieter now.

"We have seen them mark their lands by worse means than this," said Noah.

"Bah. Whoever built this shabby thing did so long ago," said Eroch, dismounting his dragon. His tone was dismissive, but he gripped his great cudgel tightly. "The mortar has crumbled." He pulled a long bone from the tower and tapped it on his cudgel, knocking off chalky chunks that clung to it, and made a sound of disgust. "Odd. Some of it is still moist."

Noah, both in youth in Eden and in his travels as a missioner, had built a city's worth of altars through his years. The giant's two statements were incongruous. He wished to look for himself, but he had taken only a few steps before the desire evaporated in a chill of realization. His heart dropped so hard his teeth ached, and his eyes bounced to the shadows of the trees above them.

"Smell your hands, Eroch."

With an odd glance at Noah, the Naphil obliged. His nose wrinkled ridges about his eyes and forehead. "That," he said, "is a pile of sh—"

Pure reflex drove Noah to jump back as Eroch was enveloped by leathery wings and bony, jutting angles. A sharp, man-length beak, set at the end of a long and gangly neck, whipped down furiously. Eroch's pained roar echoes among the trees.

"Wyverns!" cried Tehama as another wide-winged shape swooped down from the canopy. Her elk's great antlers crashed back and forth, beating the beast off, but a third one targeted Phiaphara, who was not so fortunate. She screamed as it clutched at her cloak-clad shoulders with thin claws; writhing, she somehow avoided being impaled by the beak. Undeterred, the creature spread its sail-like wings and lifted Phiaphara from her mount's back, but not before the river dragon's thin jaws had torn a piece off the wyvern's left wing.

The wyvern's wings, neck, and beak would have been comically oversized compared to its hind legs, but for the fury with which it had attacked the girl, who struggled still. The wound the beast had suffered was not incapacitating, clearly, but it struggled momentarily to gain altitude as it headed to the ridge's edge, and Phiaphara's striving against its grip slowed it further. Again on reflex, Noah took his chance.

He sprinted past Tehama, who was in the process of loosing her quiver's contents into the creature that had attacked her. He ignored Eudeon in the corner of his eye, the other giant running to Eroch with an arrow nocked to his longbow. The wyvern's wide wingspan made a huge target, but a moving one and hardly unmissable. Noah leapt, fully outstretched, off the ridge.

He hit hard on the wyvern's back. The beast's body was all skin, bone, and muscle, with no fur or feathers to grab. Beating wings bucked him up once, then again, and he used the motion to propel himself forward. The creature's neck was too thick to wrap his arms around, so he clutched handfuls of the loose skin at the base of it and held on tight.

"Phiaphara!" Noah shouted over the wyvern's cries.

"Shoot it!" Phiaphara shouted back. She sounded more defiant than scared or pained. "I cannot reach my—augh!—my bow!"

"No!" Every flap of the wings threatened to knock out Noah's wind, so he spoke in breathless grunts. "If I kill it—we drop!"

"Then what do we do?"

"Just wait! Together—we are too heavy! Do not—allow it—to let you go!"

Over the wyvern's elongated head, the swells of treetops rose up. The beast was big, but it was losing height even as it flew away from the forested ridge. The mists were no longer a field of solid grey; now Noah could see them move and swirl, though still as opaque up close as from a distance.

The wyvern's flight wavered as it approached the tops of the valley's canopy. "Get—ready!" yelled Noah.

The beast tried its best to slow itself, opening its wings and straightening to vertical before it broke through the canopy. Noah slid off, drawing his bow and firing an arrow as soon as his feet hit solid wood. It flew true, burying into the base of the wyvern's neck. It released Phiaphara, or Phiaphara released it—Noah could not tell—but either way, she fell through a mass of leaves and thin branches and out of his sight.

The wyvern's size worked against it as it tried to take flight within the foliage. Its thrashing set leaves falling in flurries, and through them Noah did not see the arrow Phiaphara fired from below until it was lodged in the wyvern's thorax.

Noah shot again. Screeching, the wyvern crashed downward and disappeared into the mists. Noah put his bow at his back and began climbing down. Obviously Phiaphara had been well enough to use her weapon, and he prayed that the wyvern's fall had not changed that for the worse.

He found Phiaphara upon a thick limb, halfway around the tree with her back against its bole. She was breathing hard, eyes closed, one white-knuckled hand around a branch beside her and the other securing the bow and quiver upon her lap. Her eyes opened and locked with Noah's. Slowly, and from a mix of emotions he was too exhausted to identify, his mouth curled into a smile.

"Man," Noah said, "was not meant to fly."

Phiaphara leaned her head against the tree and grinned. "Woman managed it rather well."

◂ CHAPTER 35 ▸

Phiaphara's grin turned to a grimace. She sucked in a breath through closed teeth and put her fingers to her shoulder.

"May I see?" asked Noah. Phiaphara nodded. She unclasped her cloak, tattered where the wyvern's claws had gripped it, and put it over her bow, then pulled the neck of her tunic down over her shoulder. Angry red streaks marked her skin, but no blood had been drawn. The other shoulder had been protected by the leather straps of her satchel and quiver, now rent and nearly torn through.

"It could have been much worse," reassured Noah.

"I cannot believe it wasn't," said Phiaphara, looking down at the sea of mist. Nothing was visible, but the rasping cries of the wounded wyvern drifted up to them. She straightened quickly, shutting her eyes. "My hand is trembling. Why am I trembling?"

"The body responds in such a way after an experience like that." Between both of his, Noah pressed her hand still. "Or if you have a bad aversion to heights, which I suspect you do. It will pass."

"When it does, can we get back to the others?" asked the young woman. "I do not care to be here any longer than I need be."

"We cannot, I fear." At this, Phiaphara's eyes shot open. "Night is about to fall," explained Noah. "If the climb up to the ridge is possible at all, it would not be in the dark. And when morning comes, the mists will be at their thickest, and we would be most at the mercy of whatever predators lurk below. We need to wait until the sun burns off all the mist it can."

"So we are to spend the night in this tree?"

Noah gave her a single nod.

"But if I fall asleep I'll fall!"

"I promise you will not." Crouching on the large branch and careful not to jostle Phiaphara, he shrugged off his cloak. He tied an edge of the cloak to the branch she gripped at their side, then passed the other edge below them and secured it to two more sturdy branches.

"Can we trust it to hold fast?"

Noah reached to the bow at his back. "I can pin it with arrows to make sure."

"No," said Phiaphara. "Even then I will not sleep."

The quiet noise of the forest was broken by a chorus of unseen howls and snarls. The wyvern shrieked, but its cry was cut short by the sounds of tooth and claw on flesh. "And *that* is not helping matters," Phiaphara whispered.

"Phiaphara," said Noah gently. "I have spent more nights in trees like this than you have spent alive. I will not fall."

"Then don't let me, either," she said, almost pleading. He pursed his lips, gauging his boundaries and how firmly he need apply them in this particular instance. He placed his bow and quiver in the cloak below. "Lean forward," he said. Nimbly, Noah climbed into the branches above Phiaphara and lowered himself behind her. "Lie back upon me and sleep, and I will keep watch." His hands hovered awkwardly over her abdomen; she took them in hers and wrapped his arms tight around her. "Rest. All will be well."

Phiaphara shifted slightly. "How can you be so confident about it?" she quietly asked.

"About what?"

"All of this. The death around us. The constant danger."

"You seem to have no shortage of confidence yourself, especially for one so young."

"Seem." Her exhalation could have been a laugh. "What I mean is, Eroch is possessed of strength beyond even most giants. Eudeon is a giant, too, and Tehama is like a goddess of the woods, and all of them are part of an angel-blooded family that rules the most powerful land on earth. You, and Midash too—you are just a man."

"And both proud of our bloodlines as well," said Noah, more defensively than he intended.

"But still as human as any other."

"Humans," said Noah, "yes, but ones who believe in a Creator that has a purpose for his creatures. I do not believe mine has been accomplished yet."

"So . . . faith in a god. Most have that, yet lack your assurance."

"Not a god. The God."

"The one you speak to in your prayers. Always the same one?"

"Yes." Noah had not realized she listened to his prayers.

Phiaphara quieted. A few seconds passed, and Noah prepared himself for a sleepless night's watch, but she spoke again.

"Is it not like speaking to a hound, or a horse?"

"What? Praying?"

"Yes. I mean no offense," Phiaphara said. "I only wonder. My cat is trained; I tell it what I wish, and if the thing is simple she will perform it. Perhaps your words, if you are skilled, can result in the desired outcome, but the conversation is still one way, is it not? Does he speak to you?"

"He has. In His words." Noah pulled one hand away, and Phiaphara tightened her grip on his other. He pulled a copy of the toledoths—thin vellum, folded twice—from his belt and held it where she could see.

"It isn't much."

"Perhaps one day He will add to it. Keep it. Read it." He closed her hand around it. "But for now, sleep."

Bright moonlight filtered through the canopy, painting the leaves around Noah and the girl slumbering in his arms; what passed in shafts through the trees was swallowed into the swirling grey below them. Faint, violent noises from all around—rips and tears, guttural sounds made by hungry bestial throats—made wakefulness easy for Noah. A sudden shriek of an animal in its death throes caused Phiaphara to stop breathing in the rhythm of sleep. Noah felt her tense up, awakened.

"Back to dreams, child," said Noah.

"I am not your child," murmured Phiaphara, relaxing her head on Noah's chest and already half-asleep again. "You are not my father."

⟨ CHAPTER 36 ⟩

Night passed into quiet morning, and one by one the nocturnal hunters that prowled and predated below Noah and sleeping Phiaphara crawled back into their hidden holes. The rising sun thinned the mists, turning them to dreamlike spiderwebs drifting among the trees. Noah doubted that the mists would dissipate entirely, even after the sun passed its midday zenith; as they were now, they would not impede movement through the woods much beyond what undergrowth and rough roots would anyway, and he could not allow himself and his companion to be caught on the forest floor at nightfall. Now was the time to move, so move they must.

"Phiaphara," Noah whispered, and he hoped the dreams he disturbed were peaceful. She stirred.

"Is it time?" She sat up slowly, leaning forward until she could peer down through the branches to the ground barely visible. She grabbed back at Noah's arm and drew a long breath.

"You can do this," said Noah.

"I know," she answered. "I will go first."

"Let me take your bow and cloak," Noah offered. "Just worry about the climb." She nodded her assent. Carefully she began to make her way down. As she did, Noah gathered their weapons and gear to himself and descended behind her, his maneuvering among the branches stretching arms, legs, and back stiff from the long night's watch.

The drop to the ground from the lowest limb was longer than he liked, but a cushion of damp detritus broke his fall and nothing else. Phiaphara appeared fine, too, brushing leaves and moss off a short tunic and leather trousers that fit her form well. Noah blinked, noticing that he noticed such a thing and being rather surprised at it. He moved his eyes from her and took inventory of their surroundings. Green grew upon green; vines and mosses carpeted and climbed upon every surface. Shelves of fungi that wrapped around the bases of the trees might have shown ianthine, crimson, or honey hues in the daylight, but in the mists and shadows they were the color of bruises and rust.

"Come, Noah, don't leave me naked over here."

Again Noah startled. He met her stare and outstretched hand with a half-furrowed brow.

"My bow and quiver. I do not wish to be caught unarmed in these woods." He nodded and handed her gear to her. "Thank you," she said. "For the night. For not letting me fall."

"Of course. I need you with me," replied Noah. "If we are to get out of here unharmed," he added too quickly— or perhaps he paused too long.

"Then let us waste no time in doing so," said Phiaphara, pointing. "This way?"

"This way." Noah corrected her course with his own finger. "Arrows out," he prompted, and off they started.

For sheer size, the architecture of the forest rivaled anything man-made that Noah had ever seen, with massive, looping roots and branches wide as bridges. The world beneath the canopy was lush and verdant with plant life, but also dark with decay, both of those a function of the perpetual wetness provided by the near-constant mists. Noah and Phiaphara endeavored to move quietly through it, though the droning of uncountable insects that filled the air from every direction drowned out any sound they might have made while they went. Undergrowth erupted wherever trees, so big around their trunks seemed more like walls than pillars, gave it room to. It slowed Noah and Phiaphara, but they dared not try and follow a game trail; both of them were well aware that prey in a place like this were likely bigger than they, and the predators more so.

They moved through the trees with as much care and haste as they could muster. The going was hard, the air humid and hot. Noah took note of the sun's position every time they passed under an opening in the canopy, which was less often than he wished. He was confident in their direction, but the forest showed no sign of ending. Four centuries and four-score years had not much sapped his stamina, but his breathing began to become labored and his quiver grew heavier against his sweat-soaked tunic. Phiaphara, young and fit as she was, seemed to be struggling more too. They could not afford to rest, but then again, the time quickly approached when they could not afford not to.

The underbrush thickened, and the noises of the forest changed. Noah slowed and motioned to Phiaphara to keep quiet. A faint chorus of windy bellowing, unmistakably animalistic, broke through the perpetual hum and chirp of the local entomological varieties. They crept to the edge of the thick ferns and fronds that blocked the source of the new sounds from view. Noah peered through a tangle of verge and grinned. He turned back to Phiaphara. "How would you like to ride out of here?"

He clambered up a gnarled trunk and beckoned Phiaphara to follow, stopping just high enough for both of them to escape the press of the thick understory, but not so far up as to make her nervous. He did not bother pointing out the beasts, for she could not help but see them: crested dragons, an entire herd, clustered around a long pool, drinking at the edge. For a few minutes, they watched the dragons, some wading to where bright green flowered plants floated on the surface to scoop them into broad, flat mouths and others pulling at branches hanging above the pool, stripping them of round yellow fruit, sometimes rising on hind limbs. Several stood watchfully beside their young, small compared to their elders but still the size of a lion or a drake.

"How in the world can we capture one?" asked Phiaphara.

"Animals are driven by two things: a drive to eat, and a drive to mate." Noah flushed when the words left his mouth, but he hoped the mottled shadows on his face hid the fact. "The latter comes only so often, and we certainly have no means to exploit it, so we must use the former." He pointed at the nearest fruit tree, as yet untouched by hungry dragons. "Can you gather as much as you are able?"

"I can."

"We will also need rope of some kind, long and strong, if you would prefer a task with less climbing." Noah wished not to seem patriarchal to the girl—"Woman," he corrected himself—but he also knew what needed to be done.

"No, I can do it," Phiaphara said. "I know not how to make rope."

"To work, then. Bow ready, always. There are reasons even dragons keep watch here."

Quietly Phiaphara dropped from the tree and set about her task. The dragons seemed to ignore her; when she was sure of it, she began to work more quickly, plucking

the low-hanging fruit and making the beginnings of
a pile on her outstretched cloak. Noah admired her
industry, but only for a moment, since he had much
to do as well. Vines hung all around, but for a rope
meant to harness a dragon, he needed to find something
tougher, fibrous, perhaps dead but not rotten. He did not
intend to put distance between himself and the young
huntress, but plants grew where they grew, and he soon
became obliged to search deeper into the forest. A few
tall reeds looked promising, but clusters of sharp leaves
at their bases turned him away. A woodbine-wrapped
trunk caught his eye; the tree was unfamiliar to Noah,
but it struck him as a type of willow, with broad nodes
ending in thin, shooting branches. Perhaps their bark
would prove good material, even without means to boil
it or time to dry. Bending a branch down toward him, he
peeled the outer bark away, indeed finding an inner layer
suitable for his needs. Thanking the Creator, he pulled
himself up to the nearest copse, unsheathed his knife,
and began to cut.

The work was mindless, requiring effort, but not
focus. When a pile of branches had grown below him,
he paused to rest. He was glad he had found a cordage
source with a vantage point: there was the herd, thus far
unmolested and surely the more docile for it, and there
was Phiaphara, having stripped her tree near bare of fruit
now piled high.

A motion in the understory caught the edge of his
vision and froze him still. He had been a woodsman
for far too long to question if he had merely imagined
it. Something was stalking toward Phiaphara, dark and
hard to follow, but certainly there. His eyes darted to
her, climbing down with another armful to add to the

fruit that had begun to attract the looks of the closest dragons. He almost shouted, but a cry might cause the crested dragons to panic and disperse, uncaring of what or who they might trample in a retreat. The furtive creature moved faster, barely setting ferns rustling. There was no doubt where it was heading: Phiaphara.

"Blood and death," cursed Noah, and a fiery rage lit in his chest. He dropped from the tree, forgetting the willow and nocking an arrow at full speed, ignoring branches that cut his face and whipped his shoulders.

Now on the ground, he had lost sight of either the beast or Phiaphara. If he was not too late—and this was the only outcome he would countenance—he would burst from the undergrowth in time for a clear shot. If he was—if the predator's hunt was successful . . . He refused to form a clear plan of action on the subject, but by Abel's broken head, he felt sure he would be brutal beyond what his conscience could bear, even to an animal.

As he burst from the underbrush into the clearing, another thought struck him. The creature moved silently; he did not. If Phiaphara was at all as wary as she ought to be, as he warned her to be, she might fire at him before she could know to stay her hand. Noah accepted it. As long as he could fire faster, fast enough to protect her, he would be satisfied. Part of his comfort came from having lived a useful life, to his fellow man and his Creator, if not yet an overly long one; part of it, though—most of it, perhaps—was her.

What a strange feeling.

Now reflexes overtook conscious thought. His vision narrowed to his target as it erupted from the wall of green behind the young huntress and devoured the final distance between it and her. Phiaphara's eyes, wide and white, swung in Noah's direction, rather than to the long, dark shape with open jaws that helped Noah see just where he needed to place an arrow behind them. He let his arrow loose, and Phiaphara did, too, to her great credit. He shut his eyes, wondering how an arrow's head would feel as it pierced his flesh. Balling up in the hope of protecting vital targets, he hit the ground hard. The arrow struck like a battering ram to his lower back, above his hip. It felt oddly blunt, when naturally Noah had expected a sharp sensation. It added a surprising amount of force to his forward motion, and he tumbled into the pool. The pain from the wound hadn't come yet; he could not even yet tell precisely where the arrow had hit him. Ah, there it was, but it remained quite dull, although . . . How *had* the blow come from behind him? That made no sense. Another second passed. He sat up and wiped wet hair from his face.

"Noah!"

Phiaphara splashed though ankle-deep water toward him. She leaned to him and pulled him to his feet, and he found that he needed little of her help to stand. "Are you alright?" she asked.

Noah regained himself and looked around, unsure yet of the answer. His shot had been true, the shaft of his arrow buried in the neck of an unmoving beast that seemed as if a crocodile had taken a wolfhound's form. Phiaphara was looking past his shoulder with a furrowed brow. Noah turned and, wondering, saw another of the same kind of creature, scaled and black green, with two sharp spines sticking out from its slumped shoulders and an arrow protruding from its left eye.

"That thing came out right behind you," said Phiaphara, trembling. "I was afraid I would hit you, then it knocked you into the water." Not knowing what else to do, he pulled her to his chest.

"Deep breaths," he told her, and himself as well. "Basilisks hunt in pairs. The danger is passed."

"Twice in two days I cannot stop shaking," said Phiaphara, trying to hide her voice's wavering. "Is life always this exciting with you, Noah?"

"I had not thought it was," he replied. "Perhaps it is you making it so." Even while he held her, his gaze swept from carcass to carcass, looking for any movement, but the rest of his senses were fully engaged in appreciating Phiaphara's closeness.

A crested dragon had approached Phiaphara's pile of fruit. It nosed at the dead creature beside it, then, apparently satisfied, nonchalantly looked their way and began to eat.

Noah separated from Phiaphara, though he did not want to. The bait she had collected was ample, but it would not last long with a beast that size. "Come with me," he said, taking her by the hand. "Let me teach you how to make rope."

‹ CHAPTER 37 ›

The ropemaking went quickly, strips of wood becoming cord as soon as they passed through Noah's fingers. He did teach her, as he promised, but Phiaphara insisted that her unpracticed hands must not slow their progress, so she contented herself with watching. Soon two lengths of rope were coiled on the ground. Noah bid Phiaphara hold them and follow him to where three dragons leisurely fed from the fruit she had piled upon her cloak. Noah circled behind the beasts to pick from a branch she had not touched, then approached the closest dragon and offered it the fruit in his hands. It snorted and tossed its head as if Noah were a bothersome insect, so he moved to the next beast. This one bent its neck to eat, and with a few whispered words from the missioner, it was Noah's. The change in the dragon's demeanor had been near immediate; Phiaphara had never seen anything like it, neither in Mizraim or with the Wa-Mizhan, and had she not witnessed the taming for herself, she would not have believed it possible.

Noah beckoned her over, taking a loop of rope from her and securing it around the dragon's curved crest.

"The crest is a sensitive structure," Noah explained. "Not so much that a rope will cause it pain, but the dragon will be more responsive to the reins." Another whisper, a gentle hand on a massive scaled haunch, another offering of fruit, and the animal crouched down. He threw his cloak up and over its broad back. "Climb aboard?" he asked Phiaphara. For anyone else, she would have hesitated. For Noah, she stepped into his cupped and waiting hands and, with his help, took her seat upon a newly tamed dragon.

Like that, they were on their way. Bows, bags, and quivers hung at either of the dragon's sides from the second length of rope. Thus freed from the burdens at their backs, Phiaphara could hold Noah secure around the waist as he sped their mount through the jungle. They soon made up in distance for the time they delayed in making the rope and taming the dragon, both far shorter than Phiaphara had anticipated, and, though the spread cloaks hardly proved the most comfortable saddles, riding was far more restful than another dangerous day of pressing through roots and underbrush.

"The dragon will not rest the night with us, so far from its herd," said Noah. "It will certainly be gone when we wake, so we must go as far as we can while we may."

Barely listening, Phiaphara kept her arms wrapped around Noah, much like he had held her the night before in the tree. Then, because of her fear, she had not wanted him to let her go. Now her fear was gone, replaced by something she wished not yet to name, something that just as strongly told *her* to not let *him* go. She rested her head on his back and watched the woods speed by.

The forest thinned and the ground rose. Predators could move more quickly in terrain like this, but ones big enough to take a dragon down would be easy to spot among the sparse trees. Of more concern to Noah were signs of outcast communities, bandits and the like, who were savvy enough to hide themselves until spears and arrows were already flying, but he saw none.

After a time, Phiaphara pointed to their right, to a streak of rushes drawing a golden line under the horizon, toward which the sun had already dropped near. "A river bank?" she suggested. "A spring?"

Their dragon needed little coaxing to veer over, and Noah was suddenly struck by the need to drink and rest that his zeal to escape the forest had suppressed. A spring it was indeed, cold and briskly flowing. Noah let the beast drink its fill, then prodded it to follow the water to a suitable place for him and Phiaphara to make camp. In short order they found one, at a pool bordered in broad, flat stone. The pool—not the spring's source, merely a widening on its way—overflowed on its north side, sending water trickling down a slope that was worn in a manner that gave the stone itself a flowing quality.

"Let us rest for the night here," said Noah over his shoulder. "There is water, obviously, and we can eat the mace-reeds." Phiaphara voiced her agreement. He slid from the dragon's back and helped the young huntress down; the animal paused long enough for them to retrieve their things, including the harness rope, then loped away. It turned once at a bow shot's distance to give a trumpet-like call as if in farewell, then was lost from sight.

The relative safety of their dragonback respite thus ended, Noah and Phiaphara rearmed themselves. "I will gather fuel," said Phiaphara.

"Wait," said Noah, grabbing her hand before he had realized he had done it. He thought she would pull it away, but instead she let it be and stepped closer. "Zuthi, outcasts, whatever nocturnal hunters live here . . . we ought not build a fire. It may draw far worse than moths to us."

"Very well. But you, Noah of Eden," she said, stabbing a finger at his chest, "had better teach me how to eat mace-reeds, because I never have." Her eyes twinkled, and

Noah's head momentarily felt as if he had drunk one too many cups of wine.

"As long as you, Phiaphara of Mizraim," he replied, gesturing to the nearest of dozens of reed patches that bordered the pool, "promise to leave some for me."

"Hello there!" A man's clear voice rang out below them, from the foot of the flowing slope. By the time Noah freed his bow, Phiaphara already had hers in hand. Two heads came into view, both smiling broadly, neither seeming concerned that a pair of armed strangers stared at them with arrows nocked.

"Can we come up?" asked the taller one, himself with a longbow and quiver at his back. "We have food better than reeds for you, Noah."

Noah hoped his furrowed brow was answer enough to Phiaphara's questioning glance: he did not know these men. "How do you know my name?"

The shorter man, sheathed sword at his side, answered as he advanced. "Long have you been known to us, Noah. We serve the same master."

"You are from Atlantis?" Phiaphara called.

Both men laughed. "Is Atlantis master of you?" asked the swordsman. "Of either of you, Phiaphara? I think not."

"Light a fire," said the other. "Nothing will happen to you tonight, but that you will sleep with fuller stomachs than you anticipated."

Noah made no move to do what the man bid, although he sensed no treachery. Beside him, Phiaphara remained tense. "You know our names," said Noah. "What are yours?"

"In your tongue, I am Aia," said the bowman. "He is Colselph." The other man inclined his head. Both of them walked with sure steps up the wet stone as if it were a paved path.

"In *our* tongue?" Phiaphara kept her tone cold, but she lowered her bow. "There is but one tongue of man."

"Yes," said Aia.

"Shall we eat?" asked Colselph, holding up a full-looking bag with one hand.

Not waiting for an answer, the two men set about preparing a meal, mixing dry beans and spices and pastes in several shallow bowls they took from the bag. Noah saw no better course of action than to gather fuel for the fire. He went quick about the task. Phiaphara worked with him, staying close. Aia and Colselph kept their distance, which Noah appreciated; the young woman's discomfort was not hidden.

"I do not trust them," she whispered.

"All will be fine," answered Noah, almost entirely certain that were true. "Stay close to me."

"I plan to," said Phiaphara. A thrill danced across Noah's chest unbidden. He felt a jealousy well up in him, a feeling decades upon decades absent. Striking his flint, he caught a spark to the kindling they had gathered and carefully coaxed it into a flame, then he stood to face the strangers.

"We would know your intentions," he called. "Put us at ease."

"To feed you and set you on your way," said Aia.

"But you worry still," said Colselph, fixing a steady stare on Phiaphara. "Why?"

A strange feeling struck Noah, a desire for complete transparency in his every word; in that moment, his greatest wish was for Phiaphara to answer the man's question as honestly and entirely as she was able.

"Because you might want a fire as a beacon to draw your fellows," she said, "or perhaps you plan harm to us, to Noah, and I will suffer the loss of yet another person I care about." She seemed surprised at her own words. "Or perhaps you want to take by force what does not belong to you." Her voice cracked.

Colselph held a palm out for her to stop. "My lady, you have nothing we desire, including your womanhood, which you do right to guard." The plainness of his speech cleaned the scandal from what he said.

"And do you trust us, Noah?" asked Aia.

"I do."

"Good," said Colselph. "We are worthy of it."

"Now let us eat," said Aia. "These bodies have become hungry."

Whether the nature of the food or the satisfaction of a satiated hunger, Noah could not recall a meal he so enjoyed. The two other men provided simple, substantial conversation as pleasant as the meal, and he was gratified to see Phiaphara relaxing as it went. As she did, her eyes rested more frequently on Aia's bow; after she had emptied her bowl, the archer asked, "Would you like to see it?"

She nodded yes, and Aia handed her the weapon. Noah ran his eyes along the bow as Phiaphara did her fingers. It was simple, unadorned, and the wood looked to be untreated except for whatever tools had shaped and smoothed it, but never had Noah seen a more beautiful weapon. Compared to it, the filigree and gems on the bow Midash had given him seemed like gaudy baubles masking a shoddy mimicry of the real, perfected version that Phiaphara held. Noah glanced to the sheathed sword rested upon Colselph's crossed legs. By the hilt alone, he could tell that it too was an exemplar of its kind, and he almost wished the group right then to be attacked by some beast, only that he might see the sword freed from its scabbard and in action.

"You approve?" asked Aia after a few moments, amusement on his face.

"It is . . . extraordinary."

"Yes, it is that."

"Phiaphara is an excellent shot," said Noah, feeling a strong urge to justify her momentary possession of such a weapon before its owner decided she was unworthy to touch it any longer. "She put an arrow through the eye of a charging basilisk at a full run." Phiaphara blushed.

"Very impressive," said Aia to the young woman. "Please, show me. No, try out mine."

She might not have jumped at the chance, but she certainly rose quickly. While Aia quietly instructed her on the finer distinctions between her shorter hunting bow and his longbow, Colselph leaned to Noah. "Are you finished with that rope?" he asked, gesturing to the discarded cords they had removed from the dragon.

"Yes, help yourself."

"Thank you." Colselph took an end and began making a tight spiral around it on the ground until he had a round mat about the width of a man's shoulders. He continued spiraling the rope to make another layer, going outer to inner, then made yet another, inner to outer. When he reached the edge, he secured the three layers together with two vertical loops and two more horizontal. The entire effort had taken only a minute or two, and at the end of it, Colselph had made a thick, round, circular target divided into nine sections by the intersecting loops that held it together.

"Shall you hold it," he asked Noah, "or shall I?"

"I said she was an excellent shot," Noah replied, gripping the knot of rope that Colselph had tied on the final end for a handle and extending his arm, seeing how far away from his body he could hold it.

Colselph smiled. "Never one to lack faith."

"Come, Noah," said Aia, seeing the ready target. "Phiaphara, since the bow is new to you, let us start at an easy distance." Phiaphara took a shooting stance, nocking one of her own arrows and waiting for Noah to position himself. He had planned on standing ten paces or so away, but Aia took him by his shoulders and quietly directed him to a spot no more than a man's length from where Phiaphara stood.

"An easy distance," the archer said, smiling. Noah and Phiaphara shared a glance, but something about these strangers rebuffed second-guessing, so Noah raised the target high and Phiaphara drew.

"Center square," said Aia. Phiaphara fired. The arrow hit dead center, piercing the rope layers to the very end of the fletchings.

Colselph clapped. "Good!" said Aia. "Now aim just to the right. Stay there, Noah." Though a child could hardly have missed at such a short distance, Phiaphara still practiced good technique, breathing evenly and aiming her second arrow carefully. Again, it found its mark precisely.

"Now the left," said Aia, "but this time, after you aim your arrow, close your eyes. Keep them closed and fire when I tell you."

The left of the target was the side closest to Noah's body, so these instructions made him slightly nervous, but as long as Phiaphara remained steady after she aimed—and he knew she would—he had nothing to fear. She raised her bow, focused, and shut her eyes.

"Keep them closed," said Aia again, and as he did, Colselph, finger to his lips, came up to Noah. Silently he beckoned him to walk straight backward. With the other man's help he did so, not wavering even a step to either side, until he stood perhaps twenty times further away from Phiaphara than he had before. Colselph stopped him with a hand on his back and nodded to Aia.

"Fire!" said the archer.

Phiaphara did. Her arrow flew fast and straight and, at this further distance, wildly to left of Noah. It skipped off the rocks by the pool and disappeared into the reeds across the water.

"What was the purpose of that?" asked Phiaphara, unable to keep the irritation out of her voice. She had opened her eyes at the crack of the arrow on stone, soon enough to see it vanish beyond finding. Noah wondered the same thing. He looked at Colselph for an explanation.

"The time will soon come," said the man, "when your Master, Noah, would have you understand this: when one's aim is true to center, the distance traveled does not matter." They walked together to where Aia and Phiaphara stood, the latter still with the shadow of a scowl on her face. "If one's aim is off, however, things are different. You have seen it matters little if the end comes soon."

"But if the end is far away," continued Aia, taking his longbow back, "even the least deviation will lead to utter failure."

"This is true for the distance to an arrow's target," said Colselph, "and it is true for the length of a man's life. Remember our words when you hear those of One far greater than us."

"You had me waste an arrow so you could tell a riddle?" asked Phiaphara.

"Yes, quite so," answered Aia, "but I will make it right. Here, take these." He loosened his quiver and handed it to Phiaphara, keeping a single arrow—silver tip, ivory-colored wood shaft, white feathered fletchings—for himself. "I only need the one." The young woman could offer no objection.

"Now, did we mention that we have bedrolls?" asked Colselph. "Among the supplies we left below, with our horses. Did I mention we have horses? Phiaphara, will you assist me?"

"You happened to bring more than two bedrolls into the wilderness?" asked Phiaphara.

"No, just the two," the swordsman said. "But we will not be sleeping tonight."

Phiaphara looked at Noah. "Better than a tree," he said.

"We can take the easy path down," said Aia.

Colselph piled the bowls and motioned Noah to join him. They walked to the pool's edge, where the other man bent down and began washing out the dishes.

"Mankind was created, Noah," said Colselph, "with the second-most powerful force in the universe: free will. The problem is that it was placed inside a weak vessel: flesh. Since Adam and Eve and that primal sin, that vessel is cracked, and the longer one resides inside the other, the greater the likelihood of it breaking. She does not understand—not fully. You must."

"I think I do," said Noah.

"I think you will." Colselph looked up and met Noah's eyes. "Things are about to change, Noah. The workings of the world are about to change, perhaps for better, perhaps for worse. All depends on you."

"Me, myself?"

Colselph laughed. "Mankind. You are not that important—not yet, and perhaps never, I pray. Although some change does depend on you ... and perhaps another person besides." He looked over Noah's shoulder at the backlit forms of Aia and Phiaphara cresting the sloping edge of the rocks. Noah turned to see them; Phiaphara smiled.

"I wish you to know, Noah," added Colselph. "We are not alike to those others you knew long ago."

"I know."

"Good." His tone suggested that he was personally gratified to hear Noah say it. "Aia and I will keep watch. Rest now. You and she have a hard road still ahead."

The advice proved easy to follow; Noah fell asleep the moment he lay down.

‹ CHAPTER 38 ›

Noah awoke from a dreamless sleep to the quiet of a new morning. The rocks upon which they had made their beds were too high up for the mist to be thick there; instead, it drifted in wisps over the surface of the pool. He watched until he heard Phiaphara stir in the bedroll across the dying fire from him. He sat up and looked around for Aia and Colselph, seeing no sign of them, but he did see provisions set out, as well as two three-toed horses saddled and drinking at the water's edge. Beside the food was a leather cylinder, of the kind used to protect parchment from the mists that rose every morning, ever threatening to ruin a careless traveler's unprotected documents or maps. Indeed, a map was inside. Noah had drafted many of his own, doing so with a simplicity that he believed imparted clarity, but this one was detailed beyond any skill he could recall ever seeing. It spanned the vast lands from Atlantis to the edge of Havilah, with features depicted in their natural hues, interrupted by place-name script and one dotted line that began with "follow this," all done by a sure hand in a bold orange ochre.

"Where are we?" asked Phiaphara.

Noah scanned the map. "Here." He placed his finger on the letter at the beginning of the marked line. "It appears this route is meant for us."

Phiaphara looked for herself. With a nod, she confirmed her agreement. "It is very exact," she said. Noah concurred. Although the line ended in Atlantis, it did not take a straight path, meandering in places and snaking around spots where a direct route seemed better.

"It seems circuitous. We need speed," said Phiaphara, not emphatically.

"The horses will provide that," answered Noah. "I would trust Aia and Colselph still. If they marked this path for us, they must have done so with good reason."

"They were . . . certainly perceptive," said Phiaphara, and Noah wondered what she and Aia might have discussed on last night's errand to the horses.

"No time to lose, then. To Atlantis?"

"To Atlantis."

Rumination on the words of Aia and Colselph kept Noah taciturn at the journey's start. Phiaphara stayed quiet, too, and Noah surmised it was for much the same reason, so her midmorning question was almost expected.

"Do you really believe that the Creator will cut short the lives of men?"

"If it pleases Him," he answered.

"Do you not think that . . . inhuman?"

"Inhuman? Men do that very thing to other men already."

"Yes, they do." Noah could hear the frown in her tone. "And we call it murder and banish those who do it."

"So, if our Creator, Who gives all life to begin with, did such a thing," said Noah, "for reasons He will not share or we would not comprehend, ought we banish Him?"

"Not I," Phiaphara said. "Some might."

Noah's smile mimicked mirth, but the truth of what Phiaphara said—a truth he had seen played out— allowed no humor in his eyes. "Some do already, from their lives and minds. And if no God, there is no author of conscience, no rules to follow for how one acts toward his fellow man, no boundaries one must remain inside. I would wager that whatever even now drives Zuthi traces its roots to that very calculus. That is precisely why God would cut short the lifespan of men, if I understand last night's scene correctly. By rejecting Him, we will have brought such a judgment upon ourselves." He sighed. "Once again, humankind brings trouble upon this world, and the consequence will be Elohim's mercy."

"Trouble. Eve, you mean? Her temptation?" she asked him.

"Just so. Midash would be proud that you remember what he told you."

"I remember it from you, actually." In reality, Noah knew perfectly well that all three of the missioners— himself, Eudeon, Midash—had talked often on such topics, but it gave him pleasure to have the credit from her. She caught his eye with a sideways glance.

"And what do you mean by judgment being mercy?" asked Phiaphara.

"Just that. Eve and Adam brought death into the world, into their own bodies, and lost paradise because of it. It was a horrific thing to happen. Imagine this, though: they had stayed, eaten from the tree of eternal life, and became immortal in their sin. What might they have become? Who is strong enough to walk for an eternity without falling? Perhaps we have grown even weaker than they, and another cutting-short must be made."

"And you believe all this to be history, not mythology?"

"I do."

His young companion retreated into thought again. A few minutes later, she spoke. "Humanity may be the source of trouble, Noah, but we can be the source of good things too." She kicked her horse ahead. He watched her sinewy shoulders rise and fall with her animal's steps, watched the wisp of hair that had escaped her high bun to blow along the nape of her neck.

Good things.

Phiaphara's appetite for weighty conversation was satiated after that first day's conversation, but she felt a desire to remain the object of Noah's attention, else he retract into the guarded temple of his mind. In an attempt (successful, she thought) to do so, for three days they took turns asking one another questions about themselves. Phiaphara ran out of answers first—naturally, since Noah had done four centuries and half again more living than she, give or take a few years. Noah was free with his responses about himself, although they often turned to thoughts and musings about Elohim. She found it neither stifling nor imperious, although before she met Noah and his companions, she might have used both words to describe the God she had believed existed. In Mizraim, when a Creator was talked about, and if he were discussed at all, he was like an absent father who had sired children, then demanded them to run his household in a certain way, except he made no mechanism to punish disobedience to him or cruelty toward weaker siblings. In contrast, Noah talked about Him—Elohim—like He were a beloved friend. At first it induced pangs of near jealousy in Phiaphara, but as Noah spoke—of his observations of nature's workings, of various fortunate happenings he attributed to the Creator's intercession, of other people's moments of belief proving to be inflection points in lives that corrected their courses from ill to good—she found herself wishing to know Elohim as Noah did.

They came to a stretch of windswept plains devoid of vegetation except coarse, short grasses and tangles of plants
that clung close to the ground. The travel was slow here.
Vents and cracks forced them to pick their path carefully,
but outbursts of steam, erupting violently and quickly
blown away, made avoiding such pitfalls easy. Still, the
crossbacks and weaving became frustrating.

"Does this strike you as a good way to have directed
us?" asked Phiaphara.

"It strikes me," said Noah, "as a way that an army of
Zuthians would not be able to come."

"True enough," she said, and voiced no more
complaints.

When the sky took on twilight's palette, they found
a place to stay, making a camp in a shallow crevasse that
at least rose high enough to protect their standing horses
and let them light a fire. They ate together and talked
until full dark fell. Their fire dwindled to embers. Noah
knew he ought to drift to sleep, but he and Phiaphara sat
together instead, looking up at the band of sky between
the crevasse's edges, ribbons of green light flowing across
it in waves. Neither spoke, both in awe; the celestial
display was truly the most beautiful thing Noah had ever
seen, but even so, he kept taking his eyes from it to look
at her. She finally noticed him. "What is it?" she asked,
her smile just visible in the darkness. He was spared from
answering when she tilted her head to look behind him.
"What is *that*?"

Noah turned to see as well. They had not bothered
to follow the crevasse's floor as it sloped down. Now, as
his eyes followed it as far as they could, he saw that at
the curve of the earthen walls where the floor's course
disappeared from view, the rocks faintly glowed.

"Come on," said Phiaphara, rising and taking his hand. Past the curve the walls widened, the ground dove sharply, and Noah and Phiaphara stood at the edge of a pool lit up in blue-white as if the moon itself had descended to inhabit its waters. The water was deep, clear as crystal, everything within visible due to walls illuminated by the substance that coated them. The more Noah looked, the more he saw: chalky, flutelike columns rising up and tapering to rounded, hollow points that ended just under the surface; glowing, tubular strings of some sort of organism—plant? worm?—attached to the pool's sides, drifting and contracting lazily; tiny crabs with phosphorescent shells scuttling on hairlike legs almost too small to be visible. These he pointed out to Phiaphara, who watched them for a long while in amazement.

"Life persists," said Noah, mostly to himself. "Even dark and drowned, life persists."

A muffled rushing sound rolled around them. It was difficult to tell, but to Noah it seemed to come from beneath the water. "Back up," he cautioned Phiaphara. They both stepped a ways back from the pool's edge.

From the submerged columns erupted white streams of water straight upward, dispersing and widening when they rose high enough to be caught by the winds above them. Sheets of spray, then droplets, fell upon them. Phiaphara shouted in surprise; the water was warm, not scalding, Noah noted thankfully.

"Water from the sky!" said Phiaphara, loud enough to hear above the hiss of the eruptions. "Such a strange sensation!" She laughed.

"Strange indeed!" Noah could not help but laugh along.

"I like it!" She twirled, head thrown back. The thought crossed Noah's mind to warn her from the edge. He stopped himself. This woman was not his daughter or his ward. She was grown, she had agency and free will as much as he did, and she could be anything she wanted to be, even . . .

The outbursts of water subsided and stopped, then Phiaphara did as well. "Noah, you are *glowing!*"

He examined the backs of his wet hands; veins and creases outlined in the same blue-white as everything else around him. He looked back at her. "So are you!" The realization set her laughing again; the spurts began anew, and so did she.

Phiaphara capered and spun. Despite her invitation, Noah declined to join, but she knew he watched her. It pleased her to know his eyes were upon her, though. Hers caught him, too, when they could, his dampened tunic showing the outline of his shoulders and clinging to his chest.

She danced close to Noah just as another shower erupted and fell upon them both, wet and warm and heavy. Ducking her head, she pressed herself into Noah's chest without thinking. She felt as she had when she was a little girl sailing with her father, squealing and seeking his protection as the spray cascaded over the prow, but with the feeling came two thoughts that had crossed her mind before, but now were definite: first, that she was not a little girl anymore; and second, that this man was most certainly not her father.

Noah's strong arms pushed her away, but only just; his hands, however, gripped her firmly, as if he were afraid she might escape. With his eyes locked on to hers, she felt she could not, even if she had wanted to.

She did not want to.

The first time, their lips met only briefly before Noah pulled away.

"I know I am young," whispered Phiaphara, her mouth pressed into Noah's neck, "but I am old enough to know what I want."

Their second kiss lasted longer.

"We have each made vows," said Noah, after they emerged for air.

"I have made no vows to Tehama that I cannot break with no damage to my conscience."

"But I ha—" She pressed her mouth to his, interrupting his protest. He gently pulled her head away. "I have made no vows either, but . . ."

"Emzara. Eudeon told me."

"I need to tell her, though she cannot understand." Eyes closed, he rested his forehead on hers. "I promise, you will become mine. Please be patient."

She kissed him again, and he took it as an assent that she would be.

‹ CHAPTER 39 ›

Eventually, the beckon of sleep before another hard day of travel became stronger than Phiaphara's amative appeal. Noah took her hand and led her to the dying fire, where he held her until their clothes became dry enough not to ruin the fur lining the bedrolls.

"Will you cleave to me?" asked Phiaphara. She said it as a question, not an invitation.

"I will marry you first."

A part of Noah asked whose consents were needed beyond his and Phiaphara's to take her as his wife, in whose eyes but Elohim. Then again, how could he "leave his father and mother"—metaphorically, obviously—if they did not know? And Phiaphara . . . He wished not to doubt her feelings, fervently so; then again, how could he be sure that they would remain the same surrounded by the young men of Atlantis as in the wilderness alone with him? Those thoughts were easily chased away by more pleasant ones. He looked over at her one last time, closed his eyes as hers were already, and let sleep take him to such dreams he had not had in half a lifetime.

Two things powered the haste at which they traveled: the urgency of reaching the safe bastion of Atlantis, and the desire to be wed to one another, properly and truly. Hard days' rides imparted physical exhaustion that greatly helped Noah stave off any temptation to cross boundaries that would besmirch Phiaphara's honor when night fell, but seldom did they fall asleep without hands clasping one another's. Following the angels' map, they saw no Zuthian, and at last crossed into the lands of Nod and signs of civilization.

"A road, at last," exclaimed Phiaphara, spying a thread of white in the distance. "Where does it lead?"

"The seat of the southern lands of Nod is called Athan," said Noah, consulting their map, "so I imagine we cannot be far. And then to Atlantis, I pray."

They rode on with renewed vigor, buoyed by every new sighting of a silo, house, or plowed field, but they saw no people. If the outskirts were not abandoned entirely, whoever lived there stayed well hidden. At least, Noah thought, there were no indicators that Zuthi had come through, and the abandoned farms denoted warnings well heeded, so they continued on the road.

Athan had no walls. Its entrance was marked by a marble arch that was guarded by a line of Atlantean warriors, who met them with hard faces and spears and shields at the ready.

"You have been watched," said one.

"We are aware," answered Phiaphara, although Noah had not been.

"From whence have you come?"

"We were part of a group of emissaries sent from Atlantis and were separated from our group," said Noah. "We traveled with Eudeon, son of Samyaza, and Tehama and Eroch, children of Dyeus."

The soldiers exchanged looks and voiced murmurs. "That claim is verified easily enough," said their leader. "Follow me. You may keep your weapons, but do not draw them."

They obeyed. The soldier led them to a building that looked to have once been administrative, now repurposed as a base of operations, and bid them enter a windowless room with a single door. The couches inside looked comfortable, and they complied without complaint.

The door shut. With a sigh, Phiaphara relaxed into Noah, who put his arms around her. He closed his eyes, letting a sense of peace fill him and hoping Phiaphara— "My betrothed," he thought, with an intense spark of excitement—felt the same.

"Phiaphara!"

Noah's eyes snapped open as a woman in the garb of a Wa-Mizhan huntress burst into the room. Phiaphara pushed away from Noah, sitting up straight.

"Kiah!"

The woman answered her with a disapproving frown. "Tehama will be so pleased I found you." She glared at Noah. "Though perhaps not so much *how* I found you."

"Kiah, this is Noah, of Eden," said Phiaphara, uncowed by the other huntress's cold demeanor. "He traveled with me and Tehama and protected me when we were separated. He guarded me." Defiance tinged her tone. "He guarded *everything* about me."

Kiah's glare softened. "Well. Glad to hear it. Noah, I am Kiah, *beth* of the Wa-Mizhan, Tehama's second-in-command. I have been hoping both of you would appear. Tehama bid me listen for word of you."

"She returned, then?" asked Noah. "Eudeon too?"

Kiah nodded. "With that brutish giant as well, two days ago, just ahead of the Zuthians."

"They were here?"

"Not here. They sack farms and villages for food like a swarm of locusts, but only those that lie in the path between them and Atlantis, and those we warned with ample time to escape. Most of our forces amass in Atlantis waiting for them. Soldiers were left in this city on the chance any of scouts or envoys still unaccounted for appear. Few besides you have."

"They do not turn aside?" asked Noah.

"No," Kiah replied. "They aim for the heart of civilization, to kill it in a single great blow. They think Atlantis is weak because it values peace. They will soon discover how wrong they are."

The huntress assured Noah and Phiaphara that they were free to move about, and they gladly accepted her offer to lead them to where the soldiers had set up a commissary stocked with food left behind by citizens who had absconded from Athan. Much meat had been prepared that would have otherwise spoiled, but Noah found more than enough flatbreads, fruit, nuts, and hard cheeses to satisfy a palate from Eden. Phiaphara chose the same, and they sat down to take a meal with company other than themselves for the first time in days uncounted.

Noah's ears were pricked to overhear any news in the conversations of surrounding Atlantean soldiers, but his eyes were fixed to the face of Phiaphara. He tried to make his infatuation less overt when Kiah and two other Wa-Mizhan women sat to join them, asking them of tidings from Nod, little of which they could give. "We have been in the wilds as much as you," Kiah said.

"News!" A man in a soldier's cape and falconer's leathers strode into the room, bird perched upon his arm. He gave a small scroll to the warrior that stood up to meet him, who opened and read it before booming, "Move out!" In a flurry, tables were cleared and the place was emptied. Noah and the huntresses—did Phiaphara still count herself among them, he wondered?—joined the flow.

"What news, commander?" asked Kiah to the man who had received it.

"The Zuthians move slowly, but the path to Atlantis closes," he answered her. "We must return now. Soon enough, Athan will be safe, or else nowhere will be."

Troops poured out of the city in a rush onto the road north, Noah and Phiaphara with them. Kiah bid Phiaphara ride with the huntresses, so Noah did, too, an allowance no doubt due to Tehama's good report and bolstered by Phiaphara's confirmation of his conscientious treatment of her, though she left out (wisely, to Noah's mind) details of Aia's and Colselph's visit and their night at the glowing pool. They travelled hard, stopping in towns along the way; the days passed swiftly, aided by restful nights spent in empty dormitories and abandoned beds instead of under the stars. Huntresses and hidden scouts orbited the fast-moving column, advancing forward and reporting back, but none saw any part of the Zuthian hordes, and on the fourth day the bright walls of Atlantis appeared.

The relief that Noah felt upon seeing that white sculpted stone was quelled immediately when the war-camps came into view. A dark band extended along the entirety of Atlantis's great moat, thickest at the entrances to the gate-bridges, and curved around the city to either side into imperceptibility. Some of the raised banners, though, were Atlantean, and as the warriors around him continued to advance, he surmised that the forces were friendly.

Friends or no, they were stopped thrice before being allowed to pass over Wide Bridge into Atlantis. At each pause, ranks were exchanged and stations confirmed, and Noah loosed prayers like a flurry of arrows: of thanks, that they had reached the walls of Atlantis—of warriors and of stone—before the Zuthians did, and of supplication, that neither would be overwhelmed by the forces that would soon be upon them.

The flow of trade, usually robust and rapid on Wide Bridge, was the merest trickle, almost entirely smiths and leatherworkers selling services to soldiers. Here, Noah and Phiaphara stayed close. Their group moved slowly; rather than passing them as a unit, the guards at the gate were taking names of every individual and letting each through one at a time.

"Do we know that Tehama is even in the city?" asked Phiaphara.

"Everyone useful to this fight should be," replied Kiah. "Even the colleges at Armon have emptied it of the fruits of their labor and brought them here."

Inside the wall, Noah saw no one dressed in less than full military attire, though many were soldiers from elsewhere than Atlantis: spearmen in sharkleather and shell plate, giants clad in furs and iron, hooded archers in similar bearing and dress as the rangers and scouts of Eden, though Noah greatly doubted his grandfather would lend any martial aid to this endeavor, no matter how justifiable.

"Man of Eden!" called Kiah. A man in forest green trotted over; she pointed at Noah. "One of your country-men. Know you where your leaders are?"

"At the palaces of state, at the war council." He nodded at Noah, then ran back to where other lightly armored bowmen, all in various styles of appearance, conversed quietly.

"Good woodsmen, those," said Kiah, kicking her horse to a walk. "Come. If a council of war is being held, Tehama will be there." Noah caught Phiaphara's eye and smiled. His pulse quickened, and he hoped she had the same thought as he: in all likelihood, she would be meeting his family much sooner than anticipated.

The state palaces of Atlantis had worn the centuries well. The *bene Elohim* had had many faults, but poor workmanship was not among them. The small crowds filling the spaces between columns and statues were composed primarily of warriors from dozens of tribes and peoples, most in clusters of countrymen. A common foe and cause promoted some mingling, though; Noah guessed that some bloodlines there had not shared words since the generation of Adam's grandchildren.

"Come on," said Kiah. "Halls of dead stone do not impress me." She strode up stairs and past warriors as if she was the mistress of the place. "I am *beth* of the Wa-Mizhan. Let me through," she told the pair of Atlantean high guards at the door to the council chambers before they could ask. She was met with spears crossed before her.

"The council is closed."

Kiah opened her mouth to argue, thought better of it, and turned away.

"Do you want to try?" she asked Noah. He shook his head. The guards did not seem particularly persuadable.

"Very well," said the huntress. "There is a lodge in the city, Phiaphara. Will you come?"

"I will stay here with Noah," she replied. "To wait for Tehama," she added hurriedly. "I would have her know that we are well." Kiah pursed her lips, but she nodded. With a wave, she loped away like a dog freed from a kennel.

While they waited, Noah and Phiaphara strolled about the plaza at the palace's foot. Other similar buildings

surrounded the open space; as far as Noah knew, they
served the same administrative functions they did centuries ago, and the time passed had only given the majestic
structures an even greater air of authority than they had
possessed when the city was still called Enoch. Phiaphara
spoke admiringly of their grandeur as they walked,
but it was a bitter beauty to Noah, who had known the
bene Elohim who had made them. The reality of war's
imminence could hardly be felt here, so Noah put such
thoughts from his mind and simply enjoyed being with the
woman—the notion was still unfamiliar—that he loved.

The square had its share of pleasing features, too, and
when they had finished looking at the buildings' facades,
they meandered among its fountains and sculptures.

"Look at this one," exclaimed Phiaphara. It was a
golden statue of a man, too big to be life sized even for a
Naphil, set upon a tiered pedestal of sky-blue marble as
tall as Noah. "Who is it?"

Noah approached the stone to see if an answer was
inscripted upon in. It was, and it read

SAMYAZA GRIGORI
BUILDER OF ATLANTIS
FROM THE HEAVENS HE CAME
TO THE HEAVENS HE ASCENDED

"Blood and death," swore Noah. He stepped back
and noticed small, folded pieces of parchment and silver
trinkets occupying a ledge of the pedestal. He opened
one, read it, then crumpled it and tossed it to the ground.

"What is it?" asked Phiaphara, concern on her face.

"This," answered Noah, "is Samyaza. Or, rather, what
the passage of time has made of him."

"Samyaza." She said the name like she had tasted a fine wine and found it spoiled, which satisfied Noah's pique.

"And those." Noah gestured to the scraps and silver. "Petitions written to Samyaza in hopes he might grant them." He shook his head. "How could Pethun countenance this?"

"I suppose a son wishes to think best of his father when he is gone."

"I cannot believe it. Man's memory is short, Phiaphara, but . . ."

Her hand touched his shoulder. "For you, it is not."

"No. Not for me. Not with him."

"Noah." She pressed into him, taking his hand. "I want to understand. Perhaps I cannot help the pain you feel, but . . . will you let me try?"

In that moment, Noah realized just how much pressure had built up, over scores upon scores of years, against the dam he had built to contain his sadness, his rage, his resentment, and now he felt the full weight of it. Here, though, in Phiaphara, the Creator God had provided a channel that might at last relieve it, one that he had long abandoned hope of finding.

"Come," said Noah. "Let us find a place to sit." He gently pulled her away from the blasphemous image of Samyaza, toward the palace whose broad steps would serve perfectly well as benches. "I will tell you about a woman named Emzara."

⋅ CHAPTER 40 ⋅

The story of Emzara was told in full; like a key, it opened Phiaphara to share her own hardships: growing up without a mother, the difficult dichotomy of praise and social shunning that came with a father both brilliant and eccentric, the sudden onset of Zuthi aggression that introduced her to the evil of which man was capable. Despite the sad subjects, Noah could have talked with her for hours, but when the doors to the council opened, the conversation ended.

Waiting aides ran in, and runners rushed out. Noah hailed one he thought might be from Eden. When the man confirmed that he was, Noah asked him, "Who is your commander?"

"Greatfather Methuselah has come himself," the man replied. "He still speaks with the inner council inside." He paused. "You are from Eden as well?"

The simplest answer was yes, so Noah gave it.

"Do not fear," the man said, a kind smile on his face that Noah sensed he did not genuinely feel. "We shall retrieve them." He gave both of them a reassuring nod, then ran off.

"What did he mean?" asked Phiaphara. Noah frowned in response.

They entered the palace unhindered by guards. Noah needed a moment to adjust to the dimly torchlit chamber, its upper skylights closed by canvas covers; he had not realized how brightly the sun really did shine upon the gold and white stone of the palaces. The expansive room was circular and sloped steeply downward, with a dais in the center for the speaker. There were the giant Atlantean lords Dyeus and Pethun, as expected, although he again failed to see their older brother Dedroth. Phiaphara looked for Tehama; for himself, he wished only to see if Methuselah or Lamech or another of his kin was indeed present, but the more his eyes wandered the bottom rows of seating, the more they widened in surprise at everyone there he knew.

His grandfather Methuselah spoke with animation to Eudeon, close to the front. Dyeus's son Mareth stood in full armor, arms crossed, and unexpectedly beside him was Gilyon, arrayed for battle as well. Each of the giant warriors had a human in simple robes beside him, neither of whom Noah recognized. Tehama talked with Tiras the Naphil, his father Hoduìn, and a woman in a hooded cloak with light pauldrons upon her shoulders. A handful of leaders from foreign lands—Noah remembered the name Doude, the islander—huddled together in discussion; one of them, to his surprise, was Caiphes.

"Grandfather!" Noah exclaimed, waving. When Methuselah saw him, the old man took the steps two at a time to reach him, joy on his face. They embraced.

"I have prayed so very much for your return since Eudeon told me what happened," said Methuselah. "Jumped on a wyvern! This is the girl you saved?" He took Phiaphara's hand.

"Phiaphara of Mizraim, sir," she said.

"She saved me as well, in the jungles," said Noah. "And she is more than just a girl. Grandfather, we mean to be—"

His declaration was cut short by a flood of reunions. Caiphes and Eudeon embraced him, and Tehama and Tiras greeted him warmly. Even Dyeus, Pethun, Hoduín, and Mareth gave him friendly salutes; his ties with the Nephilim lords, though forged briefly and half a lifetime ago, were not easily broken.

"Noah." Gilyon put a gloved hand on his shoulder. His bright eyes said everything.

Noah gripped the giant's gauntleted forearm. "Good to see you, old friend." He peered around the Naphil to the robed man. "Well met, sir. My name is Noah of Eden." His introduction was not met in kind; instead, the somber straight line of the other man's mouth twitched up.

"Clearly, Noah, it has been too long. I am Merim."

"Merim?" Noah laughed, stepping up to the man and clasping him with both arms. "Phiaphara, come, meet my cousin Merim, Emzara's—" His exuberance sobered at the name, as did Merim's. "Emzara's brother."

"The young huntress." Merim nodded. Content for Phiaphara for now to be defined as such, Noah asked, "What part have you in this, Merim?"

"I represent the Scribes of Enoch," he replied. "Everyone that can must stand against these monsters. We use no blades, so Gilyon has agreed to lead us as our bloodletter against the Zuthian heathens."

"Bloodletter? This will be a war among men, not sacrifice."

"Every death is a sacrifice."

"We mean to kill animals only," Gilyon quickly said. "Zuthi fights with warbeasts, feeds slaves to them— scouts have seen dragons, pigs, gorgons, wolves."

Noah felt sure there was more to be said, but he was a newcomer here, his tongue stilled by a certain lack of understanding. He decided to try to rectify it. "What is the strategy here?"

"It was Hoduín's idea," said Gilyon.

"The land here will not be ruined by blood," said the Nephilim mystic, hearing his name. "It is barren already."

"But this is where the refugees have amassed. Do you not put them in the same danger from which they escaped, by allowing Zuthi to come to Atlantis?"

"Many of those have passed north to Assyria," said Tiras, "beyond the fortress city where my brother Tevesh keeps guard. Many have stayed to fight, or to share the fate of their kin who do."

"And besides Tiras, who fights with your friends the Scribes, and our healers in the Wa-Kirhai, who will stay in the city," Hoduín said, inclining his head to the hooded woman, "the children of Barkayal stand together in Assyria as a bastion, if the unthinkable happens."

"It will not happen," said Mareth. "Zuthi will come to Atlantis, and they will not escape. They will not flee and scatter to fester among our people, as they would if we had beaten them back as they advanced."

"Enough." Dyeus held up his hand as one accustomed to being obeyed. "We need not justify our course to anyone. It is chosen, and we will see it through. Come, there is much work yet to be done." He and Pethun enjoined Doude and several other foreigners in discussion, and Mareth drew Tiras aside.

Tehama stepped between Noah and Phiaphara, a smile adding still more splendor to her austere beauty. "Phia, your father may be the one person in Atlantis happier to see you than I. Let us go find him."

"I would go with them," said Noah to Methuselah. "Grandfather, you must come too. Gilyon, Eudeon, Caiphes, Merim—I have much to say to all of you."

"I regret, I cannot," said Merim. "Our forces must be prepared."

"Nor can I," Caiphes said. "Pellu the Seer arrived at the gates of Atlantis ten days ago with a few hundred men of Phempor, claiming I was their leader and wishing to join the armies that stand against Zuthi. Dashael's kin and I are doing what we can to make sure they will not all be killed."

The remainder agreed to come, and Noah began to formulate the start of a conversation that both thrilled and terrified him: how to tell his grandfather that he would marry a young woman from Mizraim.

Outside, Kiah joined the other two huntresses in earnest, excited conversation that began when the *beth* presented Phiaphara's lithe cat familiar to her. Gilyon and Eudeon talked with one another as they followed the Wa-Mizhan, no doubt to enjoy being able to speak with someone who could actually look them in the eye. Noah walked with Methuselah and Elebru, who had been waiting for them in the shadows of a column. Noah had not seen him in ages, but burns like his could belong to no one else. The oddest effect of the pitted-wax scars was that the man—his face, at least—was apparently impervious to gathering the signs of time's passage. His tongue worked, though, and his reports to Eden's greatfather demanded the elder man's attention. Noah listened, his betrothal pushed from his mind. Never would he have dreamed that so many of Eden's men, from so many places, could have been motivated to join such a violent cause, even behind Methuselah's leadership. Perhaps—a sick pang accompanied the thought—Eden had suffered an insidious injury, like Havilah. He waited for a lull.

"Grandfather, what brought Eden to this war? Are you simply giving aid to old friends, or did Zuthi attack?"

"Attack! Indeed they did, Noah, and at our very soul. Their agents took the toledoths—the very words of the Lord God Creator!" The volume of Methuselah's voice climbed. "I know I risk my blood, and that of many of my kin, but nothing else will do. I will see the toledoths returned, no matter what."

"But . . ." Too many of Noah's thoughts battled for access to his tongue, so he picked the simplest. "Why?"

"Why?"

The thoughts settled and ordered themselves. "You lead men away from their families, to war—to death— for the words of the Creator? But . . . they are here." He put a finger to his temple, then a hand to his heart. "They are in the parchment at Phiaphara's belt." Methuselah's eyes narrowed, so Noah sped toward his point. "I, and Eudeon, and Gilyon, and countless others, have spent nigh on four hundred years spreading them to every corner of the earth we could find where man has filled the land, where those words have taken root and seeded themselves even further. And all this time, the toledoths remained in Eden. Has my work been fruitless, then? Grandfather, the tablets are nothing compared to the words upon them. Elohim—"

"Stop!" Noah had heard that tone seldom, and not since boyhood. "You have long been absent from Eden, Noah. Perhaps, when *you* are greatfather, you will better understand her important possessions. That is, if you even bother to return when the role passes to you. Come, Elebru."

Methuselah speeded his steps; Elebru turned his head to Noah as he passed, but his featureless face was unreadable. Thus repulsed, Noah dropped behind to his Nephilim comrades.

"We heard," said Gilyon. "I agree with you about the toledoths, but he need not rely on that reason alone. Zuthi has made them plentiful."

Tehama had known where to find Phiaphara's father, but Gilyon was the one who suggested traveling to him on Atlantis's outer wall. Built at the behest of the *bene Elohim* by their instruction, it was both the crown that encircled the city's head and the iron helm that protected it, a sculpted wonder of beauty and strength. The entirety of its top was as wide as a plaza, broken by parapets and towers through which it passed as an arched tunnel. Walking along it, Noah was afforded an incomparable view to either side, and he could see why Gilyon had wanted to come this way: more soldiers and warriors were immediately behind the wall than outside it, milling about in loose groupings that nevertheless would make for slow passage through them. While the forces beyond the moat were mostly Atlantean, obvious by the bright banners and gleam of speartips and scale, those along the wall's inner edge were motley and nonuniform, comprised of men, and occasionally women or Nephilim, of different refugee nationalities.

Gilyon noticed him staring down at the assortments of warriors. "It was decided that the remnants of other peoples' warriors should remain hidden to mask our numbers, and able to be deployed wherever they might be most needed."

Noah nodded. Peals of rough laughter rose up from a knot of giants clothed in skins, and they reminded him of another of their kind. "Where is Eroch? Kiah mentioned a brute." His question was for Eudeon, but Tehama heard it—naturally, with her acute ear—and answered for him.

"He has been bouncing between brothels and the ruefully given hospitality of Atlantean nobles possessing large winecellars and more regard for his father than dislike for him."

"Poor behavior, to be sure, but I am glad he is well," said Noah, ignoring her disparagement. "When the wyvern fell upon him like that, I feared that even he might not withstand the assault." Something in the way the huntress's eyes darted to Eudeon made Noah glance back at the Naphil, whose face was stone, lips pressed in a thin line. "What is it?" Noah asked.

"Eroch . . ." Eudeon started. "No, I cannot say."

"He withstood the assault," said Tehama, her tone dripping disgust. "Let us leave it there. Phiaphara, here we are."

They had rounded the wall until it crossed the coastline and overlooked the sapphire-blue sea that mirrored the sky until the two met at the horizon. The top of the wall had been active as they walked, replete with archers, birdmasters, and messengers running to and fro, but here, above the waters, that activity had much changed.

If the machines—Noah had no more specific word for them, and they were not all of a kind—could be moved at all, it would not be easily, and he wondered if their architects had assembled them upon the wall. Leather-capped figures, certainly not warriors, hustled about, peering at parchments and shouting at one another. Tehama seemed to know where she wished to go, so Noah simply followed with the rest and did his best to ascertain the nature of these huge constructs. Some reminded him of Midash's crossbow, but of a size that would be near comical except for the iron-headed bolts, longer than he was tall, set into them. Others were indecipherable arrays of beams, ropes, and metal hinges, but their purpose was made obvious when two men lifted a stone block from a stack of them, put it into a leather hammock at the end of one of the constructs, and released a mechanism that sent the block soaring into the air, splashing into the sea farther away than a bow could shoot. Of their group, only Phiaphara's cat remained unimpressed.

"Phiaphara! Phiaphara!" His betrothed beamed when she saw the man waving. She returned it. "Father!"

Noah took stock of the man from whom he would ask to take his most precious possession.

Ninniachul struck an odd figure, even among the other ingeniators. His cloak hung too loosely over a belt heavy with thin tools and pouches. He wore a tall cap of loose leather, dipping in at its crown, and his eyes were covered with two large lenses set into a eyemask of polished bronze. The overall effect was one of a tall-headed owl, but the imposition Noah felt upon seeing him was as if he were a lion who did not know his meal was about to be stolen.

Phiaphara ran ahead to meet him. Noah caught Methuselah's eye, wishing they were in Eden, drinking wine after a finished harvest. Elebru's audience could not be helped; this was Noah's opportunity. "Grandfather, I have something I must tell you," he quietly said.

"You wish to marry that girl," said Methuselah.

"One hardly needs the gift of prophecy to ascertain that," echoed Elebru.

"Obvious from the moment we saw both of you."

Two shadows fell over Noah, and a huge hand engulfed his shoulder. "Congratulations, Noah," said Eudeon.

"Congratulations? Are we sure she has agreed?" asked Gilyon, winking.

"He is of *my* bloodline," said Methuselah. "Of *course* she agrees."

Eudeon bent to Noah's ear. "She follows Elohim?"

"She does, and more so every day," said Noah, "but please, quiet." Tehama and Kiah stood away, talking between themselves, and gave no sign that they had overheard. When Phiaphara brought her father over, the banter stopped and introductions flew.

"Come, my dear, see my work," Ninniachul said. "All of you, p-please." He led them past more slinging machines to a large, complicated array of mirrors and lenses. "Careful, please," the ingeniator cautioned. "Especially you." He pointed at Gilyon. "I have heard about you, sir. You have a certain reputation for breaking contraptions made of mirrors, you know." Noah filed the comment away to ask the Naphil about later.

"What does this do?" asked Kiah.

"It harnesses the sun . . . better to watch." Ninniachul removed a lens from one pocket and a scrap of parchment from another. He held the latter below the former and an arm's length away. A point of light appeared on the scrap, then burst into flames. "This," the ingeniator said, waving the lens at the apparatus. "Zuthians." He held up the parchment, then calmly walked to edge of the wall and tossed it over, sea winds carrying it away as it burned to ash.

"That . . . is rather amazing," said Eudeon.

"If it works," Gilyon added.

"I-it works. Let me show you how we will make it do so."

"Actually, Ninniachul," said Noah, stepping close to the man and speaking with a calm his racing heart contradicted. "I had hoped to discuss a matter with you."

"Oh?" He motioned another leather-capped fellow over. "Reshus, show these . . . ah, gentlemen our designs."

As the two men walked away, Noah glanced back at Phiaphara. Though she pretended not to notice them, she could not hide the blush in her cheeks or the smile pulling at her mouth's corners.

Phiaphara suppressed her smile, since it did not seem appropriate to let it blossom among such machines of war, but despite all of the anxiety obscuring the future like mist, her heart rejoiced in that moment. She inhaled. Noah was having his talk. Now Phiaphara needed to have hers.

"Tehama, may we speak?"

"As I am far from blind, I can guess the subject," the huntress answered. "Kiah tells me that you kept unspoiled during your accidental detour."

Phiaphara took deep breath. "Yes, but I am betrothed to Noah. I wish to be with him. Which means . . ." She left the end unspoken: she could not remain with the Wa-Mizhan.

"Noah of Eden is a good man," said Tehama. "And our Wa-Mizhan insistence on a woman keeping her own council must extend even to her leaving us. You could do much worse with your life . . . but are you sure you cannot do better?"

Before Phiaphara could determine whether an answer was expected from her, a lean, long-legged giant sprinted up to them. His golden skin glistened with sweat, but his speech was not broken from breathlessness. She had never seen the Naphil before, but Tehama obviously knew him, as did Methuselah and the other giants, who greeted him as "Hamerch."

The giant nodded in reply and turned to Tehama. "I have been searching all over for you. Father wishes to discuss the roles your rangers will play in the battle. Gilyon, Methuselah, your forces are ready?" At their assurances, he nodded again, then ran off like an antelope.

"Duty calls," said Tehama. "Kiah, I will meet you at the lodge. Phiaphara, let us speak more about this later. I want only the best for you." Taking her leave of the others, she followed Hamerch's path back around the top of the wall.

Kiah stared after her for a while. "That woman is the very emblem of devotion to a cause," said the *beth*. She faced Phiaphara and lowered her voice. "I do not think ill of this Noah—far from it. Tehama speaks well of him, and alone with a fertile female, most men revert to the animals from which they came. I will not attempt to dissuade you from your feelings, but . . ." She seemed to rethink what she had been going to say.

"Do you know," Kiah continued, "that Nephilim females are barren, as beautiful as they are? Proof that of what gods there may be, at least one is partial to irony. This lonely life is easier for Tehama, who does not share certain human longings. Phiaphara, the wilds . . . alone with another, under skies never seen by those who live within walls . . . it does strange things to one's heart that often do not last. Take my council: take this respite, while we have it, find a garden or pool or wherever seems best, and think about *you*." She took a half step closer and brushed Phiaphara's hip with her hand. "While you do, remember this, for at times it has kept me from straying from this path: your sisters in the Wa-Mizhan can provide everything a husband can. Companionship, safety . . . love . . ." She whispered, lips nearly touching Phiaphara's ear but for the younger woman's pulling her head away. "Everything."

The *beth* stepped away. "I am needed elsewhere. Think about it. Pray to your gods, or what have you." Phiaphara nodded, not trusting words to her trembling lip. Ignoring the men, who were still either engaged in conversation or engrossed in examining the mirrored machine, Kiah, too, ran off.

Phiaphara felt flustered. She was not tempted by the huntresses' offer—whatever it may have been—but between them and Noah, never before had she been the object of such desire, and by ones so far above the esteem in which she held herself. Her father had doted on her without spoiling her, making her part of his work in Mizraim, and that had been sufficient. She did need to think and, yes, pray as well.

She wished not to interrupt Noah and her father. "Eudeon," she said, "I would find a washroom." Stairways were set into the great wall's inner surface at regular intervals, and she gestured at the nearest. "I will return shortly."

"Do you wish me to accompany you?" the giant asked.

"I am fine, thank you. No doubt a guard will be taking names of everyone who enters a public bath." She meant it in humor, but then again, it might be true.

"Take your cat, at least."

"No, she prefers the sun. Stay here," she commanded her familiar.

In truth, Phiaphara would have been glad to use a washroom, but she neither knew where one was nor cared to search it out. From the stairs she saw a low building with a mosaic that marked it as a bathhouse, open to men and women alike, but the modesty that Eve had learned in the Garden had not yet abandoned Mizraim as she had heard it had among Cain's people. Atlantis was famed for its waterworks, though, and rightly so; the street she walked (and she seemed to be the only one) turned its corner at a three-bowled fountain, benches surrounding. She sat and looked around her. Apparently, the citizens who bore no arms had well heeded the call to stay inside. She saw no guards, either, which suited her. In this moment, she desired privacy.

Phiaphara dipped a finger in a basin and touched it to her tongue. Finding the water fresh, not salty, she splashed her face. It was hardly a proper bath, but those had been rare of late, and at least it refreshed her. After drying her hands on the cleanest part of her tunic she could find, she took from her belt the small copy of the toledoths Noah had given her. She read it, lingering on Eve's origin and Adam's declaration after it.

"Bone of my bones and flesh of my flesh." The words sounded mythical, but she knew—honestly, the realization surprised her—with complete confidence that they had been spoken by the man from whom the world descended.

She closed her eyes and spoke aloud, her prayer's words hidden by the sound of cascading water from every ear but hers and, she trusted, Elohim's.

"Creator God, Noah tells me that You listen and give wisdom to whoever asks. I have not spoken to you often, but I have much to say to you now." Admitting that fact freed her to pour out everything she felt—her gratitude, her fear, her desires, all of them at once—in hopes that the Maker of the world would be able to take and assemble them into coherency.

Absorbed in her orison, she never saw the figure that clamped the sweet-smelling cloth over her face. Her eyes flew open, but all went black before she thought to scream.

⋅ CHAPTER 41 ⋅

"Noah, you have convinced me of your sincerity," said Ninniachul. "But I need to s-say something before you go on. I will never agree to a marriage unless Phiaphara agrees as well."

Noah frowned. "I am sorry. I do not understand."

"I mean I will not even countenance your offer unless my daughter wishes to marry you as well. I have rejected wealthier men than you. I may not have much of worth, but I have her, and my own honor, and these I will not cheapen."

"I would not ask this if Phiaphara did not desire it as well."

"I w-would hear that from her. If it is indeed true, what is your offer?"

"Nothing, sir, but myself. In Eden we do not barter for marriage."

"In Mizraim, we do," said the ingeniator. He adjusted the lenses over his eyes. "But then again, we are not in Mizraim, are we?" The way he said it intimated to Noah that the man was hardly tethered to the customs and practices of his homeland. "Very well. If Phiaphara wishes to marry you, Noah of Eden, I will bless the union."

"It is easily accomplished," said Noah. He looked around, ready to call Phiaphara over, but he did not see her. "Where is Phiaphara?"

"Down the wall," answered Eudeon. "She ought to return in a moment."

She did not, and Noah's patience was quickly exhausted, as was Ninniachul's. "Shall you go fetch her?" he asked Noah.

"She was looking for a washroom," said Eudeon.

"Only bathhouses and inns open theirs to the public," said Gilyon. "Plenty of those are nearby, this close to the ports."

Noah raised a hand in thanks, already to the stairway's head. The streets below were barren of people, including Phiaphara. With a skip in his step, he followed the main way, head turning to the left and right; the longer he went, the more inclined he was to break the eerie silence by calling her name.

He stopped at the corner, looking once more down the paved stones he had just walked, then up the street that intersected it where he stood. He sat, perplexed, on the edge of a fountain, one of many that had sprouted up around old Enoch. For a moment, the marvelous cleanliness of Atlantis—even its harbor district, hardly the first stop for tourists in any major port city—imposed itself upon Noah's worry. His entire vista, even the byways and alleys, was pristine, a state more obvious for the absence of commerce. He amended his assessment: a single piece of detritus marred perfection. Noah would have thought it a leaf, had there been trees about, but for its rectangular shape too exact to be natural. A gust of sea breeze sent it scurrying along the stones, and something about it caught Noah's attention, then dropped his heart like an anchor from a ship. He ran to pick it up, to prove to himself it was not as he feared, that it was just a bill of cargo or a misplaced bit of captain's log.

It was the toledoths he had given Phiaphara.

"Not again," said Noah. "Not again. Damn this cursed city." He bit his tongue. Imprecations would not bring him help, but he certainly needed some. First, he prayed; next, since he was barely beyond the shadow of Atlantis's wall, he shouted up to it. "Eudeon! *Eudeon!* Gilyon!" He yelled until a helmeted head looked over.

"What?" called Gilyon.

"I need you all! Come down, please!" He felt loath to tell Phiaphara's father—what was there to tell?—but then again, if it were he, he would wish to know. "Bring Ninniachul!"

Noah resisted the urge to crumple the toledoths, but his pacing was wont to wear a rut in the stone beneath his feet. His wait was short. The two giants, the ingeniator, and Methuselah and Elebru hurried to him, faces questioning. He explained.

"She cannot have disappeared," said Gilyon. "Methuselah, Elebru, check there and there." He pointed at the bathhouse and an inn past it, marked with the picture of a crab with a palace for a shell. "There is a guard station at Sea Bridge, not far from here. I will tell the guards to send runners to checkpoints. If she passed any, she will be recorded. If she did not, she is here somewhere."

"What shall we do?" asked Eudeon.

"You and Noah? Stay here and wait for me. Pray. Look around, but do not go far. Ninniachul, as a commander of Atlantean forces, I need to ask you to return to your device." To Noah's surprise, he nodded in agreement.

"Worry not," he said, patting Noah on the shoulder. "Study all you like, but even a learned man cannot fathom the ways of a woman, especially one as headstrong as my daughter. Within these walls she must be, and I will do my part to protect them." With a wave, he went off, cloak flapping and belt jangling.

"He is not wrong. Remind me to tell you," said Methuselah, "what your aunt did two days before she wed." He gripped Noah's arm, their quarrel forgotten, and departed down the street with Elebru.

"I will see you soon," said Gilyon, and he left as well. Less bolstered by hopeful words than their speakers intended, he sat with a sigh on the edge of the fountain. He had not noticed, but apparently Phiaphara's cat had followed them down and was now lapping up water from the fountain's basin. Noah stroked its back. "If only you were a hound," he said absently, but then he jumped up. "Tehama! I must find Tehama."

Eudeon extended an arm, bidding him stay. "I will find her."

The Naphil left; Noah stayed, but he did not sit back down. Crouching, not hopeful, he scoured the street for a sign of Phiaphara's passing. In Phempor, an entire day of a man's movements could be traced in the muddy clay, but here the stone took no tracks upon it. He rose. What commotion they had made had drawn nobody outside, and he still saw no one around him.

He was not alone, though. He began to pray.

Methuselah and Elebru returned, having discovered nothing. Gilyon arrived soon after. "She has not passed any guard," said the giant. "She *must* be here."

Elebru spread his hands, palms up. "Where, then? We are no fools. We would have found her." Never gregarious, the scarred man seemed especially sour. "Noah, perhaps you ought not keep bringing to this city the women to whom you are betrothed. It does not seem to agree with them."

"Elebru!" Methuselah burst out angrily, and Gilyon scowled, but the sharp words had cut deep. The older man had been fond of Emzara, and had she never accompanied Noah to Enoch all those years ago, they might now be longtime neighbors. Indeed, so much now was the same as then; he had even just been surprised by the unexpected appearance of a Scribe . . .

The light came gradually, more akin to a dawning than opening a door into sunlight, but it shone on Noah's face nonetheless as his eyes grew wide and bright. "Gilyon, can you find someone who knows the underground?"

"What?"

"Inside the palaces, underneath the city—this place is riddled with hidden passages!" Perhaps he was grasping at the straw too tightly, but it was the only one left. "Jonan and I escaped the *bene Sheol* with the Scribes through them. Where is Merim?"

"The Scribes have not had a large presence in this city in ages," said Gilyon. "Certainly not beneath it."

"How would Phiaphara know these places?" asked Methuselah. "Why would she go there if she did?"

In that moment, such questions seemed of little importance to Noah; a low horn sounded in the distance and multiplied until it seemed to flood the city, and he knew that they had suddenly diminished in Methuselah's and Gilyon's sight as well.

"Zuthi approaches," said Gilyon, his voice suddenly stone. "Noah . . ."

"Go."

"I may be too old to fight," Methuselah said to Noah, "but I am needed still."

"Grandfather . . ."

"I know not what I can do here. I would stay with you if I did. I know my place against these savages, though. I will pray that the girl returns."

They stood there—the Naphil warrior, Eden's great-father, old Elebru—as if waiting for Noah's permission to depart, and he considered that he had no cause to deny it. "Go," he said. "May your paths lead far from Sheol's mouth."

"And yours, my son," answered Methuselah; with that, they departed.

His solitude—despite Phiaphara's cat, whose feline aloofness Noah hardly counted as companionship—was brief. Eudeon's unseen calls came to him from the staircase on the wall. He answered, and the giant soon appeared, and with him Tehama behind two shaggy, sharp-nosed wolfhounds on leather leashes. Unexpectedly, massively muscled Eroch was with them as well, cudgel in hand.

"Have you something of Phiaphara's?" asked Tehama. She had not been one for unneeded pleasantries on their travels, and Noah appreciated such directness now. He held out the toledoth to the hounds' noses; he was embarrassed when they pressed their sniffing snouts into him as well.

"Better you than the cat," said Tehama, noting his discomfort. "You have spent far more time with Phiaphara than it has of late, and you will suffer the dogs to take a scent without biting or scratching." It was a fair point.

Like arrows aimed straight down, the hounds' noses hit the street. Immediately they began to pull the huntress past the fountain, through a gap between buildings, and to the foot of the great wall itself.

"Unless she flew away, this is where her trail ends," said Tehama. "You were right, Eudeon."

"*Noah* was right," said the giant.

"Pethun often tells of his exploit through Enoch's underground to save it," said Tehama. "But he and my father had the passages closed, or so he says."

"Perhaps not all. The entrance must be found first, if we are to contradict him," said Noah, hope rising, and worry with it. "Come, help me. There must be some mechanism." He pushed a great block of stone, then another, both solid as a mountain.

"Allow me," said Eroch. He approached the wall, petting the wolfhounds on the way, and tapped it gently with his great weapon. He did it several more times elsewhere, coming back to where he started and doing it again. Noah listened. The tapping was indeed more hollow where the wolfhounds had stopped. He was so close; while the key to the passage's access was secret now, it would certainly fall to Noah's determination to discover it, he had no doubt. He went to the wall again, searching for the slightest crack where it ought not be.

"Excuse me, Noah. Eudeon, if you will?" Eroch said. The other Naphil unslung a huge hammer from his back. With one terrible strike after another, cudgel and hammer, the stone cracked until a blow broke through. Eroch reached a hand in and, straining, simply ripped a section of wall out to crash at their feet. Twice more, and the opening was large enough to accommodate entry.

Eroch's grin was as wide as his shoulders as he stooped to enter the passage. "Well met again, Noah, by the way. How exciting!"

Tehama followed, shrugging. "He wanted to come. Was there any point in attempting to stop him?" She disappeared into the ruined wall after the pair of hounds.

Eudeon gestured for Noah to follow. "Thank you," Noah told him.

"I could not help with Emzara," answered the giant. "I can help you now, and mine is not the greatest help you have. Elohim goes before us."

"And behind," said Noah. With that thought of comfort, he plunged into the darkness.

Scouts poured into the city, and with them detailed reports. Atlantis and her allies were quickly mobilized to their optimal positions. Slowly, like a creeping ooze in a dying swamp, Zuthians seeped into sight of the great wall of Atlantis, both on land and by sea.

Gilyon stood beside Mareth, high commander of the Atlantean army, above Wide Bridge. He had accepted his role and would soon join battle along the Scribes and with a clean conscience, but the red, fiery light that kindled in Mareth's eyes was absent from his own.

"I cannot see the end of them," he solemnly said. "There are so many."

"Soon," replied Mareth, "there will be none." He raised his war horn to his lips and blew.

‹ CHAPTER 42 ›

FOWL BRIDGE

In the misty distance, the amassed Zuthians took on a single form, like a swarm of flies on carrion, a solid field of black until disturbed. Methuselah did not yet know where the toledoths were, nor could he; the falcons would help, but retaking the tablets would take the violent efforts of men. He prayed for two things over all else: that the inscribed generations of Elohim and of Adam remained unblemished, and that they were with the Zuthian army at all.

He trusted that the primary driving force of the Edenites who had come with him—more than three thousand, mostly woodsmen with no fields to tend—was the desire to regain the toledoths, but he was also aware that without the force of his convictions, few of those would have replaced their velleity with the actual action that had brought them before an army in foreign lands. He and his lieutenants had divided them among their allied forces arrayed around Atlantis's six bridges, in hope that wherever their stolen quarry proved to be, it would be quickly discovered.

The mass in the mists began to move. A murmur rose up; a restless shudder passed through his countrymen. Even though only a portion of his men were with Methuselah now, they needed a Greatfather, and especially in this moment. Now was the time to steel their resolve with the strength of his own. He faced them and raised his voice.

"Men of Eden! Words matter! We are here to retake those of Elohim, priceless beyond measuring. I give you some of my own words now.

"The lives of men are short! Though we must ensure that it is through no fault or doing of ours, some will end today. The words of Elohim, however, last forever. We must reclaim them! This is our only goal. The Zuthians have monstrous mounts, war wagons, beasts of battle, and these we will slay with no quarter! Protect yourself, but remember: even in this cursed land, it is not ours to send a man to Sheol, nor to spill his blood, no matter how much the justice of our conscience might cry for it. One of these heathens has the toledoths, though, and when the Lord God allows him to be struck down this day, we will pick up what he leaves behind on his way to the pit."

Someone unseen shouted, "You want us to be vultures when we could be eagles." Voices of assent sprouted and bloomed.

"We are neither," replied Methuselah. "We are human! We are above the beasts and birds, and it is not ours to take a life."

The Zuthians moved faster now. The Atlanteans strode forward in shining silver, stepping to the sound of their mail's metallic rhythm. "In this, as in all things, let Elohim be praised," shouted Methuselah. He drew an arrow and put it to his bow.

BULL BRIDGE

The Scribes *had* warriors, thought Gilyon, but looking over them—literally, down upon the tops of their hooded heads, as no Nephilim besides himself and Tiras were among them—he would not characterize them *as* warriors. They were scholars by their passion, and only placed themselves at the battle lines today because the object of their study had been taken; that some of them knew how to bear arms well was a matter of statistics. Their fervor gave them boldness, to be sure, and their sober minds would help keep them from recklessness. Many rode upon great shaggy unicorns, and some handled the rams and stone-skulled drakes that would be sent out as the first wave to meet the enemy. None but he had a bladed weapon, since he was the lone bloodletter, so all others carried staves, mallets, or maces. Tiras drove his chariot, drawn by four stout spiral-horned sheep, down the line of men, encouraging and advising them and bolstering their spirits with the sight of his enormous bronze-headed hammer that would be fighting alongside them. In his angelic grandfather Azazyel's crossblade, returned to him by Tubal-Cain on the eve of battle, Gilyon had a weapon even more impressive, and he believed he had better words that would speak truer to the Scribes' devout hearts as well.

The Zuthians advanced, details of their kinds and numbers yet obscured by the lingering mists. This was the moment when courage needed reassurance. Gilyon raised his weapon, three polished blades catching the sun and calling all attention to himself; even Tiras stopped.

"Many of you," said Gilyon, "like me, are descended from Cain. He built this city out of fear—fear that men would come and take his life. Those men have come, and they are before you! Today let us cast down that fear, and forever let this city be a symbol of hope instead! Let us be a light to our comrades in darkness—let them see that those who fear the Lord God Creator need fear nothing else! For Elohim, for Enoch, for Atlantis!"

Black Bridge

Mareth looked down his nose at the raucous rabble of Zuthian fighters that had approached near enough to Black Bridge for their unintelligible cacophony of jeers and howls to be heard. These were Zuthi's rank and file, just as the scouts had reported, and their strength lay in the sheer number of them. If Mareth could see them, then they could see his own men, and the disparity between the two forces—a few hundred warriors with the Naphil guarding the bridge from many thousands of the southern marauders—no doubt provided fuel for their loud and increasingly maddened bluster. Ibon-Azazyel, master of the *bene Sheol*, was silent beside him, the deep lines of his face betraying neither fear nor compassion.

"It is time," said Mareth. Ibon-Azazyel barked a command in a tongue not of earth.

Gathered close, the lightly armored assassins of the *bene Sheol* and the Atlantean high guard barely spanned the width of Black Bridge. Spreading out at Ibon-Azazyel's signal, with enough space among them to swing a chain or long spear without fear of harming their fellows, they formed a front wide enough to meet the crush of Zuthians that had devolved into a great rushing, screaming mob, weapons raised high.

"They are waves," called Mareth, "and we are the jutting rocks upon which they will crash. Let them come. If any one of us falls, we will pay them back seven times seven again."

No other words were needed. Mareth unsheathed his massive sword and waited for an army to fall upon them.

Scuttling echoed around Noah as rats, and who knew what else, retreated at the unexpected human intrusion into their dark domain. His party moved quickly behind the hounds, eased by an unexpected visibility inside the passages. Thin shafts of sunlight pierced the darkness at intervals and faintly lit their path, their footsteps sending motes of dust spiraling in sparse clouds within the beams.

The bit of light was welcome, but it abandoned them after two stairwells and a sloping length of passage so narrow that Eudeon and Eroch were obliged to turn sideways to traverse it. The air became damp; the dust turned to grime that Noah felt with each step and every time he placed a hand on the wall to steady himself, since it also cost his boots traction upon the slippery stone. Underfoot became rougher. The air moved more freely—foul, not fresh—and Noah could no longer feel a wall to either side. Weak light high above them barely illuminated stone ducts that surely were the source of the dripping echoes around them, and Noah recalled a moment long ages ago underneath Enoch, in the caverns through which ran the city's sewers.

The hounds slowed and stopped.

"Well?" Eroch vocalized the impatience Noah was trying to suppress.

"I think they cannot smell anything in this filth," said Tehama, sounding frustrated. "And although I know this foul ground must be covered in tracks, I cannot see to follow them."

"Call upon your God, Noah," asked Eroch. "Or you, Eudeon. Ask him to grant a boon."

"We will," said Eudeon. "In the meantime, keep walking."

They did. Noah held out a hand as he walked; he could still see it, like a dark shadow on a field of pure black, but nothing beyond it. The near-total darkness was doing strange things to his perception of time, making him feel like he had been trudging for days.

"There is a light ahead," said Eudeon. Noah trusted the giant's eyes, though his own failed to confirm it.

"I see it too," said Tehama. She picked up their pace. A glowing point of orange did indeed appear far in front of them, although Noah had to step to the side to see beyond Eroch; with a curse, the muscled Naphil halted, and Noah ran full into him and almost slipped in the muck.

"There is a stream here," said Tehama.

"Dare I ask what runs within it?" asked Eroch.

"No doubt what you smell."

"I think I see the far bank," said Eudeon. "Too far to jump across."

Tehama and Eroch spoke at the same time. "Do we go upstream, or down?" asked the huntress; "How far across?" asked the big giant.

Eudeon answered Eroch. "Perhaps four times your height, or six or seven of a human."

"Oh. Excuse me." Eroch moved his bulk past Noah and Eudeon as if he were retreating the way they had come, then ran back toward them, near unseen in the dark but loudly heard, his heavy steps slapping the wet stone. He leapt. Noah held his breath. From the sounds, he could imagine what was happening: Eroch's grunt of exertion, the quiet second in midair, the absence of a splash that would have proven the giant had fallen short.

"Disgusting!" Eroch called. "I slipped when I landed. Hold on, friends!" The distant light was blocked by the

Naphil's body, his steps sounding fainter as he loped toward it to retrieve it. He did, and his return with a torch and a quick exploration of the far back discovered a small, flat raft and a long push pole.

"Catch, Eudeon." Eroch shoved the raft halfway across the filthy stream, then threw the pole to the other Naphil, who used it to guide the raft to their side.

"Noah, Tehama, you two go first with the animals," said Eudeon. "My weight alone will be test enough for this rough craft."

Carefully, Noah stepped aboard, wishing for at least a rail to hold. Tehama followed, then the wolfhounds; the hunting cat came last, after a pause that made clear her disdain for the effort. The stream below them was made all the more foul by the glowing torch that made it visible. A layer of foamy sludge was pushed and swirled about by the faster-moving current it floated upon, broken by myriad bobbing islands of filth and the occasional bloated, fur-covered carcass. Noah choked back the bile that threatened to add itself to the miasmic milieu.

"The places we go for love," said Tehama nasally.

"She is worth it," replied Noah.

"She is that." The huntress stroked the head of the cat pressed against her legs. "This voyage is rather crowded with animals."

"At least it is short," said Noah, giving one last push and reaching a hand to Eroch's outstretched arm. The giant pulled the raft flush to the edge, wood scraping against stone, and helped them debark. In a few minutes more, Eudeon was across as well.

"It is clean and dry up ahead," said Eroch. "Another passage."

"I hope the wolfhounds can find the trail again," said Tehama. The animals began tugging and sniffing as if on cue. The group picked up the pace, entered the passage—indeed dry, with a slow outflow of air that purged it of much of the stench—and followed it along its curve to another torch, then a third. The eager, near-fanatical fire in Noah's bosom driving him toward Phiaphara had been threatened to be dampened by the darkness and filth, but now it was rekindled with new strength. He longed to look upon his newly betrothed and felt in his spirit that that moment grew close, although right now his view consisted primarily of Eroch's broad back and thick arms; when the giant abruptly stopped, he pushed around them to Tehama to see what had halted their progress.

The passage had ended at a door, or a gate. Noah was unsure what appellation the barrier deserved. It was iron and bronze, stretching from wall to wall and floor to ceiling. The entire thing was layered with circles and semicircles laid upon and around one another, with no obvious handles or locks. Tehama handed the leashes to Noah and reached out a hand.

"These move," she said, rotating a crescent to the clicking of a hidden mechanism.

"Must we manipulate them in order, do you think?" asked Noah. "Eudeon, you are skilled at puzzles. Might you decipher it?"

"I cannot fathom this, but we have no other way forward."

"Between this and the sewer, I think whoever is inside likes his privacy," said Eroch. "But maybe we could knock."

A squealing, otherworldly cry from within, faint as if loosed from a distance but unmistakeable, froze their wondering. Head and chest above Noah, Eroch and Eudeon shared a glance. Each reached to the weapon at his back.

"Yes, Eroch," said Eudeon. "We should knock."

· CHAPTER 43 ·

Even after Eroch and Eudeon had rent a hole in the gate, it took a good while for the two Nephilim to enlarge it so they could enter. The woman inside stared at them the entire time. She had been beautiful once, no doubt, but her gaunt cheeks and sunken eyes prevented the descriptor from being applied to her now. She ignored their hails and pleas for help as they worked against the metal gate; she just stood watching them, silent as the grave. Finally, with one last, great effort and the squeal of bending metal, they were through.

Eroch stomped up to the woman, his frustration overwhelming his usual manner toward the gentler sex. "Why," he growled, "in the great grey depths of Sheol, did you not open that gate?"

"I know not how to," she answered. Her voice lilted, with an absence of emotion that gave the impression that she was either astoundingly simple or absolutely fearless.

Noah climbed through the ruined gate. Indeed, it seemed consistently complex throughout its considerable thickness, as difficult to decipher from the inside as the out for one who was not privy to its secrets. He hurried to the woman. "Have you seen a young wo—"

"Introductions first," she said. "Else I set the servants upon you." Her voice held no malice whatsoever, nor was it polite. Regardless, introductions were quickly made.

"And I am Belseraphim."

"Belseraphim," repeated Eudeon. "'Mistress of the angels?' Are you Naphil?"

"No," the thin woman replied. "I could not be my master's womb if I were."

"We follow a young woman who was taken," said Tehama. "Against her will, we think. Have you seen her?"

The first shade of emotion flitted on Belseraphim's face. "One of the master's dogs brought her through. Come, I will lead you." She turned and called, "Servants!"

Three shambling figures emerged from the shadows, dressed in long, dark skirts, so fleshy and fat that gender was difficult to tell. They stared with stuporous faces at Belseraphim, and Noah noticed, with some unease, that each of them had hollow sockets where their right eyes should have been.

"Guard this entrance," instructed Belseraphim. "Let no one exit, not even the master's dogs." The servants grunted and moaned, apparently in understanding, and took up places by the ruined portal.

"Come," she said again. Wary but eager, Noah fell in behind her, and his companions followed.

The still silence of the dead, dim halls asked not to be broken, but eventually Eroch did so. "So," he said. "Your . . . servants. Their eyes."

"Yes?"

"What happened to them?"

"They were put out, of course, in order for my master to fix what lay beneath. So as to make their owners *useful*," replied Belseraphim, as easily as if she were describing the ingredients in bread. "That is what my master does: make broken things useful."

"From where do these 'broken things' come?" asked Tehama. Her eyes darted around to every shadow; if city walls put her at unease, Noah could only imagine how she felt in this subterrane.

"From exile."

"Exile."

"Yes. This is exile. My master is over it." Belseraphim looked to each of them with her blank face, but her tone took on the slightest hue of wonder. "You come here, and you do not know this?"

"I know of exile, certainly," said Tehama. "Atlantis sends her irredeemable criminals—its murderers, its debauchers and violent defilers of women—beyond its borders."

"*Beyond* its borders? And spread disease where it was not before?" replied the flat-affected woman. "No, no. The host must heal itself, and the master is Atlantis's great physician."

Tehama laughed, although Noah heard the uncertainty in it. "Atlantis exiles outside its borders," she repeated.

"How would you know?"

"Because I am mistress of Atlantis's border guard, and my father is Dyeus, son of Samyaza!" Tehama's voice was rising. "Eroch, tell her."

"She speaks truth," the big Naphil said, "as far as I know."

The air grew cooler as Belseraphim led them onto a bridge lit intermittently by lanterns of clouded glass. "So both of you have seen these places, beyond Atlantis?" continued Belseraphim. "Or have your border guards ever stopped any incursions of outlaw colonies that perhaps became homesick?"

"Mm. No, I cannot say I have," said Eroch, after Tehama did not speak to answer. "Noah? Eudeon? You wander about."

"Exile colonies? From other peoples, yes," said Eudeon. "But . . . no, never from Atlantis."

The bridge—proving to be far longer than Noah would have guessed, perhaps due to how keen he was to cross it to Phiaphara—widened into a courtlike circle. The lamps around it were brightly lit, enough to cast to the ground far below. Belseraphim walked to the edge. "Here. You can see for yourselves what I say is true."

A fog drifted below them. Through it, Noah saw figures trudging about, and past those, holes of doorways set into piled structures that Noah supposed were shelters.

"What are they harvesting?" asked Eudeon, seeing details Noah could not.

"Mushrooms," answered their hostess. "It is sustenance enough, usually."

"Your 'servants,'" said Tehama coldly, authority in her voice. "They come from these people?"

"These killers and sadists. Yes. The master performs the metamorphosis himself, to make them more . . . docile."

Head and chest above Noah, Eudeon frowned. "Your master takes an eye, and this calms them?"

"No, not the eye itself. The brain behind it." Someone sharply intook a breath; Eroch cursed. Belseraphim began walking again. "The procedure works almost every time now."

"*Almost?*" Noah was loath to estrange his guide to his betrothed in any way, but he was beginning to feel much as he did with Phempor's prince. "Your 'master' experiments on criminals?"

"He *fixes* them. After all, if one can *do* something so wrong," Belseraphim said, "there surely must *be* something wrong. Must it not be so?"

"Surely, but that thing is the sin of man's soul, not the contents of his skull."

"Yes. Precisely. We are come. You may bring your animals inside. Open!"

The gate before them rose, unseen chains and gears moving in a staccato of iron. More of the macabre servants, most of them corpulent, wandered aimlessly about in the wide hall beyond, making no notice as the group passed. The blue-glassed lamps here shone brighter and colder. Shadows were sharp, shrouding alcoves and arched portals in deep black. In one of them, at the end of the hall and raised above the others, a hidden, seated figure was denoted by a pair of legs that were unmistakably Naphil.

"My master," addressed Belseraphim. "I bring you unexpected company."

Silence met her pronouncement; Noah noticed the hallways had become clogged with the strange attendants of the place, every good eye fixed upon his party.

"Shall I introduce them?" continued Belseraphim.

"No," said a voice that creaked from disuse. "No, my womb, there is no need. I have not had the pleasure in a very long time, but I must say, it *is* nice to receive unexpected visits from friends and family."

The shadowed figure leaned forward.

Ninniachul tended to gravitate to the outcast, and it had always seemed logical to him: the most improvement could be had with what needed most to be improved. In most contexts of society, he himself had never fit in well, but the fact never bothered him; it simply meant that he was a component of a different machine. The trend held true when he had arrived in Atlantis. While the other Atlantean ingeniators built their brute war machines designed to fling large things long distances, Reshus and Orrin merely pored over drawings and models. Ninniachul had instantly seen the potential in their ideas, and he had attached himself to the project, despite the derision directed at the "mirror men" and the encouragement from the other ingeniators to apply his mind to a more worthwhile endeavor.

They had done it, however, and they had won their array a place on the wall. The value of their work, and his contribution to it, would soon be seen by all, peers and soldiers alike.

The Zuthians had arrived.

The sea mists had already retreated to the shore, and the view from the wall was clear, even to Ninniachul, thanks to the lenses over his eyes. That they allowed him to see detail at a distance beyond his outstretched hand had not ceased to be wondrous, true testimony to the power and potential of the technology. Spotters shouted as small ships came into sight around a horn of land almost at the horizon. The sailed vessels were shabby in appearance, but Ninniachul knew boats, and these looked fast and sturdy; in many arenas, crude appearance did not necessarily mean poor performance, and the ships at the leading edge of the Zuthian marine assault seemed to him like sharp stone knives, just as deadly as any made of polished bronze.

Behind these came a vessel that was larger by far, boxy and black, with a blunt prow armored in iron plate and large, open porthole windows set high above the water-line. Low double rows of oars on either side propelled it ponderously forward. Its sheer size and slow, steady approach gave it an ominous, inexorable look. Ninniachul wished he could see through those windows to what was hidden inside.

"Ignore the black ark!" shouted the Atlantean lieutenant who had been placed with the ingeniators to coordinate with their naval forces, amassed and waiting unseen at the mouth of Atlantis's great moat. "Focus on the sailships! Fire when they come within the range of your machine!" Ninniachul drew a deep breath, steeling himself with images of old friends, corpses charred by the work of the Zuthians, and readied to set his deadly engine to work.

One by one, the teams fired. Ingeniators called out distances and adjustments; Nephilim loading crews hoisted huge stones into buckets and winched back iron arms of gargantuan bolt throwers. The first volleys were mostly ineffective, but as the machines discovered their ranges, they wrought absolute destruction upon the Zuthian fleet. Soaring blocks rained down to crack ram-shackle ships in half; bolts impaled sailors and pierced hulls, causing terror among the crews or sinking vessels outright. Zuthians died—Ninniachul watched them

die—but the distance and silence made it a far different
experience than the horrors he had witnessed up close,
and those at Zuthi's hands, and he felt no conviction or
hesitation.

What he did feel was frustration. Cries and cheers
went up every time a missile struck true, but none rose
from the ingeniators manning the mirror machine. The
Zuthian ships were too swift, the lens array too difficult
to quickly adjust while remaining focused on its target
long enough to kindle a fire. The lieutenant called a halt
to the ingeniator schools' barrages. A few blackened holes
in sails were the only scars from Ninniachul's team upon
the few ships that limped or lucked through.

Indistinct shouts with the cadences of military
orders came up from the moat. Most of the men on the
wall, Ninniachul with them, went to the edge of it and
looked down at the Atlantean navy below. Reshus looked
glum and in no mood to talk, but Orrin grinned at the
Mizraimite. "Watch," he said, "and witness why Pethun of
Atlantis claims dominion over the sea."

Even if the other man had not pointed him out,
Pethun would have been unmistakeable. There he stood,
at the prow of the lead Atlantean frigate, calling out
orders that were passed back from ship to ship, and to
other craft Ninniachul had no names for. The Nephilim
lord did indeed seem like some ocean deity imagined by
the most inventive oracle and painted with a master's
brush: long, white-blonde hair curled by saltwater into
waves, silver-scaled armor that left tanned, muscular
arms bare, a three-pronged spear of bronze and gold
held aloft in anticipation of a victory that was certain
to come. He finished speaking and dove into the water,
apparently a signal for the Atlantean sailors to set sails

and work oars, and the entirety of the navy started up at good speed. Ninniachul scanned the water for a sign of Pethun, finally finding the giant far ahead of where the ingeniator would have thought him to be. He was moving fast, faster than arms and legs could possibly propel him on their own; both realization and awe simultaneously struck Ninniachul when he spied the tall black fin moving at the same speed behind the Naphil.

"That . . ." He looked again to make sure that his eyes, for so long untrustworthy, did not now deceive him. "Th-that is a *whale*."

"It is," answered Orrin. "And not just Pethun is partner to one. Look. And here come the dolphin chariots!"

Dozens of thin wakes traced the paths of other Atlantean whale riders, pushed along at a fantastic pace by the noses of the lustrous black-and-white creatures behind them. After these came high-helmed men balanced upon rounded, flared white coracles like enormous shells, javelin in one hand and reins in the other, pulled along by teams of dolphins of pink or grey. Galleys and frigates followed, with every simultaneous stroke of their oarmen gliding closer to the decimated Zuthians. When splashes at the ships' sides prompted Ninniachul to discover their causes, he saw yet another trained Atlantean warbeast as seal after seal, spotted and streamlined, dove from the decks into the water to swim alongside the fast-moving boats.

The remnant of the Zuthians was overwhelmed from every direction. Orcas thrust human and Naphil partners high into the air and into the midst of Zuthi's panicked crews before submerging and ramming their battered boats from below. Seals leapt up and knocked or snatched enemy sailors into the sea, where they were quickly ended by charioteers or the surprisingly vicious dolphins. Once the Atlantean galleys engaged, the battle was all but over. The few surviving Zuthian ships were boarded, their sails lowered, their arms laid down.

A cheer went up among the ingeniators, pleased to have done their parts well. Ninniachul braced himself for the derision he expected to be sent his way; in that moment, it did not come, but he had no doubt that when victory's elation subsided, his peers would mock. The celebration quieted. Men murmured and pointed as the Atlantean navy began to stir again. Their purpose was obvious, their battle not yet complete.

The black ark had never stopped moving.

Frigates pulled up along the ark, trying to cut the steadily rowing oars, thick around as cedars' trunks and more than matches for hacking swords. A few intrepid Atlanteans tried to climb up the oars' shafts, but only one avoided slipping off, and he was dislodged—or dispatched, Ninniachul could not tell—at the ark's hull when long spears darted in and out of openings like maddened serpents' tongues. Apparently no one else of the ships' crews cared to be skewered on the cusp of triumph, so they backed off to give the whale riders room. One by one, orcas breached fully out of the water, the Atlantean warriors upon their snouts shot above the oars. The ark's jutting plates and spikes provided ample handholds, and a score or so of Atlantis's finest began to climb to the larger portholes above.

The first of them gained his goal, and all on the wall cheered, until snapping draconic jaws pulled him violently inside. The next one to reach a porthole could not hear the cries of the sailors below, and certainly not the ingeniators, but his screams were loud enough to give the rest of the climbers pause enough to catch a glimpse of his scrabbling hands torn from their grip on the window's edge. When a spined dragon's knobby, thin-snouted head flashed out to grab a third Atlantean warrior hesitating several cubits below a porthole, the remaining whale riders dropped into the water, one of them caroming hard against an oar on his way down.

All except Pethun.

The Naphil held his position below the window, gripping an iron plate with one hand and holding his tri-tipped spear at the ready with the other. Again, a dragon struck, but Pethun's strike was quicker. He plunged his spear into the bottom jaw of the monstrous beast, three barbed ends preventing the thrashing head from freeing itself. Pethun hung on, letting it carry him up to the window into which it was trying to retreat.

Suddenly, the entire section of hull around the port-hole fell away, dropping like a drawbridge around a hinge on its bottom edge. The thick slab of wood slammed into the side of the ark, crushing both the Naphil and dragon's head between and pulling the beast's body out with it. The weight of the dragon—now limp, like a carcass—ripped its head back through the porthole, and the enormous animal fell into the sea with a tremendous splash, cracking two oars to splinters as it did. Ninniachul could not tell if Pethun had fallen as well, but when the enormous gate was pulled back up and closed, he was nowhere to be seen.

The ark continued toward the port.

Atlantean soldiers took up oars of two of the Zuthian ships that still floated, rowing them in front of the ark and diving to safety. The huge ship pushed through unimpeded, crushing the boats to splinters. The lieutenant on the wall shouted, not yet in a panic, but not far from it, for the ingeniators to recommence firing. Stone after stone flew to the black ark, only to clang off its armored hull into the water.

Orrin swore. "The port has no wall. Those savages plan to run aground and release a barge full of dragons into the city!"

"You needed to say that aloud? Do you think us blind?" asked Reshus harshly. "An obvious observation, and one that I wish not to see closer."

Orrin grabbed the other man's coat. "Where will you hide?"

"Not your concern."

"Let me come with you!"

"Stop!" Ninniachul shouted. "Take your places! The *wooden ark moves slowly.*"

Even sluggish minds would have understood, and theirs were agile. Orrin and Reshus adjusted mirrors and checked angles while Ninniachul aligned the proper lenses. Distance was gauged, gears rotated, and one last great lens was turned to face the shining sun overhead. When it did, every glass surface of the machine glared or flared brightly, capturing the power of the sun itself and redirecting and focusing its energy at a single point of bare wood midway up the ark's broad bow.

In the seconds in which nothing seemed to happen, Ninniachul prayed to whatever gods might be listening for success. Survival had pushed professional vindication from his mind; there was no way to know exactly, of course, but if dragons truly filled a barge that size to its capacity, he could not fathom Atlantis victorious, no matter what other forces attacked or defended it.

A thin plume of smoke appeared, then grew bigger. Reshus began talking to himself excitedly under his breath; finally, a yellow flame came to life. Orrin yelled in triumph. Ninniachul adjusted ever so slightly, keeping the focus, continuing his silent, aimless prayer.

The Atlantean lieutenant ran over. "What is it?" he demanded. "See for yourself," said Orrin, pointing to the small fire.

"Praise to the Sea Mother," whispered the soldier. He turned to call down the line of ingeniators. "Get to the ports! Get barrels of oil, blubber, anything that will feed a fire!" Ingeniator crews sent men and Nephilim rushing down the stairs.

"You," he said to Ninniachul and his fellows. "Keep up that flame. For the sake of Atlantis and free men, *keep up that flame.*" Ninniachul needed no telling twice.

The new ordinance was loaded into the catapults and hurled away. A few barrels exploded near the fire caused by the mirror machine, and a direct hit caused the flame to spread angrily. Ninniachul called to change the target point. This time, the oil-soaked wood burned easily, and still the barrels flew.

Smoke billowed thick and black now from the ark's prow; if there were Zuthian observers inside it watching the ports of Atlantis approach, they could see no more.

The big boat slowed, but it had not stopped. Ninniachul set a third fire. The first one was burning through the hull; armor plates dropped into the water with splashes and hisses of steam. Now merchants ships were leaving their docks at the Atlantean ports, coming alongside galleys to deliver their wares—perfumes in jars, oils for cooking or lamps, anything that might spread a flame—to be thrown and dashed at the fire's edge, leading it along the black ark's side. Zuthian spears futilely arched out of the openings by the oars, not intended for ranged use and impotent to stop the authors of the conflagration. One of the ark's great gates fell open and a maddened dragon barreled out, but as soon as it hit the water, orcas and dolphins were upon it, battering it mercilessly and pulling it under the surface to drown.

The thick oars moved disjointedly, then none at all. The flames engulfed the ark and burned almost to the waterline. The ingeniators watched the scene play out in silence, as did the sailors below them, the only sound across the water the muted cries of man and beast inside the ark as it began to sink.

Such cries awakened no pity in Ninniachul. He smiled and stared until the burning ship disappeared into the sea.

CHAPTER 45

Noah searched for familiarity in the Naphil face that emerged into the light. He did not find it in individual features—sharp and beardless cheeks, close-cropped head, furrowed brow that kept his eyes shrouded in shadow—but in the whole, he recognized a person he had known long ago, or at least what had become of him.

"Dedroth?"

"Noah of Eden. I must say, you have aged tremendously. I mean tremendously *well*. You also, little brother." Eudeon nodded. "And you, Tehama, look as hale and beautiful as ever. It must be the sun, the open air. Of course, one cannot do *all this* out in the open, eh?" He spread his hands, in thin black gloves at the end of tight black sleeves.

"Dedroth." Eroch said the name like he was tasting it. "You are my father's brother?"

"That depends entirely on who your father is."

"Dyeus of Atlantis."

"Ah! Another bastard! Then indeed I am—though I am eldest, so I would say that *he* is *my* brother," answered the Naphil, stepping down and moving within a handspan of Eroch, examining him. "Mm. You *are* an interesting specimen. What is your name?"

"Eroch." The younger giant was bigger by far than the other, but to Noah he almost looked like prey under Dedroth's intense, probing gaze, like a wounded mammoth under a lone, patient buzzard. He disliked it. Eroch was crude, but he was familiar; everything about Dedroth, about this place, felt strange.

"My master." Belseraphim's featureless voice was even so like a bell for Dedroth, who instantly looked up and smiled at the woman. "One of your dogs fetched for you another womb," she said, "but it is wanted by someone else." She inclined her head to Noah. The black-clad Naphil frowned.

"I know not of such a thing."

Noah noticed no change in the pale, waifish woman, and from their confused looks, neither did his companions, but something Dedroth saw in Belseraphim prompted him to stride forward and clutch her to himself, picking her up like a father embracing a sobbing child with a skinned knee. "My womb, my womb, you know I do not tell falsehoods, least of all to you."

"I am pleased. I was worried so." Her face pressed into Dedroth's shoulder, Belseraphim's words were muffled, and *still* her voice was to the ears as unsalted bread was to the palate. The scene was somehow touching, but it was bizarre.

Their embrace ended, and Dedroth put his . . . wife? . . . down. "Now, Noah," he said. "Explain." Noah did, in succinct, thorough, rapid fashion, and all the while the Naphil's face darkened to match his garb.

"I have heard you tell this tale before," he said, "as well you know. My father was the source of your misery last time, and I could do nothing. If an agent of mine has done this now, I promise you it shall be undone." He motioned for several of the shambling attendants to follow. "Come with me, all. This shall soon be ended."

Noah expected Dedroth to lead them through cramped, winding hallways, dreary and damp. Instead, the Naphil had taken a great deal of effort to make his abode spacious as befit the great stature of his kind. Wide pillars supported tall ceilings in rooms that seemed to go on and on. Where they walked, lamps were few, but bright light poured from myriad entryways. Noah supposed these led to more comfortable quarters, as this main thoroughfare was cold and sparsely decorated.

"Your animals are beautiful," said Dedroth. "That cat in particular. I must say, the lack of interesting fauna is a decided downside of my duties underground. Few creatures here but vermin." He snapped his fingers. One of the servants drew to him. "Bring me my pet," he said, and the servant lumbered off. They started again.

"What is all this?" said Eudeon, watching the servant go. "What happened to these people's eyes?"

"Let me start at the beginning, little brother," Dedroth replied. "I regret I have not known you, the youngest child of my mother, who died birthing you. You left when you were just a boy. This being so, you have not known me either. From my youth I have studied the ways of all living things, and I do so still. Beasts have always fascinated me." As if on cue, the attendant returned, panting. He held out a small animal, which the giant gingerly took. Tehama cursed, and Noah may have made a sound as well. It was a three-headed pup, four paws in front and two in back. Dedroth ignored them and began to softly stroke its triple heads with three giant fingers. "Beasts have always fascinated me," he repeated.

"Humans," said Eudeon.

"Hmm?"

"I ask about humans," Eudeon repeated. "Humans are not beasts."

"No?" Dedroth gave him a curious glance. "But neither are they *bene Elohim*. Or Nephilim."

"Come, Dedroth, humans have *souls*."

"Yes, they do."

From some hall beyond them, a faint cry chilled the air. Dedroth, Belseraphim, and the fleshy servants seemed not even to hear it, but the others shared a discomfited glance, even Eroch. Unease settled on the back of Noah's neck and stood the hairs up; Tehama hitched up the quiver on her back, as if reassuring herself it was there.

"Do you ever wonder where resides a man's soul?" asked Dedroth. "At one time I thought it might be the eyes, but the eyes are only a window to it, or at least to *part* of it. How to explain? Atlantis sends me her broken sons and daughters, some beyond fixing. Others, though, can be repaired, can be made to function once more. Never to leave exile, mind you—else why exile them at all?—but here, I can put them to useful work, once I heal their soul."

"Heal their soul?" asked Noah. This was a phrase missioners used commonly, but Noah had no doubt that here, it meant something far different.

"Indeed, with care and precision, and at the mere cost of an eye. Once I reform what lies behind, impulses are restrained, appetites are changed, the savage is rendered docile. Would I let such violent beings into my very home, to wait on the woman who has borne my children, if it were not so?"

"Brother, the soul can be healed by Elohim, and no other." Noah knew Eudeon well; the giant's voice was calm, but only with great effort.

"But you declare that out of your *belief*," answered Dedroth. "I am a man of science, and I make my statement based on evidence."

"What evidence?"

Dedroth smiled. This time he sent two attendants, with instructions to meet them in some hall beyond. "Give a man an excuse to display his work, and he invariably will."

"What 'work' is that?" asked Tehama.

"Knowledge," replied Dedroth. "Knowledge of mankind's limits, so we might better them. I wish to know how much a man needs to eat to survive yet remain always starving, how little he might drink and stay alive but never quench his thirst, how little he can sleep without succumbing to exhaustion though he may be ever tired, how much pain he can endure without his body surrendering his mind entirely."

"Dedroth, you describe torture," said Noah.

"Torture? You misunderstand, my old friend. I make them *useful*, when the world above declares them to be useless. I give their lives *meaning*. The knowledge I gain I do not keep for myself. It disseminates, through various means I have devised, to the physicians and healers in the city above, who spread it far beyond these walls."

A burbling noise came from ahead. Noah saw the pair of obese, grotesque servants wheel some sort of cart or cradle into the main hall. The odd, disconcerting sound came again, from inside the cradle.

"We have no time for this, Dedroth," said Tehama. "We must find Phiaphara." Noah guessed she wished to see Dedroth's "work" no more than he.

"It will take but a moment. Eudeon, do you want to see the essence of a man? Here it is—or, at least, it will demonstrate what it is *not*."

Holding his breath, Noah peered into the cradle. It was of a size made for an infant, but the figure within was no newborn; it was a person, naked, armless and legless, with no nose, ears, or eyes. It writhed about on silken sheets, somehow sensing an audience and ululating horribly as if calling for help. Noah stepped back, closed his eyes, and prayed. He knew not what else he could do.

"The jaw and tongue can be removed as well," said Dedroth, "but it takes quite too much trouble to feed and water on my part. So, you see: whatever makes a man is somewhere still *in there*. Perhaps the head, perhaps the chest, and there is a *small* chance it is near the stomach. Interesting, no?"

From the way Eudeon looked at his elder brother, Noah could tell that his dam of civility had been sundered. "Our mother called you Dedroth," he said, in tones so low and cold that the words seemed to freeze in the air. "I name you Sheol, for you have embraced the grave and given it a home on earth. You consort with death, the final enemy."

"How dare you judge me, in my abode."

"I do not judge you," said Eudeon. "But I leave you to the One who will."

Dedroth's face went stony for a moment, then relaxed. He chuckled. "Death is only your enemy if you strive against it. Death is only your enemy if you are not on her side—for now, at least. One day, all those with the blood of angels will thank me for what I do here." He considered Noah. "Perhaps even you, descendant of Enoch the Undying. Who can say?"

"My lord," interjected Belseraphim, "should we not be moving on? These people wish to find their friend, and you know how eager your dogs can be." Thankfully, she waved the servants with the macabre cradle away.

"Quite right, quite right." Dedroth motioned the entire procession forward, seeming to forget the preceding conversation entirely. "We near the dwellings of my agents and associates. You shall be reunited with your . . . Phiaphara, yes? . . . shortly." He smiled at Noah, who caught a fleeting, tragic glimpse of the awkward naturalist the Naphil had once been. "I am certain we will find her in one piece."

Noah did not know if he meant it as a joke.

‹ CHAPTER 46 ›

The cavernous pillared halls transitioned to the cramped, winding warrens that Noah had initially expected. As they went, Dedroth sent servants down every fork and branch with instructions to find a girl matching the description given by Noah and Tehama and to fetch her back to the entrance to these confusing passages.

When only two attendants remained, Dedroth beckoned the rest to continue with him. "It would not do for you to become lost yourselves," he said, rounding a corner. He stooped to avoid hitting his head on a hanging lamp, turning to look behind. "Do watch yourselves, Eudeon, Eroch. These tunnels were not made for gi—Oh!"

Something, or someone, had run full on into the Naphil's leg hard enough to jolt him. Whoever it was had been silent and stealthy, but still running hard, now on the ground and panting, scrambling for a bow that had been knocked away. Heart in his throat, Noah peered around the giant's big body, then pushed past Belseraphim and Dedroth when he saw who it was.

"Phiaphara!"

"Noah!" she said breathlessly. She jumped up and threw her arms around him with a sob that he could tell she tried hard to stifle. Noah had no words; he just held her.

"Are you hurt?" He broke their embrace and looked her full in the face. A thin ribbon of blood, not quite yet dried, ran from her nose to her the corner of her lip, and her hair was disheveled, strands pulled loose and stuck with sweat to her temples and forehead. Despite all that, she shook her head no.

"I *am* so pleased this ended with no trouble," said Dedroth. "My servant will see you out to the old Grigori palaces. You should be safe there."

Eroch scratched his head, appearing grossly unsatisfied. "If I had known that all we were going to do was ask for Phiaphara politely and wait for her to arrive, I would not have come. At least in battle there is *some* glory, even if it is only against Zuthian rabble—more than in mucking through human waste in the dark, anyway."

"Zuthi?" Belseraphim asked, tone inscrutable. "Zuthi fights Atlantis, above us?"

To Noah, she might have been standing a bit stiffer than before, but she looked as vapid and trancelike as ever; Dedroth, however, strode over to her and bent on a knee. "Now, now, my womb, please—do not become hysterical, especially in front of guests. Here, lean upon me." Staring into nothing, she rested her head listlessly upon his shoulder.

"Our sons," she said.

"The most useful tools are used up most quickly. It does not mean they were wasted."

"I would not worry about your sons, madam," said Tehama, infusing confidence into her words. "Atlantis's unrivaled strengths have been united by common cause. By the time the battle ends, nothing of Zuthi will be left, and your children will be safe once more."

At this, Belseraphim whipped around and started walking briskly back the way they had come.

"Go after her," instructed Dedroth to a pair of attendants. Pursing his lips, he looked disapprovingly at Eroch and Tehama in turn, as if they were misbehaved children from whom he had expected better. He opened his mouth, but before he could speak, angry sputtering and uneven footsteps drew their attention down the passage.

A man made the corner, hobbling with haste, face reddened in rage beneath bolder red welts running across it. He spit blood as he cursed, one hand on the wall and the other clutched between his legs. Like Phiaphara, he did not see Dedroth until he ran into the giant, who allowed him to do it.

Phiaphara's hand reflexively went to her quiver. Instead of drawing an arrow, she raised an accusatory finger. "That is who accosted me and dragged me here! He tried . . . tried to dishonor me, by force." Rather than cower in fear, she sneered. "He was unsuccessful." Undisguised pleasure flitted across Tehama's face.

"Is this true, Pirdan?" asked Dedroth.

"I . . . But this is the girl who . . ." In raising his head to address his stuttering defense to Dedroth, the man saw who was with him, and his features froze into perhaps the most bizarre expression Noah had ever seen. It was a mixture of surprise, fear, and fury, and as he studied it, he realized that, underneath the scratches and flushing, he recognized it.

Apparently, Eroch did too.

"*You!*" the muscular giant shouted.

"Havilah's plague bringer," whispered Tehama. "So this is the hole you crawled back to. You will regret it."

"Master, I . . ." That this cringing figure was the same one that had poisoned the wedding wine of Havilah, killed off entire families, brought a nation to its knees, was clear, but gone was the arrogant defiance he had shown in front of Midash's peacekeepers. All emotion had fallen from the man's face but fear. He tried to back away, keeping Dedroth between himself and Noah's party, but several of the Naphil's servants had come behind him, giving him nowhere to go.

"Pirdan. *Pirdan.*" Dedroth placed his hands together in front of him, calm and thoughtful. "You were useful once, and for that I am grateful, but something about this girl has broken you. I fear you cannot be repaired." He turned his back to Pirdan, who bent over and screamed. Noah wouldn't have thought Dedroth's undramatic statement deserved such a violent reaction from the man, but it did, and it escalated. As his breath ran out and brought his cry to a close, Pirdan's eyes widened; he straightened and tried to shove through the wall of meaty servants, who seemed to be expecting it and coalesced around him. He pushed again, and they lifted him bodily off his feet.

"Bring him here," commanded Dedroth. Pirdan strained against pairs of clutching hands that brought him close, his effort in vain.

"Noah," said Dedroth, "this man took your betrothed from you, as did my father. I did nothing and thus cannot apologize for either, but could I, no number of words would be enough. We both know you must have thought much on what revenge you would wish on Samyaza. Say what you will, and I will visit such upon this man."

The Naphil was right. It had been the prayerful work of years to dismiss the horrifying images of pain and torture that Noah visited upon the *ben Elohim* in his daydreams and nightmares about Emzara, every time he imagined the life he would have had with her in Eden, instead of as a perpetual nomad in strange places. Now those images came to him at once, bright and vivid, with-out the dullness that time imparted, and Dedroth was offering any and all of them to a being who more than deserved them. The answer was easy.

"I would have you do nothing on my account," said Noah. "We have who we came for, thank you. Could you have someone show us the way out?"

Dedroth nodded. "Good. Mercy suits you, Noah, as it always has. I would not have wished the fate of this worthless creature to be on your conscience, and now it is not. Servants! Eat!"

Pirdan screamed again as human teeth tore him apart with shocking ferocity.

"Oh," said Eroch.

Dedroth placed giant hands on Phiaphara's and Noah's backs and steered them away. "No need to see this, friends, nor do we need to emerge above ground just yet. Let us find a place to wait in safety until we discover who prevails in the battle above." Shaking her head, Tehama followed, pulling at Eroch, who was watching slack jawed. Eudeon, though, stood stone still, as if he had not heard.

"You." Eudeon sounded stunned, or drunk, and it made Noah pause. "Dedroth. It is *you*. Zuthi. Your sons. Pirdan." In two strides, the giant was face to face with his elder brother. "Did all of this come from *you*?"

Dedroth straightened to a handspan taller than Eudeon. "Yes. All for Atlantis. If nature has taught me anything, the strong weed out the weak. For myself, I hypothesize that Atlantis is stronger than the rabble assembled by my children. Yes, some good people have died, but you have culled herds before, have you not? You have sacrificed?"

"You started a war!" yelled Eudeon. "You have destroyed sacred places, brought death to entire *cities* that did *nothing* to you!" Though his fists were clenched and shaking, he made no move to assault Dedroth physically, but Eroch did. The powerful giant roared, grabbing the front of Dedroth's black tunic and lifting him high against a pillar. Anger flew across Dedroth's face, but it instantly settled into calm. He raised his sleeved arms, then brought stiff-fingered hands down hard to strike at Eroch's locked elbows. With a cry of pain, Eroch dropped him.

"Feeling will come back in a moment, nephew. Touch me again, and its loss will be permanent." He turned from the cursing giant and addressed them all. "I left my children and my agents to their own particular methods. I will not accept blame for them."

"Oh, you will be blamed," said Tehama, fitting an arrow to her bow. "I will make sure of it. My father and Pethun will send waves of warriors to drown you down here."

"Drown?" Dedroth narrowed his eyes and loomed above the Nephilim huntress. "I will tell you about *drowning*. If my brothers come against me, I will stop up the sewers until Atlantis's streets turn to rivers of filth and pestilence. If a single soldier enters my domain, I will empty the underground of every murderer and man of violence here, and they will paint your gleaming white stones red with blood. And, after all that, if I am *still* beset upon, I will destroy the very foundations of Atlantis and sink her into the sea. Or . . ." He straightened, impassive once more. "You may leave without rancor, and enter once again the jewel of earth, the city without peer, now and forever in peace, because I have brought the barbarians of this world to dash themselves upon the strength of Atlantis. Either way: goodbye." He waved and departed, leaving behind one attendant who shuffled over to the wall, removed a torch, and stared at them expectantly.

"Come," said Eudeon. "There is nothing else to do."

Eroch grunted; with a sigh, Tehama replaced her arrow.

Noah watched Dedroth disappear into the darkness, then took Phiaphara's hand and turned to go.

‹ CHAPTER 47 ›

NORTH BRIDGE

Over the centuries, the riches of Atlantis and its people multiplied too greatly to be constrained by the great wall around it, or the massive moat beyond that. Outside North Bridge, through which flowed the riches of Assyria and beyond—herbs and spices, exotic drakes and stocky, shaggy oxen, gems and stone found nowhere else—the land sloped down, so the city did as well. The buildings were staggered, one's roof another's front court. Staircases for pedestrians rose along wide roads that provided a last gentle obstacle for traders and merchants, none of whom plied their trades today.

Instead, here Mareth had placed the disparate forces of the nations displaced by Zuthi. His reasoning had been twofold: first, the high ground would be easier to hold for troops that the Atlantean commander viewed as less trained and less equipped that his own; and second, scouts had reported that the mass of the Zuthian army approaching North Bridge consisted of captured countrymen of the refugee fighters, who surely would switch sides when given the opportunity.

Elebru had taken several hundred Edenites to bolster the defenders of North Bridge. He wore a leather pauldron and sheath over his drawing arm, bow at his back and sword at his side. He had kept his face and head bare, displaying his brutal scar; that, along with an air of superiority he had cultivated as ardently as he had his gardens in Eden, marked him as a man who demanded respect, and others gave it to him, both his own countrymen and the foreigners he would soon fight alongside. He loved the feeling. He would have smiled to himself, but the burned, immobile flesh around his mouth did not let him.

For his position, he had chosen a high rooftop bordered on two sides with tall pots of fiery flowers that reminded him of his Eden estate. He knew it was sentimental, but he was too old to care, and the vantage was excellent regardless. He scanned the hills in the distance; his eyes were aged, but he trusted them. A line of men crawled over them, slow and plodding, no doubt fatigued from the long march from Zuthi, or wherever they had been conscripted.

"They have numbers," observed Rescal, head of his huntsmen. The man was a mercenary from Cush, and Elebru paid him well to keep his flocks well guarded. Since Elebru's gold went with Elebru, now Rescal was here.

"I worry less about them," said Elebru, "than about whatever keeps them compliant. I guess those." He pointed at one, two, three wide, wheeled platforms interrupting the assembled army. He squinted. Thick smoke belched from uncovered cauldrons in the centers, while similar ones remained lidded around the edges, every one attended by a near-naked figure whose whole body gleamed with oil. Grey-robed individuals in bizarre angular masks, genders impossible to assign, roamed among the oiled ones gesturing and shouting. Surely these were Zuthi's commanders, which meant the first targets for the arrows and darts of Eden would be the knobby reptilian beasts that pulled the platforms. Alas, a few might very well miss their marks high and dispatch the platforms' occupants instead, but surely Elohim knew that even the best intentions are not immune to accident.

"We may soon find out their tricks and methods," said Rescal. "Look there."

The leading edge of the Zuthian slave horde had reached the outer buildings. When it did, a cluster of men broke from the pack at a sprint; the cries and shouts of the fisherfolk arrayed a few blocks over marked the runners from Mame. They seemed safe enough from the cauldron platforms, which Elebru doubted could maneuver quickly at all, much less among suburban streets.

How horribly wrong *that* notion proved to be.

A contingent of fighters from Mame rushed out to meet the aspiring escapees. As they did, the grey-robes shrieked and waved their arms madly. In response, the smoke-spewing cauldrons were covered, and the outer ones opened. Now the wild flailing became more precise, more intentional, and Elebru became sure that the masked and shrouded figures were sorcerers of some kind. At first, as dark plumes rose from the newly opened containers, he guessed they were a sort of wind charmer, since the billows moved against the breeze. That idea lasted for just a moment when he realized the black smoke was, in fact, *alive*.

Incredulously, the smoke—insects, in truth, beyond counting and big as chestnuts—was directed by the sorcerers on the great wheeled platforms to fall upon the men of Mame, their reunion brief. The free warriors wore skirts and thick strands of shells and teeth around their necks and nothing else, and the slaves were clad only in rags. Fat beetles enveloped all of them. They dropped to the ground wailing, their screams mingling into a single hideous noise that reached a crescendo and stopped almost at once. The swarms drifted up, hovering over skeletal remains that glistened red in the bright sunlight. Their secret revealed, the sorcerers on each platform—now Elebru saw at least a score of them among the captives—released more swirling swarms of the black beetles. With guttural howls and violent, definitive motions, they sent the vicious insects in thick waves toward the defenders of Atlantis.

A few shouts of horror and the clattering of dropped weapons echoed about the emptied buildings. This was something to make even brave men flee. Elebru recognized the feeling in himself, as he had felt it before, only once, when his hubristic foolishness had sacrificed the lives of good men to the flame-spewing jaws of a leviathan. He was no fool now.

"We cannot fight this," he said to Rescal. The Cushite shook his head in accord. With regret that it had to be, but with no guilt whatsoever, Elebru shouted the call for the Edenites to retreat.

His cry was drowned out completely by the clarion peal of a trumpet.

The sound had seemed to come from everywhere at once. Elebru spun around, looking for its source. Two figures stood atop the highest point in the vicinity, a soaring monumental spire thrice as tall as the surrounding structures. They were strangers, dressed in pure white, and certainly not a part of any of the factions gathered before North Bridge. Elebru did not even see a means to ascend the monument.

One of them raised a sword. The blade shone more brightly than it should have, as if it was luring rays of sunlight and capturing them. Inexorably, it pulled Elebru's eyes to it, and somehow he was sure the same was true for each pair within sight of it. The other figure had a bow, arrow fitted to the string and pulled back. Elebru could not be sure which one said the word, but nevertheless he heard it as clearly as if it had been spoken directly into his ear.

"Fire!"

This was a command that none dared disobey. Elebru did not even pick a target; he simply drew an arrow and loosed it into the air. His arrow joined hundreds more: feather fletched from fellow Edenites, finned and tooth tipped from fishermen of Mame, short shafted from Eazor, long atlatl-thrown darts from the longfooted hunters of the plains of Temmen-thurah. For a moment, Elebru was aghast at what they had done. No number of arrows would be effective against the beetle swarms, but even if a few of the insects, or many, or all, were speared, the projectiles would still fall on the captives, struck down by their kinsmen as surely as if the Zuthians had done it themselves. He shut his eyes, unwilling to watch.

"Behemoth's blood," breathed Rescal. Elebru snapped his scarred lids open at the Cushite imprecation, just in time to see the arrows cease to be arrows anymore. Fletchings turned to tailfeathers, arrowheads became beaks, every speeding shaft morphing into a bird of prey that took a flight of its own. Falcons and kestrels, gulls and frigatebirds, hawks and swifts, met the beetle swarms in swoops and dives, dispersing and devouring them with unrestrained savagery. The howls of the Zuthian sorcerers changed to wails of disbelief. Elebru was a simple man of the earth and could not know what powers were in play here, but he was certain of two things: this struggle had ascended beyond the mere physical, and the strength of the two white warriors was greater by far.

After a few minutes of watching the birds' aerial onslaught in amazement, it struck Elebru that it was over.

The insects were gone. The power of the grey sorcerers was spent entirely. Cheers erupted all around him as his men realized it as well.

The captives realized it too.

With cries of rage, they climbed the platforms. The oil-covered Zuthians fought back hard, but sheer numbers overwhelmed them, and they likewise cried out, but in terror. Bodies were pummeled and passed back in the rush for the robed magicians, who had nowhere to flee. Some were ripped apart by bare hands; others were thrust screaming and thrashing into the great smoking cauldrons. Free men ran into the streets, reuniting with family and friends, their enslavement ended, dread turned to joy. Still somewhat dubious, Elebru looked up at the spire. The two men were gone.

"Gather the men," he said the Rescal. "Let us see if we can be of help elsewhere."

"If elsewhere is anything like here," said Rescal, "the battle is already over."

‹ CHAPTER 48 ›

BULL BRIDGE

What are they waiting for?"

Merim looked over at Maban, who had asked the question, as he pulled the reins of a unicorn as impatient as he apparently was.

"I assume that was rhetorical, Maban, as I am no prophet."

"Let them take all the time they wish," said young Uzti, a converted war priest of Peag. "Those dragons' stunted arms will grow no longer to protect its belly from being impaled upon the horn of my unicorn."

"I have no authority among you to tell you to be quiet, but: be quiet," said Tiras. He stood in his chariot—at least, he called it a chariot, though it was more akin to a war wagon—behind his rams, alert, eyes fixated on the stuttering line of lance-wielding warriors from Zuthi astride minor dragons that strutted obnoxiously back and forth, bobbing their scaly heads like chickens in a feedyard.

"Your concern is noted, angel-blood." Uzti smirked. "You carry quite the big hammer, giant. Overcompensating?"

Gilyon wheeled on the man. "Blood is meaningless. Actions are everything. Calm your nerves with prayer, not frivolous, unbecoming banter."

Uzti nodded. "Yes, Bloodletter."

Gilyon faced the line of dragons again, their sharp yellow maws only slightly less imposing in the distance. Their riders, tattered cloaks flapping behind them, had taken them to the crest of a ridge and no further. Perhaps Zuthi hid some war machine beyond, but it was impossible to say whether wisdom dictated risking an advance to find out. So, despite a growing, gnawing hunger to fight that could only be sated by engaging the murderous Zuthians, Gilyon held his holy knights in position.

Gilyon alone among the Scribes was unmounted. His trust extended to himself, his Creator, a few friends, and no one else, and certainly not to some dumb beast meant to bear him into battle, even ones as suited for such a task as the unicorns. Mounted or not, he did not relish the prospect of facing such creatures as those dragons, though neither did he fear it. The stoic Scribes' forces were greater, bolstered by the Atlantean militias behind them. Still, it was a good question: What *were* they waiting for?

"What was the report from the scouts?" asked Tiras.

"None," replied Gilyon. "None of the scouts sent to this column came back."

"That bodes poorly," said Maban.

"But we are not *scouts*," said Uzti. "We are soldiers of the Lord God, and the tool He shall use to smite His enemies!"

"Our enemy is *death*," said Merim. "And it is not your place to purposely introduce another human to it. Remember that."

"Ah ha. Here is something," said Tiras. He pointed his hammer's blocky bronze head toward the ridge.

The back of an enormous wagon climbed into view, wheels creaking. Chains lay thick on top of it, and some encircled it entirely. Sweaty, hooded figures surrounded it, clutching axes or metal hooks on long poles. Some of them—Gilyon counted seven—struggled to carry squealing, leather-wrapped bundles a third their size but difficult to hold with all the squirming, despite obviously secure constraints. These the men tossed before the wagon's back gate; immediately, all seven of them started to writhe madly, snapping leather straps as they did. A few managed the free one or two legs, hobbling about blindly, and the rest wriggled and hopped on the ground.

"Are those . . . pigs?" asked Merim.

"They are strong and angry," said Tiras, just as one of them loosened its bindings enough to gain its feet and begin charging toward the line of Scribes like a bull. "Amazingly so."

"But . . . still *pigs*. What is Zuthi playing at?"

Suddenly, Gilyon knew.

"Merim, get your casters," he ordered. "All of them, to the front, *now*." Merim gave the command, quickly passed down the line.

"What is it, Gilyon?" asked Tiras.

"There are demons in those pigs," Gilyon said. "Seven pigs, seven demons."

"And that wagon . . ."

"Large enough to carry a mammoth."

Tiras nodded. "Or a dragon."

Impiously, Uzti cursed.

The Zuthians with axes and poles fell to chopping at chains and pulling them away. The gate crashed down. Scaled, splayed feet stamped out, and the beast within rose to its full height.

"That," whispered Maban, "is a very big dragon."

Voices—Gilyon characterized them as *fervent*, not *panicked*—shouted, "Baledragon!" For the benefit of the Atlanteans behind his knights unable to see, he did not silence them. He raised his crossblade high, yelling "Hold!"

"No, charge!" urged Uzti. Tiras's glance showed he agreed.

"Not yet," said Gilyon.

The Zuthians by the wagon had scrambled out of view; the dragon riders' lances were all pointed at the baledragon. The creature was kin to the spined dragon, a thick sail on its back and elongated jaws, but Gilyon had never seen one this large. It dwarfed the minor dragons in both length and mass, and its clawed arms possessed far greater reach. The enormous reptile noticed three bundled, bouncing pigs before him. Their squeals increased, then were muffled as they were devoured. Its interest piqued, the baledragon searched for more of the swine, three of which it found and snapped up quickly, bindings and all. It turned its black-slit eyes, great yet beady, to the single remaining pig that still sprinted straight toward Bull Bridge.

"I do not understand," said Tiras. "It eats the pigs?"

"No," said Gilyon, comprehension dawning. "It eats the *demons*."

"Then the demons . . ." Maban did not finish, so Gilyon did for him.

"Are inside the *baledragon*."

The baledragon's taloned feet shook the earth as it raced to catch the last pig. When it did, it stopped, statue-still. It was common knowledge among anyone who had ever been in the slightest proximity to dragon lands that such beasts required motion for sight, but this creature, despite the ordered, unmoving composure of the Scribes' long front of unicorn knights, ran its eyes down the entirety of it.

"On second thought, get the casters back," Gilyon told Merim. "You *must* protect them. Tiras, Maban, Uzti . . . *now* we charge."

With Tiras and his ram chariot in front, the Scribes spurred their unicorns into a stampede, sending up a corporate roar that was matched by the demon-possessed baledragon. The Zuthian dragon riders finally set into motion, as did the Scribes' fleetfooted stone-skulled drakes and the club-tailed tarasques lumbering after them. As fast as he was even in full armor, Gilyon was left behind.

The clash of battle was epic in its violence. Though a few unicorn knights fell prey to the Zuthian dragons' jaws, Uzti proved right: the scaly beasts were ill suited to face the unicorns' massive horns, which kept the cautious ones at bay and eviscerated any that became too aggressive. The lancers were better fighters than the Scribes, however, and their long weapons were still deadly if unseated; more than a few Scribes felt the thrill of victory as their beast bested a dragon, only to feel something very different as a Zuthian lance darted up to pierce them through.

The Zuthian warriors did not last long on the ground, though. The big-headed drakes were too fast, the tarasques too well armored, and the human skeleton could not withstand more than one bludgeoning from creatures like those. None of the unseated warriors dared face Gilyon; when any saw the Naphil, they ran for the ridge.

Gilyon turned to gargantuan footsteps pounding toward him. A dragon lancer bore down, leaning into a thrust aimed at Gilyon's neck. The giant spun his blade through the weapon's shaft, then pivoted and cut through the passing dragon's ankle, almost severing its three-toed foot. It hit the ground hard, screeching, its rider thrown past Gilyon, who ignored the Zuthian to spear the beast through the head with the top of his crossblade. The rider scrambled off.

Gilyon scanned the battlefield for another target worth engaging, but the only fighters Gilyon could see who remained mounted were Scribes. For a few minutes, Gilyon thought the battle was going in their favor.

Then he came to the baledragon.

The ground around the enormous beast was the site of absolute carnage. Unicorn carcasses made shaggy islands in a sea of red, of blood and offal and shredded meat. Bodies barely recognizable as human lay among them: half-eaten, ripped apart, stomped upon and crushed. The remains of Tiras's chariot, shattered to pieces, was tangled with the mangled flesh of the rams that had pulled it; Gilyon saw Tiras's furred, bloodstained cape past that, the body beneath unmoving.

At the center of this crimson corona of death, the bale-dragon was still doing its terrible work. Uzti was gripped in its jaws, screaming as the monstrous beast thrashed its hideous head about until the man was bitten through. Uzti's upper half flew away, the Scribe still shrieking until he hit the hard dirt with a sickening crunch. The baledragon dropped the remains from its mouth. Gilyon noticed that it was missing a section of teeth—perhaps Tiras or some other brave soul had struck a true blow before the end—but it otherwise looked untouched and unsatiated, with a malevolent madness in eyes that seemed less bestial than before.

Those eyes turned to Gilyon.

The fighting had stopped. The Scribes had retreated to a vanguard position in front of the bridge, with the

militia packed behind, while the Zuthians had gathered
in a tight group at the ridge. Gilyon felt the demons inside
the dragon. They were no princes, but neither were they
mere imps, and he sensed that the seven together were
more than capable of resisting the righteous casters who
even now struggled against them. The Zuthians began to
chant: "*Lo*-tan, *Lo*-tan, *Lo*-tan."

To be the object of that beast's gaze would have frozen any man alive in fear, but Gilyon was Nephilim, not
man, with the blood of angels in his veins and the favor
of Elohim upon his soul. More than that, he was son of
Gloryon of Enoch, and his entire life had prepared him
for this moment, for this conflict of both flesh *and* spirit.

Like a gift from the Creator, a riderless unicorn meandered by. Gilyon leapt astride it, kicking it with iron heels
into a barreling run and pointing its huge horn straight
ahead. The baledragon roared in response, stooping with
maw agape to meet the attack. Gilyon had no delusion
that the unicorn would survive; then again, what was
animal sacrifice to a bloodletter?

The baledragon—Lotan—did not attempt to avoid
the charging unicorn. As the great horn lowered, Lotan
turned its head sideways and closed its jaws around the
unicorn's face, then twisted, snapping the animal's neck.
The unicorn careened forward in a wild tumble, obliging
Gilyon to jump clear. As he did, he ran his crossblade down
Lotan's neck, drawing a line of blood on a rough canvas of
blue scales. At the same time, he tore away two demons in
a blazing flash of exorcism, invisible to terrestrial onlookers
but blinding to the dark spirits within the dragon.

A clawed hand swiped at Gilyon's head. His helm
prevented the blow from being fatal, but it twisted
around his face so he could not see. He rolled with the

momentum and ripped the helm off. Only four demons remained inside the baledragon now; the Scribes were hard at work.

He gripped his weapon with both hands. Lotan was angry, and even more dangerous because of it, but rage often led to opportunities for cooler heads, so Gilyon prayed for calmness.

The monstrous creature changed strategies, and the Naphil noticed it immediately. Lotan broke into a thunderous run, *around* Gilyon and straight toward Bull Bridge. An epic clash of champions was never its aim, nor Zuthi's. Gaining Atlantis's gate was the only goal, and Gilyon saw nothing to prevent that except himself. He darted in front of the baledragon, brandishing his angelic blade imposingly enough to give it pause. It went to the side, and so did he, stepping over corpses as he gave ground. He held up a palm, as if *that* would halt Lotan's advance; when he clenched his gauntleted fist, another demon disappeared.

The unexpected banishment enraged Lotan past games or caution. Quicker than a viper, it shot its snout forward, knocking Gilyon down. A hundred thick fangs clamped down on his iron armor, and Gilyon gritted his teeth as he was lifted into the air.

Spined dragons, no matter how big, were natural piscivores, with relatively weak jaws meant for snatching fish. Buttressed by demonic strength, however, they gnawed and rent through the plates protecting his flesh and worried at the leather beneath, drawing blood in a score of places. Malformed metal bent around his body, but his arms and chest were free.

As long as Lotan had him trapped, *Lotan* was trapped with *him* as well.

Gilyon flipped his grip on the crossblade, pointing it down—or, in his present orientation, right at the baledragon's eye. He thrust the endblade into it; Lotan reared its neck and Gilyon dropped further into its jaws, taking his weapon within reach of the dragon's neck. He stabbed again, and again and again, as fast as he could, like a sapsucker on a tree trunk. An iron or bronze blade would have surely broken after one or two thrusts through the rough scales and flexing, spasming muscles, but the crossblade, forged by one of the *bene Elohim* by methods known to them alone, pierced hide and sinew over and over as if it were fruit flesh. He willed all his waning strength into his arms. His armor was failing, the clothing underneath it warm and wet with his own blood and Lotan's saliva. This was to be a race to deliver death to the other.

Gilyon won.

Lotan's head was half-cloven from its body before it finally slumped to the ground. With effort he could barely afford, Gilyon rolled out of its limp jaws. He breathed, but not as heavily as he needed to, his crushed cuirass constricting his chest. The presence of the three remaining demons, now without a living host and denied entry into another by the Scribes' casters, dissipated.

Gilyon used one last bit of energy to pull off his chest plate and sit up on his elbows. He looked at his torso, a field of blood to match the one he lay upon. Past his feet, he saw Tiras's huge hammer, bronze head half-buried in the dirt, handle pointed up like a marker for a grave; if he died today, and at the moment it seemed a definite possibility, he would not be the only mighty warrior to do so, but the knowledge was small comfort. He thought of his mother, and of his long-dead father. He thought of his Creator and hoped he had been a useful tool for Him. He coughed. It hurt, badly.

Slow footsteps approached. A blurry figure stood over him, tall and gaunt, Naphil.

"You *pissant*," the strange, skinny giant said. "That was a life's work you destroyed." He stepped over to Tiras's hammer's handle and wrapped a hand around it. "You are hard to kill. I imagine this should do it." The wiry muscles of his thin arms strained into sharp relief. The weapon did not budge. He tried again with two hands, grunting, barely raising the blocky bronze head off the ground.

Another figure, even taller and far broader, came behind the Naphil and cast him into shadow.

It was Tiras.

"You may be Nephilim," said Tiras, "but that does not mean you have strength to lift my hammer."

Exhaustion and injury overtook Gilyon, and his eyes shut of their own accord. He heard a cry cut short by a wet crack and felt a body drop beside him, then all went dark.

◂ CHAPTER 49 ▸

WIDE BRIDGE

The Atlanteans fought for family and home, for sons and daughters, mothers and fathers, for everyone with a drop of Cain's blood within them. They fought for their city and their nation, bound together by common culture, with cosmopolitan connections that snaked along rivers and trade routes to every other civilized people on earth. They fought for freedom: to protect their own, to regain that of others stolen away.

They fought for him.

Dyeus, resplendent in shining armor fit for an Atlantean Nephilim lord, watched the fighting from a rise beside Wide Bridge. His honor guard, composed of both Nephilim and humans, surrounded him, letting in runners who gave reports from the different battle sites. All seemed to be going well. Already heroes had emerged—some to be honored posthumously—and legends forged.

Not Dyeus's legend, though. Not yet.

Before Wide Gate, the ordered strength of Atlantis stood against the frenzied chaos of Zuthi. The guardsmen and soldiers of Cain's people commanded volunteers who had poured from the city, and from every other corner of the land of Nod. Dyeus had needed a while to decipher the ebb and flow of forces, the small skirmishes and little victories, that wove together to create the battle's tapestry, but now that he had, he realized something, a truth that his son Mareth had declared many times, but he himself had never felt.

War was glorious.

Mareth, with the Atlantean high guard and the reformed *bene Sheol*, was already approaching around the moat. The reports from the victory at Black Bridge were almost too favorable, too one sided, to be believed. For every fighter for Atlantis fallen to sheer numbers, *hundreds* of Zuthians had been cut down. The forces from Fowl Bridge were on the move too; Dyeus had been worried about the Edenites' resolve to bring arms against humans, but they had no qualms about using them on mere animals, and now Zuthi's beast masters, unmounted and fled, knew it well.

Far in the distance, over the heads and helms of humans clashing in mortal combat, through the clouds of dust kicked up from ground cursed on ancient Cain's account, Dyeus finally saw foes worthy of his attention. They were Nephilim, eight or nine of them, attired of a kind: long-snouted masks like a wolf or a jackal, bodies wrapped all the way to the hands and feet by dirty, dark strips of ragged cloth. Their weapons were as ornate as their clothing was shabby, serpentine black blades finely decorated with swirls of pinkish gold that flashed in the sun as they slaughtered Atlanteans and their allies without challenge.

With a wave of his hand, Dyeus beckoned his guard forward. The Atlantean forces parted before him; the only Zuthians this close to the bridge were corpses. His grandson Demeth raised the standard, Cain's symbol in bold red on a field of sea green. It was a warning, and a promise: spill the blood of an Atlantean, and the death that followed would be yours, borne by your guilt alone.

It also served as a beacon to the jackal-masked giants. They howled. Dyeus's honor guard shouted,

"For Atlantis!" Both groups closed quickly, all combatants between melting away to avoid being caught in the titanic clash. Then, in the midst of the cloth-swathed Nephilim, Dyeus at last saw the face of the *true* enemy, for it could be no one else.

He was a Naphil, too, hooded, wearing a mask like the others but of rose gold. Bleached bones, intricately linked together and etched in strange symbols, sheathed his arms. Several knives hung at his broad belt; with disgust, Dyeus discerned that their sheaths were formed from skinned human faces turned upside down, handles emerging from open mouths. His robes and tunic were as red as Cain's symbol, but Dyeus doubted it was dye, and over his chest, in a setting of iron and secured by chains around his neck, shoulders, and waist, were two tablets of stone, one rougher than the other. He wielded a wooden pole ending in a crescent made of material Dyeus did not recognize, but the gleam and polish of it, and the way it so easily decapitated the honor guardsman that charged within its reach, confirmed that it was strong and sharp.

"You must be Dyeus," said the macabre figure. His voice was surprising in its gentility. "I am Marduch. You are in my city. Call off this opposition and leave."

Incredulous, Dyeus barked a laugh. "Madness is the only explanation for hubris so detached from reality. *Your* city?"

"Eldest son of the eldest son of Samyaza, architect of Atlantis. In the natural order of the world, his inheritance is mine!"

"Eldest son . . . Dedroth? *Dedroth* is behind all this?"

The Naphil's mask hid his face, but Dyeus could imagine the putrid sneer that surely was beneath it.

"Your forces are fallen," shouted Dyeus, "your filthy hordes beaten and broken upon this shining nation!"

"My faithful adherents and worshippers have proven their fealty by persevering through these trials you have set before them," said Marduch. "Now their god has come to deliver them."

"You talk far too much."

"The words of god," said the giant. "You would do well to heed them."

In response, Dyeus hurled a javelin.

Only a small area remained uncovered between Marduch's metal mask and the stone plates at his chest, and the short spear pierced through it. The Naphil dropped his weapon, making a noise between a cough and a croak. He would have crumpled to the ground, but Dyeus was before him and held him up by the javelin transfixing his throat.

"Have you any more words now?" whispered Dyeus. He pulled out his javelin, letting Marduch topple with a gurgling exhalation.

Seeing their leader—their deity?—fall took the fight out of the surviving masked giants. They dropped to their knees or lay down prostrate, wailing with cries that a few of the honor guard viciously kicked silent, until Dyeus commanded them to halt and bind their conquered foes. The surrender rippled outward. The battle subsided, the outcome assured, the vast majority of Zuthians still alive unwilling to continue a futile fight to a death so far away from their native lands.

Dyeus stood above Marduch's all-too-mundane corpse. He reached down and found the clasps that fastened the chains of the Zuthian leader's bizarre breast-plate and undid them, then ripped it off his chest.

"I know someone who has been searching for this," said Dyeus to Demeth's questioning look. "One more sin these savages must answer for."

"What now, Grandfather?"

"We have conquered," answered Dyeus, standing tall, proudly surveying the triumph his people had achieved. "Now we reign."

CHAPTER 50

W e could have helped," said Caiphes. Pellu the Seer
stood to his left, Dashael to his right, and neither
looked as bothered as he was.

"Placing us here was a mercy," said Dashael. "Here we
are safe."

"When I cried no deaths if Phempor went to war,"
Pellu chuckled, "I took it as a sign of our unrivaled
strength. I would never have guessed it was actually a sign
of our insignificance."

That perceived insignificance had caused the
Atlantean commanders to position the volunteers who
had made the trek from Phempor at the mouth of a
thin ravine formed long ago and forgotten, a remnant of
Atlantis's ever-improving waterworks. Not even Dashael
had known of its existence, but since it conceivably could
be used as a means to surreptitiously funnel a small force
almost to the city's walls, it needed guarding. The men of
Phempor had arrived carrying staves and sticks, pouches
and slings, and wearing protective caps and vests of
leather and clay. Atlantean forges were long since emptied
of metal arms and armor, so the consensus had been that
they were, and must remain, woefully ill equipped for
the battle ahead. What was a newly named leader of a
land to do, but to accept a meaningless station that would
nevertheless keep his people in safety?

No sooner had Caiphes reconciled himself to this
thought than that safety evaporated.

A parade of silent figures moved down the ravine in
a winding line. They were dressed, but barely, males and

females alike, and certainly not for battle, although every one of them wielded a long, sharp knife of glass in either hand. The first of them spied the band from Phempor at the same moment Caiphes and his fellows did them. The near-naked strangers stopped, impasse obvious, a sling's throw away.

Three giants pushed their way to the front. The first carried a tall, ornate shield, carved in curves and spirals, and the pair behind held spears twice their height. All of them wore close-fitting clothing of patterned snakeskin liberally accessorized with ivory and bone.

"Go no further!" yelled Caiphes, hoping to calm the men he could hear shifting uneasily behind him.

"Who are you to order us about?" the shieldbearing giant called back. "Move aside or die!"

"I am Caiphes, leader of Phempor, blood ally of Atlantis, and you cannot continue."

"I know not you, nor your land, little man. I am the serpent's tongue. My breeding is of angels and warriors, and you will die if you remain. Pay my words heed, lest you feel the bite of the fangs behind me." The pair of Nephilim spearmen lowered the points of their weapons.

"And my breeding is of potters and plant growers," said Caiphes. "You still cannot continue."

"Fie on your promises of death!" yelled Pellu. "The Lord God Creator alone gives the gift of prophecy, and you do not have it!"

The giant laughed. "Claim you to have a god on your side? Show me yours, for I will show you mine."

"Your god has heard your call," said a nasal, silken voice, "and answered you." A being emerged from behind the Nephilim, swaying with each slow step. Draped in gauzy, iridescent robes and hairless from bald pate to bare arms, it was not immediately recognizable as either male or female, very tall for a human but small for a Naphil. Pale green tinged the skin under its half-shut eyes, and it smiled at Caiphes with lips painted the color of spring grass.

"Choose," said the enigmatic figure. "Pain, or pleasure." It gestured to the scantily clad women, dozens of them, with characteristic coloration from a score of different peoples, who filed out from behind and formed a new front of flesh.

"This is pleasure," said the so-called god. "My sisters and daughters will happily provide it to all of you, in whatever form you wish, should you stand aside. If not, my acolytes are well prepared to deliver pain instead." The women melted back; the lithe, knife-wielding warriors in loincloths came forward. "What is the wise choice? I leave it to you to decide."

Caiphes glanced at Pellu, who scowled, then Dashael, looking lazily impassive as usual. He took several steps forward.

"Here we stand, impelled to guard this pass at the sore expense of having to cause your deaths," Caiphes shouted, "and I cannot say that the God of life would be with us in that. But I tell you this with absolute certainty: He is *not* with *you*. Go back. Do not burden our consciences with battle."

"Then you have decided. So be it." The figure slithered back, and the giant with the shield advanced, pulling a sickle-shaped blade from his belt.

Kenan's ancient sword was at Caiphes's hip, but he did not draw it. Instead, he whipped his sling around once and let fly the missile within. The serpent's tongue raised his shield. The round shot struck it in a cloud of dust that showered to either side, the shattering of clay prefacing a burst of mocking laughter from the giant.

"Is . . . is that your best? Could you not even find a simple solid stone?" He smiled smugly, looking over to his fellows surely sharing his amusement. His face fell. The other two Nephilim had dropped their spears, rasping and hoarsely screaming, tears flowing in agony, and a few of near-nude knife-wielders past them began to cough too. The shieldbearer looked again to Caiphes and the drab, shabby men standing with him as spheres, unable to be counted, flew toward him, dark against the morning sun.

‹ CHAPTER 51 ›

The way to the surface was long, the passages confusing, and made more so by the utter lack of illumination. The portly attendant that led them to the Grigori palaces did so in the pitch dark, so they had to hold hands. Noah held Phiaphara's tightly, thanking the Creator all the way. When they reached a chamber where natural light filtered through small, circular windows above them, Dedroth's servant pointed at a protruding block in the far wall. "Press that," he said, and left.

Eroch put his ear to the wall. "I hear nothing." He pushed in the block, and the ground beneath him dropped away into steep stairs. He ducked into the passage, Tehama, Phiaphara, Noah, and Eudeon behind. They hurried, and it was a good thing; as soon as the stairs finished their descent into a dusty storeroom, whatever mechanism moved them immediately brought them up again, and Eudeon had to crouch almost to a ball to exit.

Eroch was already bounding out of the room, club in hand. "Come at me, you worthless filth!" Noah heard shrieks of terror from beyond the door. He rushed out to see that Eroch, mustering the fiercest countenance he could, had frightened a kitchen full of cooks and porters who were either retreating in a mad scramble or pressing themselves against various columns.

"Hold, Eroch!" said Tehama, storing her bow.

"Yes, obviously." The brawny giant frowned, disappointed.

Noah went to the woman who straightened up and regained composure most quickly. "What of Zuthi?" he asked.

She told him. The battle, and thus the war, had been won on all fronts. The victorious lords of Atlantis had gathered the leaders of all displaced nations together here, at the ornate palaces of the *bene Elohim*, to feast, celebrate, and discuss what was to be done next. They were toasting now in one of the Grigori's great halls.

Tehama took a silver cup from a tray of them held by a servant in Dyeus's colors. "And does this wine go to them?"

The woman affirmed it did.

"Then, as a daughter of Dyeus, I command that these excellent beasts be fed and watered," she said, indicating the pair of hounds and the hunting cat, "while I go make an urgent report to my father." The huntress extended a graceful hand to the wine-bearing servant. "After you."

They walked in while the chiefs and captains of the refugee lands were raising glasses in turn and pledging partnership to Atlantis, a cheer going up as each one did so. Dyeus held his cup aloft to them with a bright smile when he saw the five of them.

"I know not what errand kept you all from the battle," he loudly said, "but glory is reflected upon each of you regardless. Eudeon, my brother! Tehama, Eroch, my children! Many songs will be sung of the deeds done by Samyaza's heirs this day! My dear girl . . . Phiaphara, yes? Your father's machine saved the ports, and perhaps the city! And even you, Noah, have much reason to be proud: I have just now received word that your kin has captured more than six hundred Zuthians, many elite warriors and a self-ascribed deity among them, without a single casualty on either side!" He spread his hands wide and beamed. More loud encomiums came forth.

"Sit, sit," Dyeus beckoned. Led by Eroch, who took two goblets from the server they had followed, the rest obeyed. Dyeus whispered to Pethun, who looked as if he had just stepped out of a bath, then addressed the assembly. "We here have faced many enemies together, my friends, and we have conquered them. Peace is here. We, the leaders of the free earth, are here. Let us together face the world's *final* enemy—one which has introduced itself far too often as of late." He placed his knuckles on the table before him, straight armed and leaning forward. "Let us conquer death."

A fiery-skinned man in a headdress of bold feathers cocked his head. "Explain, Lord Dyeus."

"I will, Apin-api. I mean this: a man might live nine hundred, perhaps a thousand years, and no more. We Nephilim, though, born of the angels . . . How long might *our* lifespans be, if we do not suffer mortal insult? None of us have yet reached that age. Atlantis, and your nations as well, grows in knowledge of every kind, and that *growth* grows. Can we not direct that knowledge . . . to one day stave off death itself?"

The very question struck Noah like a slap to the cheek, as it must have Eudeon as well, who stood. "My brother, with respect, what you say is ill thought and impossible."

"Is it?" Dyeus waved his hand to everyone around the hall. "Many of you have mediums in your lands who can pull up spirits of the dead. Is it not so? And a woman, no matter how humble, has the ability to *create life* within herself! That it is commonplace makes it no less magnificent. So *no*, I will *not* say that what I propose is impossible. Consider, too: our glad hearts are tempered with grief at the many lives lost this day, but what if those brave souls could *live again?*" He rose to his full height, voice pregnant with magnanimity and purpose. "My friends, there can be no greater work."

"If man and Naphil could live forever . . ." mumbled a stout, bare-chested man—Noah remembered his name as Doude—sitting beside Tehama. Others bent toward their fellows, murmuring. Drunk on victory and strong wine, they were actually considering it.

"This is wrong," said Phiaphara. "Do none of these people know the history of the Garden? Does no one read the toledoths?" Noah could only shake his head. Eudeon rose again to speak, despite a discreet cautionary glance sent his way by Dyeus.

A thrown-open door made an echoing crack that drew the hall's attention to a balcony above to another unexpected entrance.

"Aia and Colselph?" Phiaphara said. Noah took her hand, uneasy, feeling certain that the angels' presence would not prove as favorable as his first meeting with them.

"We have a word to deliver to you all, O leaders of men," said Aia in crystal tone. "Thus saith the Lord God, Maker of earth and heaven: 'My Spirit shall not strive with man forever, because he also is flesh; nevertheless, his days shall be one hundred and twenty years.'"

"The word of the Lord God," repeated Colselph. As one, they turned their back and exited the balcony.

The whole hall buzzed. "Retrieve those men!" shouted Dyeus to several seated Atlantean commanders, who jumped up and ran from the hall. A few moments later they appeared on the balcony.

"We saw no one, my lord," one called down. Dyeus's lids grew heavy for an instant, but he quickly readopted his previous celebratory air.

"We will speak of this later, my friends," he said. "Right now, we feast!" He motioned the servers to begin bringing food, which prompted another round of cheers.

"Somehow," said Eudeon, "I find I do not have an appetite."

Noah knew exactly how he felt.

They agreed that Tehama ought to give the news about Dedroth to Dyeus, who took it accompanied by Pethun and Mareth. Her report back to the companions who had been with her in the scheming Naphil's dank lair was ambiguous and tentative.

"They already knew he was behind Zuthi's aggression," she said. "One of his sons boasted of his heritage on the battlefield, before my father struck him down."

"I pity Belseraphim," said Eudeon, empathetic beyond what Noah could muster.

"I told them of Dedroth's threats, and they promised to deal with him," continued Tehama. "They could give nothing more precise than that."

"At least his treachery will not go unknown," said Noah. "Midash will appreciate that."

"As will Gilyon," added Eudeon.

"How is his convalescence?" Tehama asked.

"It proceeds apace," said Noah. "The Scribes are perhaps not as masterful in the healing arts as your brother is, but they come close."

"Good. He did a great thing at Bull Bridge."

Eroch crossed his corded arms. "I could have equalled him, had I been there." Tehama opened her mouth, no doubt to issue a stinging rebuttal, but closed it again. "Perhaps you could have, at that," she said instead.

"We will miss you all, terribly so," said Phiaphara.

"And we you," replied Tehama, "though the work our father has planned will keep both Eroch and myself busy enough to keep the pang of it at bay."

"You cannot marry here?" asked Eroch, not for the first time. "Weddings do make women so . . . romantic."

"My mother would cripple me for doing it," said Noah, "and then you for suggesting it, and even your great strength would not withstand her. One night here at my brother Hadishad's home, then we travel with my grandfather back to Eden."

"I will send news of the wedding back with my father," said Phiaphara.

Tehama kissed Phiaphara on the cheek. "Dear girl, grown a woman. You will always have a place with the Wa-Mizhan."

"Virgin huntresses?" Phiaphara grinned and winked at Noah. "Not for much longer." Noah's face grew hearth warm as Eroch roared with laughter. Even Tehama smirked as she mounted her great elk in a single lithe motion.

"Farewell, my friends!" said the musclebound giant. "Until we meet again!" He and Tehama went off together, his tussled mane of hair reaching the height of the tips of the elk's antlers, volleyed banter between them reminiscent of Noah's own siblings. A longing for home—his real home, Eden, not simply another place to eat and slumber for a few years—gripped his heart, and he knew his decision to return there was right. He gripped Eudeon's hand—his finger, really—and was pulled by the Naphil into an enveloping embrace.

"You will not come with us, will you?" asked Noah, once released.

"I look around at the place of my birth," said Eudeon, "magnificent, shining, splendid, and I see naught but rot and decay, as barren as if Cain's curse had been on his descendant's very spirits, and not merely the ground they lived upon." He covered Noah's shoulders with both huge hands. "I have neglected the place of my birth, of my blood, for far too long, and I would rectify it."

"And I will pray for your success," said Noah. "Every day."

"I know you will," said Eudeon. "Now, Noah, Phiaphara . . . Obey our Creator. Cleave together, be fruitful, multiply, and go fill the earth."

Noah found himself eager to get started.

‹ CHAPTER 52 ›

S he usually wanders over here," said Jonan. Noah and
Phiaphara held hands as they followed him through
the groves, her grip on him keeping him tethered to
the expectant present even as his thoughts drifted to cruel
past. Noah had held out hope for Emzara's healing for
decades. It finally had faded, but what remained had been
bitterness at the choices that she had made that kept her
from him, anger at the *ben Elohim* Samyaza and the witch
Lilith, and even, strangely, sorrow that Emzara was hurt
when Samyaza was banished and their single flesh was
rent. He harbored no anger at God, though. She suffered
upon herself the consequence of sin, both hers and those
of others, and the pain of the fact was what had compelled
him to dedicate the prime of his life to help everyone he
could to avoid that fate. As he did, he strived to model his
faithfulness to Emzara—one that she could never return
in kind—on the Creator's faithfulness to him.

Now that path was ended, with this one final stop to
make.

"There she is." Jonan pointed through the trees at a
thin figure walking in the soft grass between two groves.
Phiaphara did not appear nervous; indeed, she looked
almost reverent when Emzara glided into view. The
woman wore a simple, undyed dress that drifted in the
faint breeze, and her long hair was unadorned. She faced
ahead with half-closed eyes, the slightest smile gracing
her parted lips. She still looked extraordinarily young, as
if Elohim had alleviated the childlike simplicity that had
been forced upon her mind with an equal effect upon the

features of her face. Noah and Phiaphara had to approach her within arm's length before she gave notice of them.

"Emzara. It is I, Noah."

Emzara looked at him with empty eyes, as if he had woken her up from a deep dream. "This is Phiaphara," said Noah. "She is brave, strong, beautiful, and filled with a love for the Creator that increases daily. She . . . she and I are to be married. I wanted you to know."

Zara slowly stretched out a delicate hand, as if reaching for a butterfly she did not wish to fly away. Noah took it in his; at his touch, her fingers clutched upon it. He tried to gently pull it from her, but with a strength he would not have guessed, she pulled it back, staring at him intently, smile gone.

"I cannot do this," breathed Phiaphara. She turned to go to Jonan, waiting in the shadows of the trees, but Emzara gripped her wrist and tugged her back. She held Phiaphara's hand in hers, examining it as an infant does a new plaything. A smile, a true one, with the light of intent and understanding behind it, blossomed upon Emzara's face. She drew her hands together, Noah's and Phiaphara's with them, until they were joined, then she took them away. When she did, she went on her way again, fallen once more into whatever waking dream she lived.

"It is done," sighed Noah. "Praise be to Elohim. And now, dear Phiaphara, your life will be my life."

"Your God will be my God," echoed Phiaphara.

"Yes." Noah kissed his beloved on the forehead. "Just as He always was."

⟨ CHAPTER 53 ⟩

The refugee camps around Armon emptied, their inhabitants returned to their homes to rebuild, bearing with them the charity and well-wishes of their hosts. Atlanteans went with them: scholars, merchants, craftsmen and builders, political ambassadors and liaisons of state. At the suggestion of the Nephilim lords of Atlantis, however, the grateful kings and chieftains remained behind.

With promises and persuasion, Dyeus had made to them a proposal: they, with their families, wives and paramours and children, would join him at the peak of Mount Armon, the abode of the angels themselves, to form a council that would secure amity over all the earth. Their edicts, formed with wisdom and by consensus, would descend from on high and disperse to every one of their nations. None refused such an invitation, nor wanted to . . . except Hadishad, ambassador from Eden.

At the foot of Armon, where Dyeus, Pethun beside him, had made this great appeal, only Hadishad met it with something less than enthusiasm. Dyeus noticed it immediately and took the man aside.

"Hadishad, old friend. What concerns you?"

"I am no leader of Eden, Dyeus," he said. "My grandfather is, to be followed by my father, then my brother Noah. I have no right to a place among these people here." Disappointment weighed his words, but more did also.

"But you have the ear of all of those, and always will," argued Dyeus. "You *have* a place with us, and have worked hard to gain it. Will you and your family not come take it, without doubt or misgiving?"

Dyeus thought Hadishad's pained pause might reflect a change of mind, but it was simply him steeling himself for a final refusal. "I cannot," said the Edenite. "I will stay in Atlantis and continue to help you as I can, as I have."

"Reconsider, please."

"It is decided," said Hadishad, even as he cast envious eyes up the mountain.

Dyeus tried to dilute his displeasure with gentleness, but he feared he did so poorly. "Then . . . you will *not* stay in Atlantis. If Eden will have no part in our plans, then Eden will be *set* apart. Take your wife, take your family, and leave the lands of Nod."

Surprise parted Hadishad's lips, but he bit back a response. He nodded. "Perhaps this is best. Until we meet again, my friend."

Dyeus voiced no promises, and he did not watch Hadishad depart.

"Come, friends!" boomed Pethun, herding the assembly of potentates into the hall that adjoined the great amphitheater of the colleges of Armon. "Let us ascend to your new home in a paradise built by the hands of heaven, where reason and goodwill shall overflow and flood the world!" Strangely, the Naphil's warm words were at conspicuous odds with the hall's interior, so changed from when they had previously seen it. The once-festive space was empty and dark, not a lamp or torch to be seen, stone tables bare. Towering statues, names illegible in the gloom, loomed ominously at every turn. A chill draft that set some of them shivering carried with it a remnant of incense, but something distasteful as well—yeast, or mold—traveled with it. A chieftain's child began to cry.

"Dyeus?" asked Doude of Mame, gooseflesh upon his bare chest.

"Peace, friends," the Naphil answered. "It appears the servants have not yet arrived to welcome us. Ah! I believe I hear them now."

Nightmares of flabby folds and lumpy flesh limped and shuffled out of shadows, saying nothing as they clutched at clothes and limbs with yellow-nailed fingers. The leaders of earth's free nations, and their families with them, screamed and fought in vain, dragged into the darkness until only echoes lingered.

Dedroth stepped out from behind the statue that bore his likeness. "Hello, my brothers." Dyeus and Pethun embraced him in turn.

"Shall we meet the rest at the summit?" asked Pethun.

"Not I," said Dedroth. "This excursion has taken me further from my abode than I ever plan on going again. I must return."

"Give Belseraphim our regards," said Dyeus.

Pethun laughed. "I remember when you would traipse to every people on earth, bringing back your bits of creatures and bottles of smashed berries."

"Indeed," said Dedroth. "Now you can bring every people on earth to *me*."

Bowing, he returned to the darkness.

The very air inside the Grigori palaces at Armon's peak seemed divine. Dyeus inhaled deeply. "Do you smell that?" he asked.

"My apologies, father," said Deneresh. "I must *reek* of ambrosia." His fat hand raised a crystal goblet to florid lips. "Every time I come here, I wonder why I still bother with mere wine."

"Hardly that, my son. The incense from the altar houses below . . . it indeed rises. To *us*."

Mareth stood behind Tubal-Cain, resting his bad leg after the arduous climb. The courtesan Voluta lounged upon Pethun's lap. Lean Hamerch reclined beside Deneresh's sprawling corpulence and slight, pretty Edenah. The sisters Eila, Temethe, and Asathea clustered together like the matriarchs of a hen coop. Peleg sat at the chamber's wide window that stretched the length of it and, from this great height, seemed to show the whole world all at once. The sun shone full upon him and showed him hale, none the worse for his time in plague-haunted Havilah. In his shadow hid Tehama, gazing longingly at the swaths of green forests below, hoping her daughterly obligation would soon be fulfilled so she could return to them.

"My apologies as well, father," said Tehama, "but what have you called us for?"

"To tell you, Tehama, that you need not concern yourself with the border any longer." Her only response was to narrow her eyes, shifting them from Dyeus, to Pethun, then up to Peleg.

"We are the lords of earth now," Dyeus continued, looking past Tehama, out the window before which she stood. Atlantis was just visible, the far distance tinting its white spires pale blue; beyond, the sky and sea blurred together at the horizon. "Your place is here, to help us rule it."

"Rule it." Her skeptical tone bordered on disdain.

"Not all of it," said Pethun. "Not yet. Hoduín and his sons hold Assyria as our firm allies in the north. Cush has chosen to be a hermit kingdom, Havilah is crippled, Eden is small and unambitious. Most others are now under our sway."

"*Most others* already *have* their authorities: gods, priests, rulers, judges. We are not those."

Dyeus and Pethun met eyes in a way that told her that they were *not* telling her something.

"Many such rulers have . . . recently retired, leaving their peoples in our charge." Dyeus seemed to satisfy himself with that explanation, but it burned in Tehama's ears. "As for gods: What gods? Marduch thought as you. He stole the most precious holy relics from every nation he burned down, and even wearing them all upon his very person did not protect his throat from my javelin."

Edenah rose and took her arm, smiling softly with eager eyes. "Dearest sister," she said, "I see you doubt the nobility of our father's intent, but understand: we can be more real 'gods' to the needy of this world than the invisible deities worshipped elsewhere, and we can do more good. Tangible good, *quantifiable* good."

"Elohim does tangible good," said Tehama. "I have seen it. I know some of you have too."

"'The so-called 'Creator,'" scoffed Dyeus, "acts sporadically, arbitrarily, taking the glory when the battle is won. Our fathers were right to descend from the heavens and better the world, and now it falls to us, their children, to continue."

"Speaking of Elohim," said Deneresh, coming up from his drink, "I like not that prophecy, or what have you. Man's days shall be a hundred years and twenty? Edenah, you are wise, as such things go. What does it mean?"

"It is unclear," said the Nephilim girl. "A shortened lifespan, perhaps. Hoduín thinks it is time until judgment of some sort. Then again, it might be ramblings without meaning."

Deneresh tittered. "I choose the latter. If Elohim was so powerful, Hamerch would have been struck down on the spot when he stole Eden's toledoths!"

Hamerch laughed along. "I thought that idiot Naphil gave the whole charade away when he called me 'my lord.' I hope Dedroth bears me no ill will that I had to kill his grandson."

"*Charade?*" Tehama's disdain had kindled to ire; Deneresh and Hamerch snapped their mouths shut.

Pethun sighed. "I knew we ought not to have involved her, Dyeus."

"She is my daughter. She has the right to know."

Tehama almost asked, "Know *what?*" A flash of insight made the question unneeded. "It was not Dedroth," she breathed. "It was all of you."

"And what will you do, you little bastard?" snapped Eila, her aunt by blood and her mother by marriage.

"Eila . . ." cautioned Dyeus, but she ignored him.

"You will tell . . . who? Your friends in Eden, or Havilah, whose eyes have already proven those deeds were accomplished by Zuthians now dead? Will they come against us? Will anyone believe you, when all of us here insist otherwise?"

Frowning, disbelieving, Tehama looked to Peleg for support, and Eila saw it. "You will find no aid there," she told her. "Your brother was the provider of the means to bring down Havilah. How do you think he made you all immune, or could concoct a treatment so quickly?" Peleg chose to face the sun rather than meet her eyes.

"Tehama," said Dyeus. "Dearest Tehama. Do not imagine that the Zuthian hordes were driven by our ideas alone. Dedroth has been among them. Squabbling, petty, quick to trade blows over trifles. They were a raging river that would have eventually overflowed whatever dam Atlantis could build. We simply . . . redirected it, to the least-destructive path we could, and at the same time culled the weak from the herds of humanity in its way." He stepped to her, hands pleading. "I know you dislike how this power was acquired, but I offer it to you anyway, along with these of our kin, to do with what you will. Be with us. Shape this earth to the betterment of all within it."

"You cannot refuse such an offer, sister," said Peleg quietly.

Heart heavy, head hanging, she knew he was right.

‹ EPILOGUE ›

Phia, he is perfect."

The midwives, Noah's mother among them, had performed admirably, as had Phiaphara, but the birth had been troublesome. Brave in the face of hardship as always, his wife had plainly told him she would likely be unable to bear him further children, but now, gazes fixed on the newborn face of their third son, neither of them cared.

"He does look like a Ham," said Phia, hair plastered to her cheeks by the sweat of labor.

Their eldest, Japheth, peeked into his mother's arms on tiptoes. "His face is squishy."

"Tikka tikka tikka," added his little brother Shem happily.

"Our three sons," whispered Noah, filled with a rested joy he would have never thought possible had he not felt it for himself. "The Creator God is going to use them in mighty ways."

Phiaphara smiled at him, eyes sparkling, beautiful despite the tired circles around them. "Is that a prophecy?"

"No," answered Noah, "but I am sure of it just the same."

Borin clapped his hands in anticipation. Few Nephilim lived in the river valleys west of Cush, so nearly everyone in the village packed the antechamber of the birthing temple. His child's mother, stout and sturdy and ample of hip, had come full term after two months, belly tight full near to bursting. That wasn't a normal length of pregnancy, of course, but he was hardly normal.

"He's going to be a big one," Borin grinned, watching the gathered folk perform a traditional fertility ritual. These were not an attractive people as far as humans went, but what they lacked in aesthetics they made up for in enthusiasm.

"You're hardly a prophet," said the innkeeper good-naturedly, flopping beside him, spent for the moment and trying to catch his breath. "How can you be certain it'll be a boy?"

"I just am!"

A woman's pained scream of one last great effort stilled the whole room. Every ear cocked to hear the baby's first cry, but the one they heard was the priestess's. She burst from the motherhood sanctum, pushing over two men, a woman, and a tall incense burner in her haste to escape the temple. Scowling, scared, Borin waded through the chattering villagers, a dozen of them falling in behind him.

In a bed stained with blood and afterbirth, his lover heaved in gasping sobs. When they saw what lay between her legs, wet and mewling, some of them gasped too.

"It is a horror," said the goatherd.

"No," replied Borin, and despite the sickness that settled upon him as he said it, he knew it was true. "It is my son."

◀ ◀ ▶ ▶

‹ GENEALOGY ›

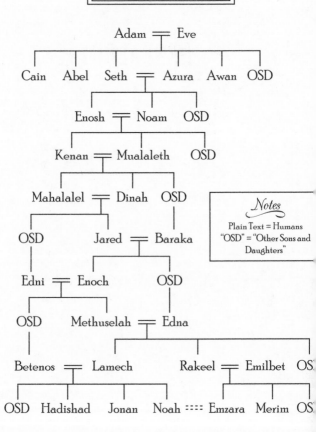

GENEALOGY of ADAM

Notes
Plain Text = Humans
"OSD" = "Other Sons and Daughters"

GENEALOGY of CAIN

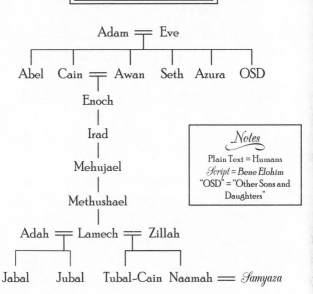

Notes

Plain Text = Humans
Script = *Bene Elohim*
"OSD" = "Other Sons and Daughters"

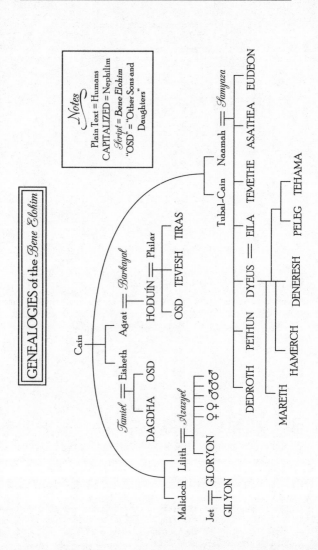

GENEALOGIES of the *Bene Elohim*

Notes
Plain Text = Humans
CAPITALIZED = Nephilim
Script = *Bene Elohim*
"OSD" = "Other Sons and Daughters"

‹ ILLUSTRATIONS ›

ATLANTEANS
(human/Naphil)

DIRE PIG
MODERN: *ENTELEDONT*

RIVER DRAGON
MODERN: *BARYONYX*

SCRIBES
(HUMAN/NAPHIL)

UNICORN

MODERN: *ELASMOTHERIUM*

WA-MIZHAN
(HUMAN/NAPHIL)

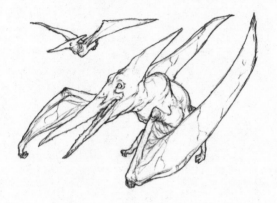

WYVERN
MODERN: *QUETZALCOATLUS*

YALE

MODERN: *SYNTHETOCERAS*

ZUTHIANS
(Naphil/human)

BALEDRAGON

MODERN: *SPINOSAURUS*

PREVIEW FROM

REMNANT

BOOK THREE
IN THE ANTEDILUVIAN
LEGACY TRILOGY

‹ CHAPTER 1 ›

It could hardly be called a garden. The word was too tame. The breathtaking aesthetic of the place defied any suggestion of human design. No orchard grower could ever imagine planning such an effortless array of fruitbearing vegetation; no man, no matter how keen an eye for beauty, could hope to create beds of buds and blossoms as naturally perfect and pleasing as were found here. One might imagine a human hand finding useful work to do, perhaps pruning here, gathering there, but the overwhelming grandeur of the garden did not demand such a thing. The branches of each tree seemed to flow into those of the next and hung low with ripe fruits of every kind. Flowers, of varieties both common and extraordinary, bloomed outrageously from leafy green canvases. Every so often a ray of sun stealing through the verdant canopy above would highlight rolling patches of lawn, quiet pauses in the ardent symphony of color and bounty surrounding. The whole of this place, and every part of it, was utterly *alive*.

Despite its wild, unfathomable beauty, the place was obviously and absolutely benign, almost gentle. No stalk or vine had a single thorn. No bur hid in the soft grass. Conspicuous, too, was the utter absence of decay. Fruits and seedpods exploded from every tree, but none of them were fallen on the ground or showed any sign of rot. Not a single leaf was absent from its perch in the branches above. Dead greys and wet, spoiled browns were simply not part of the palette here; it was as if all had been made before such dull colors had even come into existence.

Faint paths wandered through the trees. Every one seemed to lead, however casually or indirectly, to a central clearing in which stood two trees, if such specimens could be properly called so mundane a thing. The first and largest tree erupted from the ground like a geyser, its enormous mottled trunk spraying branches that arched hundreds of feet into the air and back down almost to the ground. Clusters of black berries, each the size of a child's fist and perfectly round, clung to the ends of the branches. Their faintly translucent skins suggested a light-colored pulp inside, and they smelled of cinnamon and honey. The draping limbs encompassed ground blanketed by soft grass and patches of clover.

Rising gently next to the great tree was a small knoll, upon which grew the second tree. This tree was smaller and straighter, its white trunk wavy with ridges continuing from the root to the very top. Slender, strong boughs progressed evenly outward, every so often sending smaller offshoots ending in pale blue-green leaves. From each of these hung a single teardrop-shaped fruit. The fruits shimmered in the light, appearing almost liquid. Variations in their crimson colors made one seem as a drop of wine, another as a drop of blood. Had a man stood beneath, he would have found the lowest-hanging fruit to be just out of reach. He would have kept trying.

At one end of the garden were several large pools, fed by springs from underground. The clear waters of the pools filled raised basins of white stone; overflowing rivulets streamed down around the chalky rocks to form successively larger pools until all met in a wide, slowly flowing river. Trees at the water's edge cast fruited branches over lilies that floated between curling roots that dove from the green bank to the sparkling surface.

Eventually the river met the garden's boundary, cascading down a sheer face of vine- and rose-covered rock to the valley below and splitting into four streams continuing their separate ways to the horizon.

The rosy cliffs below the garden circumscribed the entirety of it but for one sloping path entering from the east. A curious vision would have met an outsider climbing the path. An undulating, burning form swept across the entrance, rolling this way and swelling that, sometimes pausing just long enough to appear as a massive sword bathed in flames. A far more fearsome sight, however, were the beings at either side of the way. Each had four faces, a man's peering ahead between those of a lion and bull, an eagle's facing backwards, none of them turning or looking aside. Two glorious wings with no analogue in nature stretched behind the creature to the heavens, and two more covered a gleaming, powerful body. Legs like bronze pillars ended in split hooves. The creatures looked to be on fire, as if they were themselves torches bearing some supernatural flame. They made no motion, but flitted from one spot to another in flashes of lightning, leaving blazing trails of fire.

Such were the guardians to the lost garden in Eden, empty of man for more than fifteen hundred years.

◀ ◀ ▶ ▶